THE VALIANT

Savanna Fowler

As bold and as beautiful as the ungentle land before her,
Savanna was too busy to feel the need of a man. Until passion found her, and changed her mind.

Captain Thomas Brook

Older than Savanna by thirty years, he was her husband
while she was yet a girl of sixteen. But his untimely death
left her wiser, older, and fully a woman.

Abe Lathrop

Behind his water-cool gray eyes was a smoldering fire that
burned white-hot for Savanna's touch.

Doctor David Holt

A young army surgeon, he would care for Savanna in his
own way . . . and in his own time.

> "You'll wait a long time to find a
> more exciting, more honest, and better
> done book than SAVANNA."
> *Dallas Times Herald*

THE STIRRING, AUTHENTIC NOVELS
OF THE BOLDSPIRITED PIONEERS
WHO BRAVED THE SAVAGE ELE-
MENTS TO FIND A NEW LIFE IN A
VIRGIN WILDERNESS

by

JANICE HOLT GILES

From Hannah, the iron-willed frontier woman, through
four generations of Fowlers, their saga is as rich as
the vast untamed land they settled—Johnny Osage, who
was made an outcast for befriending the Indians;
Savanna, twice-widowed and alone in the wild; and Joe,
who roamed the Rockies in the great westward adventure of the age—their lives interwoven, their destinies
bound up with the relentless onward march of a nation.

* Coming soon from Avon.

JHG 6-77

SAVANNA

JANICE HOLT GILES

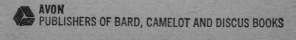

AVON
PUBLISHERS OF BARD, CAMELOT AND DISCUS BOOKS

To my mother
Lucy McGraw Holt
who made it easier for me
to write this book

Author's Note: With one exception, all of the characters
in this book are fictional save the known historical figures.
The exception is my own kinsman, David Holt, who was
post surgeon at Fort Gibson during the period of time
covered.

AVON BOOKS
A division of
The Hearst Corporation
959 Eighth Avenue
New York, New York 10019

First Avon Printing, July, 1977

Printed in the U.S.A.

With hard young strength ebbing, but still serving her, the girl set the pirogue against a drowned log and with one last shove of her paddle sent it wedging into the mud of the riverbank.

She felt the paddle drag on the shallow bottom and dug it deeper, letting the boat drift and hold against it. For a moment longer she remained bent, clutching the paddle, trying to get one deep, good gulp of air. Her breath was coming in short, fast pants, dragged in hoarse rasping sounds out of her throat. They were rough, animal sounds, like nothing human and, hearing them, she made an effort to control them. Her heart was pounding until she thought it would burst out of her chest and the pain in her lungs was almost cutting her in two.

She collapsed onto the narrow board seat and leaned her head on her knees, gripping the sides of the boat. She opened her mouth and made the air go deeper with each breath. She forcibly slowed it and felt the good, sucking draughts begin to ease the pain.

Soft, she thought, with contempt for the condition. She had gone plain soft. There was a day when she could have done a three-mile pull up the river without working up a sweat, much less bursting her lungs. She had lived on a river all her life and paddled herself where she pleased—but there had been so little time for any river or any boat lately.

She scrubbed at her face with her skirt tail. She was soaking wet and all the blood in her body must have swarmed to her face. Her cheeks were as hot as if she had been burning with a fever and her head was pounding with the thumping and thudding of her heart. She kept her forehead on her knees and closed her eyes. She hung her arms limply from the shoulders, wondering how they could be so cramped and stiff unless she had knotted the flesh around her bones. She would be so sore tomorrow she couldn't move. She tried to make all her muscles go lax.

At least she wasn't angry now. There was that much to be said for pelting down the river in the clumsiest boat, save a buffalo bull skin, ever made by man. It worked off your rage pulling back upstream. There wasn't any room for anger when you had to concentrate on a deep, dragging current in an awkward, tipsy boat.

Foolish! Foolish, she thought. But she had been in such a frenzy with the colonel. There was a time when she had believed that only God was more important and powerful than Colonel Matthew Arbuckle. This morning, though, when he

5

wouldn't listen to her, when he wouldn't let her explain, she had felt only this surging, helpless rage at his amiable, elderly, courteous stubbornness. If he had only listened to her! That was what had been so maddening. At her very first sentence he had held up his hands and shaken his head. "It's impossible, Savanna! Utterly impossible! I cannot discuss it. It cannot be done."

And he would not discuss it. So, after only five minutes with him, when she had marshaled her arguments so carefully, she had gone storming down the river in the first boat she could lay hands on. One thing was certain—next time she would make sure the boat she took was no pirogue. She wondered whose it was. Some Indian's, likely, and she grinned thinking how astonished he must have been to find it gone and how much more astonished he would be in the morning to find it tied up again where he had left it. Spirits at work, he would be certain to think, taking his boat and bringing it back.

She could breathe more deeply now and her face was cooling. She would rest a little longer, then tidy up and cross the river to the fort.

Her eyes closed, her head on her knees, she began to hear, one at a time and separately, the sounds all around her.

There was first, and still a part of the feeling in her body, the river sounds—the suck and sough of the sliding current, the mewl of the water as it reached, parted, and flowed round the boat, the faint rippling cascade over the drowned log— the mild but eternal fuss of the river Neosho as it slipped downstream to its meeting with the Arkansas.

She became aware, then, of the sounds from the woods on the bank so close by. There was the rustle of October-dried leaves, the creak of a limb now and then as it rubbed against another, the swift patter of nuthulls dropped by a squirrel onto the ground, the drone of insects near the water, and overlaying it all the chirping and chuckling and chattering of the birds. There was the singing whistle of the parakeets, the sweet trill of a towhee, the pipe of a lark, and so soft as barely to be heard the throaty, contented cluck of pigeons. There was no more peaceful, no more lulling or drowsy sound on earth, she thought, than the full-throated, half-swallowed sound of pigeons talking together.

Farther away in the woods a crosscut saw was rasping back and forth. It would be two soldiers, she guessed, detailed to cut logs to patch up one of the fort buildings. Colonel Arbuckle's dream was to get a sawmill working so as to be able to mend and repair the log buildings less tediously. Only five years old, they were already falling into decay and disrepair. But his dream was still a long way off.

From across the river, from the fort itself, there came other sounds. There was the ringing of the blacksmith's hammer on iron. There was the quick yelp of a dog kicked out of somebody's path. There was the blunt sound of an axe chopping wood. There were the high, excited voices of some children playing. There was the raised gruff voice of a man in barking protest. And, as she separated the sounds and identified them, there came the soft, muffled ruffle of a drum.

Her eyes flew open. Sweet heaven, it couldn't be time for Retreat already! She looked quickly about.

The sun was gone and the fort across the river was catching only a saffron light reflected by clouds. Robbed of any touch of crimson by a dark clot of clouds in the west, the air was filled with a soft, pale light and the water was dark and oiled with shadow. The blockhouse roofs had a blurred, bruised look and the trees on the campus were fuzzed and feathery. Savanna swept her hair back. How long had she been gone? All day—more than eight hours. It made her feel foolish. Black Kizzy would think she had lost her mind.

She squared about on her narrow seat to look at the stockade.

It was a pretty place.

There was the fort itself. Built on rising ground seventeen feet above the Neosho River, it was a great palisaded square with bulky blockhouses at opposite corners and heavy wooden gates set into its stout long walls. It looked squatted and neat and wholly businesslike.

It was relieved from grimness and given some grace by the tree-shaded campus surrounding it. In the narrow area to the west, between the fort and the river, were several buildings. These were storehouses, the carpenter's shop, a blacksmith shop, and at the closest end, just on the river, her own store and home and warehouse.

On the other three sides, rising higher than the fort on the gently sloping incline, the greenswarded campus stretched. Here were the officers' quarters, the council house, the homes of married soldiers, the mess houses, the hospital, and Colonel Arbuckle's quarters. At both the north and south ends of the campus were vegetable gardens and cornfields, both now dry and stripped except for pumpkins and fodder stacks.

It was all very neat, although the log buildings were beginning to decay. The grass was kept clipped, and all summer the gardens and fields were worked by fatigue details. The dead branches and twigs the wind occasionally blew from the trees were picked up almost as fast as they fell. Nothing littered the grass.

The principal buildings were properly parallel and some of them were whitewashed. Though it was a frontier post, pushed like a great fist into the heart of the Indian Territory, Colonel Arbuckle kept his men busy trying to make it, within reason, a proper military reservation. No spit and polish martinet, he was however an old campaigner and he knew that idleness makes for discontent and mischief. There was enough of both in the isolation of the post without adding long hours of free time for the men to brood. The colonel made them work.

Five years before, in 1824, Colonel Matthew Arbuckle had chosen this location for the new post he was ordered to establish. At that time he had been the commandant at Fort Smith, on the Arkansas, for two years. Fort Smith was built on the old Osage line; but when the line was moved forty miles farther west the fort no longer served the purpose for which it had been established. A new stockade, on the new line, was needed to mediate between the Plains Indians who had claimed the land since time began, and the eastern Indians the government was slowly removing to the area.

Fort Smith had been the first military post to be built west of the Mississippi and it was unique in military history, for its purpose had not been to protect white settlers from Indians. Instead, the regiment garrisoned there was to mediate between the Indians themselves and to provide protection for them from the encroachment of white squatters. Fort Smith, however, had served its time.

Colonel Arbuckle chose the east bank of the Neosho River. Some three miles upstream from where it flowed into the Arkansas he had found a broad ledge of shelving rock which made an excellent landing place. Here the steam packets which would provision the fort could tie up. Here the water was deep, and in the great curving elbow of the Arkansas there was plenty of room for the buildings and grounds the post needed.

Savanna had heard the colonel say that he would have preferred to locate the new cantonment on the Verdigris, which also flowed into the Arkansas only a few miles away. But the trading settlement of Three Forks was already established there and every good landing place was taken. Of necessity, then, he had explored the Neosho and was delighted to find so good a place so near its mouth.

Farther to the south and east of the fort were the vast canebrakes and swamps which even in the droughtiest summer never wholly dried up. No one gave them a thought except for their nuisance. It was true that mosquitoes swarmed out of them from the first warm day in the spring until the last one in the fall, but insects were always a plague in this country and you put up with them as best you could. No fort had ever been built under perfect conditions, the colonel said. The best one could do was make certain of good water, of plenty of wood, and of forage for the horses.

This new cantonment, Fort Gibson as it was named, had been Savanna's home for nearly three years.

As she looked, the drum ruffle began to quicken and roll, louder and louder, slowly building up to a frightened, solid sound where the sticks were lost in a steady crescendo. At its height, it stopped. Then the evening gun was fired, with its great crash, and as the flag, limp in the windless sunset air, began its slow, impressive descent of the tall pole in the center of the stockade, the sweet, clean-blown notes of the bugle drifted over the water.

She had been hearing the bugle of the regiment for years, but no bugler she had ever heard had been able to push army calls out of a horn as full and as mellow and as sweet as Sebe Hawkins. He was just a squatter's boy from the mountains north of the reservation, but he blew a beautiful horn. "My pa taught me on a fox horn," he had told Savanna once. "I could blow his fox horn as long and as loud as he could when I wasn't but ten years old. You ever hear a fox horn, Miss Savanna?"

"Yes."

"But not, I expect, the way my pa could blow one, or me."

"Perhaps not."

"You take," he had said, "a clear, cold, frosty night, and the hounds have got up a fox and they're driving hard, and they're sounding loud. And you blow to send 'em on and to give 'em heart and wind. And it sounds over all the hills. It's a little bit sad and low and a little mournful, and you hold it as long as you can and it blasts out loud and clear at the first, and then it dies away and the cliffs in the hills hold it and give it back to you, dying but real sweet."

Savanna, watching his face, had shaken her head. "No. I have never heard a fox horn blown that way."

She grinned, now, remembering the time some of the men had played a joke on Sebe. They had stolen his horn and he had chased them to the river. There, cruelly, someone dropped it into the current. Sebe could not swim and he was crying and wringing his hands and pleading when Savanna came onto the scene. Immediately enraged she had taken her horse crop and flogged one of the men into the stream to recover the horn. Sebe Hawkins had never forgotten it. From that day he was wholly devoted to her, her loyal and unquestioning slave.

The belled tones died away. There were no blackjack hills

9

here to hold the sound and give it back. There was only the last beautiful, perfect note, lifted, held a moment, and blown away.

The Seventh Infantry Regiment of the United States Army, garrisoned at the farthest west military post in the land, had officially ended its day. There would follow Mess, Tattoo, and Taps, but Retreat and the sunset gun brought the day to the close of fatigue duty, work details, and even garrison punishment. The men in the stocks would be released for the night. The man caught running whiskey would have his heavy pack lifted from his shoulders and would quit pacing the stockade square until morning. The rawboned Texan caught stealing a ham from the commissary, lashed and left tied to the post this morning, could ease his sore back on his bunk now. He had got off light this time. A second offense and he would be branded with the letter "T" on his forehead and drummed out of the service.

All the men were dismissed now, and they would scatter. Some would make for the doggeries run by the halfbreed Indians on the fringe of the reservation where they would drink too much illegal whiskey, gamble too much, and make a little too much love too promiscuously. Others would drift over to Three Forks, the trading settlement on the Verdigris, and do the same things in only a slightly different environment. Still others would stay around the post, gather in small groups in the barracks or the billiard room or the council house. According to his own temperament each man would find his own way of amusing himself, where amusements were so scarce, in his free hours.

There would be a few officers, Savanna remembered, who would call by her own home for a glass of wine or a game of cards. They would borrow her guitar and sing a few songs and try to recover in a small way the feeling of home once more.

Duty at Cantonment Gibson was exile for many of them and, for some of them, just out of West Point, the first duty of any kind. It was so far from home, they told Savanna, it was like being sent to another land. It was so hot here in the summer and so raw and cold and windy in the winter, and there was so much sickness and it was so beastly uncomfortable in every way.

The duty was so wearying. They were expected to build roads, chase whiskey runners, recover stolen property, listen to the monotonous councils with the Indians, do details on the prairies, and there was forever and ever the grinding routine of drill and drill and drill. And there were so few pleasures—a little racing on the track they had laid out, amateur theatricals in the council house, cards and billiards and too much drinking.

10

There were so few women, so few nice young girls, and now the government was even moving the settlers out of the Lovely Purchase, their daughters with them, to make way for the Cherokees who were moving in. There were the Indian girls, of course, but the young officers did not mention their visits to them.

Nothing about any of it squared with their lives as young gentlemen. They spoke so often of home, and of the girls they had known there, and of the comforts and graces of life "back in civilization where it was beautiful and clean and orderly." They were so homesick for a year or two.

There was no doubt that Gibson was a place to make or break a man. Those who did not die of the fever, or crack up under its bleak monotony, became tough enough and hard enough for anything for the rest of their lives—and no man who ever served there forgot it.

Savanna knew that some of the officers' wives, that handful of women who, out of ignorance of what they were getting into or nerve to face it, had followed their husbands to the frontier, did not approve of her hospitality to the young bachelor officers. "A widow only two months," they whispered, "and already entertaining men in her home. Shame!"

Savanna dismissed them contemptuously. They were only tongue-clattering women. Let them talk. She had no intention of closing her doors to homesick men because of the gossip of a few women.

The only one among the wives for whom Savanna had much respect was Major Short's wife, who was as good a soldier as her husband. There was little love lost between them, for Martha Short no more approved of Savanna than the others, but Savanna admired her because she did not wail or complain and, when she was allowed, she took to the field with the major with a crisp efficiency which no one could help respecting. She made no attempt to hide the fact that she thought this a God-forsaken country, but she had been an Army wife for a long, long time and duty was duty and that was that. "In the Army," she lectured the younger wives, "your man has his job to do. Your job is to take care of your man. Do it and don't whine."

"If she had children," the younger wives told each other, "she couldn't pack and go with him when the major goes to Towson, or Natchitoches or St. Louis."

"Yes, she could," Savanna told them, "and I think she would. She would pack up her children exactly the way she packs a horse and they would be taught what *their* duty is."

Savanna had little understanding of the desolate feeling the frontier brought to these more fragile, delicately reared wom-

11

en, and because she lacked understanding she lacked patience with them. She respected Martha Short because she buckled down to her job and wasted neither breath nor time complaining and comparing. Certainly the country was hard on newcomers, men and women alike, but it was harder if you gave up in the beginning and sat on your hunkers and kept eternally looking back over your shoulder at what you had left behind. Over and over she told the young officers who came to her home, as she told the young wives when she had the opportunity, "Forget what you left behind. Make the most of what you've got. This is a wonderful country if you take it as it is."

"But you grew up here," they reminded her. "You have never known any other life. It's easier for you."

When she fumed to Colonel Arbuckle once he said to her, "Don't be too hard on them. It is a harsh land here, and it does make heavy demands on human beings."

Quickly, out of her passionate love for it, she defended it. "It's a beautiful bone-bare land. You can see its shape and form and its skeleton. It isn't larded over with the fat of foliage and growth."

"Life is gentler in other places," he said.

"Who wants life to be gentle?" she retorted.

"Ah, Savanna," he had smiled, "you are as tough as a whang-string. Be a little tender with them."

I

She was born Savanna Fowler.

Her mother was Piney Cartwright, the eldest daughter of Cassius and Tattie Cartwright of the Green River valley in Kentucky. Her father was Matthew Fowler, the second son of Hannah and Matthias Fowler, of the Hanging Fork.

She was born in her grandmother Hannah's log house and her grandmother Hannah's hands had caught her and spanked the breath of life into her. She was the youngest child of four, and the only daughter.

When her three brothers were brought to stand in a ring about her bed the morning after Savanna was born, their mother was still weary and pain-racked, for this last child, this tiny daughter, had given her a hard night. She came quickly as though she had no time to waste, tearing and thrusting herself with frenzy into a strange, but what was ever to be exciting, new world. "I never seen a youngling so bent on bein' birthed," Hannah Fowler said to her son's wife. "This 'un is in a tearin' hurry about something."

The mother smiled mistily. "This one," she said, "is in a tearing hurry to begin living by herself."

By herself—it was always to be the key to her character.

Struck dumb with awe, her brothers gazed at the new sister. She lay on her mother's arm, her round black eyes blinking, her mouth puckered as though tasting wryly of this new climate. She was amazingly unwrinkled by her long enwrapment and unbruised by her rapid journey.

She was small-boned, her hands and feet delicately formed, but she had been so greedy in the womb that she was plumped roundly; her wrists and ankles were hidden in deep, wrinkly creases and her neck was sweetly dimpled with the baby fat she had accumulated. It was the only time in her life Savanna was ever to have an extra ounce of flesh on her body. It was used up early and was never to return.

She had a fine, peachbloom skin and deep black eyes already sparked and splintered with light. She lay with one small hand, fisted, thrown challengingly above her head.

When they had looked and touched, their grandmother shepherded the three little boys to the door. "You'll be wearyin' yer ma. Go to the kitchen an' I'll be along directly to give you breakfast. Manifee," she said to the five-year-old, who was the oldest, "set out the plates. Tully," to the middling son, who was three, "set the spoons around. And Jeffie." she smiled on the youngest who was not quite two, "jist try bein' good, will you? Now, you rest," she told her daughter-in-law, "an' sleep if you kin."

At the door she turned again, nodding at the baby. "She's got yore ma's scant frame an' likely her sperrit from the way she birthed herself, but I'm afeared she's took my dark looks."

"I hope," the mother said, "she has taken more of you than your looks. I wish she might have your courage and strength and endurance."

Her heritage was good.

Born into Savanna was much of the lustiness for life of her grandmother Tattie, who had been a waif in the Philadelphia gutters when Cassius Cartwright found her and befriended her—and much of her storminess and quick cleverness. But born into her also was the good, strong health of her grandmother Hannah, the enduring energy, the undefeated will. The strains did not always live at peace in her but all, in their way, were to serve her well.

But the one characteristic which from babyhood was strongest in her was a fierce self-reliance, a conviction that she could do anything she set her heart and mind and will to do.

When she began talking her first words were those garbled

13

sounds which fond parents always interpret as meaning themselves. The next two words Savanna learned were clear and distinct and unmistakable—they were "by myself." She scowled when she said them, shaking off the hands stretched to help her. Before she could walk she took a bad tumble down the stairs because she would have no help. "By myself," she said, pushing away the anxious hands, "by myself."

When she had learned to walk she stubbornly refused ever again to be carried. "By myself," she would say, shoving impatiently at the arms which would have lifted her. Doggedly, putting her feet down firmly, often dawdling and delaying but always moving on her own feet, she progressed to suit herself. In despair her family, her father, her mother, her three brothers would call, "Savanna, we must hurry. We'll be late. Let Father—Mother—Manifee—carry you."

The small mouth would set, the chin would jut, the little head would shake vehemently. "By myself."

She was four the first time her father set her on the back of a horse. "Now, Savanna, I will lead the horse around the back lot."

"No!" she screeched, "not lead! Not lead! By myself! I can ride."

She kicked the horse's flanks and he took off across the meadow, alarmed by the screeches and her flailing heels. She stuck like a small burr in the saddle and came to no harm, though her mother fainted dead away in the dooryard.

"By myself," her mother said to her one day, fondly shaking her head at her, "is going to get you into trouble some day, Savanna. You must learn you cannot do all things by yourself. Life must be lived with others. No one is sufficient unto himself. Be self-reliant. It is an excellent quality. But do not be self-centered. Temper your independence with love, my dear, or you will come to grief."

But Savanna was too young to believe her.

She was never to know any of her grandparents or to remember any part of her life in Kentucky. Tired of surveying, which was the only calling he knew, racked with rheumatic pains in his limbs, and fevered with the same westering urge which had taken his younger brother, Johnny Fowler, to the Indian Territory earlier, Matthew Fowler decided his own destiny lay on the Arkansas.

Neither he nor his wife nor any of his children ever saw their native state again.

Though Johnny Fowler had left the Indian Territory to go into the Santa Fe trade, he deeded to his brother one hundred and sixty acres of land to help him make his start on the frontier. It lay on the north side of the Arkansas River, five miles from the stockade at Fort Smith, and near the tiny settlement known as Phillips Landing.

Here Matthew Fowler brought his family to a double log house—two rooms with a dogtrot between downstairs, two loft bedrooms above. Here Piney Fowler, reared in the luxury of her father's great brick mansion on Green River, with her father's blacks to wait upon her, a tidy, loving, and gracious lady, tried to accustom herself to a harsh land peopled only by Indians, adventurers, soldiers, and squatters. Here, on the muddy, sprawling Arkansas, Savanna grew up, loving passionately the wild land her mother never ceased to hate.

The land was fertile, but Matthew Fowler was a feckless man, dreamy and impractical, given to much studying and reading and philosophizing. He was also inexperienced and slow to learn that this hard, dry, droughty climate would not grow tobacco, hemp, indigo and flax—that it was made for cotton and corn. The hundred and sixty acres yielded him, therefore, the barest living for too many years. Piney Fowler made do as best she could. The children roved the prairie, rode their mustangs, hunted and fished and thought they lived in paradise until they were old enough to know what poverty meant.

What Matthew liked best to do was gather around him men who also liked to discuss and argue and converse endlessly. Early he made friends with the more literate men of the country—Elias Rector of the village near Fort Smith; John Rogers, who kept an inn in the same village; Colonel Matthew Arbuckle who commanded the stockade; the young post surgeon, David Holt; and Captain Thomas Brook, perhaps the widest traveled, the best read man of them all. From her childhood Savanna knew them, saw them often in her father's home, was petted and spoiled by them all.

When she was a child Savanna liked best the young surgeon. He was a bare twenty-one when she was a leggy, colty ten, but she thought him as old as the others. All adults were old to her. She liked him because he would ride recklessly with her over the prairies, would pole the scow up the river to her favorite fishing hole with her, would hunt walnuts and chinquapins and pecans in the river bottoms with her.

No one else, save her brother Manifee's good friend Abe Lathrop, a scout with the regiment, had enough energy to keep up with her. She liked David better than Abe because he loved the land as much as she did. "It's a beautiful land," he would say, "a terrible, bare, gaunt, grand, lovely land."

Abe hated it.

"Then why are you a scout for the regiment?" Savanna stormed at him.

"Because I mean to take good care the damned country doesn't kill me. It's an unfriendly land and you can't know too much about it or take too much care."

"Oh, fiddlesticks."

Abe took Manifee onto the plains one spring to hunt wild horses and Savanna cried to go. "You're a girl," Manifee said scornfully. "Girls can't go onto the plains. It's too dangerous."

"I can do anything you can do," Savanna wailed.

Abe laughed at her temper. "Manifee's right. The plains are no place for a woman. My God! A girl on the plains!"

Savanna made her hands into fists. "I'll go! Someday I'll go! You'll see. You'll see where a girl can go!"

"You'd faint if you saw a Pawnee," Abe taunted her.

"I wouldn't!"

"You'd perish with thirst."

"I wouldn't!"

"You'd get trampled by a buffalo."

She flew at him and kicked and flailed. "I wouldn't! I wouldn't!"

With one strong young hand Abe held her off. "Think you can do anything, don't you?"

Manifee hauled her away. "All her life she's thought that."

David also teased her but with such twinkling good humor and understanding that she was never angered. He teased her out of temper tantrums, teased her into smiles when she had been weeping, teased her into obedience when she was stormily rebellious.

And he ministered to her. David could get the bitter Peruvian bark down her when she had the fever and her mother despaired. David set her arm when she was thrown by one of Manifee's young mustangs. "I told her he was a broncho," Manifee said, torn between sympathy for her pain and anger at her disobedience, "I told her to leave him alone. But you can't tell the little brat anything."

"I'll ride him yet," Savanna said defiantly, "and I'll break him, too."

"Not," Daivd said, rolling down his sleeves, "until this arm has healed."

He was there to watch her when she did break the broncho and to give her an approving grin when she slid, flushed, and triumphant, off the winded animal. "I did it, David. I did it."

"Of course you did. I never doubted you would."

But he was not there the year Savanna's world turned upside

down. He had gone back to Philadelphia to study.
He was not there when Savanna's mother died.

II

Piney Fowler had never become reconciled to the new country. She never ceased feeling she was an exile in an alien land, a stranger among strangers, a wayfaring pilgrim in a terrible wilderness. Though she set herself grimly to what it required of her, she never quit thinking of it as a savage place, inhabited by heathen Indians, cutthroats, brigands and outlaws, a place where the scheming and ruthless, the unscrupulous, preyed on the luckless, and she carried a deep and abiding fear that Matthew was among the luckless.

Accustomed to cupped and sheltering hills about her, she hated the look of the land, its faceless stretching prairies, its sprawling muddy rivers, its short-topped blackjacks, its blue, glaring skies. She hated the everlasting winds, hot in the summer, cold in the winter, and the sudden, tornadic storms. It was a land of such violent extremes. She longed for the tranquillity of home, for the soft greenness, the gentler sun, the sweet, clear streams. She could not understand her husband's liking for this raw brash land, nor her children's passion for it. She hated it and she could not hide her hatred for it, but she would not admit defeat, although on every side she was vexed and frustrated. No amount of effort could make the log cabin into the gracious home she wanted, and her children could not be wrenched and commanded into the pattern she wanted them to follow. They loved her, they did not wish to make her unhappy, but their young energies directed them with more truth than her wishes—and they did not understand her.

When Savanna had helped her clean the kitchen one day, the child looked at the rows of shining pots, the clean-scoured floor, the swept hearth, and said, "Doesn't it look nice, Mother?"

Bitterly Piney had said, "The blacks on my father's place live better than we do."

But there was a pride in her which would not let her settle into the easy, slovenly ways of other settlers' wives. Despising the log house, even the land on which she walked, she yet refused to be defeated by it. Furiously she kept the house and the yard spotless, her mahogany bed and cherry chest from her father's home shining, her windows gleaming and her own person as neat and trim as always. She could never be content with a house less than perfectly kept and keeping this house perfect left her with never a moment's rest. The chinking between the logs crumbled and a dozen times a day she swept it up. In the winter the mud was deep and the boys tracked it in. She mopped after them constantly. In the summer the dust blew and she went about all day with a rag to keep it from grinding into her few nice pieces of furniture. She felt as though the country itself had a grudge against her and she was facing it in a desperate battle.

In February, just before Savanna was fourteen, her mother got up one morning with a sniffly nose and a slight, rasping cough. Never one to bow to illness, she was only provoked at the onset of a head cold and went about preparing breakfast as usual. It was just another of the vexations of this vile climate. Everyone had catarrhs and colds the whole enduring winter. You never knew what to expect from the weather. One day it would be mild and sunny, almost warm, the next day a norther would blow in across the prairies and freeze you to the marrowbone. And this was such a day, slashy with wind and rain, rattling with hail and sleet. Looking out on it, Piney felt further vexed. She had meant to scour the floors downstairs today. They were grimy with the mud from the last rain and she had determined yesterday she could not abide them another day.

She looked bleakly at the mud the boys and Matthew brought in from the barn and when they had eaten and gone out again anger and vexation and frustration rose up within her and she determined she would not be brooked by the weather. It did not occur to her that she was like many another taut, tense woman who, the worse she felt, the more compelled she was to work. She *had* to scour the floors. She felt tight and angry and prickly. The floors were somehow something which would bring her relief.

Savanna had gone to the barn with her brothers. She did not see, therefore, that when Piney needed fresh water she went out to the well with only a thin house shawl thrown carelessly over her head. She did not see that as trip after trip was required her mother got wetter and wetter, her shoulders soaked, her hair sodden, and her dress and apron draggled.

No one saw it, no one knew it, until Savanna came to the house. She found her mother crouched in front of the fire, the scouring abandoned, the water circling everywhere. She was horrified at her mother's condition. Piney was as wet as a storm-caught hen; she was shaking with ague; her eyes were glazed with fever, and her mind was a little wandering. She did not oppose Savanna when she urged her to bed. Like a child she was suddenly docile and, their roles reversed, she obeyed her daughter as if she had been her mother.

When she had got Piney into bed, with a hot stone at her

feet, Savanna flew to find her father. He was aghast. "Scrubbing floors on a day like this? What in the samhill got into her?"

Savanna was so frightened she was shaking. Her mother was invincible. Her mother was like the solid earth under her feet. Her mother was the verity and the hope of life. But her mother was queerly felled and suddenly helpless. "She must have been fevered. Surely she didn't know what she was doing, Father."

Matthew could not tell whether Piney was in a stupor or asleep when he stood beside the bed. Her face was very red and seemed swollen. Her breathing was short and heavy and he could not rouse her. "I must go for help," he said tersely.

"Where?" Savanna asked.

Until two months ago they could ride to the post at any hour of the day or night and David would have come immediately. But David was gone now, and the new post surgeon had not yet arrived. "Where?" she echoed.

"Mrs. Hadley's, I guess."

Lena Hadley was their nearest neighbor, a young widow whose husband had died only a short time before. Piney had befriended her then by keeping her three small children during the worst of the crisis and until after the funeral. Matthew had continued to befriend her by helping, with other neighbors, with the roughest outside work. Unhesitatingly Lena Hadley came now, and after one swift look said the words that shot an arrow of fear through the whole family now gathered about Piney's bed. "Lung fever," Lena Hadley said. "Same as my man died of."

Later, Savanna believed that she never really had any hope after hearing the fateful words, though she hid it from her father and brothers.

They did what could be done, but without ever recovering consciousness and in a pitilessly brief forty-eight hours Savanna and her brothers lost their mother and Matthew Fowler lost his wife.

III

Overnight Savanna Fowler became a woman.

Returning from the graveside, she laid off her wraps and helped her father to his bed. Then she went into the kitchen.

Feeling infinitely bereft and forlorn, small and lost, she looked dully about her. She would never hear her mother's quick footsteps across that scrubbed floor again. She would never hear her mother's voice, a little edged sometimes, raised to call her to some task again. She would never be able to fly to her mother's arms, in fear or temper or love, and be scolded and petted and comforted, again. She felt a sudden moment of deep panic. How could she live without her mother? How did one manage? What did one do? She wanted to run and run and run and find those safe, loving arms again. She wanted her mother to be there, to tell her how to manage, to tell her what to do.

Her father's voice cut across her panic. "Savanna? I believe I could eat some of that stew if there's any left."

Savanna stood very still. It was as though her mother had spoken to her. You manage, my love, by doing what must be done, one thing at a time. You manage right now, this exact moment, by building up the fire, by heating up the beef stew, by making a pot of coffee, by mixing a batch of johnnycakes. You manage these next hours by feeding your father and your brothers, and by washing up when they have fed. You will manage tomorrow by rising early and doing all day, one thing at a time, those things I have always done for my husband and sons and daughter. You will manage the weeks and the months ahead of you by taking my place. You will manage the years by growing up.

Savanna squared her shoulders and answered her father. "There's plenty of the stew and I'll have it warm for you in a moment."

She was three months short of fourteen years old.

IV

She managed very well for a year and several months.

It was May and she was just past fifteen.

The day was almost over but the sun was still warm and Savanna had dropped on the top step and was leaning against a porch post drinking up the last of the heat. She was tired. She had done a tremendous washing that day and then she had helped the boys set tobacco. She was simply glad to sit and breathe and have no further work to do for a while.

A horseman rode out of the woods and turned up their lane. Savanna smiled. It was Captain Brook. She liked him so very much. She was glad he had drawn so much closer to her father and came so much oftener than he used to do. She thought perhaps it was because he had lost his own wife long years ago and understood what her father was feeling all during this long year. He came nearly every week to play at cards or draughts with Matthew and to have a meal with them. She rose now to greet him, but he motioned her to sit again. "Let me tie my horse," he said, "and I'll join you there in the sun."

When he had lowered his long frame onto the step beside her he gave her a closer look. "You're tired, Savanna?"

"Dreadfully," she admitted. "I don't know of anything more wearisome than setting tobacco. My back has got kinks in it yet." She stretched and yawned. "But we got through today, thank heaven. No more of it this year. And if I have my way," she added fiercely, "we'll raise no more of it. It's Father's notion to keep trying to grow it here. And the climate's not fit for it. I hope Manifee will put the whole place in cotton next year."

The captain plucked at a loose splinter in the step and pulled it free. He twiddled it between his fingers. "Where is your father?"

"At Lena Hadley's. He's laying her a new fence."

"He helps her pretty often, doesn't he?"

"No more than the other men, I guess. They all have to help." Savanna ran one finger over a long red scratch on the back of her hand. She added, almost absently, "What Lena ought to do is marry again and get a man of her own to do her work. It would take a load off the other men in the settlement."

Captain Brook's long, lean fingers stopped their twiddling for a second, then began again. "Perhaps that's what she means to do."

"If she does," Savanna said, "I've not heard of it."

The captain was silent for a time and then he said, hesitantly, "Savanna, I may be wrong, but I think I should warn you that your father may be thinking of marrying again."

If the earth had opened at her feet Savanna could not have been more astounded. She sat bolt upright. "He's not! He couldn't be! Who?"

Captain Brook took her hand, which she jerked away promptly. He smiled at her wryly. "I think it may be Mrs. Hadley."

"Oh, sweet heaven, no!"

"She's a very attractive young woman, my dear."

"She's a cow!"

"If your father marries her . . . "

"He won't! We won't let him! The boys and I have worked too hard!" Stormy-eyed she faced him. "You can't believe how hard we've worked and we've just started to manage . . . just begun to get a little ahead. Just one more crop and we can pay off that great debt of his. You don't know how that debt haunted my mother and how it has haunted the boys and me. He couldn't do such a thing to us!"

"I know how hard you have worked, Savanna," Captain Brook said, "I have watched you."

21

"Then if you have seen it, tell him. Tell him we won't have him bringing her here to change everything. He has no right! It will spoil everything. Nothing will be the same. This is *our* home. Since my mother died I have kept this house and I have kept it well—my father knows that. He doesn't need anybody else—I have cooked and washed and ironed and made him comfortable. My mother taught me well—I can manage . . ."

To her dismay her voice broke and the tears began to flow. She had not meant to cry but she couldn't abide the idea of her father marrying Lena Hadley. It was intolerable. It was somehow not even decent. It was callous of him, after all his grieving, to think of putting another woman in her mother's place. And it was footless and foolish and useless. They didn't need Lena Hadley or anybody else. They were managing perfectly well as they were.

She was sobbing now, bent over, her face hidden in her hands. It was too dreadful and terrible to be borne. She felt as bereft and forlorn as she had the day they had buried her mother, as lonely and friendless and forsaken. Thomas Brook, pierced by her hurt, by the small narrow shoulders which had carried such a heavy load so uncomplainingly, shaking so helplessly, moved beside her and took her in his arms. He held her and buried his face in her hair. "Don't cry, little love. Don't cry. It will come all right. It will be all right in the end."

"It can't be. There is no way it can be."

"Yes, it will. You'll see."

He talked to her quietly, saying nothing much, smoothing her hair, holding her, until her sobs ceased and she lay still, only a shudder or two running through her now and then. At last she sat up and he gave her his handkerchief. She wiped her eyes and blew her nose. "Why must he? How can he think of putting Lena Hadley in Mother's place? Mother was so dear and sweet and wise and clever. Lena is just soft and fat and white. I suppose," she said contemptuously and coarsely, "he wants her to warm his bed."

"Well," Thomas Brook said, putting his handkerchief away and hiding his amusement, "there is that, of course."

"Men!" Savanna exploded, "they can be such fools!"

"My dear," Thomas Brook arched his fine brows, "there is nothing foolish about your father's wanting a wife again. He is not an old man though he may seem so to you. It is natural he should want a wife. When a man has been married for a long time he gets into the habit of marriage. He is very lonely without a woman . . . "

"You haven't married again," Savanna burst out, interrupting, "and your wife has been dead much longer."

Thomas Brook looked at her a little sadly. "Which does not mean," he said, "I don't want to marry again. The truth is Savanna, I would like to marry very much—some day."

She was startled. "But you won't, will you?"

Thomas smiled. "Not right away. But some day, if she will have me—yes."

"Not you too!" It was a wail of woe.

Captain Brook caught her hand. "Savanna, I promise you that if you do not approve I will not do it. I promise you. But you will approve. I'm very certain you will."

She shook her head vehemently. "Never. I don't want you to get married."

"Very well. I shan't. Not until you give me your leave."

She looked at him suspiciously. "You're not just fooling —because I'm a child."

His mouth quirked. "You aren't much of a child nowadays, Savanna. And very soon you'll be a young lady. No, I'm not fooling you."

She felt better, and somehow she even felt better about her father.

It was not more than a week later that Matthew Fowler called his children together and told them he meant to marry Lena Hadley. He did not ask their counsel. Bluntly, and with some bravado as though he had a chip on his shoulder and dared them to knock it off, he told them.

"When do you expect to be married?" Manifee asked, when he had finished.

"On Saturday," Matthew said. "We plan to go to the village and be married there by Brother Chapman. We shall stay over Sunday at Captain Rogers' inn and return home on Monday." His eyes pleaded with them with his next words. "I would like for all of you to come . . . to witness the ceremony . . . it would make me very happy."

Savanna looked at her brothers. It was more than she felt any of them could do. How could they watch their father being married to Lena Hadley when the ghost of their mother would be standing beside him? She had prepared them for this knowledge and tried to ease their unhappiness, but Manifee had said promptly that if his father married again he would feel his duty had been done and he would join up with a fur-trading expedition to the Rocky Mountains. Tully said he would get a job clerking in John Rogers' store in Fort Smith. He wanted to read law at night. Jeff and she were the only two who must stay on and bear the brunt of the change.

Manifee shook his head. "I'm sorry, Father. I'd rather not."

Jeff echoed him. "No, sir, I couldn't."

23

Tully spoke up. "I'll come, Father."

And Savanna felt she should also stand by. "I'll come, too, Father."

It would kill her, she believed, but this was still her father and although she didn't think he had taken his children's happiness into much consideration, she could not deliberately make him unhappy.

She saw her father's eyes grow luminous with tears, and his voice stumbled with clogged words. "You must not believe," he said, finally, "that Lena can in any way take the place of your mother. No one can ever do that. Your mother will always be my beloved wife. But I am fond of Lena and she is fond of me, and she needs a husband and I am not an old man yet . . . barely forty-four. It is but natural that I should have . . . well," he finished lamely, "I am lonely without a wife."

Embarrassed, their eyes on the floor, none of the boys said a word. It was Savanna who cleared her throat and spoke gently. "We understand, Father. We do not blame you."

They did—they certainly did, but it would do no good to say so. It could not mend matters to storm and rant at their father, to cause a rift between them and him. All they could do was accept it, and manage as best they could. But this much said, now, they could not stay in the room with him, watch him, try to make conversation on other subjects or listen to him amplify on this one. In a body they stood, said goodnight and left him.

Had they looked back they would have seen Matthew sitting dejectedly, watching them file out of the room. They would have seen the bleakness in his eyes and the trembling of his mouth. He knew he had driven a wedge between himself and his children, that because he could not bear his loneliness and because he lusted after Lena's white flesh intolerably, he had lost these four young bodies which his seed had planted and which Piney's sweet young body had nourished and borne.

When the door closed behind them he wiped his hand over his face and for a moment wished he had never got himself into the affair. They would never feel the same toward him again. Slowly he rose out of the chair and went to the bed, undressed and lay down. His arm brushed the wide space beside him and the emptiness he had felt nightly since Piney died overcame him again. No, by God! He would fill that emptiness. He would put Lena's soft white body here beside him. Children grew up and left the home nest. His boys were old enough to be going any day and Savanna was nearly as old as Piney when he married her. She, too, would be marrying before long and going. He had himself to think about. A man could not live through his children forever. It was not right for them or for

24

him. It was good for him to take a wife.

Deliberately he called up the memory of Lena's soft moist mouth when he had kissed her today, the feeling of her plump flesh in his arms, the warmth of it and the softness of it and the whiteness of it. He brought her into the bed with him and broke into sweat with the vigor of his lust. Saturday, he told himself—Saturday night, and he grinned to think she was no virgin and he need not be gentle.

V

It enraged Savanna to see her mother's neat, tidy house slowly deteriorate under Lena Hadley's rather lazy, slothful ways. Mother, she would think, finding Lena sitting and rocking and fanning and laughing, would never have been so idle—not even in the family way, for Lena was quickly pregnant—mother would have been stirring, at some task or other. Mother never sat and rocked and fanned and laughed. Mother's hands were never idle. She was always busy, always working.

And she was jealous, a little, though she tried very hard to put it down, of her father's infatuation with his new wife. Savanna had no way of knowing how utterly Lena satisfied him physically, how abandoned she was in the night hours and how new and gratifying this was to Matthew. Piney had been wholly his, she had loved him devotedly, but there had been something prim in Piney, something which always held back, which believed that a lady did her duty but without pleasure. Lena held nothing back. She had none of the traits of a gentlewoman.

So, Matthew, immensely happy physically, became more and more foolish about his new wife and had less and less time for his two children still at home. Jeff was constantly occupied about the place. Tully was gone. Manifee was gone, and with Manifee gone his friend Abe Lathrop ceased to visit any more. David was gone. Savanna was lonely much of the time.

When Captain Brook began to spend more time with her than with her father, therefore, she welcomed him gladly.

Thomas Brook was a tall, slender man with fine gray eyes, a sweet, winning smile, and thinning sandy hair. He was forty-five years old but looked younger. He came from an old Virginia family and had been reared to live graciously. Since manhood he had rarely been able to. Savanna's mother had been much attached to him. "He is a gentleman," she said.

As a child and lad he had been sent to schools in England and Switzerland. Then, because of his family's failing fortunes, he had entered West Point. He had since, for twenty years, served faithfully in the army. He had been posted to Fort Smith with Colonel Arbuckle's command, the Seventh Infantry, in 1821. He did not like the duty or the frontier country, but he was accustomed to hard duty on any post and he made no complaint. He did like his commanding officer, and he did like the friends he had made in the village.

Once he had been married, but his wife had died long before he came to the Territory. There had been no children.

He came, as he had got in the habit of doing earlier, at least once a week and where before her father's marriage he had spent his time with Matthew, he now devoted himself to Savanna. He rode with her. He fished with her, he taught her some games of cards and played them with her, listened to her woes and comforted her, brought her little presents to cheer her up, told her innumerable stories of his adventures, counseled her, and was the one bright spot in her life.

"Don't you ever marry!" she told him fiercely one day.

"Why not?"

"You couldn't be my friend. Everything would be different."

"I promise," he said solemnly, "that if I ever marry it will be with your consent. I promise you will like the woman I choose."

One day Lena said to her, "I believe Captain Brook is courting."

"Who?" Savanna said, startled, remembering instantly his promise. "Is it someone I know?"

"Somebody you know mighty well," Lena said, laughing. "He's courting you."

"Oh, fiddle," Savanna said, "he's older than Father."

"Makes no difference," Lena said. "I know courting when I see it."

It did make Savanna think, and it did make her look at him differently when he came next. Was he? She couldn't tell. He had always been pleasant, thoughtful and courtly. It was his way. If he was courting it was a queer courtship. But then, she didn't know much about courtship. Boys grabbed and kissed and were hot and eager, but perhaps a man as old as the captain courted differently. Inevitably, though, her mind rummaged the possibility. And she began to think, maybe—maybe. It would be so exciting to be Thomas Brook's wife. And it would be so wonderful to get away from home and Lena and three squalling young ones.

And she did like him so much. And she was dreadfully fond of him. He was good and he was kind and he was such a gentleman.

It was the first day of December, 1825, with a snow as light as goosefeathers falling, that he came, entering, surprisingly, from the back as though he had been at the barn with her father. "Let's go into the parlor," he told Savanna.

She protested. "It's cold in there. We never use that room."

"I think there is a fire," he said, smiling at her.

She was amazed to find there was. Who had lit it? Who had known the room would be needed?

She wasn't left in doubt long for Thomas Brook went to the point at once. "Your father knew I was coming today and knew I wanted to talk with you alone. He made the parlor comfortable for us."

Savanna sat down near the fire, her heart beating up in alarm. Was he going to ask her to marry him? Or was he, perhaps, going to tell her he was going to marry someone else? If he did that, she determined swiftly, she would remind him that he was not to marry without her consent, and she would *not* give it. She would not. He was all she had left these days.

She did not know how appealing she looked, her dark eyes wide with fear, her mouth a little quivery, her hair so youngly tumbled and unkempt. She had grown a good deal the past year and her figure had become more mature, the bosom high and full, her waist slim, the hips curved roundly.

Thomas sat beside her on the small sofa which accommodated only two and took her hand. He held it a moment, looking at its roughness, the calluses in the palm, the broken fingernails, the evidences of the hard work she had had to do for so long. He closed his other hand over it protectingly and looked up to meet her eyes. "Savanna," he said, "I think the time has come. I think you have grown up enough. I would like you to marry me."

Her heart lurched, but her first thought was, Lena was right, he was courting me. Her second and joyous thought was, I will. I will do it! I will marry him!

Then she swallowed hard. There was a thing he must know first. And when he knew it, he might not want to marry her. She swallowed again, "I am honored, sir," she began, "but I think I should tell you—" she broke off suddenly. "Oh, God's britches, Captain, I'm not all mushy and moony about you the way my father is about Lena, and I don't know if that's love or not, but if it is you might not want to marry me if I don't act silly . . . " One hand covered her mouth and she looked at him over it, her eyes as round as a child's, regretting already her outburst and wondering what in the world he would think of her.

He eyed her solemnly, nothing of his inner amusement

27

showing. "Suppose you tell me, Savanna, just how you do feel about me. Just tell me, in your own way, and do take your time and forget what you think a young lady should say."

She relaxed. She should have known he would be sensible. She scowled, trying to sort out her thoughts. "Well," she said, at last, "I *am* dreadfully fond of you. I believe I am fonder of you now than I am of my father, and maybe even of my brothers. I do like you immensely. And I think you are the kindest man I've ever known. And of course you are the cleverest man, too, and so wonderfully wise. You know almost everything. And we do have such good times together. You are never dull. I admire you tremendously. I think you are the very best friend I ever had—except maybe David, but David isn't here now. That's why," she told him trustingly, "I didn't want you ever to get married."

He smiled. "Do you remember that I told you you would approve of my choice?"

She giggled. "Was it me, all the time?"

"It was you. But you were a little girl and I had to wait a while. Now, then, let's see." He named off on his fingers. "You feel fondness for me, affection, friendliness, liking, and I think we might say trust and respect, don't you?"

"Oh, yes," she hurried to agree. "Did I forget those?"

"Well, you implied them."

"I meant to. I do trust you and I do respect you."

"Thank you, my dear. I believe we may take it, then, Savanna, that the mooniness and mushiness and silliness are not necessary. The things you have mentioned are more than enough for me. But there is one other thing you should carefully consider. I am thirty years older than you."

"Fiddle," she said, "what difference does that make?"

"It may make a great deal of difference some day. When you are thirty and still vigorous and lively, I will be an old man of sixty."

Herself at thirty was beyond Savanna's imagination. She dismissed it airily. "I don't see any use crossing that bridge until we get to it."

"You're probably right," Thomas said, laughing. "One other thing and I am done warning you. You are certain there is no young man?"

"Oh, of course not. You would have known if there was. I tell you everything. But God's britches, Captain, why wouldn't I be glad you're a grown man? What would I do with a callow youth?"

He laughed so hard the tears came and when he could speak he wiped his eyes and said, "There are a good many things you might do but I am eternally grateful you don't know them."

Savanna didn't know what there was to laugh about. She said rather stiffly, "You'll be getting no bargain, sir. You know I am tempery and headstrong and whither-wayed about many things. I like having my own will, as you well know. I loathe keeping a house though under necessity I can do it and do it well. I know how much the comfort of a home means to you and if we marry I will promise to see to it you do not lack your comforts, but I don't promise to learn to love doing it save for your sake."

"Black Kizzy keeps my house, Savanna," he said. "I want a wife."

The heavens be praised, Savanna thought. Her heart almost burst from her body with joy at his words. How much, how very much of what she most wanted and felt the need of, he offered her. "Then I will be your wife, Captain," she said.

"Can you learn to say Thomas?" he asked gently.

"Yes, sir ... yes, Thomas."

He searched his pocket and brought out a tiny box, opened it, and took from it a ring—a gold ring with a green set. Taking her hand he slipped it on her finger. She watched him wonderingly, but the ring excited her. How she did love baubles and gaudies, and it was a lovely ring. "What is it?" she asked.

"An engagement ring," he said, smiling, still holding her hand.

"I know that. But what is the set?"

"An emerald. I thought it would match the green lights in your eyes. Did you know sometimes there *are* green lights in your eyes?"

"Silly!" She withdrew her hand to look at the ring. She held her hand off and admired it. "It's a lovely ring, Thomas. I do love it."

"I'm glad. There will be a pair of the longest, jingliest earrings I can find to match it on our wedding day."

Impulsively Savanna threw her arms around his neck and kissed him noisily and heartily half a dozen times. Thomas suffered the kisses, knowing they were yet a child's generous show of gratitude. But, he told himself, patience. Patience. The time will come.

"When are we going to be married?" Savanna said, the ring still holding her attention.

"Your sixteenth birthday?"

She felt let down, disappointed. She would have liked to be married at once. "Why must we wait? That's not till April."

Thomas chuckled. "A time of betrothal is more seemly, sweet. A hasty marriage causes talk. I wouldn't like that, and you wouldn't, really. Besides, you have put up with Lena this long and a few more months won't hurt."

Savanna's face grew hot that he should see through her, but she said stubbornly. "You aren't the one that has had to put up with her."

"I know, my darling," he soothed, "I know, and soon you will be free. But do let us observe the proprieties."

And so they did.

VI

Never for one moment did she regret her marriage to Thomas Brook.

Their wedding day fell out right as for weather, the day brilliant and bright and lucid with sun. It was a good omen, Savanna felt—happy the bride the sun shines on—and she set the house in order that morning with cheer and good humor.

Her father had managed in some way to provide her the funds to buy the material for two new gowns, one in which to be married a beautiful emerald-green silk, only a little gaudier than her mother would have liked, with slippers and a satin bonnet to match. Thomas, seeing her; had got a strange, queer look on his face, as if something pained him suddenly. "You are exquisitely beautiful, my darling," he had said, and his voice had been thick and a little rough.

At sixteen Savanna had little vanity and she had no idea how radiantly and glowingly lovely she was. Her skin had not turned out as dark as her grandmother Hannah's. It lacked Hannah's brown swarthiness and was of finer grain, firm but not coarsely textured. Tempered by her mother's frail paleness, her color was more like that of a ripening peach, a glow under gold which gave it a tawny look.

Her face was rather square, with a strongly modeled jaw and chin, a clearly formed, well-articulated mouth. Her eyes were splendid, brilliantly black and lit by splintered lights. They were so intensely expressive that they were always a guide to her moods. They could blaze hotly, lower mutinously, gloom stubbornly, or deepen tenderly and softly. Her eyes always gave her away and it had early become a byword in the family, her mother's warning, "Don't look at me in that tone of voice, Savanna."

Her hair was as black as her grandmother Hannah's, a little coarse in texture, and so curly that it was always flyaway. No pins, no ribbons, no caps, no nets could contain it long. It had been her mother's despair, but it gave Savanna no problem. It was simply hair. She combed it and forgot it.

The other gown Savanna bought was of a sturdy brown stuff which she did not like but which, sensibly, she chose to last her several years. She did not wish to become an extravagance to Thomas immediately and she did not mean to ask him for clothing for a long time. She would go to him, in pride, with what she needed.

They both found it comical that Thomas should abhor the gown as much as she and make her give it away immediately. "Colors are for you," he told her, "good, strong colors. Never dull yourself with drabs."

They were married in Savanna's home and went immediately to Thomas's home in the village near Fort Smith.

There, Thomas brought Preacher, his black man, and Kizzy, Preacher's wife, and Widgie, Kizzy's young son, to be presented to their new mistress. "In all things," he told them, "you are to be as mindful of Miss Savanna as you are of me. Her word is law in the house now. She will order it as she pleases and I'll skin the lot of you if you give her a moment's trouble."

Oh, but Thomas spoiled her.

It was as though he could not pamper her enough, as though he must make up to her somehow the lean, hard years. He was devoted to her, wholly, totally devoted to her and he petted and adored her. Her father shook his head over it. "It can never be said of you, Savanna, that you drove your geese to a poor market. You could not have done better than Thomas."

With her whole heart, Savanna agreed.

In her turn, she managed his home thriftily, capably and for her, with an amazing order and neatness. She gave him comfort, excellent meals, her entire loyalty, her good humor and cheerfulness, her deep and profound affection. She felt wonderfully secure and happy with Thomas and she bloomed like a flower that is lovingly nurtured and fed.

Because Kizzy also adored her and, under Savanna's management, ran the house so well, she had many free hours to do with what she pleased. She tagged along with Thomas, who was always delighted to have her, went fishing or riding about as she had always done, and felt everlastingly grateful that Thomas Brook had come courting her. He never bored her because he had a vast fund of experience and knowledge to draw on and he was always willing to share it with her. He was never irritated with her questions, he took them seriously, and he paid her the compliment of believing she had an excellent mind. He was not only witty but he had also, which was much better, a fine sense of humor and he met her own frequent and joyous laughter with a quieter but just as appreciative chuckle.

31

The only faults Thomas had were a gentleman's faults. He drank too much occasionally and he sometimes gambled for higher stakes than he could afford. These things were never mentioned between them. Most of the men in the country did the same and Savanna took it as simply the way of men and felt that a good wife would keep her silence and accept it. She helped Thomas to bed when he came home in his cups—he was never troublesome—and the next day, however ill he might feel, he got up and went about his duties with the quiet dignity of his usual manner.

Savanna knew that she made him deeply happy. He never left her in any doubt of it. If occasionally she felt a troubling sense of guilt because she did not love him with the ardor and passion she saw in the eyes of other wives for their young husband, it passed swiftly. She believed she and Thomas had something better, for she knew that ardor and passion dwindle and perish and their comfortable, old-shoe friendliness and affection would continue to grow with their clearer understanding and mutual esteem.

She sometimes wondered why he had chosen her. An older woman could have made a home for him, after his long widowed years, and could have been a companion for his loneliness. She thought perhaps it was because she was young and full of strength and energy, because she amused him, and because, she admitted it, she had a lot of common sense and a shrewd, practical mind. Thomas once told her, "You are a constant and delightful surprise to me. I never know which way you're going to jump next, but I am always eager to learn. When you put your mind to it you can be as hardheaded as a businessman, but put a fishing rod in your hand and you're a child again."

"What's childish about fishing?"

"The pleasure you take in it."

She did not mind the demands he made on her body. Even in bed, Thomas was a gentleman. She came to her marriage with an acceptance of a wife's duty and if Thomas's not too frequent calls upon her left her unawakened, they also left her without any restless and unsatisfied stirrings. Unawakened, she had not yet the imagination to know there could be any difference. She continued to use her hard young body and her boundless health and energy in the ways of her girlhood and was delighted to find that marriage made so little change in her ways. Most of the time she was blissfully happy and thought herself the most fortunate of girls. She envied no young wife the drudgery of her devotion to a young husband with its complement of babies every other year. She was free, blessedly free, and she exulted in it.

In addition, not long after they were married there came about a change in their circumstances which occupied much of her energy and time and thought.

Thomas Brook was far from a wealthy man when they married. He was a regular army officer with no money on the outside, caught helplessly in the army's system of slow promotion. He was still a captain after twenty years of service. During the War with Britain in 1812 he had been brevetted major, but when the war ended he reverted to his regular rank.

When the regiment's sutler died, Savanna pondered the issues and finally suggested that Thomas resign from the army and apply for the post. "Colonel Arbuckle would appoint you in a minute," she told him. "You've served with him for so long and he knows you so well. There's money to be made in provisioning the army, Thomas. You worked in the commissary all during the war and have good experience. Why don't you turn it to your own advantage now?"

Startled, he replied, "I have never thought of it."

"Well, do think of it."

"My dear, I will retire in a few more years."

"All the more reason for resigning now. What will you get from serving few more years? Nothing."

"Savanna, I was trained for the army."

"But in the army you also got a lot of training in provisioning. Thomas, you've given twenty years to the army."

"I have given nothing but my duty, since I got a free education."

"You paid that back long ago."

Thomas looked at her thoughtfully. "Savanna, are you greedy for money? Don't I do enough for you?"

Swiftly she replied. "Oh, Thomas, yes, of course you do. And I'm not greedy—not really. But I was dreadfully poor a long, long time, Thomas. I had to scrabble too long, maybe. As long as I live I'll never forget all the cotton it took to pay off Father's debt. Being dreadfully poor isn't nice, Thomas. You never have been. You don't know. It . . . " she searched for words, "it sort of makes an animal out of you. There's no time for anything but scrabbling. You're too tired for anything but working and eating and sleeping. Oh, I know Father always had time for reading and talking and dreaming. But do you think the boys and I did? Or Mother? Never. From daylight to dark it was scrabble and minch and slave. I don't want to be poor like that again."

She was young enough to be brutal, but too tenderhearted

33

and too loyal to be, so she did not add that his meager captain's pay was enough for them to live comfortably but not luxuriously, nor did she remind him it would end when he died. But she had found, anyhow, the one argument to move him. He stretched out his hand, "And you won't be poor like that again, my darling. I promise you won't. I will attend to this immediately."

Savanna's mind raced like a busy squirrel the rest of the day. It was still racing that night when, in her dressing gown, she stood brushing her hair before going to bed. There was only one candle in the room and she had set it before herself on the cherry chest.

Thomas surveyed her from his narrow cot across the room. He had been ill again of the chills and fever which regularly attacked him. It was part of his consideration for her that when the intermittent came back on him, as it did chronically, he disliked disturbing her sleep and insisted on having the cot brought in for him. He watched the brush make the short black hair fly and bristle. He watched the small, bothering frown which pulled the winged black brows together and said, finally, "Don't scowl, Savanna. You are too pretty to frown. Dearest Savanna, do you have any idea how kind the candlelight is to you, who need no such kindness?"

She flung him a quick smile. "I was thinking, Thomas, that we shall have to move to Gibson."

Thomas was silent. "Not necessarily," he said then. "I can put a man there to operate the sutler's store."

"It wouldn't do," Savanna said briskly. "To make the most of it, a sutler needs to be with the regiment. No, it wouldn't do." Her fingers tapped the back of her brush. "But the thing is," she continued, "the thing is you would rather stay here. You like Fort Smith."

"And you don't," Thomas said, mildly.

"Oh, I don't mind it. It's dull and I think Gibson would be more exciting, but I don't honestly dislike it. But I do believe, Thomas, that if you are going to apply for the sutler's post and if the colonel appoints you, we ought to be practical about it. There isn't any use paying a man to operate the store when you can do it so much better. And I can make you just as comfortable at Gibson. Most of the regiment is already there, too. I truly don't see why you wouldn't like it just as well in the long run."

Thomas looked at her quizzically. "Savanna," he said, making a temple of his long fingers as he often did when he was thinking, "the cantonment is no place for a lady. There are some refinements here. There is the nucleus of a pleasant and

34

cheerful social life, the beginnings of culture and grace on the frontier. There are none at Gibson. There is nothing but the stockade, the trading settlement at Three Forks, some trappers, traders, hunters, halfbreeds, whiskey runners, loose women . . ."

Savanna banged the brush down. "Oh, God's britches, Thomas, I grew up on this frontier. I know what it's like. It may shock you, but it has never shocked me."

"Nevertheless, my dear, my instincts are to protect my wife from such rudeness and coarseness."

"Now, Thomas . . ." she began mutinously.

"Don't say it," he said, putting up a hand, "you have said it a thousand times already. You are not a lady and you have no wish to be one. But to me you are a very great lady."

She grinned at him from under her hair. "Even when I swear like a top sergeant?"

"Even when you use your grandmother Tattie's favorite oath." He laughed. "I do believe, however, that not only would it be possible for you to live happily at Gibson but you would actually thrive on it."

Savanna went back to brushing her hair. "I expect so."

"Yes. You like all manner of people and you rarely sit in judgment. I think it is perfectly true that nothing shocks you. My instincts are wasted on you. You would be capable of making friends with an enlisted man's prostitute or with Auguste Chouteau's two Indian squaws. Or with Polly Walker for that matter."

"Who's Polly Walker?"

"A halfbreed who runs a doggery on the edge of the reservation."

"What's a doggery?"

Dryly Thomas replied. "A place, my dear, that furnishes illegal whiskey to satisfy men's thirst and Indian girls to satisfy their lusts."

"Oh." She dug the brush strongly into the scalp and made her hair fly. "What are you leading up to, Thomas? You would be there, wouldn't you? It's not as though I'd be alone. What possible harm could there be in a wife accompanying her husband wherever his business or his duty take him? Some of the army wives are coming."

"Who told you that?"

"Colonel Arbuckle. Major Short's wife is already there. Lieutenant Felt is sending for his wife. Captain Hammond is sending not only for his wife but for his children. Jim Haverty is bringing his family, as well as Aaron Cleet."

Thomas chuckled. "The place may be too respectable for you, Savanna."

"Don't tease, Thomas. I do think we should make this move."

"Very well, my dear." Thomas gave up. "Perhaps the only reason I like this place is because I am accustomed to it. I have been longer in Fort Smith than any other duty. But it doesn't matter, really. Any place, with you beside me, I should be content. As soon as I am stronger I shall look into it—all of it."

Savanna flung the brush down and flew to his side. "Thomas! You meant to all along."

"It is sensible."

He freed the hand she had clasped and ran it over the fly-away hair. "How old are you, Savanna?"

"Why, you know, Thomas. Sixteen."

"No. You are at least a hundred and six." Bemused, he wound a curl of hair about one finger. "Such a sound head on such a young girl." Abruptly he changed the subject. "I wish, a little, you would let your hair grow again. I have never got used to seeing it short. It makes you look like a boy."

"Does it? Truly?"

He looked at the opened dressing gown where the pale cleavage below the brown throat swelled into a soft roundness, and he laughed softly. "No, not truly. You could never look like a boy. But your hair was so beautiful when it was long. I liked seeing it spread on the pillow at night."

"Then I'll let it grow again, Thomas. I'm sure it will. I didn't know you disliked it short. You've never said so before. It was so heavy that it sometimes made my head ache and when I had the fever and had to cut it, it felt light and free as it used to do when I was a child. I wanted to keep it that way. But I won't if you'd rather I didn't."

He reached up to bring her face down to his and kissed her forehead. "You will leave it short, my dear. I did not know your head had ever ached. It's very pretty as it is and it's just an old man's fancy, not to be humored at all, to see it spread on the pillow. Your comfort is far more important."

He went into her bed then and, afterward, told her he felt less ill. It was such a sturdy, warm, compact young body that lay beside him that, like King David with the handmaiden, he took warmth and comfort from it. These and other things he whispered to her. "I think your heart is as stout and willing as a little prairie mustang's."

"And my hair as shaggy," she giggled.

He set the wheels into motion which took them to Gibson

where, in the almost three years that followed, they did exceedingly well.

Out of uniform, Thomas threw off all its constricting regulations and the native merchandising talent which had made him such a good quartermaster officer also made him a successful sutler and merchant. He expanded rapidly. Within a year he set up a store in Fort Smith, which served the village and did some Indian trade, also jobbing for the traders and Indian agencies farther up the river. The following year he established a trading post at Crown Falls on the Cherokee reservation. Within twelve months he found himself with three thriving stores with more details than he could manage alone.

To her delight, he asked Savanna to keep the accounts for him. She went with him often to oversee the stores in Fort Smith and Crown Falls and she kept excellent and accurate accounts on all three stores. It was as companionable as their entire marriage, Thomas buying and selling, Savanna keeping the figures, each concerned for their mutual affairs.

When no children came, though she wondered a little that they did not, Savanna came to feel it was meant that her life should follow these lines and she was content that they should.

There was one additional compensation for leaving the army, about which Thomas was rather saltily humorous.

Upon his resignation he received the majority for which he had so long waited. But only Savanna knew he found it ironical. Gravely he allowed himself to be addressed as Major Brook and when, as he was occasionally called upon to do, he had to dress again in his uniform, he meticulously pinned on his major's insignia. He might denigrate the service to his wife but he would never fail to honor it in public.

VII

But Thomas was gone now, dead eight weeks.

Savanna rocked the pirogue and switched at the soggy tail of her calico dress. She must rouse herself and go home. It was almost dark and Kizzy would be worried. But the house was still so empty. She always dreaded coming back to it.

She smoothed her skirt over her knees. The faded but still gaudy colors made her smile, then misted her eyes with tears. When she had sewed up this dress Thomas had puzzled his brows together. "You are like a Creek Indian, Savanna, or a gypsy. You have the most abominable taste in colors. Did no one ever tell you that bright orange and red don't go together?"

Pertly she had sassed him back. "On me, they do."

He had considered it and conceded the point. "On you, they do. And on you, I love them." Then, in a slumbrous embrace

37

he had whispered to her, "When I die, Savanna, don't wear black. When they bury me, wear your emerald silk that makes your skin look like honey and your eyes like oak leaves and your hair like a crow's wing. And wear all your bracelets, Savanna, and your jingly earrings. Just at the last, when Sebe finishes blowing Taps, hold up your arm so your bracelets will jangle and hold up your head so your earrings will jingle and I'll swear that dead though I'll be, I'll hear them and I'll see you looking like the brightest green parakeet that ever nested on a blackjack hill."

"Hush!"

"Ah, Savanna, you are a beautiful gypsy."

"I am not beautiful, Thomas."

He had punched her chin lightly with his fist. "Perhaps not. You have too much jaw and chin for real beauty, I expect. They are much too determined. And your mouth," he had tilted her head to look, "is a little wide, perhaps." He had bent and kissed it lingeringly. "But very soft and red and warm and exactly right for mine. Your skin is like . . . what is your skin like, Savanna?"

"Skin."

"Honey—sun-ripened honey. And your eyes are long and bright and tipped here," touching the corners, "most interestingly."

There had been so little time left to them even then, and now he was gone and she was alone and it was a misery.

There hadn't been time at the last for Thomas to advise her. He probably would not have tried, anyhow. If he had had one minute for one final word, he probably would have said: Jingle your earrings, Savanna.

He had been ill with the same old intermittent fever with which they were so familiar and about which they thought so little. He had weathered so many attacks. Everyone had it, some worse than others, and some it killed, and some, like Thomas, had it chronically. Few entirely escaped it in this country. But Thomas had been getting better, as they expected he would, and then she awakened that morning two months ago and found him dead beside her. David Holt said his heart had simply stopped beating in his sleep. "It is a good way to go, Savanna—painless and easy. I wish when my time comes it may be that way."

David had come back to the Territory the year after Savanna was married. If it puzzled him to find her married to a man older than her own father, he did not mention it. He became post surgeon at the new cantonment, Gibson, and slipped easily back into the fold of her friendship. Savanna, adoring the life

38

Thomas opened up to her, accepted him joyously but casually. It was nice to have David home again, to go on rides with her and Thomas, to pole up the river, to talk to endlessly in the evenings about the fire. David was always the nicest friend she had, but it was Thomas who had made her life wonderful.

Now, Savanna was numbed by the suddenness of her loss. Thomas could *not* be gone. Only last night he had got up to have supper with her and to visit with the officers who had stopped by to inquire after him. He had looked wan and tired, but he always did after these bouts with the fever. And she *had* sent the officers away early. Thomas had gone to bed then and when he complained that his back was cold she had climbed in beside him and curved herself around him and warmed him with her own warmth. The very last words he ever spoke to her were, "You are like a slow-burning fire, Savanna. Don't move. My back is so comfortable now." Then he had dropped off to sleep, never to waken again.

The next day when he was buried in the little post cemetery she did precisely what he had asked her to do that night several weeks before. She wore her emerald silk and all her bracelets, and she wore the jingly earrings he had given her on their wedding day. Kizzy was horrified. "Miss Savanna, you cain't do dat. All de ladies an' all de gempmum on dis post be scandalized you do sich a thing."

Savanna wheeled on her hissingly, her nerves raw with shook and grief. "Let them! Do you think I don't know what I'm doing? The major asked me to wear these things when he died, and I mean to wear them if the Lord himself is scandalized!"

Kizzy was meek then. "Yessum. That's diff'runt, if de major done want it. He know whut please him, de major did."

Savanna dissolved into the hard tears she could not seem to control these last hours. "Kizzy, Kizzy, what am I going to do without him?"

Kizzy held her and rocked her against her ridiculously, but somehow comforting, scrawny breast and smoothed Savanna's hair and kept her silence until the tears stopped once more. "I'll wear de black for bofe of us."

"You do that."

She held her head high at the funeral and she lifted her arm when Sebe Hawkins finished blowing Taps and her bracelets jangled and her earrings jingled. David knew why, and he stood beside her and smiled down at her when she lifted her arm and held up her head. She was grateful for David's understanding, but she was fiercely scornful of the others. Whatever the ladies of the post thought and said, she meant to

39

do what Thomas wanted her to do.

And she meant also, she thought, bringing her thoughts down to the moment, Good Lord how she meant to save that tremendous stock of goods they had ordered for the sutler's store just before Thomas died. They had gone deeply in debt for it and she was not going to slough off ten thousand dollars' worth of goods to the army. Nor was she going to absorb it in the other stores. She couldn't. They were full-stocked already. Some way, somehow, she had to get herself appointed post sutler in Thomas's place. What if it was unheard of? What difference did that make? If she could just get that stubborn old idiot to *listen* to her! All he could hear was "woman sutler" and all he could say was "impossible."

She sighed heavily.

She did miss Thomas so much. The whole pattern of her life was broken up. When she waked each morning now all the spring and bounce which had made bed intolerable another moment was gone. There was no urgency to rise now, no reason to make the small flat wheat cakes, served with honey, and the pot of rich-smelling coffee. That was the bad time of the day, waking to emptiness: facing so lonelily the three meals which must somehow be eaten, and with so little appetite that she sometimes retched, without Thomas across the table from her; facing the ghostly stillness which lay over the house without Thomas's small rituals of shaving and washing and dressing to fill it; the absurdly small but at the same time enormously great loss of his one habit that had exasperated her when he was living—his tidiness. He had been as fussy as her mother and had said, as did her mother so often, "A place for everything, Savanna, and everything in its place." Her heart was sore at the thought of all the times she had fumed over those words.

The very worst moment, she thought, had not been at the graveside, though that had been bad enough, but when she had come home alone. There was such a silence in the house, such a lot of silence. At that moment she had felt a wild and almost unassuageable sense of desolation, and she had fled the house wailing Thomas's name.

The next day when she found his old houseshoes under the bed where he had placed them neatly, the very night he died, out of sight, she had been completely broken up. They still wore the shape of his feet, the toes outlined, the heels a little flattened, as if they were waiting, with an enduring love and patience, to be worn again. She had sobbed for an hour, holding them in her lap. She had knitted the houseshoes for him and the wool had been too coarse and they had scratched his tender feet, but he had insisted on wearing them because she had made them for him.

She was still sitting, her thoughts like long black plumes and a cold place where her heart was usually warm, when David came by. "It isn't good for you to sit here and mope, Savanna."

David, who had been slim enough at twenty-one, had become a solid, chunky man now, with a heavy dark brown beard and a thatch of rough brown hair to match. He went about in a preposterous linsey jacket and an ancient peaked cap. Preferring to keep a civilian status, he was attached to the regiment as post surgeon but at an assistant surgeon's pay. He had not married, he drank too much occasionally, he swore with an abandon and eloquence that even the sergeants admired, and he still loved going on a detail on the prairies better than anything in life. That, he said, was why he wanted to keep his civilian status. No army orders were to prevent his being free. "When I get onto the prairies," he said, "and see nothing but distance and sky, feel the long wind blowing on my face, sleep at night on short grass and feed on buffalo hump, my strength is restored. I become a man again. God, I wish I never had to come back to Gibson then."

It made Savanna dreamy. "Some day I'm going, too."

David was the only person in the world who insisted there was no reason why she shouldn't. "You'd love it and you'd do fine."

But Thomas wouldn't hear to it.

Savanna lifted woeful eyes to David now and pointed to the houseshoes.

"Yes," he said. "Well, Savanna, my advice to you is to give all Thomas's effects away as soon as possible. Don't keep souvenirs to weep over. He wouldn't have liked to see you weeping."

He sat down near her and took out his evil-smelling old pipe. "I know, but David . . . "

He waited for her to go on. One of his virtues was an utter lack of restlessness. He could sit as still as an Indian.

"David, do you think Thomas really minded leaving the army? He hadn't thought of it until I suggested it."

"So you're gnawing on that old bone. He may have missed some things a little, but I don't think he ever really regretted it. He hadn't thought of it. The army does things to a man's mind when he has been in service as long as Thomas was, Savanna. It often cramps his mind as much as it does his life. Thomas had settled into army life as one does into a feather bed. It never occurred to him to make any change." David stroked the bowl of his pipe thoughtfully. "I have often thought Thomas

41

would have made an excellent schoolmaster and I have often wondered why he chose the army."

"His family had no money left. It was the only way he could get the schooling he wanted—at West Point."

"Yes. Of course. And then he felt obligated. Thomas would."

"Yes." Savanna took a deep breath. "Do you think he would have died of the fever if we hadn't come to Gibson?"

David hesitated. "Savanna, it's impossible to know. Of course he died of a heart stoppage, but he had had intermittent for many years. Maybe he would have died as he did any place, at any time. Surgeons just don't know enough about these things. Gibson," he went on slowly, "is a sickly place, but so is Fort Smith. All these rivers throw off a miasmal air that causes sickness. We don't know why. We just know they do. Pests of all kinds, insects, mosquitoes, dampness, heat, raw cold in the winter—the climate is abominable. Only the strongest can live equably here." He grinned. "Thank God I'm one of them, for in spite of its climate I love the damned place and wish never to leave it."

It wasn't very much comfort, but she clutched it. Thomas had had the intermittent for a long time, and both Fort Smith and Gibson had always had long sick rolls among their men. Surely he was no worse off at Gibson—but she wished David could have been more reassuring.

"I miss him so much, David."

"Of course you do. And you will for a long time. But don't sit here and mope. You made one man happier than he had ever thought to be. Cherish that and then get on about the business of living. You are only nineteen. Keep busy. Thomas left you three thriving stores. What do you intend to do about them?"

Drying her eyes, Savanna said, "Run them, of course."

David laughed. "That's what I hoped you would say. That's what Thomas expected you to do."

And it was exactly what she still meant to do and she was not going to begin by sacrificing the sutler's store.

She smoothed her hair and wiped her face on her skirt tail again. Her shoulders were so stiff. She raised her arms and stretched. Her back felt cramped and sore and there was a dull pain between her shoulders. With her arms still upraised, she took a few deep breaths and let her hands go limp at the wrists. Idly she flexed them. They felt oddly swollen. They felt twice as big as they should, tight and itchy, and her wrists seemed to have no bones. She rubbed them together, scratching them. Oh, great gobs of mud! Suddenly she jerked them down and examined them, turning them over and over, looking closely at backs and palms. She groaned. No wonder they felt sore and swollen. The mosquitoes had bitten the backs until great welts were raised up and the palms were chafed and blistered from the paddle. She scrubbed them against her skirt.

Sweet heaven! You'd think her brain would work once in a while! Blistered hands when she had to ride tomorrow! How could she have forgotten, even in the rage she was in, the Cherokee annuity payment and the races and Lieutenant Felt's new Tennessee horse and the wagers she had covered? Lord, Lord—that's what getting so mad at the colonel had done— sent her paddling like a deserter down the river, every sensible thought driven out of her head. If only she hadn't gone to see the colonel this morning! If only that pirogue hadn't been tied up so handily! If only Kizzy had made her stay with the housecleaning!

She looked at her hands again. Maybe Kizzy had some salve or ointment that would heal them. Or maybe David had some medicine. Or maybe that horse ointment she used on saddle sores would help. Dismally she looked at the big blisters already full of water, and faced the truth. There was no use fooling herself. Nothing would heal them in time. Blisters had to be opened and bandaged and they took at least a week to heal. The Duke was tough-mouthed and she wouldn't be able to saw a rein against those sore places tomorrow. She had already broken one of the blisters scouring her palms against her skirt.

Widgie would just have to ride. And lose the race, she thought miserably.

All those bets! Why had she covered so many of them? But she knew why and it still made her head come up and her eyes narrow and her gold hoop earrings jingle to remember it. Everybody on the post was certain Bill Felt's new horse could beat the Duke; and there were some that were hoping mightily that Savanna Brook was going finally to get her comeuppance. How much had she covered? Ten to Captain Hammond; ten to Aaron Cleet; twenty-five to Bill Felt himself; ten to Major Short and heaven help him if Martha found it out; twenty-five to Lieutenant Bonneville . . . oh, at least a hundred dollars and most of it at two to one. What a mess her frenzy had got her in!

It was such a mess that all at once she began to laugh. All right, my girl. You have ruined your hands and can't ride tomorrow. With Widgie up the Duke will likely lose the race, but there's no use crying over spilt milk. Pay up and shut up, and next time keep your head. But it was such a pity. She grinned ruefully. How Thomas would have laughed at her. She could hear his nice deep chuckle now, and hear him saying, as he had said at least a hundred times to her, "Have a temper, Savanna, but keep it."

He had given her the Duke on her last birthday. Loving any kind of horseflesh as she did, she had yearned for a really good horse to race. "From Kentucky, Thomas. I want a Kentucky thoroughbred. Do you think we can ever afford one?"

"We'll see."

With much secrecy he had arranged it and had led her to the stables the morning of her birthday, delighted with her wild excitement when she saw the horse. "He is the Duke of York, my dear. Got by Sir Templeton of Kentucky and a fullbred on the dam side."

He was a sorrel and he had proved to be a nervy, sensitive horse, difficult to ride. But she had loved him as if he had been human right from the start and Thomas had watched her race him with enormous pride backed up by enormous wagers.

It was just too bad.

She shrugged. Well, the ladies at least would be happy. They had been horrified that she meant to ride so soon after Thomas's death. As if they knew one thing about her and Thomas. It was no dishoner to his memory to ride. From where his soul had gone she knew he would be looking down and saying, "Take those bets, Savanna. Take every last one of them, and then ride like fury and win." And he would himself be betting on her as high as heaven allowed.

It never ceased to puzzle her that so few people understood how different their marriage had been. David had told her one time, "Thomas could afford to give you a loose rein, my dear, because he left the service. It didn't matter if you scandalized the post and he rather enjoyed it. But if he had remained in the service he would have had to make you conform. The army can break a man and he's unlucky if he has a rebellious wife."

Savanna was aghast. "Then why on earth did Thomas marry me? He must have known I wouldn't make a very good army wife."

David's tobacco-brown eyes had searched her face. "Savanna, don't you have any idea what you are?"

"Myself."

"And one of the most exciting persons Thomas ever knew. He did the most illogical, inconsistent, adventurous thing of his life when he married you."

She giggled. "Heavens, what a risk!"

David's eyes had softened. "And what happiness."

Savanna picked up the paddle now and winced as her palms came in contact with the wood. She stared at them as if they were traitors. Why, she couldn't even paddle across the river! Silly, soft things to chafe so after a three-mile pull. You'd think all the riding she did would have kept them tough enough for that. She'd have to yell for the government flat to come over and get her.

Her head came up. I'll be swizzled if I do, she thought. The whole post would laugh at her. They would know, nothing was ever kept a secret for long on an army post, that she had gone raging down the river, and they would whisper, were already whispering, about what had sent her. They would put their heads together. "She went to see the colonel this morning. First day he's home from that two months's trip down the river. Couldn't wait to see him. Couldn't give him a chance to rest. Had to see him right now."

"What for?"

"Jacob said she came tearing out of the colonel's quarters like a flybitten mustang."

"Went skedaddling down the river to that island she's so crazy about and blistered her hands. Had to yell for the flatboat to get herself home."

Buzz, buzz, buzz.

She put the paddle down and ripped off her petticoat. Thank goodness it was an old one and worn thin. She tore it into strips and wound them around her hands. Savanna Brook was going to get home under her own steam, blisters or no blisters.

When she shoved the boat out into the current she was surprised to find that her hands hurt hardly at all. All that padding of cloth, of course.

She almost dropped the paddle as another idea dawned. Why couldn't she pad her hands heavily under Thomas's big leather gloves and ride tomorrow? Of course she could. She and Kizzy would work over those blisters tonight and bandage her palms an inch thick in the morning. And nobody would ever know. "We'll just see," she said, sending the pirogue a full length forward with a long stroke, and whooping with glee, "who wins that race tomorrow after all!"

II

Savanna went onto her back porch early the next morning to see what could be expected of the weather.

The day was brilliant, glittery, gold-dusty, with the light, dry, fine air which sent one heady with the sheer pleasure of breathing it. There were a few fat plushy clouds drifting across the sky looking like ruffled white geese on a wide blue lake.

45

The purple banks over the sun last night had been only a threat and had blown away during the night.

You couldn't ask for a more perfect day, nor expect to get it anywhere but here, Savanna thought, happy with the sun and drawing in deep draughts of the day-fresh air. It tastes like fruit, she thought. You could almost drink it and get drunk on it. She licked her lips as though the air could leave its taste on them. How wonderful that the rain had held off.

It was going to be a lucky day. She could feel it in her bones. With such beautiful weather only good things could happen—she grinned—except, she hoped, to Bill Felt and his big Tennessee horse. She couldn't possibly lose the race on a day like this. It was the kind the Duke liked best, winy, cool, with no trace of moisture. The track would be dry and fast, he would be edgy and nervous but he would run like a streak of lightning.

From the back porch where she stood, Savanna looked down on the river. It was wide and deep at this point, only three miles from its mouth. A thousand feet downstream was the ledge of rocks where the steamboats tied up. Speculatively she looked at the great iron ring sunk in the rock for their convenience. The *Robert Thompson* was due next week—its last trip for the season—and on it would be that big load of goods Thomas had ordered. She tapped her booted foot restlessly. She had to know what disposal she could make of them soon. In some way she must pin the colonel down and get his ear more attentively. She had to make him understand that if she had to let the shipment go in a lump lot to some trader she wouldn't raise enough on it to pay off the debt on it. She had to make him understand that she must have time to dispose of the goods in the usual, orderly way. She had some way to change that "Impossible" to "Very well, Savanna."

She looked at the sun again and moved away from the post. Abe was late. She was pleased that the colonel had assigned Abe as her handler for the race today, though she had protested at the time. "No, no," the colonel had said, waving off her protests, "you will need him since Thomas won't be with you."

"I'll have Preacher, Colonel Arbuckle," she had reminded him.

The colonel had chuckled. "Abe will be happy to serve you, Savanna. It will be a pleasant change of duty for him."

She was really very grateful because Preacher was slow and fussy and a little scared of the Duke. No one handled a horse better than Abe. He had horse sense built into him and he could feel the skittishness in an animal quicker than anyone

46

she had ever known. He knew how to work a horse out before a race without working off his edge, leaving him just tense enough to get off smoothly and run well. "Isn't Abe running one of his own horses today?" she asked.

"I believe not."

Savanna knew she would never know, from either the colonel or Abe, whether he had been ordered not to race today so he could be of help to her. She would hate it if he had been made to sacrifice his own pleasure. He had a string of good mustangs, any one of them a formidable horse in a race. But she could do nothing about orders, so she said, simply "Thank you, sir. I shall be happy to have Abe with me."

She was already dressed for the ride over to Bayou Menard where the Cherokee annuity was to be paid and the encampment held. Her heavy crimson skirt flowed about her boots and the jacket was buttoned severely to the chin. "What color shall I have my habit, Thomas?" she had asked.

"Red," he had said unhesitatingly, "as red as the scarlet tanager. That's what you'll look like on the Duke—a redbird on the wing."

She touched her jingly earrings. Sometimes Thomas had made her wear them to bed. "It's like sleeping with bells," he had said.

They'll bring me luck today, she thought, rubbing them. Thomas will be riding with me.

She left the porch and went into the house, her boot heels tapping briskly on the floor. "Kizzy, let's get these hands bandaged. Abe is late and I want to be ready to ride."

"Yessum."

Kizzy brought the fresh strips of cloth and went to work. She had punctured the blisters the night before and salved them and wrapped them against injury while Savanna slept. Now she unwrapped the night bandaging and examined the palms. Savanna bent to look also. "Sweet heaven, Kizzy! They look like raw beef!"

"I done tole you. You rides dat tough-moufed horse today an' saw on them lines de way you has to, dem hands ain't gwine be nothin' but a mess ob mincemeat. You is crazy to do sich a thing."

Savanna jerked her head. "Do what you can for them. They'll just have to be mincemeat. I've got to ride today."

"Why has you got to?"

She winced as Kizzy pulled away the last of the bandaging and wiped off the drainings. "That's my business."

Kizzy stole an oblique look at her. "I know de Duke got to run today, but ain't nothin' say you got to do de ridin', is they?

47

Why'nt you let Widgie ride? He know dat horse good as you does."

"Nobody knows that horse as well as I do. Besides, I've got to be up today. It's important. I know what I'm doing, Kizzy."

"Hmmmph. Sho' doan look lak it, wid dese hands."

The black woman finished winding one hand and began on the other. "Reckon de major be wantin' you goin' to dis 'campment by yo'self? Gwine be lots ob trash out dere."

Savanna was silent a moment before replying. Then she said, "Kizzy, I'm going to have to do a lot of things that wouldn't be necessary for me to do if the major was still living. We've gone to the annuity payments together before, but I've got to go alone this time. Thomas always set up store during the encampment and I mean to do what he's always done. I've sent over some trading goods from here and Albright is bringing more from the Fort Smith store. I expect him to do a good business for me during the encampment. Don't start carping at me, Kizzy. Thomas left me these three stores to provide for me. He knew I could run them. But a woman at the head of three stores has got to forget she is alone."

"You aimin' to run de stoahs yo'self?"

"That's precisely what I'm aiming to do and I'll do it as well as Thomas. I would be ashamed not to."

"Yessum. Ah 'spects you will. Ah ain't carpin', Miss Savanna. Anybody say a mumblin' word 'bout you carryin' on without de major me an' Preacher an' Widgie'll claw 'em up an' shet 'em up. Jist you tell us whut to do an' we does it. Long as me an' Preacher an' Widgie is wid you, you ain't by yo'self noway."

The satiny black face looked fiercely determined. Moved to the point of a sudden clutch at her throat, Savanna touched Kizzy's arm. "You're good, Kizzy, you're good. I couldn't do without you."

"Ain't gwine have to. Ah be's right heah."

Savanna stepped back and held her hands gingerly before her. "You've got these bandages nice and tight."

Kizzy gathered up the old wrappings and threw them into the fire. "We fix 'em again when we gits dere." She cocked her head. "Somebody comin'. Mister Abe, likely. How is I gwine, Miss Savanna?"

"Why, you're going to ride, of course, the way you always do."

"Not one ob Mister Abe's mustangs, ah ain't. No, ma'am!" Kizzy backed away, the whites of her eyes showing and bulging. "Ah jist soon be pecked to death by a duck as ride one ob dem wild horses, an' ah ain't aimin' to try."

"When did you ever have to ride a wild horse? Just tell me that! Every horse we've ever provided for you was gentled."

"Some ob 'em ain't been too gentle. Lak dat gray one bucked me off on my haid."

"It was your fault. You get on a horse like he was loaded with gunpowder."

"Dem mustangs usually is."

Savanna laughed. "Widgie has got you a nice old pack horse." She picked up Thomas's leather gloves from the table and slid them over the bandages. "Make sure Widgie puts the box with my dresses on top."

"Yessum. You aimin' to stay de whole month?"

"I don't know. It depends. Did you pack my green silk dress?"

"Ah packed it, but ah doan know why you needs it at a 'campment."

"I may not need it, but if I do I don't want it left at home." She grinned at Kizzy. "The colonel may have a real celebration for me after I win that race this afternoon."

"Yessum. Mek sho' you wins it, Miss Savanna."

"I mean to. A Company has been detached to the encampment, Kizzy. The colonel has promised to set up a tent for us in the company area. Look for it if you don't find me when you get there."

"Yessum."

Abe Lathrop was waiting for Savanna at the foot of the veranda steps.

He was twenty-six years old now, no longer the stripling friend of her brother Manifee. He had become what was called, on the frontier, a middle-heighted man, which meant only that he was not as tall as those who topped six feet. Actually he stood five-foot-eleven in moccasins. He was rangy and loose-jointed and weighed a scant one hundred and sixty pounds. His leanness, however, was thongy with sinew and he was the only man Savanna knew who had never had the intemittent fever. "Too tough to ail," he told her. "Besides, I've not got the time."

She had known him for nine years, but knew very little about him or his past. He never talked about his home or his origins. He had been recruited in St. Louis and been posted west with the Seventh. For a time, during the years of friendship with her brother, he had come to Phillips Landing often. The two boys had been impatient, however, of a girl tagging after them and she had not truly got to know him well. When Manifee left home, Abe quit coming. When she married Thomas Brook and moved to Gibson, she saw Abe about the cantonment, but he was an enlisted man and her husband held an officer's rank. The barrier was very real, and she had made no attempt to cross it.

He was in uniform today, wearing a forage cap tipped down over his eyes. As Savanna joined him, he dismounted and pushed the cap back, grinning at her. "Keep you waiting long, Savanna? I had a little trouble catching up the animals."

He was riding one horse and leading another for her.

Preacher had already taken the Duke to the camp ground. The Indians raced their horses straight from a long ride over the prairies, and some of the officers and men rode their mounts to the tracks, but Savanna saved the Duke all she could.

She ran a knowledgeable eye over the mustang Abe had provided for her and her heart sank a little. He had given her a spirited mount. Today she would have preferred a gentler animal, but she grinned back at him. "He didn't like that sidesaddle, did he?"

"That one don't like any kind of a saddle yet," Abe said.

"You haven't put a burr under the blanket, have you, Abe?"

Abe's grin widened. "He'll give you a ride without it."

"I expect he will," she said dryly.

"You ready?"

She nodded.

Abe led the horse around to the porch and held the reins while she mounted by herself. With a newly broken mustang a man couldn't be gallant with a lady. She had to be ready to ride the moment she hit the saddle. Abe held the reins choked up and forced the horse to stand until Savanna had got her knee around the saddle horn. He flung her the reins and got out of the way. Savanna let the mustang raise a little dust, then she sawed the lines and brought him up. "God's britches, Abe, you just break this one?"

From his own saddle, Abe spat tobacco juice and grinned. "Thought you'd like him. I caught him last week coming back from Towson. He don't gentle easy, though, and he still shies some. Don't let up on those lines or you're liable to pick yourself up out of the bushes."

Thoughtfully Savanna looked down at the mustang now standing quietly under her firm hands. She would have loved to ride this horse to Bayou Menard—she loved to pit her strength against that of a spirited horse and her will against his—but she simply could not afford it today. Her hands would be too raw before she got to the encampment. She sighed. She would have to ask Abe to change mounts with her. Her mind went to work on a reason to give. She had not the least intention of letting him know her hands were sore.

She did not realize her mobile face was showing her regret and indecision until Abe said, "What's the matter? Don't you like him?"

She leaned forward and smoothed the horse's shoulder. "I love him, Abe, but I can't ride him to Bayou Menard. I might injure my hands." She held up Thomas's glove. "I'm wearing these to protect them."

Abe frowned. "Why, sure. Ought to've thought of it myself. Here, I'll shift the saddles and you take the mare. She'll ride you over in a rockingchair."

Savanna slid off, taking a deep breath of relief.

The saddles changed, she mounted again and watched as Abe tipped his boot into the stirrup and suddenly vaulted into the saddle. In the same moment he whooped the horse into a run and hat-whipped him across the campus. Savanna shouted and tried to knee her animal into a lope. She had been so taken with the mustang she hadn't paid any attention to Abe's other mount but she looked more closely as the mare slogged into a jolting trot and would not be budged from it. Why, drat his hide, this was the old fat mare he had put to pasture a year ago. Said she was getting too old to ride and he was going to use her only for breeding. A rockingchair, my foot! What a fine, elegant way to arrive at the encampment—mounted on a brood mare!

As wrathful and ruffled as a wet hen, Savanna finally gave up trying to nudge the mare any faster. What in the name of sweet heaven did Abe mean bringing her today? She was a strange choice for him to make when he had a dozen horses in his string. Why ride the old mare?

Suspicion began to dawn.

He was waiting for her at the edge of the woods where the military road to Fort Smith skirted the canebrakes and swamps. She pulled up beside him, her mouth tight. "I ought to horsewhip you," she said. "How did you know about my hands?"

He met her gaze and did not try to equivocate. "Preacher told me last night. Said you'd have to be careful of 'em today. How'd you figure I knew?"

"This damn mare! You wouldn't ride her across the campus, and you know it. You meant for me to ride the easiest horse you had."

"This mustang had your saddle on it," he said mildly.

"That was a trick. You knew I couldn't risk my hands with him."

"And I knew you just might if I tried to give you Bessie

51

first. Yes, ma'am, it was a trick, you being as bullheaded as you are and always have been."

Savanna almost choked and Abe grinned at her. "I've not forgot your ways, Savanna, and there's no use getting your temper up. At least I've not tried to talk you out of riding. I know you've got to ride today. I know all about those bets you've covered. But if I'm going to handle your horse today, handling you is part of the job and I aim to get you to Bayou Menard in shape to ride."

Savanna's anger died away. Her brow cleared and she broke into laughter. "Well, the joke is on me, Abe. I forgive you."

Abe spat. "Didn't ask you to. What the hell did you go high-tailing down the river for? And what made you take a damn pirogue?"

Savanna lifted her shoulders and pulled her horse around to take the path which branched off the road. "I don't know. I was so mad I wasn't thinking. It was tied up there and I took it."

"Fool thing to do. Minute I heard it I knew you'd make your hands sore."

"You needn't keep carping about it. They're my hands."

"Oh, sure."

They lapsed into silence.

The path was wide enough for them to ride side by side and Abe swung around to Savanna's right. They were going east. Bayou Menard was only ten miles away and even at a walk they would reach the encampment in good time. They were in no hurry and they let the animals choose their own pace. Abe's new mustang, his first wildness run off, was tractable now and paced along at the old mare's gait.

Around the fort, in the lowlands, the timber was tall and the growth was lush, but as Savanna and Abe trotted over the rolling land to the east they came into the long swells of treeless meadows and the short timber of the ridge lands. The sun was a warm arm around their shoulders and the grassy plains swam in its brilliant, golden light.

Out of the silence, Abe spoke. "The colonel didn't much like the idea of giving you the major's job, did he?"

Glancing at him obliquely, Savanna gave him a short answer. "No." Then she added, "Does everybody know?"

"They think they do. What did he say?"

"He said it was impossible. Said he was appalled." The anger which had sent her pelting down the river yesterday was still only barely contained and suddenly it burst forth again. "Great gobs of mud, Abe, he wouldn't even listen to me! Wouldn't let me tell him a thing. The minute I said I'd like to have the post he began shaking his head and holding up his hands and you'd have thought he was a parrot with only one word learned—impossible. *Nothing* is impossible."

"In the army a lot of things are," Abe said dryly, "and I expect a woman sutler is one of them."

"I don't believe it."

"Why do you want to keep the sutler's store, Savanna? You've got the other stores. It don't make sense to me."

"Because Thomas ordered ten thousand dollars' worth of goods on credit last spring and they'll be here on the *Robert Thompson* next week and I don't mean to lose on them. I *can't*. With a debt that big the other stores can't pay off. I've got to have the sutler's store too."

Abe whistled. "What made him order so heavy?"

"The Cherokees are moving into the Purchase, and the Creeks are beginning to arrive from Alabama. Thomas figured he needed more stock. A lot of it is perishable, too, and I can't keep it in the warehouses long."

Abe was quiet and then he said, "I reckon the colonel didn't mention somebody else wanting the post, did he?"

Savanna shot him a quick look. "No. Is there somebody else?"

"You didn't think half a dozen didn't begin scheming the minute the major died, did you?"

"Sure, I knew they would. And I know who one or two are. Chouteau would like to have it for his brother, for one. But who did you have in mind?"

"Major Short," Abe said bluntly.

Savanna felt as though she had been punched in the stomach suddenly. One of the officers would have a better chance than anyone else. "Why would Fred Short want it? He's second in command and he's not anywhere near old enough to retire yet. He's got about twenty years to go. He could get a command yet."

"Well, your husband made a mighty good thing of it. Reckon Major Short thinks he'd like to try his hand at it."

"That doesn't make sense. Fred's got a good chance of making general before he retires. I don't believe he would throw that away. There's something behind this, if he's serious about it."

"He's serious," Abe said. He added, laughing, "Maybe he's decided he'd rather make money than make general."

Savanna didn't laugh. "It's not funny."

Abe shrugged. "I wouldn't know."

They rode silently down a long, grass-bearded slope to a narrow creek rimmed with cottonwoods. In the shade they let the

53

horses drink. Savanna watched the clear, shallow water ripple over the white stones, her mind still worrying this new difficulty. Suddenly she laughed. "Of course. It's Martha. I said something was behind this, and it's Martha. She wants this for Fred. How old would you say she is, Abe?"

"Good Lord, how would I know? She looks about sixty."

"No. No, she's not that much older than Fred." Savanna gnawed her lower lip. "Fred is forty-five, I know that. The women say Martha won't tell her age because she's at least ten years older than Fred. She could be. That would make her around fifty-five."

"What difference does it make?"

"A lot, maybe. Maybe she's getting old enough to be tired of shifting around from post to post. Maybe she's getting old enough that settling down some place would look mighty good to her. And what could be more settled than the sutler's job at Gibson?"

Abe shifted in his saddle. "I dunno. If the major has got all this future ahead of him, how could his wife talk him into leaving the army?"

"You don't know much about women, do you?"

Abe exploded. "No, thank God!" He pulled the mustang's head up and prodded him with his heels.

Savanna followed him up the creek bank. "How much do you know about it, Abe?"

"Not much," he admitted. "Some of the men in the barracks began talking about it a couple of weeks ago. Said the major was after the post. Where it began and who started it, I don't know. My guess would be that the major's orderly overheard him and his wife talking and spread it around."

"What else do you know?"

"He went to see the colonel yesterday morning, same as you." Abe grinned at her. "He got there ahead of you, though. Maybe that's why the colonel was so short with you. First day he's back at the fort and two of you come sailing in wanting the same thing. And his gout's acting up. Likely he was rubbed the wrong way."

Savanna made a wry face. "Something sure rubbed him the wrong way." She sighed heavily. "Being a woman has its disadvantages, Abe."

"Has its advantages, too," Abe said. "You ever think about trying that?"

"Trying what?"

"Making eyes at the colonel."

"Oh, talk sense. I never made eyes at a man in my life and

54

I'm not about to begin with Colonel Arbuckle. This is business."

Abe ducked under a low-hanging limb. "He's pretty fond of you, Savanna. 'Twouldn't take much encouragement to make him speak out."

Savanna stared at him. "What do you mean?"

"Well, you could do worse than marry the colonel of the regiment. He's a nice old fellow and he's got that whole island down the river where he means to retire. I've seen it and it's fifteen thousand acres of the richest land in the country. Of course, you couldn't run your stores, but you wouldn't have to. You could live right handsomely down there."

Savanna kicked at the old mare's flanks. "This animal is so fat you'd need a Spanish spur to tickle her into a walk," she fumed. "I don't want to live handsomely on Colonel Arbuckle's island or anybody else's island. I want to save what Thomas left me. I've got three stores to tend, if he doesn't take one of them away from me, and if I'm just let alone I'll live right handsomely by myself."

Abe looked at her from the corner of his eyes. "You don't aim to marry again? Or is it just the colonel?"

"I've got no thought or time for it. I just want to get on with my work."

"All right, Savanna, don't take my head off. I just thought the idea might appeal to you."

"It doesn't."

"Then forget it."

He looked about and picked up the familiar marks of the trail. "We're still five miles from Bayou Menard. We better hustle a little." He kicked the mustang into a trot and Savanna made the old mare follow, though she snorted and heaved.

At the last, the spreading encampment in sight, Abe left her behind, making a flourishing and impressively noisy entrance by whooping the mustang into a hard run and weaving him between tents, lodges, and shelters, raising a dust and sending people and animals scattering out of his way. He could not help it, Savanna knew, nor did she blame him. She would have done the same thing if she could, and she was ashamed that she could not. The mare being what she was, however, she had to follow more sedately.

She was met by half a dozen young officers who spied her and came running. "Miss Savanna, your tent is in the company area."

"The colonel had it pitched near his own quarters."

Savanna slowed the mare to a walk. "Thank you, gentlemen. It was very thoughtful of the colonel."

They began to bait her joyfully about the mare. "Where'd you get the crowbait, Miss Savanna?"

"That the horse that's going to beat Bill Felt today?"

"You think she'll make it to the starting post, Miss Savanna?"

Lieutenant Joyner, the colonel's young aide, pretended to be smitten with remorse, clapping his hand to his head. "My God, I've bet a whole month's pay on Miss Savanna and this is what she's going to ride. Where's the Duke? I won't be able to pay my mess bill for six months."

Nettled, but determined to die before showing it, Savanna smiled serenely down at them and said to Lieutenant Joyner, "You can mess with me, James, until you're in funds again. I wouldn't dream of letting you starve."

Gallantly he replied, "That would be worth losing a month's pay, Miss Savanna."

The other officers took it up. "Hey, I bet all my pay too, Miss Savanna."

"And me."

"I never lost a bet on Miss Savanna before, but it would be worth it to eat supper at her house for a month."

"You gentlemen are much too nice," Savanna said sweetly. "How many of you *really* bet on the Duke today?"

"I did."

"I did."

"I did."

Liars, she thought, but not a trace of the thought crept into the pleasant smile she had fastened on her face—every blasted one of you has got money on Felt's horse and you're lying in your teeth.

Walking beside the mare the officers made an escort for her through the encampment. She kept her head high, bantered with the young men as if she hadn't a care in the world, and kept the smile on her face. Out of the corner of her eye she had seen some of the army wives sitting in the shade in the company area. Let them look. They would see Savanna Brook unworried and unafraid. They wouldn't know about her sore hands, or about the possibility of losing most of her money, or even about this last threat Fred Short posed for her. They would not see her bedeviled and beset with worries. If she died for it, all they would see would be a proud young woman, clustered about with A Company officers and staff. Let them put their heads together and whisper it was too soon after her husband's death. If they had the sense God gave a gosling they should know she wouldn't have given Thomas's little finger for all the officers in the regiment lumped together.

They passed slowly along, dogs and children and Indians moving aside, Savanna's black hair windblown from the ride but her habit neat, close-fitting, showing off her high-breasted, slim-waisted figure. Small whorls of dust rose from the mare's feet and wheeled away behind them. The young officers strode beside her with their faces lifted to her, laughing, juggling each other for a place by her stirrups, each eager to be the one to lift her off her mount.

When she drew up before her own tent, James Joyner was the lucky man. As she slid into his arms he whispered in her ear, "Miss Savanna, I wasn't lying. I have bet on the Duke, although not as much as a month's pay."

She flashed him a look of gratitude. He was such a conscientious, honorable boy. He had a round baby-face with pink cheeks and was barely able to grow a mustache. He was new at the cantonment and just out of the Academy. He replaced a member of the colonel's staff who had died a few months earlier. He was already lovestruck and mooned calfishly over Savanna, but she took it easily. He would get over it. He was still wet behind the ears. "I'm not going to lose that race today, James." She smiled at the other men. "Gentlemen—I hope you lose your shirts."

"Miss Savanna!"

It was one thing to place their small bets on Bill Felt's horse and quite another to have her find it out. Their greatest comfort was her home, and if they angered her . . .

"Do you think I am blind and deaf and dumb? Now, if you'll excuse me . . ."

"But, Miss Savanna . . ."

"Oh, scat. All of you!" But she relented enough to grin at them. "Don't fret. I'm not going to forbid you the house. But do run along now. I have a thousand things to do."

"Yes, ma'am."

"Miss Savanna, I'm sorry . . ."

"Shoo!" She lifted her skirt and shook it at them, and they fled down the street.

She stood a moment, looking around.

Below her tent, one of the last in the military row, was the big and impressive lodge of some Cherokee chief. Absently she thought, it must be John Jolly's. Her mind was intent on the things she must do. She must find Albright and make certain he had set up the trading tent in a good place. She must visit the corral and see the Duke and watch Abe work him out. She must have Kizzy bandage her hands again. She spared only a recognition of the size of the lodge, the Negro servants working about it, to determine it could only be Jolly's. He was one of the richest of the Cherokees, living in a rustic splendor at his place near the mouth of the Illinois.

As she stood, thinking, two men came out of the Indian's lodge. One of them was Jolly himself. The other man she did not know. He was dressed like an Indian but she had never seen an Indian so tall. He towered over Jolly by a foot or more. He seemed to stretch up and up to an unbelievably tall and limbery height.

Her attention riveted now, she stared. The man's back was turned so that at first she could not see his face, but as she stared he moved, circling around to get out of the sun. He was a white man, with a shaven face except for a mustache and a small goatee. His hair was plaited in a queue down his back and was so bright a chestnut that it came near being red. He covered all but the queue with a silk turban, a brilliantly gaudy silk turban such as the Creeks liked to wear.

He wore a white doeskin shirt heavily and handsomely beaded. Leggings of elaborately ornamented yellow leather extended to his thighs. Over his shoulders was thrown a bright blanket which, Savanna thought, must be for show. He certainly did not need it on this mild day. He was as gaunt as he was tall, but he still made a magnificent figure. Who was he?

As she watched, John Jolly touched the man affectionately, patting his arm. The tall, gaunt man bowed and walked away, a little unsteady on his feet. He's drunk, Savanna thought —whoever he is, he's very drunk.

She dismissed him from her mind and lifted the flap of her tent.

III

The site chosen for the annuity payments was a wide, grassy meadow near the small stream called Bayou Menard.

It was cupped on three sides by wooded ridges. At the foot of the ridge to the north the Company area had been laid out in the edge of the woods. Its wide avenue marched down the center with the precision of a measuring rod and its tents were ranked in rows like the headstones in a graveyard. It was shaded, neat, and quite military looking. It was also handily near the creek and an excellent supply of wood. A rough corral for the officers' horses had been thrown up at the west end of the street.

From the Company area the land fell away a little onto the meadow, and dead center on this rise Colonel Arbuckle had set up his quarters. He had a front porch view of the entire encampment.

Savanna's tent was at the end of officers' row. It was pitched under a great cedar tree whose drooping limbs would protect it from the weather.

She sat in front of the tent now, resting before the races began. Inside, she could hear Kizzy thumping about, grumbling and growling to herself. She didn't like the tent's location. She wanted it nearer the water. "Gwine break my back fetchin' water all dat way."

"It isn't a hundred yards, Kizzy."

"Too fur, whutever it be."

"Have Widgie carry it. He may as well make himself useful."

"Yessum." There was one last parting shot. "Ah done tuk notice de cunnel got his own tent handiest de creek."

"That's his privilege."

Savanna's hands were freshly bandaged and she rested them in her lap to hide in the folds of her skirt should someone come by unexpectantly. She had seen Albright's location and approved it; the man was sound. She had seen the Duke. She had eaten, and there was nothing more for her to do but wait until time to start for the track. There would be seven races during the afternoon, but only the fifth was important to her. It was the one in which she would ride,

She rested and watched the incredibly colorful, active, and confusing scene spread for a mile in front of her.

The whole meadow was filled. Every kind of shelter used by man, save a mansion or a cave, was represented on the wide, hill-cupped plain. There were Indian lodges of every size and shape and construction, from blankets to skins to logs and slabs. There were bark-sided huts, brush arbors, and canopies stretched from wagons. There were conical tents, round tents, rectangular tents and the plain pyramidal tent. The simplest of the camping places were those with only a ring of fire stones with a tree for a roof.

There were ten thousand people milling around down there and more coming every minute. There were the gaudy Creeks, the dark phlegmatic Choctaws, the handsome coppery Cherokees, the fierce proud Osages, all in great numbers. There were a few bandylegged Ouapaws and sinewy Delawares. There were quarterbreeds and halfbreeds, with French or Spanish or American blood mingled with their Indian. There were fullbloods and mulattoes and Negroes. There were breechclouts and buckskins and blankets. There were bristling roaches and braids and turbans. There were feathers and bells and eagle wings and bear's-claw necklaces. There were nose flutes and drums and bone whistles. There were women and children and dogs and horses. There were old men, young men, braves, warriors and hunters. It was a Cherokee payment, but not an Indian in the country would miss it.

And there were white men.

Weaving along the dusty roads already beaten out between the lodges were trappers and hunters in their dirty, stinking buckskins, bearded, weathered men with their hands knotted from icy water and their eyes bleary and whiskey-reddened. They had come from the creeks and the mountains from as far as five hundred miles away, to drink and gamble and hell around. "Gonna git me a skinful," they had said. And they would fill their skins as long as the pelts they could trade lasted.

There were the whisky runners. They were the riffraff, derelicts washed off the tides of civilization, without conscience or scruple. Most of them were as dirty and stinking as the trappers and hunters, as illiterate and tough, but infinitely more ruthless. Some of them were outlaws, hunted men, murderers, thieves, fugitives from justice. Their kind flocked to the Territory as soon as it was opened, to fleece the Indians, and they were to make trouble for a hundred years to come.

There were the traders from Three Forks—Hugh Love, Nathaniel Pryor, Sandy Mann, all with their tents and goods. There would have been her uncle, Johnny Fowler, if he had not gone farther west.

And there was Auguste Chouteau, the most fabulous character on the frontier. French, literate, aristocratic, proud, he went about with his dark, slim body impeccably clothed in white linen, a fine white hat on his silky hair. A member of the greatest fur trading family in America, he maintained one home and wife in St. Louis, and another home with two Indian wives on the Neosho. There were children in both homes. He recognized and had had baptized the several children by the Osage women but nobody, least of all himself, had any idea how many others he had sired.

His trading post on the Verdigris was the biggest and most profitable in the country. He sent twice as many pelts downriver each year as all the other posts put together. His family were long experienced in dealing with the Indians, and Auguste Chouteau had had a long training himself.

His home up the Neosho was a great log lodge which he ran like a tavern, opening it to every trader passing by. With perverted humor, an inevitable part of his famous hospitality was the offer to furnish a squaw for the night. It amused him to see the way the offer was taken. He had the manners of a prince, the palate of a gourmet, and the morals of a tomcat. He had also the greatest influence, as yet, of any man on the frontier.

There were speculators and gamblers from New Orleans, Natchez, St. Louis and Little Rock, city men with a dandy look about them. In shiny boots they strode about, their crown hats tipped rakishly, their waistcoats spanned with heavy gold watch chains. They were there to grab land or money or peltries, by any kind of double-dealing it took. This was the biggest payment ever made to any tribe of Indians. It had been owed the Cherokee for many years; and it was rumored it was to be paid in gold. It was worth coming from New Orleans for.

The speculators had brought with them most of the painted and floozy light women who were already wandering about the skirts of the encampment, although one enterprising trader from the Dardanelle had thoughtfully brought a boatload of women upstream with his other goods. It was trade, wasn't it?

They would do a flourishing trade among the enlisted men, the trappers and hunters, some of the settlers, and a few of the young officers would sneak off to them when night fell. Starved for a white woman's body they would be tempted, even if it must be bought. Some of the Indians, the quarter and halfbreeds, the mulattoes, would also visit them. But the fullbloods, for the most part, would leave them alone. They did not like white women. The mixed bloods were nearly always the result of a liaison between white men and Indian women.

Somewhere down there in that horde of people which boiled and bubbled like a simmering pot of porridge, there were also the Indian agents.

It was taken for granted on the frontier that the only reason for taking an agency was to line your own pockets at the expense of your Indian charges. Why else bother with it? The pay was meager and the Indians were unceasingly troublesome. There was no criticism involved. There was some envy and jealousy because the agents had known the right people in the government to get appointed. Almost to a man there wasn't a frontiersman who wouldn't have done the same thing in their shoes, and was doing it in his own way in his own situation. It was easy to blame an Indian for every strayed cow or horse and to collect double its worth from an ignorant and distant government. It would only be charged against the Osage annuity, or the Cherokee, or the Creek, or the Choctaw. With every man's hand in the till, each man, settler, trader, and even soldier, felt he would be a fool if he didn't get his own hand in.

It was simplest to marry an Indian woman and get your hands on her share of the bounty money, live with her on the tribal lands, make whiskey and sell it at an enormous profit in the peltry trade, the pelts being shipped downriver later.

Even Thomas had shut his eyes to the use of whiskey in his own trading stores. "You can't trade without it," he had said. "An Indian won't trade without whiskey."

Savanna railed at the stupidity of the government which had made whiskey illegal. "With the gumption of a goose they ought to have known it wouldn't work."

"Well, my dear," Thomas said, "even the government has a conscience. It was an effort to protect them. A sober Indian hasn't much chance with white men and a drunken one has none."

"It's a fool law that can't be enforced. All it does is make whiskey running one of the most profitable operations in the country and gives the army one of its most footless chores."

"And makes lawbreakers," Thomas added dryly, "out of honest traders."

But Thomas had kept it under control, as she meant to do herself. An Indian got one cup of whiskey, an honest cupful of unwatered whiskey, when he had finished trading, and no more. "I'll have no Indian saying I have cheated him," Thomas said. "If he gets drunk and gambles away all his belongings, he'll blame me for it."

Back in the woods which circled this meadow, hidden in thickets of undergrowth or in small ravines and hollows, were the stations of the whiskey runners. Paths were being beaten to the hiding places at this moment, Savanna knew. The soldiers would search out a few of them, but not even the entire regiment could root out all of them. It was a strongly forged chain which the army could not break, however hard it tried. The Indians, having learned to like the stuff, were wild for it and white men were always going to sell it to them.

She bowed as the Cherokee agent rode past her tent, lifting his hat to her. Her eyes followed him speculatively. It was that man's duty to pay the annuities to the Cherokees and the huge bounty sum. It was his further duty to protect them, to the utmost of his ability, against being cheated once the money was in their hands. That it would be impossible, perhaps he knew. Savanna wondered. She wouldn't want to be in his shoes for the next four weeks while this payment was going on. Thomas had believed him an honorable man, but he was going to need more than honor on his side. He was going to need shrewdness, a very sharp eye, and even ruthlessness if he was going to match the rascals and rapscallions who had gathered here to fight tooth and nail for everything they could lay hands on. No, she didn't envy him. Whatever happened, he was between a rock and a hard place.

"Come back to earth, Savanna. You're woolgathering."

She looked up quickly, flicking the folds of her skirt over her hands. "David. I didn't know you were here. Kizzy, bring a stool for Mister David."

"Don't bother. I'll sit here on the ground. I came over with the Company yesterday. Thought I'd look on a few days."

He lowered himself to the cool, needlestrewn sand under the cedar tree and sprawled comfortably at full length, shoving his battered, peaked old cap to the back of his head. "Abe said tell you he'd finished working out the Duke and Preacher was rubbing him down."

"Did you see him?"

"The Duke? Yes."

"What do you think, David?"

"He'll go. Abe thinks so, too. He'll go hard all the way."

"Good. He'll need to."

"How about your hands?"

Vexed, Savanna flounced on her stool. "Does everybody know about my hands?"

"No. But I do . . . Abe does."

"Well, they'll go, too," she said crisply.

"Fine." David grinned up at her. "What were you thinking when I came up? Your face was as long as a fiddle."

"The Cherokee agent just passed. I was thinking what a tough job he has on his hands."

David nodded. "Glad it's his and not mine. All hell's going to bust loose in this place when he starts paying."

"When does he think to begin?"

"Doesn't know. Money hasn't come yet."

"Do you suppose they're going to put them off again?"

"No, it's in Fort Smith."

"Gold?"

David squinted up at her. "Savanna, you haven't believed that rumor have you? Do you have any idea how heavy that much gold would be?"

"I hadn't thought about it."

"Fifty thousand in gold? I can tell you it weighs far too much. I couldn't swear to it, of course, but in my opinion they'll pay in script."

Savanna let her eyes roam from one end of the vast encampment to the other, and her thoughts went to the more than three thousand Cherokees waiting for this payment. "The poor devils," she said, finally, "the poor, poor devils."

"Yes," said David. "Hard money doesn't mean much to an Indian and paper money is practically worthless. They'll trade it off for nothing or throw it away. The speculators will get rich, of course."

"I wish," she said bitterly, "I wish the President in Washington and his precious Secretary of War who are responsible for the whole thing had to be here just one time, to see for themselves every dirty, stinking, crooked thing about it! They've got no idea what goes on out here."

"You think they'd care if they did have? Do you have any idea what kind of a deal Andrew Jackson made in the South to get himself elected President? He promised to get rid of every Indian east of Mississippi—and he's doing it and he doesn't care how it's done. He wouldn't mind if the last Indian was rubbed off the face of the earth. It'd save him a lot of bother."

Savanna looked down at David, his blocky body wholly at ease and loose-sprawled on the sand. It occurred to her that he was one of the cleverest men she knew; that he read and puzzled and thought until he reached the heart of a thing and that he was rarely fooled by surface appearances.

She wished he would shave off his beard, but mustaches and full-grown beards were the fashion for men and she supposed he never would. Even Thomas had let his beard grow the last two years of his life. And that wrinkled, baggy linsey jacket that hung on him like a sack, and the cap that was greasy and torn and so ancient it barely held together. But without them, she supposed, he would not be the same David, and she was so very fond of him just as he was, his disreputable, merry, probing, shrewd self. There were some things, she knew, a woman ought never to try to change about a man. If David ever married, some of his peculiar habits would simply have to be accepted.

He was gazing, his eyes squinted at the sun, down the slope, raised up on an elbow to look. "What is it, David?"

"That tall man going into Jolly's lodge."

She glanced quickly, in time to see the blanketed figure disappear through the opening. "I saw him this morning. Who is he?"

"Sam Houston."

"Who is Sam Houston?"

David's mouth stretched widely. "You never heard of him?"

"No."

"What a blow to his vanity—of which he has plenty. Until he came here, my dear, he was Governor of Tennessee."

"What's he doing here?"

David sat up, shrugging. "That's what the colonel would like to know."

"When did he come? How long has he been here?"

64

"Some say he's been here a couple of months—living with Jolly. They say he's been sick of the fever most of the time. First we heard of him at the cantonment was from Pryor. He said Sam Houston was visiting up at Chouteau's. Said he was living with Jolly and calling himself Jolly's adopted son. The colonel's right troubled about him."

"Why? Why should he be?"

"Well, he's a good friend of President Jackson's for one thing. Jackson sort of sponsored him in politics and backed him when he ran for governor."

Savanna looked sharply at David. "Has he been sent here officially?"

"No. No orders on him and he has presented no credentials. But that may not mean much. It's possible he's here unofficially. Or he may have some scheme of his own in mind. Nobody knows and that's what's bothersome about it."

Savanna's eyes went back to the Indian lodge. "How'd he get Jolly to adopt him?"

"That goes a long way back. Houston was a subagent to the Cherokees once in Tennessee. The colonel says he's always been crazy about them and that he ran away from home when he was a kid to live with them. Jolly adopted him then. He's just welcomed him with open arms now."

"Do you suppose they . . . the Cherokees sent for him . . . ?"

"Don't know. I do know he had to get out of Tennessee in a hurry."

"Why?"

David pulled at his beard. "Well, the little lady he married walked out on him exactly three months after the wedding ceremony and there was such a hassle and scandal he had to resign and leave the country."

Savanna's eyebrows went up. "What happened?"

"Nobody knows that, either. They married, they lived together three months, than there was some sort of ruckus and the little lady went home to her family."

"And he resigns his office and comes to the Indian Territory to live with the Cherokees. Well, Tennessee's loss seems to be our gain."

David reared himself up and hugged his knees between his arms. "Not so sure about that."

"Go on."

"He's been visiting considerably with the tribes. The agents think he's trying to stir up trouble."

"What kind of trouble?"

David met her look with twinkling eyes. "Well for the agents it would be enough trouble if he was spying on them and meant to get them removed."

"Can he?"

"There's that friendship with the President. *They* think he can, anyhow. And some of the traders are watching him pretty closely. *They* think he means to set up store for himself."

"That," Savanna said, "I wouldn't like myself. There are enough of us without him."

David nodded. "They say the man's eaten up with nerves and whiskey. They say he can't sleep."

"Why?"

David shifted his legs and spat out the cedar twig on which he had been chewing. "I don't suppose anybody could know the answer to that but Sam Houston. It stands to reason, though, he broods a lot over his bad luck. A man would. Lost his wife, lost his job, lost his prestige, lost his future. With Andrew Jackson behind him, it's not impossible he had his eye on the White House—and who's to say he wouldn't have got it. Then—whoof. Quicker than a puff of smoke, it's all gone. The wonder is that he didn't shoot his brains out."

"Well, God's britches, why didn't he stay and fight? Why did he tuck his tail and run?"

"His friends say he was too gallant to drag a woman's name in the dirt. My guess is, he was scared. Whatever parted them must have been pretty ugly and he didn't want the scandal to come out."

"Has she kept her mouth shut too?"

"Shut as an oyster."

"They sound to me like a pair of precious fools."

"Ah, Savanna, the way of men with maids was even wondrous to the Preacher."

"To who?"

The gaps in Savanna's education always amused David. He laughed. "Sugar, don't you even know the Bible?"

"I read it every night!"

"Yes, your dutiful chapter. Well, never mind." He chose another twig to put in his mouth. "There's a good story about Houston making the rounds. Seems when he was traveling this way he stopped overnight at John Linton's place. You know who John Linton is, don't you?"

"If he's the one that's always spouting the classics and has never been seen sober."

"That's him. Lives down near the Dardanelle. Well, Houston spent the night in his cabin as he journeyed to join us and the next morning Linton determined to ride a piece with him. Houston is said to be a great Latin scholar and it seems they took great joy in each other. When night overtook them

66

they camped in an abandoned hut and abandoned themselves to a couple of days of feasting and drinking and quoting the Latin poets. When it came time for Houston to continue his journey they were so sad over the disruption of their joy in each other they decided to make a sacrifice to Bacchus. The sacrifice," David added, "was to be their clothing."

"Their clothing?" Savanna's eyebrows went up.

"Their clothing. They built a huge fire and Houston opened the ceremony by casting his hat into the blaze. When it had burnt they were entitled, by the rules they had made, to have a drink. Then Linton threw his hat into the fire. This entitled them to another drink. Houston's coat went next, then Linton's."

Savanna's dark eyes were as round as a child's.

David continued. "There followed their waistcoats and then their trousers, and so on until both men were stark, mother-naked bare and drunker than hoot owls."

"David, you're making it up!"

"Upon my word and honor, I am not." He vowed with his hand on his heart. "Then Houston's black man put both of them to bed. But he only let Houston sleep a little while, then wakened him and dressed him and rode him away. Houston, of course, had luggage with him and a change of clothing. But poor Linton was left without a stitch, his clothing all burnt, and a hundred miles from home." David's mouth twitched. "It must have been right startling to waken the next morning in such a state."

Savanna's mouth quivered as she tried to contain her laughter. "What did he do?"

"The tale don't tell," David said, containing his own amusement, "but they do say that Mrs. Linton met her husband at the door when he arrived home and failed to recognize him."

"Sweet heaven, why?"

"Well, the insects are pretty bad down that way."

Savanna gave up and whooped and David released his own pure joy in the tale and raised a shout that made the old cedar tree shake and tremble.

It was a story that grew with pondering, that tickled the imagination afresh, and as they mulled it over each broke into new gales of laughter again and again. At length it was exhausted and they sat, incapable of further risibility, in a long and peaceful silence.

A small wind sighed through the cedar branches and shook a few dried needles down on them. Absently Savanna bunched those that had fallen on her skirt into a bundle and discarded them. Over the encampment the sky was like blue silk and the sun laid a golden glaze on everything it touched. The trees on the far ridges stood tranced in the soft air, their leaves glancing new scarlet and yellow in the brilliant light. A hawk sailed on lazy wings over the creek, banking, turning, rising, falling, in slow unhurried grace.

John Jolly and Sam Houston came out of the Indian's lodge and walked away together.

David and Savanna watched them go. As if his thoughts were very far away David said, softly, "Suppose a shrewd, clever man with dreams of his own, say dreams of an empire in the west, say Texas for instance, came to the Territory. Do you believe he could sway these Indians to join him?"

Savanna stared at him. "What on earth are you getting at, David?"

"Nothing. Nothing at all." He suddenly heaved himself to his feet and brushed the needles and sand from the seat of his pants. "But Texas is just a hundred miles from here. Be an awfully good place to be if a man was . . . say, dreaming." He became brisk. "About to forget what I came for. Colonel Arbuckle sends his compliments and asks if Miss Savanna will join his party at the track this afternoon."

Savanna's eyes lit with amusement and she met the surgeon's own twinkling gaze. "Tell the colonel," she said, "that Miss Savanna will be very happy to join his party."

IV

The track was a rough oval laid out on the flattest part of the meadow, west of the encampment.

It was not a good race track for the land was chucky with sand, gravel, and hummocky grass; but no one was accustomed to much better. Wild about racing as the entire country was, the races were yet run on the crudest kind of courses, many times straight across the prairie Indian fashion.

Auguste Chouteau had the best track in the country but, hospitable though he was, it was his private property and no one made free use of it. Chouteau decided when races were to be held there. The course at Gibson was fair in dry weather, but the whole military reservation was on the low ground between the Neosho and the Verdigris and when it rained the track became muddy and stayed sloshy and soft for days. The track here at Bayou Menard was one of the better ones because the Indians used it so much.

Colonel Arbuckle's party was seated inside the oval near the finish line.

Also inside the oval were most of the important personages

68

in the country. They were strung all around the track in small groups, some sitting, some standing, some sprawling in the blazing, shadeless thin grass. Most of the Indian chiefs had been invited into the oval and there were also many strangers. Savanna guessed they were territorial officials from the capital at Little Rock, merchants from downriver, and speculators from the cities. She saw John Jolly and his tall, gaunt adopted son, Sam Houston. They were with Auguste Chouteau.

Savanna was seated beside the colonel, with David Holt on her other side, Lieutenant Felt's pretty young wife, Margaret, beside him, and Bill Felt himself occupying the end stool. To the left, Captain Bonneville was next to the colonel, with a couple of unmarried officers next and finally, at the very end, Martha and Fred Short. Savanna watched the party being seated by James Joyner, the colonel's round-faced aide. With an inward chuckle she leaned toward David and whispered, "Want to bet the colonel told young Joyner to keep Martha as far away from him as possible?"

"No," David whispered back, "it's a sure thing."

It was far from a secret on the post that Colonel Arbuckle could not abide Martha Short.

She was not a comfortable woman to be around. She was as angular in her disposition as she was in her body and much too forthright and outspoken. Almost everybody on the post had suffered her prickly needling at one time or another, including the colonel, and he had learned to avoid her. The entire post knew that one of the principal duties of his staff was to protect him from Martha Short. As the wife of his second-in-command she had to be included in many social events, but after she lectured the colonel for a full hour one time on his liking for his little dram, he had vowed never to be caught alone with her again. The surest way for one of his staff to be demoted to field duty was to fail to keep Martha Short away from the colonel. Even her husband was a party to the conspiracy. It was said that Colonel Arbuckle had told him, "You are an excellent officer, Fred, and we get along well, but unless you can muzzle your wife, don't let her come around headquarters."

Fred could not muzzle her so he had had, of necessity, to be as watchful of her as the rest of the staff. Savanna could imagine, now, how anxious young Joyner must have been until he got the colonel's party safely seated. Had Martha disliked her place, or had she had some bone to pick with the colonel, she would have been quite capable of upsetting the entire arrangement. When the young officer took his place at the end of the line, Savanna saw his chest heave with a deep sigh and saw a finger run round the inside of his collar. His face was red and wet with perspiration. Savanna leaned to David again. "Well, James is safe now."

David laughed. "He must feel, each time he goes through with this, that he's laying his head on the chopping block."

"Oh, the colonel's bark is worse than his bite. He doesn't eat young second lieutenants."

"No, he just says off with their heads and they draw field duty for the rest of their assignment. You sure Joyner isn't bleeding?"

"Not this time," Savanna laughed. "I think he's brought it off."

The colonel touched her arm then and she turned to him.

He was a long, lean man with sloped, stooped shoulders that made his chest look cavernous and his uniform hang sloppy and careless on him. His face, lengthened by a balding, domed forehead, habitually wore a slightly distrait look, partly because he was so nearsighted, but mostly because he fuzzed the harsh edges of his world with, as Martha Short called it, the use of ardent spirits. He did not drink heavily, and rarely had he had been known to be drunk, but he did sip almost constantly. In no way, however, did it interfere with his performance of his duties or with his genuine efficiency. He had been a good commanding officer on every duty he had drawn, but he was an especially good one at Gibson. He not only had great patience with the Indians but he had an appreciation of their difficulties which was undergirded by affection and esteem. He genuinely liked most of the chiefs with whom he continually had to hold council and whom he had to soothe and placate.

And though they might differ with him occasionally, for the most part the people of the country loved him dearly.

Savanna had known him a long time now and she felt a deep and abiding affection for him, even though his stubbornness about the sutler's post sent her into a frenzy of impatience with him. He said to her now, "Are you very nervous about the race, Savanna?"

"I am not nervous at all, sir."

"I would be. They say Felt's horse is a winner."

"I am riding the winner," she replied calmly.

"You're very certain, my dear." The colonel bent a little toward her. "I wish you good luck, Savanna."

"Thank you, sir." She hesitated, then plunged ahead. "But I would count it better luck if you would reconsider your position on the sutler's job, sir."

He lifted his hands in protest. "Now, my dear, don't let's

spoil the afternoon. Don't bring that up again, please. You have no idea what you're asking. The army does not have women sutlers and I simply cannot forward such an appointment to the War Department. It is a preposterous notion of yours." His smile was kindly but his words were quite firm.

Savanna flushed but she made an effort to return the smile. "Very well, sir. I would not like to be another Martha Short to you."

He patted her hand. "That's a good girl."

She changed the subject. "Have you placed your bets, sir?"

The colonel laughed. "I have not yet decided to bet at all. I am caught between fires. Lieutenant Felt is on my staff and I am sure he would consider it disloyal of me should I not lay a wager on him. But you, my dear, are the daughter of my good friend and the pretty widow of another good friend and . . ."

"And I shall certainly consider it disloyal if you don't bet on the Duke."

"Ah, me, what is an old man to do?"

"Follow your conscience, sir."

The colonel shook his head, looking fondly at her. He enjoyed this kind of banter. "Perhaps I had better remain neutral. How many horses are entered in the fifth race?"

"I believe there are eleven."

A look of anxiety crossed his face. "Too many. There'll be a scramble at the start and you may be hurt. Do you think it wise to ride among so many?"

"All the more reason I should, sir. My boy, Widgie, isn't seasoned enough. He would never be able to bring the Duke out of the start. Please don't be alarmed, sir." She gave him a bright, unworried smile. "I have been racing for a year and a half now."

"My heart will be in my mouth until that race is over, young lady."

The colonel had always been fond of her and she knew that now she was a widow he felt a more pleasantly titillating affection for her. "Dear Colonel Arbuckle," she said, "I promise you I shall come to no harm."

The early races were run in the wild, whooping frontier style, Indians, soldiers, settlers, trappers, hunters, anyone at all having a horse to race, participating. The horses were for the most part the wild mustangs caught on the prairies. The crowd loved this crazy, pell-mell, hard-running kind of race and raised a roar as the horses got away each time that was held, high and wild, until a winner crossed the line.

The Indians, mad about racing and always heedlessly heavy bettors, often betting everything they owned down to their last fringed shirt, went crazy when one of their own won and poured out onto the track and pounded their own mustangs around in a kind of mounted victory dance. Brilliantly colorful, as excited and full of glee as children, they slowed the proceedings considerably and the time between races was lengthy. They could not be herded off the track until they had worked off some of their joy and excitement. David said to Savanna, "Anyone who thinks an Indian stolid and unfeeling ought to see these right now. Lord, you'd think they were all drunk."

During the intervals between races, after the first interest of watching the Indians had worn off, the people waited, the women fanning the dust away from their faces, the men wandering about from group to group, visiting. Nearly all of them came, at one time or another, to speak to the colonel.

Captain John Rogers, from Fort Smith, detached himself from a party and drifted over to speak to the colonel. Bitten hard by the westering bug, John Rogers had a festering itch to go on an expedition to the Rocky Mountains. "Beaver is played out in this country," he said, "but there's still a plenty of it in those mountains."

"And plenty to take it," he was warned.

The fur trade was, just then, in an extremely fluid state. In addition to the big companies, John Jacob Astor's American Fur Company, the Bernard Pratte Company (in which the Chouteau family had an interest), the Rocky Mountain Fur Company, there wasn't a season that private individuals didn't lead their own expeditions to the mountains to try to take their share of pelts. The eyes of the entire west-faced frontier turned on those mountain streams which yielded such wealth from the soft silky pelts of a small brown animal. That few of them except the big companies ever realized a profit from their ventures did not deter them at all. The talk was always big in the fall of the year. It was time to go if one was going. Soon the big snows would be falling on the high plateaus; ice would be webbing the rims of the streams, and a man should be camped, ready to winter, in some lovely, frosted park.

John Rogers always had a ready listener in young Captain Bonneville and Savanna watched the two men, their hands moving as if they were pointing the trail already, their eyes seeking, even as they spoke, the violet distances of the west.

Benjamin Louis Eulalie de Bonneville was born in France, but his father had fallen under the displeasure of the government. He had managed to send his wife and young son to America with Thomas Paine, who was equally unwelcome in France at the time. With Paine's influence, young Bonneville had secured a cadetship at West Point where he graduated in

1819. When the Marquis de Lafayette visited the United States, Bonneville was detailed to accompany him on his tour. Lafayette took him back to France with him, where he remained for several years. Upon his return to America Bonneville was posted to Fort Smith on the frontier. Here, listening to talk of the fur trade constantly he had become enamored of the idea of making his own fortune in it. He had not yet decided how it was to be done, but he was bent upon doing it.

When John Rogers began his interminable discussions of how an expedition could be formed, where it could go, the bales of pelts it could take, Bonneville's eyes always gleamed with interest. Savanna thought he believed, perhaps, that Rogers would one day finance an expedition and would call on him to lead it. And no one could tell. It might fall out just that way.

Bonneville sauntered away with Rogers, and Auguste Chouteau came up, bringing with him the Cherokee chief, John Jolly, and the former governor of Tennessee. The immaculate dress of the slim, dark Frenchman contrasted sharply with the gaudy Indian apparel of the toweringly tall Tennessean. Savanna watched them approach. She said, lowering her voice, to David, "What possesses the man to deck himself out like that? He looks like a peacock."

"He likes to strut like a peacock," David said. "He is an exceedingly vain man and as a politician he has learned the value of attracting attention to himself."

"That kind of thing won't go down here," Savanna said. "He is making himself ridiculous."

"With white men, perhaps, but it will go down big with the Indians. For whom do you think he is parading?"

With grace and courtesy the colonel rose to shake hands with the three men. He then presented them to Savanna. "You know Colonel Chouteau, my dear. And Mr. Jolly?"

"Of course." Savanna smiled at them.

"I believe you have not met the governor, however. May I present former Governor Sam Houston of Nashville, Mrs. Brook?"

Savanna inclined her head and Sam Houston, with a wide, sweeping gesture that brought his blanket folded about him, bowed deeply before her. "Madame."

He was very drunk, she saw immediately, so drunk his eyes were glazed and the flesh of his face was rigid, so drunk that she had a moment of panic that he might be so precariously balanced as to topple over at her feet. Her eyes fled anxiously to Auguste Chouteau who looked on smilingly. A brief nod from him reassured her. Apparently Sam Houston could carry

73

quite a load of whiskey without losing his sense of propriety. He straightened and remained standing stiffly, his long legs spraddled a little to maintain his balance.

Colonel Arbuckle was frowning and Savanna knew he was angry with Chouteau for bringing the man into the presence of ladies in such a sodden condition, but he graciously completed the introductions to the rest of his party.

Savanna's mouth twitched as she witnessed Martha Short's frigid nod. Martha was not one to appreciate drunkenness in anyone. She was a teetotaler herself and made every effort to make one of her husband.

One of the most delightful stories that had ever gone the rounds at Gibson concerned her efforts. Major Short had taken too much one night and had then tried to creep in by the window. He had been met by an irate wife with a gun in her hands, who had promptly chased him out of the house, firing a round or two at him for good measure. David had picked buckshot out of Fred's seat the rest of the night. The story had set the post to rocking and it was told and retold for weeks. It had also earned Major Short, behind his back, the nickname of Buckshot Short.

Martha must be furious at having to acknowledge, publicly, a man in Sam Houston's condition. Savanna wondered that she did not sweep her skirts aside and walk away.

Colonel Arbuckle's young officers offered stools to Chouteau and his friends, but Chouteau waved them off. "No, gentlemen. We can stay but a moment." He turned to Savanna and with his beautiful Gallic courtesy said, "Madame Brook . . . I have a small wager on your horse in the fifth."

"You aren't racing your own Aladdin?"

Chouteau smiled deprecatingly and shrugged. "He has pulled a tendon. I have had to withdraw him."

"Colonel Chouteau," Lieutenant Felt called out, "I take exception to that. If you want to win in the fifth you should have bet on my Jethro."

"Perhaps," Auguste Chouteau said, lifting his shoulders, "but I do not think, my friend, your Jethro will win."

"Why not? He's a Tennessee horse and a fullblood. He has won most of the races he has started."

Chouteau bowed slightly and said softly, "Nevertheless, sir, he will not have Madame Brook riding him."

Savanna flushed.

Auguste Chouteau was a cool one, with a face which perpetually wore an amiable expression that never gave away his inner thoughts. No one ever saw him angry or disgruntled or fussed in any way. He was cool and pleasant and charming and

74

gracious and ruthless and unscrupulous. He would cut your throat in business, but he would do it smilingly and be amazed if it threatened a friendship. "But, my friend, what would you? It is business, is it not?" With his beautiful head cocked to one side, his dark eyes twinkling, he would lift his shoulders. "You would have done the same, would you not?"

He chatted a moment longer with the colonel, Sam Houston standing woodenly beside him, John Jolly patient, silent, and inscrutable behind. Then he made his small, exquisite bow to the ladies and touched Houston's arm. "We must be going. Adieu, my friends. Madame Brook . . . my good wishes."

"Thank you, sir."

Savanna watched them walk away. She turned to Colonel Arbuckle. "Now, sir, what kind of an unholy triumvirate is that?"

"I wish I knew, my dear," the colonel said, shaking his head. "I wish I knew. Sam Houston's presence here troubles me greatly. I have no idea what he's up to, but he is a very ambitious man and he has friends in high places. I warrant he is going to cause me many moments of anxiety."

"I would keep an eye on that friendship with Auguste Chouteau," Savanna said.

"No," the colonel said, "that is one thing I need not do. Whatever Houston's purposes, Chouteau is much too clever to serve them. I think our friend is simply amusing himself with the man."

Remembering Chouteau's reputation for a perverted sense of humor Savanna nodded. "I expect you are right, sir."

The third race was over. Savanna rose. "I must leave you now, sir."

The gentlemen of the party stood and Lieutenant Felt said to her, a little mockingly, "The fourth hasn't been run yet. Do you need an entire race in which to prepare, Mrs. Brook?"

Savanna gathered up her skirt and said coolly, "Yes, I do, Lieutenant Felt."

He laughed and saluted her. "Then we will meet at the starting post. May I wish you . . ." he hesitated, "good luck, but not the money."

"Thank you."

The baby-faced Joyner touched her arm. "Miss Savanna, may I escort you to the corral?"

Colonel Arbuckle heaved himself up wheezingly. "Nonsense. I shall escort Miss Savanna to the corral myself. I'll have you know, sir, that as her host it is my special prerogative."

Joyner's round, smooth-cheeked face turned red. "Yes, sir."

There was a chorus of good wishes as Savanna took the colonel's arm and adjusted her steps to his slow, limping gait. He was still a little gouty and favored his right foot.

She smiled gaily enough and nodded to the group but she was beginning to feel the tightening in her stomach which she always felt before a race. It would increase until by the time she was in the saddle there would be real pain. "You wouldn't ride a good race without it, my dear," Thomas had told her when she complained. "It's nerves. It stiffens you to your best effort."

You would think, she thought now, feeling the fluttering in her insides, I'd get over it. I've ridden enough, goodness knows. But her stomach always felt as if she had eaten eels, all slithery and wiggly.

The colonel steered her across the track and gallantly fended for her through the crowd. They were a slow time getting through and the colonel winced when he was joggled by the mob. He laughed ruefully. "What a cripple I am becoming."

"You shouldn't have come, sir," Savanna said. "Lieutenant Joyner could have seen me to the corral."

"I am not *that* crippled," the colonel retorted. "Shall I let a young man barely out of the cradle teach me my manners?"

"No one can teach you anything, sir. You are a very wise man."

They had come through the last of the crowd now and were making their way to the crude corral in the edge of the woods. The colonel stopped to catch his breath. "Why, Savanna. That was a very pretty little speech." He shook a playful finger at her. "But I think you are a sly young minx who knows how to flatter an old codger."

"Not at all," Savanna denied quickly, "not at all, sir. Thomas always said you were the wisest commanding officer he had ever served under."

"Ah . . . Thomas." The colonel's eyes went misty. He was a softhearted man who was easily moved. "I miss him very much, my dear."

"So do I, sir."

"Yes, of course." The colonel pressed her hand.

"Shall we go on, sir?"

"Yes. Yes, I am delaying you, am I not? And you must be eager to see your horse and talk with Sergeant Lathrop."

Savanna took his arm and they moved slowly on. "Do you know, Savanna," he said regretfully, "I should have placed a wager on you. It was not very nice of me not to. I wish there was time enough still."

Savanna faced him. "Colonel Arbuckle, you are so thoughtful in all things else. You are fretting because you feel you

76

have not stood by me as loyally as you should. In all things to me, since I was a child, you have ever been so kind. Yet you are being most unkind in the one thing of greatest importance to me now."

He cupped an ear to hear her better. "I? Unkind to you?"

"Yes, sir. You will not listen to my reasons for wanting this appointment."

"But, Savanna . . ."

"Will you listen to me? Will you let me explain. If you cannot see your way then to make the appointment I promise I shall not pester you about it again. But do, at least, hear me."

His face looked resigned. "Very well. But I warn you it can make no difference."

She told him, then, hurrying her words against time, how Thomas had ordered heavily, on credit, and what a sacrifice of the goods would mean to her. She emphasized, so that he would not fail to understand, that she could not absorb the stock in the other stores because they were already heavily stocked themselves. "The goods have to be disposed of in an orderly way in the usual fashion. They can't just be dumped, sir."

"Have you thought of trying to dispose of the entire stock to one buyer?"

"Who?"

"Auguste Chouteau . . . perhaps?"

"He would drive a harder bargain than anyone else in the country, sir. I think you know that."

"Yes. Yes . . . probably." The colonel stroked his chin. "I fear I have not clearly understood your difficulties, Savanna. Are you certain you cannot move the goods and house them in one of your warehouses?"

Savanna tried to be patient. At last she was getting past the dense wall of his stubbornness which had made him refuse to listen to her, which had kept him shaking his head and saying: Impossible, impossible. He was finally hearing her, and it was no time to lose patience again. "They are full, sir—all of them are full. Thomas banked heavily on the trade this season with the Indian removals. And the debt is frightful, sir. There are perishables in the stock, too, sir. There would be so much spoilage before I could dispose of them. I might as well," she added wryly, "give the stuff to the Indians as to store it."

"Yes. Well. Perishables . . . I see. Of course. Well, my dear, let me think about this problem of yours. I shall have to give it more consideration, I see. When we go back to the cantonment I promise you I will give it my full attention."

Savanna's heart, which had begun to soar, sank again. The

77

Company would be at the encampment a full month, until the last penny had been paid to the Cherokees. She clutched his arm. "Colonel Arbuckle, it can't wait that long. Thomas ordered the goods six months ago. They arrive this week on the *Robert Thompson*. I must know what I am to do, what it is possible for me to do, very soon."

Liking, usually, to take his time about decisions, the colonel could be quickly purposeful when necessary. At once he said, "Very well, then. Now, Savanna, I cannot give you the sutler's post permanently. It is absolutely impossible. You have no idea what a tizzy the War Department would be in if I attempted it. And it would be useless because they would instantly countermand it. What I believe to be possible, however, is a temporary appointment to give you the time you need. I can send along a covering letter of explanation. I believe, though mind I am far from certain, they would allow it to stand for a few months. How much time do you need?"

Savanna knew when she was defeated. It had not occurred to her that Washington could countermand the colonel's orders. She had been intent only on persuading him to give the order. She should have known better.

Her mind quickly accepted the reversal. Very well. She could not continue to operate the profitable sutler's store. But she could dispose of the stock and she could continue with the trading stores located elsewhere. The debt, that tremendous debt which haunted her, could be paid. She calculated rapidly. "Give me six months, sir. I'm sure I can manage by the end of that time."

"Done. I will have Joyner prepare the order tonight and it will go off in the next pouch to Washington. I shall write a favorable letter to make certain the Secretary does not countermand the order and," he chuckled, "the army will have the first woman sutler in its history. But only for six months, mind. Don't ask me to extend the time, for I cannot."

He extended his hand as if she had been a man and, unthinkingly, she gave him hers. His hearty grip made her gasp as sudden pain ripped across her palm. She clenched her teeth and forced herself to allow him to pump her hand up and down. "Now," he said, "am I forgiven for being a crusty old fussbudget?"

Weakly she grinned at him and, her hand loosed finally, dropped her arm limply to her side. Dear Lord, he had made a pulp of her hand. "You are fully forgiven. Now, may I suggest, sir, that you return to your party. I see Sergeant Lathrop coming and we have much to do. Thank you, sir. Thank you very much."

He bent to touch her forehead with his lips. "Ah, my dear, it is a bright day when an old man can make a young and beautiful lady happy with the stroke of a pen. You should have made me understand sooner. I am glad to do it."

She watched him limp back toward the race track with feelings so divided she could not sort them out. She should have made him understand earlier! When she could not get him to listen! He was glad to do it! When he had sent her frenzied with suspense! She felt tenderness for his age and infirmities and impatience with his turtle-slowness; respect for his devotion to duty and frustration with his old-fashioned stiffness; liking for his cheerful amiability and exasperation with his stubbornness. How many things it took to make a man, she thought. How many mixed and conflicting things he was composed of and how many-sided he could be. You could never know the whole of any man, for the whole was a mass of inconsistency and perplexity. But the colonel had done the best he could for her and she did not propose to quarrel with him for more.

She walked to meet Abe Ltahrop.

V

Abe set the pan of warm water on a stool and stood beside her as David Holt cut the bandages off Savanna's hands. The blood had soaked through the cloth and stiffened it and the cloth itself was matted and stuck to the shredded flesh. "God," David said, "how did you stand it?"

Savanna flicked him a glance but she made no reply. She didn't know how she had stood it. She hadn't felt any pain during the race, but afterward, standing about for an hour listening to all the praise, the flattering compliments, having her hands caught and held over and over again, she had nearly died. If David hadn't brought her away when he did she thought she would have swooned, first time in her life or not. It had been dreadful. It was still dreadful, and she wondered gloomily if her hands would ever be the same again.

Kizzy, kneeling by Savanna, clucked crooningly, "Do, Lawd, dey sho' is a mess."

"Shut up, Kizzy," David said gruffly. "And get that pan of water. This is going to hurt, Savanna, but those shreds of cloth are going to have to soak. Put your hands in the water, now."

Kizzy pulled the stool holding the basin nearer and Savanna lowered her hands gingerly into it. She shuddered as the water touched the raw flesh. "Hurry," she gritted through her teeth, "hurry for God's sake, David. That hurts like wildfire."

"I know it does. Keep still and give the water time."

Kizzy, kneeling again, mumbled once more, "Jesus, dey sho' is a mess."

"Oh, don't keep grumbling," Savanna said. Then she leaned her head on Kizzy's bony shoulder and groaned.

Abe, behind, shuffled impatiently. He was moved by her suffering but it took the form of anger in him. "Damn fool thing to do," he growled, "stand around for an hour after the race."

"The whole thing was damn fool," David said. "If I had seen these hands, you wouldn't have ridden today, youngun."

"She took good care you didn't," Abe said. "She ought to have come straight to the tent when the race was over and seen to her hands. Ought to have known they'd be sawed to pieces."

Savanna raised her head and glared at him. "Walk off when I had just won the race? What do you take me for? I'd have stayed there to crow if my hands had been dripping blood all over the place." She lifted her hands and shook them in front of his face, sprinkling him and the surgeon until they ducked. "Why do you think I sawed these hands into raw beef? Why?"

David grabbed her wrists. "Put your hands back in the water!" He doused them in the basin. "And you shut up, Abe. You, too, Savanna."

"You leave me alone," she barked at him, but she suffered her hands to remain in the water. "That hour was my triumph, Abe, and I wouldn't have missed it if Gabriel had been sounding his horn. That hour was why I rode. Sure it was bad, and I think I would have died if David hadn't fetched me away, but I wasn't about to turn my back on it and walk away to take care of these." She nodded at her soaking hands. "Never!"

"Well," Abe drawled, wiping his face, "you always were bullheaded."

"Not bullheaded! No! That was pride. Don't you know," she continued hotly, her dark eyes blazing at him, "that when the betting is all against you, when people are thinking now you'll come a cropper, now you'll have to eat crow, if you've got any guts at all you get your back up and show 'em? Don't all of you know this was more than a horserace? Don't you know that since Thomas died everybody in the country has been watching me, wondering what I was going to do, talking, whispering, gossiping, traders scheming to get my stores, officers scheming to get the sutler's post? Don't you think they hoped I'd be licked and have to go creeping back to my father's farm and they could benefit by the licking? Don't you think the wives on the campus don't want to see me go, too?"

"Oh, women," Abe said, "their tongues will always clatter."

"But they have clattered most about me because Thomas had the wit to let me be different from them. He delighted in having me as gaudy as a Creek Indian and in hanging me with jangly bracelets and earrings like a gypsy. He delighted in having me with him. He delighted in all the freedom he gave me and he was proud of me."

"Thomas spoiled the hell out of you," David Holt said dryly.

"Of course he did and I am the first to own it. But you never saw a wife yet who could bear to see another wife having the hell spoiled out of her without envying her and hating her just a little. More than a little. And why not? Why wouldn't they? Lord, don't you think I know how it ate away at them to sit behind their prim white curtains and watch me riding away with Thomas so often? What other husband do you know, or ever did know, who enjoyed his wife's company so much he wanted her with him most of the time? Usually they're glad to get away from their wives as much as they can. It was like rubbing salt in a sore place to them to see a woman whose husband was so scandalously fond of her. But he's gone now, and she's tumbled into widow's weeds."

David grinned. "Did you say widow's weeds?"

"Well, sure, I don't wear them. Thomas wouldn't have wanted me to. But how they have hugged to their bosoms these last weeks the fact that Savanna Brook is a widow. No. That was more than a horserace today, Abe. That was Savanna Brook showing the whole damn world she isn't through, not by a long sight."

"Well, it was a damn good horserace, too," Abe said.

While Savanna had been blazing away with all her guns at Abe, David had got the last of the shredded cloth out of the blisters. He rested her hands in her lap, now, on a clean towel.

Savanna barely noticed. Eagerly she asked, "What did you think of the race, really, Abe?"

"You pulled a little wide on that first turn. I expected you to go for the inside there."

"I did. But Felt bumped me and I had to pull over."

"I thought that was what might have happened. I saw him unhorse an Indian that way once."

"He'd have liked to do it to me."

David took her hands and began to salve them. "You rode a pretty race today, my girl. What did you think of Felt's horse?"

"Oh, he's a beauty. A real beauty. I'd love to own him."

"Think he can beat the Duke?" Abe asked.

Savanna gave him a level look. "With me up, yes. With Felt up, no."

"How would you ride him?"

"He breaks fast, but I'd hold him until the stretch. Felt ran him hard the whole way, counting on his wind, and he tired in the stretch. That," she confessed, "is the only reason the Duke won today."

Abe grinned. "Good head."

David chuckled and said, "That's what Auguste Chouteau meant when he said he didn't think Felt's horse would win. Savanna's head wouldn't be up there figuring."

Abe nodded, shoved his cap to the back of his head and said, casually, "Want me to buy him for you?"

Savanna sat up straight. "Can he be bought?"

Abe motioned. "You tell her, Dave."

David was fastening the last bandage. He sat back and let Kizzy clear up the litter. He took out his pipe and tamped it full, lit it and puffed it a time or two. "Felt went the whole hog today. He owes everybody in the country. There isn't a gambling man around who doesn't hold some paper on him, and a lot of paper. He is in a desperate situation. He bought a Tennessee fullblood and owes for him. He reckoned to make a killing today and pay off everything he owed. It was a last, big gamble and he lost. He can't pay for the horse now. He'll have to sell him."

Savanna was thoughtful, then her head came up purposefully. "Well, a man's got no right to gamble if he can't afford to lose, but nobody can put brains into a fool's head. I'd like to have the horse and if Bill Felt doesn't ask too much for him, Abe, buy him."

"He owe you anything?"

"What he lost on the race today."

"I mean at the store."

"Oh. Yes. Thomas gave him credit. He's always been slow pay."

"You want his debts settled on the horse trade?"

"Of course not. Pay him cash. I'm not going to squeeze him on what he owes me. But that's not for his sake, it's for his wife's sake. Margaret's a nice girl, a little addlepated or she wouldn't have married Bill Felt, but she's little more than a child and it isn't her fault her husband is a fool."

"She's older than you," David said grinning.

"I don't believe it."

"Well, she is."

"How do you know?"

"I'm her doctor. She is pregnant and she is twenty years old."

"Good Lord!"

The surgeon stood. "Well, time's a wasting. Are you having dinner in the colonel's quarters with the rest of us, Savanna?"

"Certainly."

"Then I'll see you there. Have Kizzy salve your hands until the soreness begins to leave, then you can take off the bandages and begin to use them again."

"How long will that be?"

"If you're careful with them, a week or ten days."

"They'll have to mend quicker than that." Rising and walking outside with the two men she told them of the colonel's decision. "It isn't what I wanted, but it's the best he can do and it's better than nothing. So I'm going home tomorrow. I can't afford to waste any more time out here."

Kizzy, overhearing, squalled from inside the tent. "Why you goin' home? Whut you mean? We jist rid out heah so's you could mangle dem hands? Whut about all dem dresses you 'quired me to pack? Act lak you gwine stay de whole monff!"

"Oh, hush," Savanna said.

David Holt stroked his beard and Abe fingered his cap. The surgeon spoke first. "I can't say I'm surprised, Savanna, but I'd hoped the colonel would find a better loophole. Suttling is the most profitable of your businesses, isn't it?"

"By far. About twice as good as either of the other stores. But," she added quickly, "thank heaven I've got them."

Abe was awkward. "Sure will miss you on the post, Savanna. 'Twon't seem the same."

Savanna blinked at him. "I'm not going anywhere."

Abe looked at her quickly. "Thought you might be going back to Fort Smith now."

She laughed shortly. Then she took a long breath and drew herself up to her full height. "No. I'm going to open another trading store."

David Holt chuckled. "So near the post that you'll cut in on the sutler's trade, I'll wager."

"Precisely. I mean to see Jolly about a piece of land on the Three Forks Road in the morning."

Abe gave her an appraising look. "You aiming to run a doggery?"

"You know better than that," she flashed at him.

"You may get the name whether you do or not."

"I'll have to take that chance. Anyway, it's what I mean to do. I will *not* go back to Fort Smith."

The two men watched her standing there, a slim, straight little figure, but standing so straight, her chin jutted with determination, her mouth drawn tight. Abe only looked his admiration, his eyes going luminously warm. But David Holt reached out a finger and set an earring to jingling. He said nothing. Savanna flashed him a smile. He knew. He knew the day Thomas was buried and he knew now. Her heart was sore but her head was high. He was saying to her, as Thomas had said, jingle your earrings, Savanna.

Abruptly he turned away. "I'm going."

Quickly he was around the tent and out of sight.

Savanna walked with Abe, slowly, from under the cedar tree to the edge of the slope, where it began to tilt downward. The sun was just gone, the air very still, the sky streaked high with red. "Back at Gibson," Savanna said absently, "Sebe Hawkins is blowing Retreat."

"Yes."

Without more words they looked for a few moments down on the beehive encampment. Supper smokes were beginning to curl upward. There was less stirring of men and more of women as the fires were started and kettles and pots were hung. Indian lads, striplings, were taking their fathers' horses to stake out for the night. Younger children were fetching water from the creek. Men lay quietly on their blankets and smoked. For a little while, for an hour or two yet, this peace would prevail. When the night set in, it would be different. A dozen Indian dances would be going. White men, fired with whiskey, would be whooping and shouting and shooting. And the tents of the floozies would offer for each man who slipped into them a quick, sharp explosion of relief.

Savanna turned to Abe.

He continued to look out across the encampment and Savanna studied him.

His face was as lean and bony as his body, and as brown as a well-oiled saddle. He was one of the few men she knew who went clean-shaven and she liked it. The hard, good bones of his face showed up plainly. He was naturally dark-skinned, but during the summer the sun and wind burned him to mahogany.

With each dark skin you expected dark eyes and hair and it was startling, at first, to find yourself gazing into a pair of water-cool gray eyes instead and to see, when his cap was off, a head of such light hair that it was almost impossible to describe. The color of a mole's fur, Savanna thought, and wondered if it was as soft.

He had weather wrinkles at the corners of his eyes and his nose was straight and a little thin. His mouth was pleasantly full although Savanna had seen it tighten until the lips were wholly indrawn. She had also seen the cheerful gray eyes turn as hard as granite. Molded by his own instincts, whatever they were, and by his past, whatever it was, and by his country

84

which gave a man no quarter, he was hard in flesh and muscle, as tough as whang-leather, a tall, bony repository for some bleakness of the soul which he shared with no one. He had a heart easily moved by horses, children, and women, nerves as taut as fiddlestrings without the danger of cracking, and a steely courage in times of danger that gave him the reputation of being fearless. Savanna knew he was not. He had told her he was afraid of the country itself. But Abe Lathrop could calculate risks to a hair and take them boldly. He was able, skilled, braver than most men, and wholly faithful to his friends.

Suddenly he asked her, "Ever hear from Manifee?"

"Father does . . . occasionally. Not often."

"He coming back here?"

Savanna shook her head. "It isn't likely. He loves that mountain country."

Abe nodded. "I'd guessed it."

Savanna sighed. "I miss him, still. Fee was the best of the boys—in most ways."

"Like to see him again myself."

They were silent a moment, then Savanna shook herself out of her preoccupation. "I want to thank you for handling the Duke for me today, Abe. It meant a lot to me."

Abe's dark face flushed. "It meant a lot to me, too."

"Well, then, goodbye."

"You take care," he warned her, putting on his cap.

"Yes. I'll take care."

She fell into step beside him.

"There's a halfbreed Creek, name of Walkingstick, knows how to build a good log house if you're aiming to commence building soon."

"Where can I find him?"

"Lives about a mile beyond the agency. Built himself a mighty pretty one."

"I'll see him. I expect I'd better start right away."

"If I was you, I would. Can't count on good weather more than a month or two. When do you have to turn your buildings over to the colonel?"

"The first of April."

"Well, if you get that land from Jolly it might be best to get as far with your building this fall as you can."

"Yes. I'd been thinking about it."

"When the Company gets back, I'll help. Between times."

"I'd be glad if you would."

He lunged away, suddenly, into the growing darkness. "You take care," he warned her again.

Savanna laughed and then stretched, feeling pleasure in the movement, and yawned. It had been such a wonderful day. And she would never, as long as she lived, forget her sweet-tasting hour of triumph. A bubble of joy rose in her throat and for the first time since Thomas died she felt like her old self again, a surging energy rising in her, a keen intensity for the future shaping itself within her. Her sharpest worries were eased. She knew what she had to do, and she felt a complete certainty that she could do it. She had no doubt whatever that alone though she was, by herself, she could manage. She might be something new under the sun, a woman sutler and a woman trader, but her wits were as sharp as any man's. Thomas had believed it and she knew it.

Kizzy loomed before her. "You is barely got time to git into yo' dress. De cunnel'll be sendin' foh you any minnit."

"Oh, God's britches!" She fled into the tent. "I forgot that blasted feast."

VI

Savanna had been at home two days before young Joyner came with the colonel's dispatch pouch. She had begun to feel not actually worried but a little uneasy. The colonel always faithful to his word but he was also, often, dilatory.

She heard the horse coming, pounding as if the rider were in a tearing hurry, and thinking it might be the colonel's messenger she went onto the veranda to meet him at the foot of the steps. The lieutenant did not immediately dismount. Reining up he made a half salute, half hat-tipping gesture. "Morning, Miss Savanna. The *Robert Thompson* come yet?"

She greeted him. "No, but she's crossed the bar. I heard the whistle about ten minutes past."

The entrance to the Neosho River presented a tricky problem in navigation in low water stages, for the Arkansas formed a long submerged sandbar at the point and in shallow water it was always nip and tuck whether a packet could cross into the deeper Neosho. Once across, three blasts of the whistle notified the countryside she had made it. Those three shrill blasts were always a trumpet of victory, but they said other things too.

The *Sweet Sue*, for instance, always blew three short, crisp toots which spoke plainly of contempt for the crossing. Nothing to it, they said. Just part of the day's work. On the other hand, the *Robert Thompson* always blew loud and long and windy, saying, just as plainly, we've had a mighty struggle but we've made it. The *Natchez* had a Negro deckhand at the whistle who made a mournful rising and falling of the triad, wailing diss time we is ovah but it's a mean ole ribber—git us one time, foh true. The *Louisville's* whistle was strident, with a hand at the cord which yanked it hard and brooked no foolishness. This obstruction is cleared, it said, now let's get on up the river. At Fort Gibson you didn't have to know the steamboat schedule to know which boat was across the bar. You could tell by the whistle.

The colonel's aide dismounted, tied up his horse and mopped at his face with his coat sleeve. "Well, that's a relief. My orders were to catch the steamer with this post if I had to follow it downriver to the Mississippi."

"The colonel cut it pretty near," Savanna said.

"Yes. Well, things have been happening." Joyner took from the mail pouch two sheets of paper, folded. He handed them to Savanna. "The colonel wants you to have these. They are copies of his order and letter."

She scanned them quickly.

Order #2
Headquarters, 7th Inf.
Cantonment Gibson
October 18, 1829

In consequence of the death of Major Thomas L. Brook, Suttler to B, C, G, F, & K Companies of the 7th Infantry, S. F. Brook is appointed to suttle to the above named companies, until the pleasure of the Honble. the Secretary of War is known.

By order of COL. ARBUCKLE

The letter stated that the appointment was made "that his widow may hold this appointment a sufficient time to dispose of the goods on hand. This object it is believed can be accomplished by the 1st of April, next."

Savanna felt a springy uplift of spirits now that the mailbag had arrived and she knew for certain the order had been written and would actually get off immediately. She thrust the papers into her pocket, and smiled so warmly at young Joyner that he blushed furiously. "Come in, James, and let me give you a glass of wine. There's time before the packet ties up. I want to hear what's been happening."

As he drank, slowly, to make it last until the next blast of the whistle would announce the *Robert Thompson* at the landing, he gave her the news. "First," he said, grinning, "Major Short's wife has been fit to be tied—mad as a wet hen at the colonel for giving you the appointment."

"That's not surprising, is it?" Savanna laughed.

"No, but it don't make things any easier. We've been hard

87

put to it to keep her out of the colonel's way." The young officer's mouth crimped and he said plaintively, "I tell you, Miss Savanna, I'm going to end up at one of those God-forsaken Red River posts yet. I'm bound to slip one of these days."

"Maybe not." Savanna added consolingly. "If the colonel gives Fred the permanent appointment you won't have to bother with her any more—not officially, anyhow."

"And what sweet peace that would be. No more maneuvering at theatricals or the races or at dinner parties. I might grow old in the service if that happens."

"You love the service, don't you, James?"

"It's my life," the boy said simply.

Savanna refilled his glass. "Have they started paying yet?"

"No. They start tomorrow."

"In script?"

"Yes. And the Indians are pretty unhappy about it. The colonel says when they get paid in script they think they are being cheated. They have decided already to send a commission to Washington as soon as the payment is over. Sam Houston's back of that, we hear."

"What in the samhill has Sam Houston got to do with it?"

"Oh, the Cherokees have made him a full member of the tribe. Held a big ceremony and initiated him and decided to send a commission to Washington, Sam Houston to head it up, of course."

"I do believe," Savanna said, "he has charmed old Jolly right out of his senses and I always thought he was a smart old man."

"The agents are all uneasy, too. He is threatening to have them all removed."

"Really threatening?"

"Yes, he's come out in the open. Says they're all dishonest and he's got the proof."

The steamboat's whistle screamed and young Joyner jumped. "There she is!"

Savanna walked to the veranda with him. "Give the colonel my love, James, and tell him I am very grateful."

The boy's absurdly long-lashed eyes misted. "Miss Savanna, I wish it might be . . ."

Savanna cut him off. "James, you'll be late."

"Yes. Well, goodbye, Miss Savanna."

Savanna waved and ran. "Kizzy, the boat's in. Did Preacher find someone to help unload?"

"Yessum. Done down at de landin' wid 'em. He fin' hisself two Injuns."

"Good. I'm going, too."

The week that followed Savanna worked herself, Preacher, and the Creek Indians like stokers. Her hands were still too tender to be of much use so she hustled and drove the men at the job of carrying the crates and boxes and kegs and cartons from the landing to the warehouse; of breaking them open, sorting, arranging, storing the goods until Preacher grumbled at supper one night that he was "wore to the marrowbone. De major doan neber wuk us dis hard, Miss Savanna. De major tek his time fetchin' an' haulin' dem stoah goods."

"He didn't either," she snapped at him. "You're just getting lazy since the major has gone."

But her conscience accused her. Perhaps Thomas hadn't worked Preacher so hard. But then *he* had been here to see to things. It all fell to her now. And this was such a big shipment and she had so many other things to do. Surely Preacher ought to see that she had to get the stock shelved and stored quickly, in this spell of good weather, so she could turn to getting the new store and house built. She shouldn't have hurt his feelings, though. She took the time to explain.

His scowl cleared as she talked. "Yessum. Yessum." It was worth it. Her own feelings of guilt were eased and Preacher was made proud and happy again. "Yessum. Ah gwine holp wid de new house, too. Ah be's good at carpenterin'."

"Of course you will. I'm counting on it."

For days she checked and listed and rechecked and relisted, divided, sorted, arranged the great stock of goods. Into the sutler's store she put the perishables, meats that could spoil, cheeses that could go rancid, flour and meal that could get weevily and musty, molasses that could harden and turn to sugar, and sugar that could take on the taste and smell of oil and gunpowder. Onto the shelves went, also, the dry goods—the bolts of calico, domestic, shirting, strouding, madras, merino, plisse—and the crockery and glassware.

Into the warehouse went the hard goods, the plows and implements, gunpowder, nails, leathers, and the wines and whiskeys for the officers of the post. There went also the great casks and barrels the traders ordered though the sutler and stored with him.

It took her two full weeks but when it was done she knew to the last nail where to lay her hand on her stock and it was as orderly and tidy as any stock Thomas had ever stored. She gave a sigh of vast relief. Tomorrow she would ride up to find the Creek Abe had told her about and get firmly settled this business of building her new home.

89

It was cold the next morning and when Savanna led her mare onto the flatboat the animal stepped gingerly, finicky about the frost-slick floor. "She knows to take keer, don't she?" the man on duty said. He was the Texan who had been whipped for stealing. "Puts me in mind of what Sebe Hawkins is always sayin'—as uncertain as a hog on ice. That'd be mighty uncertain, wouldn't it?" The man guffawed, the sound harsh and cracked in the brittle air.

"Can't think of anything more uncertain," Savanna agreed, with good humor. She felt so fine this morning that nothing could bother her. Her hands were healed again, the pesky stores were arranged, and she felt so brisk and full of energy that even her hair crackled. "Come on, Sal," she urged the mare, "just one step at a time, and easy. Nothing to be afraid of. There's a good girl."

During the crossing she continued to talk to the mare, who was nervous and quivery. She was a pretty animal and Savanna's favorite for riding. She was part Spanish, which gave her speed and grace, and part mustang, which gave her wind and endurance. In motion, she was pure velvet.

When the Texan let down the ramp on the far shore he pointed wordlessly to the spidery webs of ice fastened to the shallow water.

Savanna was astonished. "So early?"

" 'Tain't so early, ma'am. Middle of November. Time for a little ice."

So it was. The time had fled. But there would still be good days, she thought. The worst of the winter didn't come until after the turn of the year. She could get the house well started before the deep cold set in.

She thanked the Texan and as she rode up the sloping, slippery bank she thought how, soon, it would take more than thanks to get her across the river. In six months she would have to pay the ferry toll, fishing up her pennies as did everyone else not connected with the army. How odd that would seem. Ah, well. It was one more change Thomas's death had made.

The road to Three Forks ran from Gibson to the trading settlement five miles up the Verdigris, crossing the narrow neck of land lying between that river and the Neosho. Since the establishment of the cantonment it had become a well-traveled road, rutted from oxcarts and wagons and wide enough that half a dozen horsemen could ride side by side.

Savanna had obtained the land she wanted from John Jolly. It was ten acres, higher than the rest of the land about, grassy, with one well-shaded spot directly on the road. It lay on the left side going toward Three Forks, was two miles from the ferry and the fort, and three miles south of the trading settlement at Three Forks. She could not buy the land for it was Indian land, but she liked its location. It was very near the Creek agency and she hoped to draw trade from both Cherokees and Creeks.

She pulled up at the piece of land on which she now held a lease.

There was room for pastures for her horses and a garden for Kizzy. And under the trees here, directly on the road, she would put the house with the store attached. Surveying the tract she weighed and balanced again. She would draw considerable trade from the cantonment she knew and she did not see how she could fail to draw a little trade from the Creeks and Cherokees. Auguste Chouteau might not like it, but she believed she had chosen well.

She found the man about whom Abe Lathrop had told her. She inspected his house and found it as well built as Abe had said. She then went to work to make her deal with the man.

He stood before her, a big man, head wrapped in bright silk, his face impassive, his eyes dead black and expressionless. Without restlessness he stood and listened and made his replies. Yes, he could build her a log house, a double log house with a dogtrot like his—pine logs, yes, from the hills. He didn't know when. He had things to do. A loose hand indicated many things. Yes, probably pretty soon. He would see. Probably before the cold came. He would see. Steadily she tried to pin him down. "I want as much of the building completed before cold weather as possible, and it *must* be finished by the first of April. I must move into it then."

Yes, he thought he could do that. Though, she understood, many things could happen. He waved vaguely to indicate the host of bad spirits which could interfere. How much? He would see. Not much. But he had many children to feed. Savanna kept patient. She named a figure she was willing to raise a little. Probably. He would see. The man understood that she was willing to pay a little more and Savanna understood she would have to pay it, but they had arrived at a base figure. Neither would lose sight of it.

She went home satisfied. The man would take his time. The log house certainly would not be finished this fall, and it might not be entirely finished by the first of April, but it would be nearly so. Enough that she could move into it. It was the best she could do and it did very well. She felt now as if all her arrangements were made as happily as possible. Her shoulders felt lighter than they had for many months. She was dug in, now, the way she wanted to be, and she was going to be very hard to root out.

When she reached home in the late afternoon Kizzy was just finishing the ironing. "That Miz Felt done come back fum de 'campment. Come heah. Say she lak fer you to come see her soon as you gits home."

Savanna jacked her boots off. "Is she sick?"

"No'm. Doan reckon. She look porely but she able to git about. Allus do look peaked."

"Fix a tray of food, Kizzy, and I'll take it over as soon as I change. Is the lieutenant with her?"

She flipped a dress off its peg and slid it over her head.

"No'm. That Joyner boy done bring her." Kizzy put up her sadirons, suddenly giggling. "He moughty rile you ain't heah."

Buttoning up her bodice with swift fingers, Savanna laughed. "I can't say I'm sorry to miss Mr. Joyner. He *has* gone, hasn't he?"

"Yessum. Say he couldn't linger. Lak some supper, Miss Savanna? Done turned mizzy, ain't it?"

"Yes, my hair is damp and as fuzzy as a frayed rope end. Put enough food on the tray for me too, Kizzy. I'll eat with Margaret. It's a miserable business, eating alone."

Margaret Felt was huddled wanly over a small smoking fire which Savanna hurried to mend. "Joyner!" she said. "That boy will never learn to build a proper fire."

"Oh, but I'm glad to see you, Savanna," Margaret Felt cried. "I've been so forlorn I could die—and so cold. It was such a long, cold ride."

"Are you ailing?" Savanna swept her with a frank, appraising look.

"No more than usual, I suppose."

The slight, thin figure of Margaret Felt always made Savanna feel big and buxom and healthy, though she knew she was no taller and was almost as slimly and neatly made. But in herself it was a strong muscular slenderness, a compact, firmly knitted, sturdy small body. She radiated energy and good health. Margaret's smallness was frail and wispy, delicate and fragile. She had dead white skin, tinged ocherous now with her pregnancy and emphasized by bruised-looking shadows under her pretty violet eyes. Her hair was so pale it looked ashen, unlit by any gold or red. It was straight unless she frizzed it, and at the encampment she had neglected it so that it was now stringy and streaked, darkened with dust. She does look ill, Savanna thought.

She dragged a small table to the fire and set the tray on it. "Some hot food is what you need. There's plenty for two and I'll have my supper with you."

"What an angel you are, Savanna. I was just trying to make myself get up and find something to eat and I was dreading cooking it and eating alone."

"I knew you would be. Here. Kizzy has pot roast and gravy. Eat it, Margaret." She heaped the girl's plate.

"I have such a poor appetite."

"I don't. I'm as hungry as a wolf."

"You aren't in my condition."

Savanna laughed. "I doubt I'd lose my appetite if I was."

"You just wait and see!"

"All right," Savanna said, "I'll wait and see. It'll be a long wait, seeing I have no husband."

Through the meal she talked at random, skipping from one thing to another, keeping Margaret distracted from her woes until she had eaten a fairly good meal. Then she pushed the table aside and stretched her feet to the fire. "Now," she said, "tell me what's brought you home."

Margaret curled up in the big chair opposite, tucking her feet under her like a child. "Oh, the payment is going to take a lot longer than they expected, and it's turning so dreadfully cold." She shivered. "There's been ice on the creek every morning for a week and I was nearly freezing in that tent. My poor hands and feet were blue all the time."

Savanna nodded. "So you thought you'd better come home."

Margaret fumbled with the collar of her dress. "Well, Bill thought I should. Lieutenant Joyner had to come to the stockade today and Bill decided—" Her voice trailed off and the narrow little chin which pointed the small triangular face quivered. She lifted woeful, slow-filling eyes to Savanna. "Oh, Savanna, Bill has been so hateful and mean and cross since he lost that horserace. I don't know what's come over him. He's done nothing but drink and he hardly ever came to the tent—just stayed out all the time and I don't know where he went or what he was doing with those dreadful men from downriver. And the colonel was becoming real vexed with him. And when he did come home all he did was quarrel at me because I'm sick so much." The wail lengthened. "I can't help it if I'm in the family way and if I'm sick every morning."

Savanna grunted. "He's a fine one to quarrel at you. He got you into this fix, didn't he?"

Margaret was sobbing now, talking through sobs. "He said

he didn't want this kid to begin with and now he'd be saddled with it as well as a wife and he could very well do without both. He said he shouldn't ever have married and if he'd known I was going to be sniffling and puking all the time . . . Oh, Savanna, he said dreadful things to me, and then he told me I'd have to come back to the post. Said he was sick of watching me heave up my breakfast every morning." She hiccuped and blew her nose. "I was so terribly ashamed. I'm afraid Major Short and Martha next door could hear. I was so embarrassed and I know the whole post will think—"

"Oh, fiddle," Savanna said, "the whole post will think nothing of the sort. In your condition they'll think Bill was being thoughtful of you, sending you home out of the cold."

"Do you think so?" She wept more silently now and Savanna let her weep knowing it would, in the end, relieve her. At last she snubbed her breath and wiped her eyes. "I don't know what to make of Bill, Savanna. He isn't like himself these days."

Oh, yes he is, Savanna thought. He is exactly like himself, but you are just now learning what Bill Felt is really like. Big, handsome army officer, you thought, with that affable manner and loose, easy smile, and that pretty black hair he curls so carefully into long ringlets. Now you're learning he's a big, bullying brute and you'll have to have more luck than you're likely to have not to learn he's also a cheat and a fool. She wondered again at the folly of some women. One look at Bill Felt and she had put him down for what he was. But Margaret, poor simpering idiot, had not seen an inch past the handsome, loose face and the affable manner. Slick as a greased pig and crooked as a rifled gunbarrel—that was Bill Felt. Margaret might not deserve what she was going to get from him, but she was stuck as tight as a cork in a bottle with a lifetime of misery.

"I expect," she said slowly, "Bill has been hateful to you because he lost the race."

Margaret dabbed at her eyes again. "Why did you have to win it, Savanna? It meant so much to Bill. He's such a proud man and you shamed him before everybody."

Savanna exploded. "God's britches, Margaret! I'm a proud woman, too. I don't lose horseraces if I can win."

"But it meant so much to him. It couldn't have meant so much to you. He bought that horse especially for this race. He said he couldn't lose. And he was a dreadfully expensive horse."

"You don't know a thing about how much that race meant to me," Savanna said curtly, "and I have no intention of telling

94

you. But any horse can lose a race and Bill was a fool to . . ." she stopped abruptly. The girl wasn't really listening anyhow.

"Did you know he has to sell the horse now?"

Savanna gazed at her thoughtfully. She did not want to tear any more veils of illusion away from the girl but there were some things, she thought, she had to know. "Yes, I knew. In fact, I have already bought the horse."

Margaret's eyes rounded. "You bought Jethro? You? But Bill will hate you for that, Savanna." She spoke waveringly around the hand which had crept to her mouth.

Savanna shifted her feet on the fender. "Does it matter? He hadn't paid for the horse, Margaret. That's why he has to sell him. It shouldn't matter who bought him. My money is as good as anyone else's."

"But it will. I tell you, he has never . . ."

"He has never liked me. I know that. He has never liked me because I race and because I often win and because he is foolish enough to bet more than he can afford to lose and because he so often does lose. Your husband," she added dryly, "has a habit of blaming women for his misfortunes. I can bear being blamed by him but what's more important, Margaret, can you?"

Margaret twisted her fingers and stared at Savanna for a long moment. "I don't know," she said finally, "I just don't know, Savanna, I don't know what to do."

Savanna stood and shook out her skirts. "I think you had better begin finding out. And if I were in your shoes I'd make a start by standing up to him. If you let him bully you, he will."

With fear-darkened eyes, Margaret watched Savanna cross the room. "Savanna," she said, her voice whispery, "how do you stand up to a man?"

Savanna wheeled, suddenly so angry she could have shaken the girl until her teeth rattled. "Sweet heaven, Margaret," she yelled, "haven't you got any guts at all? Haven't you got any backbone? Scream at him, claw him, scratch him, bite him, kick him! Fill his bottom with buckshot like Martha Short did! Take a horsewhip to him if you have to! Do anything, but don't snivel and whine and creep and crawl! Haven't you any pride? Must you today slink and mewl? God's britches, I'd like to see the man that could bully me! I'd flay the skin off his back!"

The girl, shrunk into her chair as if already at bay, covered her mouth with her hands. "I couldn't, Savanna. I simply could not."

And Savanna knew she could not. To some it was given to stand straight. To others it was given to crumple. Margaret

95

would always crumple. "All right," she said, her anger wilted, "I'm sorry. I have to go now, Margaret. You need to get to bed and I have some accounts to go over."

"But, Savanna, I wanted to ask you . . . I wanted to see you . . ."

Savanna waited, by the door, her head bent a little, studying the colors of the braided rug Margaret Felt had made to brighten her dull little log house. She missed the groping embarrassment, the slow rising heat to the face, the troubled, shamed look of the eyes, of the other woman. She heard, finally, an indrawn breath and looked up as the girl spoke, rushingly. "I need some food from the store, Savanna, and Bill forgot to give me any money, and . . . and I know he hasn't paid the account yet . . . and . . . but if you could let me . . ."

Savanna stopped her, ashamed and embarrassed herself now. What a fool she had been not to know at once why Margaret Felt wanted to see her. None of this wailing confessional had been intended. It had just slipped out, burst forth compulsively. Margaret's immediate needs were very plain and simple. She needed food and, without money, credit. "Make a list of what you want," Savanna told her, "and I'll send Preacher over with it the first thing in the morning."

She warded off Margaret's gratitude and escaped, feeling hot and vexed, tired and prickly with anger at Bill Felt, a little headachy from the stuffy room and too much rich food. The cold air felt good on her face. The moon was crescent and the sky was showered with stars. She walked rapidly, passing down the row of officers' homes and cutting diagonally across the lower area near the river. In this clutter of cabins lived the laundresses, the married enlisted men, some hunters attached to the regiment—all those odds and ends of people a military post must have about and provides for so ill.

The houses were dark, save one where a candle shone through a window. Savanna's step slowed. It was the cabin of Dickon, one of the hunters. His wife was a laundress for B Company. Dickon must be back from the mountains.

A queer chill fell on Savanna's heart. How joyous Ellie must be tonight. No wonder she left her candle burning, expecting her man home after a month gone. How good to feel his hard arms around her, and his cold face on her warm one, the rough scrape of his beard as in his eagerness he forgot to be gentle; the smell of whiskey and tobacco for a moment as he came close, then shut off and tasted instead, as his mouth touched. The feral, man smell, of heat and sweat and dirt. The quick, feeling hands, the whispers, the bed cold at first, then warming. She swayed a little, such a longing for these things again filling her that she pulled at her hands distractedly.

No more. No more for her. Not ever again for her. Thomas would never come riding home to her again. Gone as if they had never been were the sweet candlelit nights, her own man beside her, urgent, and she, warmed, beloved, willing—gone, the nights alone remaining. For Ellie, for all the others, even for Margaret Felt, it was still theirs—but for her, no more. Such an anguish of loneliness and longing took her that her deep, pulled-in breath was like a sob. Thomas. Thomas!

Trapped, transfixed, she looked at the square window where the warm light wavered—warm, warm, and she was so cold. Inside were a man and woman who belonged to each other, who belonged so blessedly and surely, had a right to scold and quarrel and make up, to feed and sleep and make love. She felt an extraordinary compulsion to shout to them to cherish it, to keep it well—for when you no longer belonged to someone all the candles in the world couldn't make enough light, nor all the fire enough warmth.

A man appeared at the window to draw the curtains.

Dazedly she watched him. The slow thought dawned . . . but that isn't Dickon . . . that's . . . that's . . . she didn't recognize him, the light was too dim, but she knew from the uniform it was one of the young officers.

A hand touched her arm. "Come away, Savanna. You don't belong here."

She whirled about. "Abe!"

"Come along."

"That isn't Dickon in there . . . !"

"No matter. You have stumbled on something that is none of your affair and you had best forget it."

"Forget it!" Her voice rose dangerously. Every nerve in her body was still jangled by the emotions she had felt standing outside the candlelit window, strained by the desire she had felt so strongly, by her wild, hopeless yearning to feel again the warmth and joy she had imagined within. She felt let down, betrayed, angry.

"Shut up." Abe hushed her with a hand over her mouth and dragged her away. She stumbled along, fighting to get his hand loose. Not until they were a safe distance from the cabin did he release her and by that time she was heaving and panting for breath. Before she filled her lungs to spit a torrent of indignation at him, he burst out at her. "What are you doing standing around outside windows, looking in on things that are none of your business? What are you doing down in the quarter?"

Savanna retorted sharply. "I was minding my own business, thank you."

"It looked like it," Abe said bitingly. "Playing tom-peep."

"I was not. I only cut across from Margaret Felt's and saw the light . . . and it looked cozy and warm. I was not peeking. I wasn't even thinking about peeking. I was only thinking how nice for Ellie that Dickon was home."

Abe was still short with her. "Well, he isn't at home, as you saw for yourself. Now, for God's sake, if you recognized the man have the sense to keep your mouth shut."

"I didn't, but—"

"Good. And don't come down in the quarter again. A lot goes on down here you'd better know nothing about."

Savanna soberly digested this. Abe should know. It was his own quarter. He slept in the barracks but his friends lived in this area. With a prickle of distaste she recalled Thomas's laughter one night. "That little Jolie of Abe's is as pretty a halfbreed as I ever saw."

She had been interested only enough to ask, "Who is she?"

"One of the laundresses—Jolie Perrier."

So many of the halfbreeds had French names. Perrier, Therien, Soubiran, Montaigne, Chouteau—the early French trappers and traders had left their mark all over the country.

The laundresses—almost all of them had easy morals. They came and they went. They took up with some man, soldier or Indian, went away with him, or married him and stayed on, as Ellie had done. Yes, she had no doubt things went on down here she did not need to know, or any other respectable woman. And of course Abe knew best about the officer. Likely it amounted to nothing more than the casual coupling of a tomcat come upon a female in heat. "No," Savanna said, "I'll not do it again. But, Lord, Abe, what a hassle if Dickon ever found out. He'd kill the man."

"Yes. Well," Abe commented dryly, "the young man in there tonight is commonly more careful. He must have drunk too much."

Abe went in with her when they reached her house and Kizzy brought him a bottle of wine. Abe held it up to the light. "Madeira. Kizzy, I am obliged."

Savanna pretended to be angry. "That's the major's best madeira, Kizzy."

"Fo' Mister Abe, ain't it?" The black woman poured the wine carefully, then switched across the room. "I got to set de bread, den I gwine repose myself."

Abe settled himself on one side of the hearth, in Thomas's big chair, though he did not know it. Savanna pulled up a low stool. She winced when Abe let himself down into the deep, comfortable chair and, sighing, let his head rest against its high back. Thomas had done it so often. All of the young officers avoided that chair, leaving it for her. But Abe didn't know. He was a sergeant and while Thomas was living he had not been privileged to visit freely as the officers were. In this room he had always stood, respectfully, before a superior officer. But now, Thomas gone, Abe her friend and guest, he made straight for the chair his instincts told him was a man's chair. No matter. She was so glad to see him again. For one evening a man, a man she liked, was sitting in the chair again.

She chattered away to him, telling him in detail all she had done, certain of his interest and pleased to have so much to tell him. Vivid in a scarlet dress, her eyes stealing the fire's glow, her skin flushed and pearly, she talked on and on. She had a way of using her hands much when she talked and they flew about now like small brown birds.

Abe's brown face was shadowed by the wing of the chair but she could see the flash of his teeth when he laughed and knew that she was amusing him. She felt an exhilaration she had not known for a long time and without effort was gay and merry and humorous. It was almost as good as having Thomas to talk to again, though Thomas would have pointed up every incident with one of his salty, witty comments. Abe just grinned.

Run down at last, she said, "But I haven't let you say a word! What brings you to the post?" She filled his glass again.

"Brought your new horse over."

She cocked her head. "Now, Captain Bushmyer didn't let you off tonight just to bring that horse to me."

"That's all you need to know."

"It is, is it?"

"Yes, ma'am."

She sobered. "What's been happening out there, Abe?"

Abe's voice was slow and drawling. "Well, the fat's in the fire, I reckon. Everybody but the Cherokees is getting rich. More paper floating round and changing hands than you ever saw—and none of it, you might say, sticking to Cherokee palms though some of their big guns are buying plenty. Your friend Pete Crown has a trunkful they say, and that rich Creek, Budge Pinson, has bought a lot. The agents have been buying but most of it has been going to the speculators, I guess. Sam Houston has about sixty thousand dollars in, I hear. But he claims he means to be noble with it and give it back to the Indians."

"Where did he get sixty thousand dollars?"

Abe shrugged. "Some of the chiefs are backing him, I expect. Have you read the last *Gazette*?"

"We haven't had a post since the *Robert Thompson*," Savanna reminded him.

"No, I forgot. It came to the encampment. You know, I reckon, that Houston is the one who writes those articles signed Standing Bear?"

"I've heard so."

"This week he mortally lit into the agents. Came right out and openly accused them of opening a store at the encampment to buy up script. Says they're running whiskey in at the rate of forty gallons a day. Claimed the whole payment was a fraud and that merchants who had connections with the agents bought up the script for nothing—a blanket, a flask of powder, a jug of whiskey. He showed his hand. He's out to get 'em."

Savanna's brows pulled together. "But why? What does he want out here?"

Abe twiddled with the stem of his wine glass. "In the regiment they're saying the colonel is a little worried about Texas."

Savanna sat up straight. "The colonel, too! David said . . ."

"Yes. David's had it all the time that Houston was looking in that direction. And it ain't so far away from here."

"And the Indians?"

"Well, in my opinion Houston likes the Indians all right but his big scheme goes deeper than trying to help them."

"The man's a fool."

"Maybe. But he's a big-thinking fool. And it's fools like him that aren't afraid to plunge. Texas is a pretty big plum and those people out there are going to bust loose from Mexico some day, one way or another."

"But, it's so ridiculous . . ."

"What's ridiculous about it? He's been conferencing around with all the tribes. They've sent for him, in fact, and he's listened to all their complaints. He has advised them to put their complaints into writing and promised he would deliver their petitions to the Great White Father in person. Now— what's to stop him from coming back here and convincing them they owe him something—something like backing him up in Texas. What's to stop him from promising they'll get out from under the Great White Father, who has broken so many promises to them, and have a land of their own again."

"If he made such promises," Savanna said firmly, "he couldn't keep them."

"He wouldn't need to. All he needs is to make them believe he will. And it may be he can do that." Abe rose and set his empty glass on the table. "But it don't worry me too much."

"Why?"

"You think Sam Houston or anybody else can take an army

of Indians past Colonel Arbuckle and the Seventh Infantry?"

Savanna's smile was fond and broad. The pride of a man, of a proud man, in his own proud regiment—how good it was, and how good the men who felt it. It made her own pride rise, flushing and heart-beating. It was her regiment too. "Of course not."

"Well, then."

Abe recovered his hat and for the first time Savanna noticed he was wearing buckskins. She had been too engrossed before. "A detail going out?"

"A detail of one. Me. Out your door." His eyes were merry. "I put the horse in the stable."

"Abe, you're mean."

"Yes, ma'am. Mean as a rattlesnake. Good night."

The closing door made a draft that flared and flickered the candle. Its chill blew over Savanna's bare arms and she shivered. It would be cold on the prairie tonight.

She went slowly to the fire to mend it for the night. Instead she poked aimlessly at it with her foot and gazed into it, feeling strangely melancholy.

Perhaps Abe wasn't going on the prairie tonight.

It would be warm in Jolie Perrier's room. If Jolie Perrier was still laundering for A Company.

VIII

The company did not come back from the encampment until the end of November..

Before that time Savanna had had a strange succession of visitors, beginning with Auguste Chouteau, who came one cold, blowy morning, staying to dine with her at midday.

Over the ruins of the meal he suggested, blandly, that it might be to her advantage to sell the stock of her sutler's store to him.

"Why should I, sir? Colonel Arbuckle has given me six months in which to dispose of it."

"To relieve yourself of the tedium, perhaps? I am prepared to offer you a fair sum."

"I don't find it tedious to suttle," Savanna said. She looked at him calculatingly. "What do you consider a fair sum?"

Chouteau pursed his full red lips and considered. His soft, liquid brown eyes fixed themselves on the blue milk jug. His voice was also liquid and soft when he spoke. "I should say . . . perhaps . . . five thousand?"

Savanna snorted. "I am not, m'sieu', in desperate straits, as I would have to be to accept such an offer."

The Frenchman rose. Smiling, he bowed—that slight, deferent bending of the middle—and said, "I hope you will not regret your decision, madame." The smile broadened winningly. "My grateful thanks for an excellent meal and for your own charming presence."

She paced the floor when he had left. Why should she regret it? The threat had been gloved, but it was a threat nonetheless. What could he do? What lay back of the offer? What could lie back of it but the intention to see her out of business? He had, she suspected, heard that she meant to build on the Three Forks road and he did not want her near him.

She felt an exultant lift of the spirits. If Chouteau was afraid of her, it meant he considered her a more formidable competitor than she felt herself to be. He must, she thought, be more unsure of his situation than she had realized.

But she distrusted Chouteau completely. None of his charm moved her. He would smile just as winningly with a dagger at your back. She would have to be very watchful, very careful of him. He would not, she knew, approach her again. This offer he had made constituted his one attempt at warning her. Whatever he meant to do would be done, now, quietly, cleverly, sinuously. But she did not mean to retire so ungracefully at the first warning. She was not destitute and perhaps she had more resources than Auguste Chouteau knew. She did not mean to be frightened off, by him or by anyone else.

Captain John Rogers came another morning, only a few days after Auguste Chouteau, and asked if she were considering disposing of her Fort Smith store. "No, sir," she said firmly.

Captain Rogers' eyes were neither soft nor liquid nor brown. They were a very cool gray and they were exceedingly acute. "Should you decide to do so," he said, "would you be kind enough to let me know?"

"I can't promise that, sir," Savanna said. "Should I decide to sell the Fort Smith store I expect I should be interested in the highest offer."

Captain Rogers stroked his chin. "Perhaps I could accommodate you."

He was a big man, brisk and vigorous, with a wide brow, square chin, bushy eyebrows, and a thin, down-turned mouth. He had an especially level, penetrating gaze. He was rapidly acquiring most of the land around the old stockade at Fort Smith; he operated the ferry, owned the only cotton gin in the country, ran a tavern and was the village postmaster. Next to August Chouteau, he was perhaps the most influential man in the area. Her store, Savanna decided, must be a small but needing irritation to him. But it was not for sale. Albright was a competent manager. Thomas had had an unusually soft spot in his heart for the business in Fort Smith. She meant to keep it.

Her third visitor was Pete Crown, the Cherokee trader from Crown Falls. Would she like, he asked in his husky Indian voice, to sell him an interest in her store at the Falls? Or sell to him entirely? She might find it difficult to continue its operation without Major Brook.

No, she would not be interested in doing either. She did not think she would find it very difficult to continue its operation.

But she watched the man ride away, thoughtfully. In some ways she feared this halfbreed Indian more than either of the other men who had approached her. His way would not be the slow attrition of competition. She would have to take thought of a bullet, sudden and swift, in some lonely place.

None of this was any more than she had anticipated. She had known there would be these efforts made to buy her out as soon as her intentions were known. She had expected it and long ago had determined what her answers would be. It was a man's country and it was very tough and harsh and cruel, and maybe she wasn't tough enough or cruel enough to stand up against men in it, but she believed she had to try. Being who she was, Savanna Fowler Brook did not believe she had any alternative.

What she did not anticipate was a call from Martha Short.

She came striding into Savanna's house and, without greeting, informed Savanna that she did not mean to be brooked in her intention of having the sutler's post for her husband.

Savanna blinked. "Sit down, Martha. Let me give you a cup of tea."

"I have not come to drink tea with you, Mrs. Brook," Martha Short said, in her rough, rude way. "This is not a social call. I have come to warn you not to stand in my husband's way."

"Why should you believe that I mean to stand in his way?" Savanna asked.

"I think everyone understands," Martha Short replied, "that when this temporary appointment is terminated you will use every means at your command, every wile you possess, to seduce the colonel and to persuade him into making the appointment permanent. I do not possess your youth, Mrs. Brook, or your beauty," running her eye over Savanna as if in contempt of it, "but I should like you to know we are not without recourse ourselves. I am not as persuasive as you, nor do I have the influence over the colonel. I am a middle-aged married woman, not a young widow. I am perhaps not as clever as you, either. But there is one thing I do know. I know army regulations and I know that no woman can possibly be appointed permanently to the sutler's post. I am aware of the very firm grounds on which my husband stands there. I promise you, if you are able to cozen the colonel into making such an appointment, I will see to it that the matter is taken directly to the War Department and if it is necessary I, personally, will go to Washington and I will stand at the Secretary's elbow until he has countermanded it. We should be well within my husband's rights."

The picture of Martha Short standing at Mr. Eaton's elbow, her umbrella threatening, made Savanna burst into laughter.

"I do not see anything humorous about it," the major's wife said stiffly. "I am in deadly earnest."

She had been standing all this time, in her rusty black poplin, her back as straight as though she were on the parade ground. "Oh, sweet heaven, Martha, sit down," Savanna said, "and do quit calling me 'Mrs. Brook.' For three years you have called me Savanna. Need you become formal and stiff now?"

"I do not call my enemies by their given names."

"I am not your enemy, Martha. Do sit down and drink a cup of tea. If you will cease spluttering one moment we can talk frankly."

Grudgingly the woman yielded, though she sat on the edge of her chair as if meaning to spring into action any moment.

Savanna began earnestly. "Martha," she said, "I am not your enemy and do please believe me. I have no intention of seeking a permanent appointment. I did seek it—yes. I think anyone in my circumstances would have. You are fully aware of the opportunities in the sutler's store or you would not want it for Fred. It was but natural that, having the store, I should wish to keep it. But the colonel made it very plain to me that no woman could hold the appointment permanently. Even if I wished to use all the means at my command, though I do not know what they are, and all the wiles which you say I possess, it would be footless, wouldn't it? I am not ignorant of the fact that the War Department would immediately countermand such an order. There is not a single good reason why I should make any attempt to persuade the colonel into doing a thing which would come to nothing in the end. I am not so foolish."

"No," Martha Short said, and without grudge to Savanna's astonishment, "I have always given you credit for that. You are not a foolish woman."

"Perhaps," Savanna said, a little slyly, "then that is not your real fear. Perhaps you have come here to warn me of something you are not at all afraid of. Perhaps what you really fear is that I am clever enough to see the same end you have seen."

Martha Short's hands, clasped in her lap, tightened for a moment.

"Perhaps," Savanna continued, softly, "what you really fear is that I will work toward having the temporary appointment extended indefinitely, say, from six months to six months, until it does just as well. Is that what you are afraid of, Martha?"

The major's wife flushed and she looked at Savanna sharply. "I have said you are not foolish."

Savanna admired her for not backing down. And the truth got at, she could afford to be generous. "Then set your mind at rest. I have made other plans. I am too impatient a person to live so insecurely, my certainties so dependent on another's whims. From six months to six months would not suit me at all. Besides, whether you believe it or not, obliqueness does not suit me either. I have never in my life used my wiles, as you call them, to obtain anything for myself. At least I have never done so knowingly. And I have told one other person that I do not mean to begin with Colonel Arbuckle."

No one could call what happened on Martha Short's face a smile. A smile breaking the stiff and angular lines of her face became rather a grimace. But Savanna was pleased to see it. Besides the woman's candor and courage, Savanna liked her willingness to confess herself wrong when convinced. She said to Savanna, "I think I have misjudged you." She stuck out her hand precisely as a man does and they shook. "You do not mean, then, to work against Fred?"

"On the contrary," Savanna said. "I will do what I can to help him." She could not help grinning and adding, however, "Since I cannot have the post myself, I think you and Fred would make a good sutler."

Martha Short was not dull-witted. The grimace flicked across her face again. "You think I manage my husband, don't you?"

"Some husbands need managing."

"Where his army duties are concerned I have never interfered."

"I know that, Martha," Savanna said. "Everyone knows you are as much army as Fred."

"I have my peculiarities," she confessed, "and I rub people the wrong way many times. I know, for instance, that I rub the colonel the wrong way. But I am not a foolish woman, either, Savanna. I know that Fred is such an excellent officer that my peculiarities do not greatly matter. I would like you to believe that I would not indulge myself in them if that were not true. I would wager, though I disapprove of wagering, that the colonel does not actively dislike me. I am simply a bad conscience to him, and an irritant."

Savanna found herself warming to the woman. She had always held in esteem Martha Short's acceptance of hard duty without complaint, and her quick and capable way of managing. She admired now, also, this frank appraisal of herself. "Tell me, Martha. Why do you want this appointment for Fred? I must own it surprises me. He has a good future in the army."

Martha Short's face went dull. "He has no future at all." Then she burst out bitterly. "It is a dreadful thing, Savanna, to see a man come within the grasp of his ambitions and to know that his health will not let him reach them."

So. So. Fred was ailing. Savanna reached a sympathetic hand quickly. "He must resign?"

"Before the year is out, we fear."

Savanna did not ask in what way Fred Short was ill. Instead she asked, "Has David advised him so?"

"Yes. Though I had a time getting him to see the surgeon."

"Will his health improve if he leaves the regiment?"

"David Holt says so. He says if Fred can putter about and live quietly he may live out his time. But if he stays with the regiment it means his death."

Warm tears of pity pricked at Savanna's eyes. They must have pondered much over what was to become of them, she thought. And the sutler's post would be a godsend. Martha was shrewd and if she did not drive trade away with her sharpness she could manage, even if Fred's health failed to such an extent that he could not be active at all. "Have you told the colonel?" she asked.

Martha hesitated. "No. Not yet. We have been afraid he might have some doubt about giving Fred the appointment."

"He will never accept Fred's resignation unless you do," Savanna said positively. "He needs him too badly. Let me counsel you, Martha—tell the colonel immediately. I think it will weigh in your balance. He is a kind man, you know."

Martha stood. "Yes. Yes, I expect you are right." She ordered her skirts awkwardly, a little shy now, as so many prickly people are shy when they have been touched beneath their bristles. "Well, goodbye, Savanna—and I am obliged to you. But I expect you know that." She rubbed her rough hands together, and added simply, "I want my husband to live."

As Savanna let her out into the bitter, blowing cold it struck her that she and Martha Short had wasted some years they

106

could have used better. We are kin under the skin, she thought. We are both tough and we both use our tongues too often, but we are loyal and we know how to be grateful.

She determined to let it be known that she favored Fred Short for the permanent appointment.

IX

The winter continued bitterly cold.

By the time the Company came back to Gibson, at the end of November, the cold was beginning to press hard, and the winds, which were to blow violently and ceaselessly the whole winter, had shaken the leaves off all the trees, even the blackjacks, which usually held them tenaciously until spring. They were all gone early, blown wither-strawed before the wind.

"It will drive me crazy!" Savanna cried, miserable-tempered from the constant blowing. Nothing rubbed her nerves more raw than the unending chatter of windows and the creaking of limbs and the shrilling howl about the eaves.

"Yessum," Kizzy said, "it do make a mixtie-maxtie mess of a body's brain, for a fack."

In spite of her ill-temper, Savanna laughed. Kizzy coined words recklessly, but it was amazing how often they were more apt than any others. A mixtie-maxtie mess was exactly what her brain felt like. She was so twisted with worry, too, about her house. She had counted so much on the good autumn weather holding. But there was not any good autumn weather this year. Instead there was winter, early, hard, cruel, with this furious, violent wind blowing as sharp as a skinning knife.

At best this was a windy country, for there was no barrier to blunt the wind this side of the Rockies—the earth heaved only the gentlest rise of its breast clear to the mountains—but no one had ever known such winds as came this year, blowing a gale sometimes for days on end, and rarely ceasing entirely. It howled like a thousand lost souls about the chimneys, set windows to chittering, flung shingles off roofs angrily, and drove, frequently, a smothering, blinding drift of snow before it. Then the snow itself was blown away before it had time to bank.

The land took on a naked, bladeless look. It had no shelters or barriers. Its only defense was space. It was as though the earth thought if it lay quietly enough, spread far enough and wide enough, the wind would spend itself in time. The rind of the planet, it had only its thin armor of room for the elements to play about in.

It was not strange that there was little ice on the rivers that year. They were too enraged by the wind to freeze. It boiled the

Neosho like porridge, and on the sandbars of the Arkansas it picked up the sand and sent it running in dry, dusty rivers. Only a little ice, constantly discouraged, grappled the banks.

Irking to act, twitchy with restlessness, Savanna's one consolation was that the household population of the cantonment bought generously of her and she had the pleasure of seeing the shelves and the warehouse slowly emptying. She was setting aside a portion of her goods to stock the new store with, but if trade continued healthy she thought she might dispose of the balance.

The Creek had got logs rafted down the river and hauled to the building site and he had got the foundation stones set and the walls halfway up, then he had quit. He said it was too cold and the wind blew too much. Abe told Savanna not to fret, that the house could be finished easily with a few weeks of good weather in the spring. But Savanna was unhappy about the halt in the building. "I vow," she told Abe fiercely, "I'll take Kizzy and Preacher and finish it myself if that Creek dallies about too long."

In December Sam Houston went with the Cherokee commission to Washington. It was rumored about the country that he meant to have all the agents removed. There were many uneasy heads as the rumor circulated. Could he do it? Was he still that powerful? No one could know until time had passed and the colonel received orders, or Sam Houston returned. And time dragged that cold winter.

Savanna was uneasy, too, because the situation with the young Felts did not improve. Margaret looked ill and had a bloat in her ankles and legs and Bill Felt took to drinking heavily and was seldom at home. There was scandalous talk about him—he had not paid up his gambling debts—and he was so surly and quarrelsome that even his fellow officers took to avoiding him. To what end were they coming? Savanna wondered if Margaret would survive the birth of her child, and if she did what value she would put on her survival under the circumstances. Something must change their situation, Savanna thought, and soon, but what it could be fretted at her. She wished she could take Bill Felt by the shoulders and shake a little sense into him. When she saw him he eyed her broodingly and did not speak until she had spoken first. Even then it was as though his good morning had been punched out of him. He's a fool, Savanna thought contemptuously, and passed on by.

In February, Colonel Arbuckle announced that Fred Short was to be the next sutler. Paul Chouteau, a relative of Auguste's, had wanted it and Captain Rogers had dallied with the notion. If they were disappointed they let no one witness it.

The colonel made no explanations. The announcement was posted on the bulletin board outside his quarters and that ended it. But Savanna knew that the Shorts had told him about Fred's health, that the colonel had then conferred with David Holt, and that, probably grievingly, he had determined to do what he could for his second-in-command.

The day she learned of Fred Short's appointment was the only good day for Savanna in a month which continued to make mock of her plans.

In March, however, not to be outdone by weather but unable to prod the Creek, Savanna made good on her threat and on each fit day routed out Preacher and Kizzy and made them go with her to the building site. Like most active people, she was freed from fret when she could take action. Though the black people groaned and protested, she was happy and tireless when a fine day came along and she could get a little forwarder. What she could not abide was standing still.

Sometimes David Holt went with them and with his great strength accomplished more than the rest of them put together. Sometimes Abe went, and occasionally both men accompanied them. Abe protested it all. "If you would be a little patient, Savanna, none of this would be needed. The Creek will get back to it."

"In his own good time," Savanna snapped. "I can't afford to wait on him."

With more understanding of what was driving her, David Holt made no protest. He simply went when he could get away, and did what he could, enjoying it all immensely. "Anything," he said, "even hefting logs, is a good change from the hospital."

There was the usual spate of sickness that winter and the hospital was crowded much of the time. Seeing David sometimes, his face sleep-starved, Savanna wondered how he endured it. She was glad when he could find the time to go with them to the new house.

One day of immense labor at a time they got the walls up, the roof rafters on, the floor laid, so that when there came a sudden calm and two weeks of mild, sunny weather late in the month, Abe went to find the Creek and somehow browbeat him into finishing the house. They called it finished, at any rate, though it lacked window glasses, chimneys, and a kitchen. It was a great relief to Savanna to know she could move into it and turn the government buildings over to the colonel on time.

He was unhappy over her location.

"I think it is an excellent situation," she told him.

"I'm afraid you will not find it so," he said, shaking his head.

"Oh, I know. Auguste Chouteau will do his best to drive me out. But I think I can count on enough trade from the post to offset what he takes from me."

The colonel continued to shake his head. "It is not only Chouteau, my dear. Have you not heard that Sam Houston means to set up a trading store quite near you? Less than a mile will separate your establishments."

"Damnation!"

Only the colonel's lifted eyebrows expressed amusement. "He made the arrangements with old Jolly before he left for Washington and means to order his stock while he in the east."

Savanna gave a short laugh. "I wonder that Jolly leased to me if his adopted son meant to build near me."

The old man's face was troubled. "I think perhaps, my dear, Houston determined on this *after* you leased your piece from Jolly."

Savanna took a deep breath. "So he means to cut in on the Cherokee trade. Very well. I'll fight him for it."

The colonel smiled, wanly. "I wish you would reconsider, my dear. It is not too late. Savanna, I am an old man and not much of a prospect . . ."

Alarmed, Savanna jumped to her feet. She did not want the colonel to propose marriage to her. His friendship was too valuable, she liked him too much, she did not wish to hurt him . . . there were a dozen reasons why he must not make a statement he could not retract, could not retreat from in grace. "On, no," she said, hurriedly, "no, sir. I have too much invested to be run off. Doubtless you believe, as many others do, that I should return to Fort Smith, but I cannot and I will not. I am not afraid of Sam Houston, nor of Auguste Chouteau, sir. You must not give yourself concern about me." She looked about frantically. "Now, what did I do with my carryall?"

Sighing, the colonel retrieved it for her and escorted her to the door, his long face a little longer and a little sadder, his smile, now, wry. "Perhaps you are right. Perhaps. But Houston has married Talahina Rogers, I suppose you know."

"I heard he was living with her."

"Yes. Well, he is bound to get much of the Cherokee trade."

"Perhaps. I think I can hold my own."

The colonel sighed again. "Did you know the War Department acted on Houston's recommendations and all the agents save William McClellan of the Choctaws have been removed?"

"No! I didn't believe he could."

"I was afraid of it."

"How have they taken it?"

"They are very bitter, naturally. And much of my own work with the tribes must now be done over. New agents always mean more work for me. I had got used to working with these men. I regret their removal."

"It's a pity, sir. I had hoped he would not have that much influence . . ."

"Yes. Well." The colonel nodded absently, drumming his fingers on the doorjamb. "My dear," he said suddenly, "since you insist on settling yourself in this new location, will you do me a very great favor?"

"If I can, sir," Savanna said promptly.

"Well," the colonel said, chuckling, "this won't require the War Department's permission or a written document. I am uneasy about this man Houston. Since he will be living near you, will you keep an eye on him?"

"I expect to," Savanna said crisply.

"Yes. Well more than that, my dear, will you report to me anything you see of general interest? I am particularly interested in knowing who his guests are, who he sees and talks with . . . where he goes himself."

"That's a large order, sir, but to the best of my opportunities I will do it."

"I thought you would." The old man's eyes were twinkly. He had not mistaken Savanna's liking to be in the middle of things, nor her bald, frank curiosity about them.

The following week she moved into her new home.

The new house was, as Kizzy would have said, a mixtie-maxtie jumble, and much more expressive of Savanna's many-faceted personality than any other place in which she had ever lived. She stood about the rooms the old mahogany furniture which had been her mother's. In the cupboard she set out the old silver and china. She put down her rag carpets. She stood her grandfather's cherry chest in the corner of her big main room. She had no parlor nor wanted one. The big room in which she would receive company and in which she would spend a large part of her own time was, instead, cluttered with roomy, comfortable man-sized chairs, because men would occupy them, and tables set conveniently for drawing up to hold a tray for a cigar and pipe ashes and a glass. Her saddles and bridles hung on the wall as well as a clayed and feathered Indian peacepipe and a handsome belt of wampum. For curtains she put up at the windows the beautiful Osage blankets, gorgeous in their orange and purple and scarlet, and everlasting in their endurance. Before the hearth she threw a black bear rug.

The room looked like nothing she had ever shared with Thomas, who would not have borne the Indian blankets at the windows, or the clutter on the walls. It had a heathen, barbaric look which he could never have abided. But it suited Savanna perfectly. She liked it immensely and loved to sit in it, a good fire crackling on the hearth, all the gaudy color flaming about her. It had all the force and nerve and durability of herself. It spoke for her, luminously, cheerfully, and heartily. "Good God," said David Holt when he saw it first, "you've gone a little mad, haven't you?"

"You don't like it?"

He sank into a chair, stuffed his pipe, lit it and drew on it, and looked curiously about. "You know? I think I do. It's not very restful, but then you're not either and you've got a lot of yourself in the room—and that's pretty nice."

"It's mine," Savanna said proudly, "all mine. It's precisely the way I wanted it. There isn't an uncomfortable chair in the room, David. Try them all and see."

"I'll take your word for it," he said lazily. "This one is fine."

"They're alike for ease. And there is every convenience for guests."

"Yes," the surgeon said. "You've thought of everything." He added judicially, "Except, perhaps, what people are going to say when the guests begin to fill this room every night."

Savanna jerked her head impatiently, setting her earrings to jingling. "They've always talked and I can't let it matter. I'll take care, but I am counting on those guests to fill my purse."

David Holt was suddenly sober. "See that Kizzy is always in this room, Savanna, when men are here."

"Great gobs of mud, David, I can't do that! Kizzy has work to do."

"Take my advice, Savanna. Find an Indian girl to do the work and keep Kizzy beside you. You aren't on the post now, where the proprieties are served simply by the presence of other women. You are a young and very attractive woman, alone in a trading establishment. If you don't mean to defeat your own ends, give no one room to talk. Kizzy is eminently respectable. Keep her beside you. And another thing, never, under any circumstances, sell whiskey here."

"Do you take me for a fool? I mean to serve the wine which any hostess serves her guests—to the officers who will be my guests. Enlisted men and Indians will never see the inside of

112

these walls. I am not opening a tavern!"

"Good. Stick to that and I shan't worry. And now I'll be your first customer. I need some tobacco."

X

At first Savanna missed the post so much that she could not seem to get herself sorted out. She could not get used to a day which began without the crash of the morning gun, or ended without the boom of the evening gun. The whole life of the cantonment was geared to those sounds. When the morning gun went you got up and went about your day's business. When the evening gun sounded you put your day in order. Clocks, and even the sun, seemed strangely undependable without the guns. Sure as God were the guns, but a clock could run down, and the sun could be beclouded. She found herself straining to hear the guns. She was near enough to hear them, she thought resentfully, if the wind didn't forever blow from the west and carry their noise away from her.

She missed the busyness and activity of the post. She missed seeing field details going out, four, six, eight men, counting them off—Smith, Hudspeth, Isaacs, Graham—Andy Bushmyer, Aaron Cleet, John Haverty, or some other unhappy lieutenant commanding, and knowing through the grapevine of gossip where they were going, and why they were going. Into the hills to run down a whiskey runner. To the Choctaw Nation to drive some poor white squatter off Indian land. To Fort Smith to mend the decaying buildings, or the rutted road. To the prairies, to sit for days in an Indian council, or look into a rumor that the Osages were hungry, dying of a fever epidemic, or raiding again. There was always a flurry of interest when a detail went out and over the years Savanna had learned to tell, by the choice of men, where they were going and why.

She missed the flourishes of excitement when rumors got started—someone was being promoted; someone was being transferred; someone was arriving on the next steamboat, a wife, a daughter returning from school, visitors, important army personages. She only got gossip secondhand now. She was no longer in the thick of it.

She missed being part of the regiment. She had loved her sense of belonging to it. Most women, she thought, had to make do all their lives with the pride and possession of one man. An army wife proudly possessed a company, a regiment, an entire army of men. The life was rough and wandering, often cruelly uprooting and harsh, always striped through with petty jealousies and envies and scufflings; but above all of these

113

there were days shiningly beautiful because one's own company, A Company, or B Company, or F Company, had done itself proud and its brief glory was a halo round one's own head. And however drab the duty, there was always the feeling that the Regiment itself was very special.

You might, Savanna thought, say the word carelessly, or accusingly, or even, some days, profanely, but it was the heart and luster of your life after all and you loved it and were proud of it and on those shining days you wouldn't have changed places with a queen.

She missed it. She missed being inside the close, closed circle which the very word Regiment hooped around its people. She felt outside, on the outskirts, exiled.

She missed the presence, the sight and the sounds of six hundred men garrisoned at the post.

She was always the first to admit that she liked men better than she did women—or most women, at any rate. She liked the things men did and the way they did them. They rode, gambled, swore, fished, hunted, drank, speculated, traveled, and they enjoyed them all so hugely. No woman ever had so gusty an appetite for her own occupations as nine out of ten men did. She was still of the conviction that men had the better of things.

Her life with Thomas, surrounded as it had been by men, men willing to pet and spoil her as much as Thomas, had made women go a little stale and flat for her. There were still the young officers who came almost as often as when she had been at Gibson, but the men she counted her special friends —Colonel Arbuckle, David Holt, Abe Lathrop, even James Joyner—she no longer saw daily. She felt dull and lonely without them.

Finally, she missed the river. She had not given a thought to that when she chose her new location. But for the first time in her life she was living in a place where she could not look out on water. It gave her a kind of claustrophobia. Running water, she realized belatedly, had by its soothing flow run off many of her tensions and irritations. Well—she could still ride two miles in either direction and find a river. It wasn't the same, but it had to do.

She had been facing a month of these feelings of loneliness, emptiness, and dislodgement, drawn as if by a magnet to the post and going oftener than she should, when she brought herself up sharply. This will not do! She hooted at herself. I am the one who has always preached to others, put behind you what you have to leave behind. Don't sit around on your hunkers and grieve over what is past. Look about and make the best of what you have. And here she was mooning, worse than the worst young homesick wife or second lieutenant, over what she had had to leave behind. The sutler's store, the regiment, even the cantonment, were only casually a part of her life now.

She took herself vigorously in hand. It was to end at once. She would not have it. She would not tolerate these mooning thoughts and listless ways. She would stop running to Gibson every other day. She had been neglectful of her own work in order to keep a finger on the pulse of the cantonment. She would do it no more. She would seize upon her duties immediately and keep her hours and her days full and busy. She had too much to do to mourn over what was behind her.

When she threw herself into her work she found that, as always, work and time came to her aid. Slowly the routine of her days had its settling effect and a pattern of living was evolved.

There were other little pricks and bothers, however.

Unlike Sam Houston, who was calling his establishment the Wigwam Neosho, Savanna was content to raise across the front of her store the same sign the other stores carried, and had always carried—Thos. Brook, Mcht. & Trdr. She first became aware of what it was really being called when an enlisted man told her one evening, "I just taken a notion for some good molasses and I knowed you had some so I said to myself I'll just take a little sashay over to Savanna's."

So—she was being called Savanna now and her place was becoming known as Savanna's place. She did not like it—it sounded too much like Polly's doggery. David was right. Without the protection of the military she had, inevitably, lowered her status in the country. It gave her an uneasy feeling. She did not relish any comparison to Polly Walker. She did not want to be suspected of selling whiskey and of keeping Indian girls for the men.

But she was not really frightened. She could not help this loss of status, but she could double her efforts not to feed rumor and gossip. She would take David's advice and keep Kizzy beside her and she would keep an eagle eye out for loitering girls or for any drunkenness on her premises. In time, when the countryside learned that there were neither girls nor whiskey available at her place, her position would be secure.

She did not feel entirely happy about her financial situation, either.

Her accounts at Gibson settled, her debts paid, there was not as much left as she would have liked. She had raided her warehouses to stock the new store and this took its toll of her profits. But she had not wanted to order on credit again. Since the days when her father's great debt had hung over the household and taken so long to pay off, debt had terrified her. She owed nothing now, but she had had to draw it very fine and her ready resources were so small as to give her little leeway.

It was especially worrisome since the store at Fort Smith had fallen off a little, as had the one at Crown Falls. It was seasonal, she told herself. The stores had always fallen off in the spring and summer. The spring was the time of totting up accounts, shipping pelts and honey and tallow downriver, ordering, making ready for the fall and winter season. It was too soon, she told herself, to let any fear of competition gnaw at her. Just the same, she would be glad when this first year was over and she could tell better where she stood.

She made out her own tally sheets and arranged with Auguste Chouteau to ship her pelts this year. Thomas had never used the traders' boats, preferring to ship with the steam packets. But Chouteau was cheaper and short all around as she was she did have to cut corners. She had to risk being cheated.

Though she trusted the men installed at Fort Smith and Crown Falls to operate her stores, she did not trust them entirely. Thomas had found both Albright and Minden honest, but with Thomas gone who was to say what they might be tempted to try with her? Not that she was suspicious of them. She meant simply to be careful and watchful.

Each two months, therefore, she visited the stores. She looked over the stock, made suggestions, and carefully went over the accounts. She did not expect the situation with regard to trade to improve until fall. She was satisfied that it did not seriously deteriorate. On the whole, she felt, she was doing very well. But she would be happier when she could let out a little string.

Aside from her worries about the store, Savanna's visits to Fort Smith were pleasant to her and she looked forward to them. She did not especially enjoy the village, but Tully was there and unless he had been called away, she saw him and he usually joined her in riding out to the Landing to see their father.

Tully had not married and was beginning to declare that he never would. "I'm too particular," he said. "Can't find anyone to suit me."

Savanna thought him wise and said so. "There's no hurry," she told him, "you're young yet. For goodness' sake don't saddle yourself with a family until you've made a start."

He cocked a humor-filled eye to her. "Perhaps I wouldn't have a family."

116

"Go boil your head," Savanna said scornfully. "You'd have a dozen in no time at all."

He grinned. "You overestimate me, my dear sister."

"Oh, hush. Just don't marry until you're well on your feet."

When he had passed the bar, Tully had left Captain John Rogers' store and set up for himself, but he was not getting rich in Fort Smith. He was beginning to think he should make a change. "The court is at the capital and the law business is where the court is. Unless I want to go east I think it might be a good plan to follow the business."

Savanna nodded. "I'd hate to see you go, but it will be a long time before you can make a living at law up here. What are you doing to exist?"

His eyes merry, her brother said, "I dabble in a little double-dealing in land, as everyone else does. On the side I do a little whiskey running, a little gambling, with just enough law thrown in to keep me an honest man."

Unshocked, because it was the way of most men in the country, Savanna grinned. "See that you hang on to the law."

"Oh, I mean to. My ventures on the side are solely to feed me."

Savanna was struck with a sudden idea. "Would you like to run my store here for me, Tully?"

"It's the last thing I'd like to do," he said promptly. "These nefarious occupations of mine do at least get me out into the country and among people and give me a chance to drum up a little honest business. In your store I would soon quit being a lawyer and become just another trader. I don't want to do that."

Savanna agreed. "No. I wouldn't really want you to. Some day you may be an important man in the country if you stay with the law. You might even," she mused, "go into politics."

"I might. It has occurred to me."

Jeff had not married yet either and continued to live at home, where his father and Lena had produced two more children and the house was a beehive of their babies and Lena's older children. It smelled, nowadays, of that warm, milky, and fecal smell which babies always give a place. It made Savanna wrinkle her nose but she had long ago got over her resentment of Lena and enjoyed visiting in her old home.

Jeff had come to be like Manifee in many of his ways, growing quieter as he matured, silently and capably taking over the management of his father's land. He had cut out all crops but cotton and corn, which he planted so extensively and with such profit that the family was more comfortable than it had ever been since leaving Kentucky. Savanna did not know what her father would do without Jeff. It would be a long time before her two small half-brothers would be big enough to help. But she realized that Jeff had a life of his own to live and that one day he might be impelled to live it, as Manifee had done. So long as he was enthralled with farming, however, it was a blessing for her father.

Manifee was almost wholly lost to them now. He had never returned from the west. Somewhere out there in the mountains he was living a strange and lonely life, foreign to them but apparently suiting him well. In four years there had been three letters from him. At the writing of each he was in Taos, where he seemed to go to dispose of his furs and to buy his provisions. In one letter he mentioned having been to Santa Fe where he saw his uncle and his uncle's wife. "Johnny," he wrote, "has taken out Spanish papers and is engaged in the Chihuahua trade. He is doing well and has become a regular *haciendada*."

In each letter Manifee mentioned the possibility of bringing a load of furs to St. Louis and of dropping on down the Texas Road to visit home. But they knew in all likelihood they would never see him again. The west had swallowed him up. It grieved them, but there was nothing to do but accept it.

Savanna herself always felt like a visitor at home; a welcome visitor, one whose presence was enjoyed, but her life had changed so radically, her experiences had been so various and enlarging, that she sometimes felt strange and out of place in the house she had run alone for two years following her mother's death.

She was content to have it so. She knew, now, what a boon her father's marriage had been. She would have stayed right here, as stuck as Jeffie, had her father not married Lena. She cherished her freedom and shuddered at the thought she might never have had it. A visit to her father's was always enough to send her home with new pleasure in her own establishment.

It was a sweet place.

The house, with elms and pecans and oak trees standing about it, was big. The principal room was twenty by thirty feet, and Savanna's bedroom across the dogtrot was only slightly smaller. Adjoining the big main room, with a door opening into it, was the store, housed in a shed attached to it. Savanna could step from her accounts into the store, and back to her accounts, conveniently. She liked the arrangement though it was troublesome occasionally. The Indians had a way of stealing into the big room when they did not find her in the store. They were so still with their movements, and so silent, that she rarely knew they were there. It was startling to turn

118

and find one standing, eyes dead black and fixed on her, saying nothing and doing nothing—simply standing and waiting. She tried to make them understand that they were to go into the store and to call her, but as with so many other things, they nodded pleasantly, agreed they must call her, then promptly forgot or ignored what they had been told.

"Well," Abe said when she fumed to him about it, "that's easy to remedy. Put a bell on the door. Every time it's opened it will ring and you'll know someone's there."

The flaw in that solution was that bells entranced Indians—they hung them all over their horses and even tied them on their moccasins—and, as delighted as children with the novelty of a door that rang, they would stand for half an hour swinging the door back and forth to make the bell tinkle. There was also a run on bells so extensive that not only Savanna but every trader in the vicinity was soon sold out. The Indians were going to have bells on their own lodges.

The house fronted the road but back of it and on either side a long, treeless grassy swale stretched away. It was fine pasturage for Savanna's horses and Kizzy's cow. Near the house, Preacher fenced a back lot and threw up a stable and henhouse. Kizzy had chickens, ducks and turkeys, over which she fussed constantly. From her father's home Savanna brought apple seedlings for the start of an orchard. Also from her father's she brought the little briar rose which her mother had coddled all the way from Kentucky. The meadows were sweet with love vine and honeysuckle and Kizzy brought a trumpet flower from the woods and set it climbing the front veranda. Slowly the place lost its raw, new look and took on shape and form, began to look rooted and established.

There was a certain excitement, too, Savanna found, to living on the Texas Road as it had begun to be called. Traffic was beginning to be heavy over it and many wagons, especially those of men taking their families with them to Texas, camped near her place rather than at Three Forks. Instinctively their womenfolk distrusted the crude settlement and preferred to stop where there was another woman—at Savanna's. The wagons frequently needed repair and the men would have stopped at Chouteau's where there was a blacksmith and carpenter's shop. The women usually had their way and because the men complained about lack of accommodation, Savanna had Preacher throw up another log building and installed him in it as a blacksmith. He may not have been the best blacksmith on the Texas Road but he wasn't the worst, either, and generally the emigrants were satisfied.

Savanna charged four bits for shoeing a horse all around,

six for shoeing and pointing. She charged two bits for putting a new tire on a wagon wheel, one dollar for all four. Preacher gave himself such airs over his new profession that Kizzy was thrown all out of sorts with him. "All swole up lak a toadfrog, him. I gwine whop him one do he ast me wait on him anodder time. Act lak he de king 'round heah. I gwine king him! I gwine crown him good!"

They came from Missouri, Illinois, Indiana, Kentucky—but they were all going to Texas. "Why?" Savanna asked often. "Why Texas?"

"Oh, it's the place to go, ma'am. Them Mexicans is beggin' for settlers. It's a big country and but few there yet."

"You'll lose your American citizenship."

There would be shrugs and laughs. "I don't mind taking the Spanish oath, ma'am. Not if I can better myself."

Headed for Texas. Going west. Looking for that good country, that perfect land of milk and honey. It was always there, just ahead, just a little farther west. "You'll not find it in Texas," said one, returning. "Texas is a poor country to my notion and I have traveled it from the Red River to the Rio Grande, from the gulf to the last house west and two hundred miles beyond. It is too tedious to tell about. There's nothing as good as what I left in Missouri. It's only a makeshift place."

But he discouraged no one. They had to see for themselves. It was as though the very name of Texas was a magnet drawing them mysteriously and without reason. And they were all in such a hurry. "How many on the Road ahead of us?" they would ask.

"As if," Savanna told Abe, "Texas hadn't room to house them all."

"They've no notion what it's like," Abe said. "They're thinking someone will beat them to the best land."

His horse had cast a shoe and he was waiting for Preacher to put on a new one. He looked about, noting all the improvements that had been made. "Place is looking nice. How're you making out?"

"About as well as I expected," Savanna said. "Though that Chouteau managed as slick as butter to cheat me of a hundred dollars on my shipment downriver. Said my prime pelts were downgraded, and he had the warehouse receipt to prove it!"

"You sure they were prime?"

"Certainly I'm sure. He bribed the clerk at the warehouse to sign falsely. I'm positive of it."

Abe shrugged. "Better stick to the steam packets—or ship with Cap'n Rogers. Don't believe the captain would cheat you."

"Well, I don't mean to ship with Auguste Chouteau again, that's certain."

Abe bit off a hunk of tobacco and slowly warped it into place in his cheek. When he had it softened and had spit a couple of times he said. "Hear there's been some drinking around your place."

Savanna's head came up and her earrings jangled warningly. "Where did you hear that?"

"Oh, around, and about."

"The women on the post, I guess!"

"Where there's smoke there's usually a little fire, Savanna. What's the truth about it?"

"Well, I don't sell it, you know that. They can't get it at my place, but it's so easy to get at Polly Walker's or Chouteau's, or Hugh Love's, that they fill themselves to the gills and then come drifting over here. I don't know how you can control that."

"Getting troublesome?"

"Some. Preacher has had to make a few leave."

Abe stood away from the fence against which he had been leaning. "Preacher's not enough. You've got to have a man in the store. Somebody big enough to handle the drunks and throw 'em off the place. I'll send you one in the next day or two."

"Well, that's handsome of you! How am I going to pay him? I can't afford a man."

"You'll have to. I said I'd send one."

Leaving her spluttering, Abe walked away, inspected Preacher's shoeing job, nodded his satisfaction, mounted and rode away.

The next morning the man turned up. He was a mangy-looking sample but he was huge and looked strong enough to heft an ox. A great scar across one cheek, where the beard grew patchily, gave him an evil look and he pouched as big a cud of tobacco in his jaw as Savanna had ever seen. "My name's McNulty," he said. "The sergeant sent me."

"What sort of pay do you expect?" Savanna asked brusquely.

"Same as I got in the army. My time's just up. Druther not jine up again. Gimme eight dollars a month and found."

"You know what you're to do here?"

"Yes, ma'am. Mind the store and heave the floaters off."

"I'll mind the store," Savanna said curtly. "Your job is protection."

"Any way you want it, ma'am."

"Do you know anything about trading?"

121

"Traded myself in the Illinois. Got run off by the Winnebagoes. Ain't ever got enough string together since to set up again."

Savanna looked him over carefully. He was, she decided, exactly the man she needed. If he could trade she could leave the store in his hands safely when she had to be gone. And he was so big she doubted any drunk would ever give him any trouble. She stuck her hand out. "Fine, then. We've made a deal."

"One more thing, ma'am. I'll expect a whiskey ration."

"Of course."

It was a custom of the country. Any workman expected and was allowed three pint cups of whiskey each day. The government allowed it. McNulty took her hand in his giant paw and crushed the bones. "Where you want me to put my plunder?"

"In the loft over the store. Day or night the store is your job now."

"It'll be as safe as a baby's cradle, ma'am."

Within a few days Savanna did not know how she had ever managed without him. He was dirty and he smelled and he was ugly, but he was gentle with horses, easy with Preacher and Kizzy, quick to lend a hand at any job about the place, and sharper than Savanna herself at trading. She exulted to Abe, "That was the best turn you ever did me."

"You can trust him," he told her.

"Where did you find him?"

"Oh, he drifted in and joined up a while back."

"He told me his enlistment was just up."

Abe grinnned. "It's not—but it don't matter. He's been in the guardhouse the past two months."

Savanna's eyes widened. "What for?"

"Like to killed a man. Got drunk and cut him up. Fellow had died McNulty'd have been hung."

"And you sent him here! To keep drunks off my place?"

"Best place to send him. He don't want to go back to the guardhouse. I said you could trust him."

"The first time . . ." Savanna began, warningly.

Abe interrupted. "The first time he gets out of line, just let me know. I'll want him back. But there won't be any first time. He don't like that rawhide on his back."

After he had got on his horse to leave, Abe remembered a piece of news. "Your friend Mrs. Felt has got a boy."

"Oh? When?"

"Yesterday. David says it's a little thing and scant of frame but healthy."

"I'm glad—I'm glad it's over for her. How is Margaret?"

"Doing well, according to David."

"Can you say the same for Bill?"

Abe laughed. "Hardly. He was passed out cold. Didn't know a thing about it."

Savanna's mouth curled at the corners. "Lovely for Margaret, wasn't it? First baby—husband drunk."

Abe gathered up his reins. "Coming to the races Saturday?"

"Yes. I've got to get a barrel of whiskey from the sutler's store. May as well come when I can have some pleasure, too. Make a chance to see Margaret and tell her I'll visit with her on Saturday, will you, Abe?"

Abe pulled his horse around and touched his cap. "I'll do it. Take care, Savanna."

"Oh, and tell the colonel . . . "

But Abe exploded. "You can tell the colonel yourself! It taxes my mind to remember one message. Besides, you're more welcome in his quarters than I am."

He rode quickly away, dust flowing from his mustang's heels, and Savanna laughed, watching him go. You could never push Abe Lathrop too far.

She had been about to ask him to tell the colonel she had visited Houston's Wigwam Neosho and would have some news for him. But it was best to tell him herself. She would make room on Saturday for an hour with the colonel, too.

XI

Saturday was a grilling day with the sun pouring down, the sky as wide as the world, tinged a little yellow with thunder in the south. A wind, hot as the breath of a blacksmith's bellows, blew straight off the prairie. All the little leaves and grasses curled, turned into themselves to escape it, and the dew of the morning vapored and steamed under the heat.

"You ain't aimin' to wear that ole dress, is you?" Kizzy asked Savanna, watching her dress.

"I am."

"You done lop de sleeves off to de elbow!"

"I'm not ashamed of my arms."

"Dat dress so thin it liable to cum thu' wid you."

"I'm wearing petticoats."

Kizzy screwed her eyes up and looked suspiciously at the striped blue madras dress. "How many petticoats?"

Savanna swished across the room without answering. As she passed, Kizzy snatched at her skirt tail and let out a yelp of outrage. "You ain't got on but one petticoat! I knowed it! I knowed dat dress look mighty lank. You come back heah an' put yo'seff on another petticoat, you heah me? Huccome you aims gwine to Gibson wid jes' one petticoat? Doan you know folks kin see plumb thu'? You be a disgrace."

"Let's go! It's my best one and you couldn't see through me with a telescope."

"Kin too! You stan' in dat doah an' let me see fo' myseff!"

"I won't."

"You will," Kizzy was scowling and threatening like a rain cloud, "or I gits anodder petticoat an' puts it on you if I has to calfrope you to do it."

"All *right!*" Savanna marched to the door.

Kizzy's scowl did not lift. "You ain't gwine be standin' wid yo' laigs close lak dat. Spraddle 'em!"

Wordlessly Savanna exaggerated a man's wide stance. "Well?"

"Hmmmph."

"I told you."

Kizzy retreated reluctantly. "Hit ain't nice, jes' de same. Lady ought to wear anyway three petticoats. Jes' in case."

"Just in case what?"

"Jes' in case."

The black woman went away mumbling darkly about young ladies that went about not caring how they looked, wearing old dresses with the sleeves cut off so their arms showed, when everybody knew a lady covered her skin all over, didn't have any shame for her legs showing through one petticoat, it liable to drap did she bust a string . . .

"My legs don't show!" Savanna shouted after her.

Kizzy stuck her head around the door. "If they don't it ain't kase you keers. It's jes' dat petticoat's good an' stout."

Savanna heaved a pillow at her, which Kizzy ducked easily. The two women glared at each other and then, at the same moment, broke into laughter. "I promise not to bust my string and drop my petticoat, Kizzy," Savanna said.

"Well'm." The black woman offered her own palm of peace. "It do be turrible hot. Reckon dat dress 'bout de coolest you got." She chuckled. "An' if you gwine show yo' arms, reckon you got de purtiest pair at Gibson to show."

Savanna looked at her arms indifferently. They were round, brown and smooth, but she had no vanity about them. "I hate being gloved in a tight dress on a hot day."

Her mind turned to arrangements. "Be sure to have Suzy Walkingstick make the soft soap today and watch her, Kizzy— she will boil it too long. Tell Preacher to drive the wagon over this afternoon to bring that barrel of whiskey home. And you help McNulty put up those bolts of calico. See that they're not wrinkled, and they go on the third shelf."

"Yessum."

Kizzy was accustomed to Savanna's knowing where everything was, where everything went, what was to be done every day. She herself was competent to do what she was told to do, but if Savanna had ever shown confusion or bewilderment, Kizzy's skies would have fallen in. Like a child, her world was comfortable and safe because it was in good, steady hands, Savanna's hands. "You aimin' to tek de night wid Miz Martha?"

"No. It's too hot to sleep anywhere but in my own bed. I'll be home before dark."

At the cantonment she went directly to the sutler's store to get her business done first. That accomplished, she told Martha Short, "I'm going to see Margaret and the boy and then I have some business with the colonel."

Martha nodded. "I'll set a plate for you at dinner."

The two had become good friends, though not especially close friends. Alike enough that neither felt a need to confide personal affairs, they got along well by allowing for each other's prickliness. They liked each other and were fairly comfortable together. Savanna had got into the way of making Martha's house her headquarters when she was at the post. It had been, after all, her own home and she felt easy there.

Savanna was pleased to find Margaret Felt looking much better. Her skin had lost the jaundiced look it wore before the baby came. She was white again now, still frail and wispy-looking, but the dark circles under the big violet eyes were less bruised and she was evidently taking some pride in her appearance though she was still abed. Her hair was freshly frizzed and she wore a pretty blue bedgown. It had been so long since Savanna had seen her in anything but the shapeless sacks Margaret had thought her condition required that she seemed unusually sweet-looking.

And she was foolishly fond of her boy. He was a droll little thing, long and scrawny, looking even at this early age ridiculously like Bill Felt. Savanna could not see that he had got anything of Margaret's. The color of his hair and eyes might change but not the stamp of Bill Felt's bones and features. She held the child and praised him and did not ask what the father thought of him. She already knew that. Martha had told her that Bill Felt paid no heed to the child save to require Margaret to keep him hushed when he was about. "If he's got any pride in being a father," Martha had said, "he don't show it."

As she went on to the colonel's quarters, Savanna hoped the

boy would be more comfort to Margaret than the father had been.

The colonel was delighted to see her and he seated her solicitously, growling that he never saw her any more. What did she do with herself these hot days?

"Tend three stores," Savanna told him. "They don't run themselves, you know, sir."

"Ah," he waggled a playful finger at her, "but you needn't have chosen to tend store, miss. I know half a dozen men who would have been at your feet with any encouragement at all, including," he became arch, "an old gaffer with a gouty leg."

"Dear Colonel Arbuckle," Savanna murmured, letting her eyes fall. There were always these little pleasantries he so enjoyed to be got through with. She was becoming expert at pretending she was pleased and flattered. It cost her nothing and it made the old man happy.

"You are looking as pretty and as fresh as a flower, my dear." The colonel had a store of trite phrases left over from the language of his young manhood which he used over and over again. They made his little bouquets of homage. Savanna smiled. "I am cool," she said.

"Yes." The colonel ran a finger around the neckband of his coat and grinned ruefully. "I am not." He cleared his throat.

Before he could speak again, Savanna forestalled him adroitly. "I don't know that I have learned anything you don't already know about Sam Houston, sir, but I promised to tell you what I observed."

The colonel sighed heavily.

Savanna knew he would far rather continue to pay her his small, courtly compliments, pass a pleasant hour just this side of flirtatiousness. She suspected he had asked for her help as much to give him an opportunity of seeing her as out of any real need. But he had asked her and she meant to tell him. "He rides to Chouteau's often, and to Hugh Love's, and they visit much with him. He is surrounded generally by a cordon of Cherokees and Osages and Creeks. He moved into the Wigwam Neosho recently and I visited his home this week and talked with Talahina, though I saw the man himself only briefly."

"Yes. Well." The colonel shifted his knees, easing his gouty foot carefully. "Did you learn anything?"

"Only that he has not yet begun trading. Talahina said he was having some difficulty about his license." She grinned. "Of course the longer he must postpone trading the better satisfied I shall be."

The colonel drummed on the table with his long, spatulate

fingers. He gazed thoughtfully at a spot just past Savanna's head. Coming to a decision he reached into a drawer. "Yes. He has not taken out a license to trade yet, though his goods have arrived. He is making an effort to avoid it. There is no reason why you should not see this letter just come from him. It poses quite a problem, I fear."

The letter was dated July 22nd, which was two days before. Savanna read.

Colonel Arbuckle: Sir: I have the honor to inform you of the arrival of my Boat . . . with an assortment of goods which I will proceed to open and make sale of so soon as convenient . . . My situation is peculiar and for that reason I will take pains to obviate any difficulty arising from supposed violation of the intercourse laws. I am a citizen of the Cherokee Nation and as such I do contend that the intercourse laws have no . . . bearing upon me or my circumstances.

I ordered to this point for my own use and the convenience of my establishment, five barrels of whisky (four of Monongahela and one of corn), one barrel of cognac brandy, one of gin, one of rum and one of wine. The whisky excepting one barrel will be stored with the sutler, . . . subject to your orders, and not to be used without your knowledge or consent, nor shall one drop of whisky be sold to either soldier or Indian . . . because I entertain too much respect for the wishes of the Government—second—too much friendship for the Indians and third too much respect for myself.

So soon as my establishment is opened I will request of you that you will, if you please, direct an officer or officers to examine and see that there is perfect agreement between my report and the stores on hand. I have the honor to be, sir, yours respectfully,

HOUSTON

Savanna smiled over the signature. The man always spoke of himself in the third person. Houston thinks. Houston believes. Houston says. As if Houston were too big a man, too important a man, to bother with I, myself, or me. Instead, Houston—His Royal Highness.

She handed the letter back. "He makes a nuisance of himself, sir."

The intercourse laws mentioned in the letter had to do with all trade conducted with the Indians. Any one engaged in such trade must be licensed by the government. They could not, either, keep on their premises more alcoholic spirits than needed for their own personal use, or to meet their needs in running their establishments. Such needs were not presumed to include the use of liquor in trading. It was accepted that hands and laborers were to be furnished a given amount per day. Everyone cheated on this a little. You could not keep your doors open and do business unless you did and the military, so long as the custom did not become excessive, turned its head the other way. The habit was to give an Indian one cup of watered whiskey at the conclusion of a trade. He expected it and would not have traded without it.

What Sam Houston was saying, however, was that as a citizen of the Cherokee Nation he did not come under the laws of the United States. Indians could trade freely among themselves and Sam Houston was saying that he could not be required to obtain a license and that though he was willing to do surface homage to the law by keeping his spirits in the sutler's store, there was the implication that he could not even be required to do this.

Colonel Arbuckle tapped the letter with his forefinger. "I think," he said, "I do think I must forward this missive to the War Department and ask for a decision. I do not believe this peculiar problem of Cherokee sovereignty has come up before and in my opinion it lies outside my discretion."

"Sovereignty?" She had missed that implication.

"Oh, yes. Houston has fallen back on an old treaty here. The Cherokees fought with the British during the Revolution. They were loyalists. As payment, the British made them a sovereign nation, the Cherokee Nation of Indians. There was a treaty which gave them power to declare war and make peace, and a Cherokee ambassador was invited to the Court of St. James."

"Sweet Mariah! But that was fifty years ago, sir. And the British lost the war. Surely a treaty made by them could not now be honored."

"That," the colonel said, "is what I do not know. I don't know what the government's policy might be. Houston may have the right of it." His hand slapped down on the table with a jarring thud. "Good God! If he has, it will overthrow the whole system of Indian trade. Every good-for-nothing renegade and drifter married to an Indian woman can escape the necessity for a trading license, the whiskey law won't apply, and there will be the worst state of confusion this side of Bedlam. The man has provoked a hornets' nest. I do believe it may take a decision of the Supreme Court to settle this."

"In the meantime," Savanna said, "he may not trade?"

"In the meantime he may not trade," the colonel said

decisively. "He must obtain his license like any other trader before he can open his doors."

Savanna laughed. "Good. I hope the Supreme Court takes several years to come to a decision."

"Ah, Savanna." The colonel leaned back in his chair looking suddenly old, petulant, and tired. Savanna's heart smote her. Years and years of patient work with the Indians could be undone by the stroke of one pen. This man had spent almost his entire life on the border. What good relations there were with the tribes was largely the result of his patience. "Sir," she said, "at least Sam Houston could not work his bluff on you. You are taking the matter where it belongs—to Washington, and surely Washington will not agree to this."

The colonel shook his head. "I do not mean to complain, but they are capable of some masterly illogic in Washington. I shall not be easy until this is decided." He ran a long hand over his face, from forehead to chin, slowly, as if wiping the worry away. Savanna was pleased that he could smile cheerfully at her, then. "You will see how illogical they can be, my dear. I have been brevetted brigadier general."

Truly delighted, Savanna exclaimed, "But that is wonderful, sir, and long overdue. They have been owing it to you for a long time. General Matthew Arbuckle! How fine it sounds, sir."

The colonel's face suddenly went as red as young Joyner's did when he was made shy and awkward. "I must confess, my dear," he said, his veined old hand tembling over the new insignia, "I like the sound of it myself."

"Of course you do. How happy Thomas would have been for you, sir."

Moved by a tender impulse, Savanna crossed to him and kissed the high, balding brow.

He caught her hand. "My dear Savanna." She was astonished to see tears in his eyes. "My dearest Savanna . . . "

Alarmed, afraid of what he might be going to say, he had certainly, she felt, misunderstood her gesture, she withdrew her hand and with a bustling entirely unlike herself hunted up her carryall and tied her veil about her hair. "I have overstayed," she said, "and there are so many things I must do. Dear Colonel . . ." she corrected herself, "dear General Arbuckle, I do congratulate you . . . I do hope . . ." but she was maundering and she checked herself. "No one deserves promotion more than you, sir. I am certain the entire post takes great pride in it."

The old man stood, his dignity recovered. "Thank you, my dear. I must say my staff have been appropriately generous."

"They should be. I am expected at Martha Short's very soon for dinner and am to take a plate to Margaret Felt, sir. I must go."

A stony, dark look crossed the colonel's face. "I don't know what I am to do about that young man . . . Lieutenant Felt. He is trying my patience almost beyond its limits. I only refrain from disciplining him for his wife's sake but how much longer I can do that . . . "

"What you should do is send him to Coventry, sir," Savanna said curtly. She had no patience with fools.

"No, no. He is able to carry out his orders normally, though I am not certain he is always aware of what he is doing. I should say that he very nearly equals Sam Houston in capacity. He has caused me considerable concern lately, through errors in his clerical work, but . . . " the new general winced as he stepped forgetfully on his gouty foot, "I mean to be patient a bit longer."

"Margaret will be grateful," Savanna said.

"Yes. It is for her sake."

"Houston," Savanna said. "I knew there was one thing more. Sir, the post arrived when I was at his home. There seemed a deal for one man."

The colonel fingered his chin. "Yes. He carries on a voluminous correspondence. It causes me some wonder, but . . . " he shrugged, "it is the man's right."

There was a sound from the next room, the colonel's bedroom. It was soft and sluffing as if a dog dragged himself across the floor, or as though someone in moccasins walked out. Unthinkingly Savanna turned and saw, through a crack in the door, a slight, slim Indian girl crossing the room. She got a quick impression of coppery skin, a bright skirt, and long black braids. Slung on the girl's arm was a knotted bundle. There came, then, the quick closing of the outer door. "That was the laundress, I expect," the colonel said. "My black woman has a quinsy of the throat and Joyner sent around a company laundress."

Savanna nodded. "A quinsy can be most uncomfortable."

"Yes. Well. I didn't want Delphy dabbling in water with a sore throat."

Savanna made her escape.

Coming out of the colonel's quarters onto the wide avenue of officers' row she got another glimpse of the Indian girl. She was cutting across the lower quarter, following the same path Savanna had taken the night she saw the young man at Ellie's. Laundresses. Laundresses!

The girl walked without hurry, gracefully, as almost all Indian women did, her feet planted deliberately with very little sway to her body, her toes pointed in. There was the glint of sunlight on scarlet ribbons plaited into the black braids, and it made hot the blue and scarlet pattern of the calico skirt. There was a stale taste in Savanna's mouth and her stomach felt flat and squeezed. Her eyes refused to leave the girl's figure until it disappeared into the quarter. She hurried, then, to Martha Short's. "Who," she asked bluntly, "are the laundresses for A Company?"

Martha reeled off their names. There were six, and the last of them was Jolie Perrier.

She had been certain of it, Savanna thought. As though the colonel had spoken the name she had known it would be Jolie Perrier. So—she was still here, on the post. She wished, vehemently, without thinking why she wished it, she had not had to learn that. She wished she had not seen the girl, had no notion of her slimness or brightness. She wished she had not seen the straight back and the black braids laced with scarlet ribbons. Every man who had an Indian girl gave her red ribbons for her hair. They all loved them, the Indian girls.

"Why?" Martha was asking. "You need someone to wash for you? Is Kizzy sick?"

"No." Savanna improvised quickly. "The colonel's woman is ailing. He needs someone. I thought perhaps—"

"But didn't Joyner take care of that for him? He was here this morning asking. I told him that little halfbreed, Jolie Perrier, did the best wash of any of them."

And likely, Savanna thought with a quick, brusque anger, makes love the best too. "Oh, well," she turned off Martha's curiosity, "if Joyner is in charge I needn't bother. He has probably taken care of it."

And I needn't bother about Jolie Perrier either, she told herself impatiently and angrily. What in the world is Jolie Perrier to me?

Nothing! Less than nothing! I'll never think of her again!

XII

Savanna's satisfaction with her state of affairs was badly shaken that fall. She found nothing to be satisfied about when she made her rounds of the stores in Fort Smith and Crown Falls in November. Trade should have picked up by then. The season was well advanced. Instead, both stores showed a continued falling off.

At the Falls she found Minden, the halfbreed, evasive and not inclined to be communicative. He didn't, he said, like the looks of things.

"What things?" Savanna asked.

"Nothin' much, ma'am. Nothin' to put your finger on. But there's skulkin' goin' on, and there's signs."

"What kind of signs?"

"Marks on trees around—and marks on the walls, and inside the store."

"Indian signs?"

Reluctantly he admitted it.

"Bosh," Savanna said. "What harm can a few hen scratches do?"

Minden didn't know. He shrugged, provokingly dumb. He didn't like it, and that was about all she could get from him.

"Is there any thievery?"

Minden said there was. Not much. Some. He couldn't catch anyone at it.

"You'll have to put a stop to that," Savanna said, sharp with him.

"I've not got eyes in the back of my head," the man said sullenly.

"You'd better have, or I'll replace you."

Petty thievery could grow; in time it could steal you blind, Minden himself might be doing the stealing. Perhaps he was in Pete Crown's pay. "I want your books in order the next time I come," she told him curtly.

At Fort Smith, Albright was frank with her. He was an old army sergeant. He had been devoted to Thomas. "It's several things, Miz Brook," he told her. "There is too much trading nowadays. It's not like the old days when a man had it all to himself. There is four trading stores right here in the village, and that is three too many. None of us getting the trade we'd like or need."

"But the jobbing is falling off, too, Albright. How did we lose the Dwight Mission account?"

"Cap'n Rogers, ma'am. He c'n undercut you, using his own flats. The major didn't never want to be bothered operating boats of his own and when he commenced in the trade it didn't make no difference. He could put his dependence on the steam packets and the pack horses. But with Cap'n Duval jobbing and Cap'n Rogers jobbing, and both of 'em with their own flats, I don't know as there'll be much left for you. Unless you aim to git you a flat too and take yore share of the trade."

"Do you think we can keep a share if I buy a flat?" she asked.

"Oh, we ain't plumb crowded out yet," Albright said. "If I had a flat, Miz Brook, I could undercut Duval and Rogers a little, mebbe."

But Savanna felt a great reluctance to get involved in the business of doing her own shipping. It was expensive unless it was on a grand scale. To pay out, you had to ship for others. And the debt for a good flat would be terrible. As always, she had a horror of debt. It was also troublesome. It meant the bother of hiring and keeping crews. The river was unpredictable and if a boat was sunk, or came to grief in any other way, the owner was liable for all loss. If you shipped on rates, none of the responsibility fell on your shoulders. "I'll think about it," she told Albright, but her mind was already made up. She didn't want to get into it.

She was still pondering this, feeling caught between a rock and a hard place, when, in January, a messenger came from Crown Falls. Minden was quitting. He had been shot at. His life was threatened. He was through. Savanna went boiling down to the Falls and confronted Pete Crown. Bland, silent, he heard her out, then shrugged. "I know nothing about it."

"If you didn't threaten my man, who did?"

He lifted his shoulders in the timeless, insolent, indifferent Indian gesture, than which nothing could be more exasperating. "Who knows?"

She could get nowhere with him. Nor could she get anywhere with Minden. "I will be killed," he said. And that was all he would say.

In the end she was forced to hire another man—and with difficulty. No one wanted to make an enemy of Pete Crown.

The man she finally hired was an old renegade who once worked for her uncle at Three Forks. Parley Wade by name. He was rickety with rheumatics from trapping so many years, and he hobbled when he walked. He was dirty and stinking and he wore a patch over one eye. It was said that his Osage wife, whom he knocked about when drunk, had put the eye out with a firebrand. He had the reputation of drinking heavily, but Savanna knew her uncle had trusted him and she had no alternative but to put her faith in him too. At any rate he wasn't afraid of Pete Crown and she liked that in him. "I ain't afeared of the devil himself, miss," he told her. "Cain't nobody but the Lord put the fear of God in Parley Wade. I kin handle Pete Crown or any other sonuvabitch tries to run me off."

He owned that he wasn't above trying a trick or two with her uncle but he promised to do an honest job for her. "You bein' a woman," he said.

"You'd better," she told him, "or I'll flay the skin off your back with a rawhide."

He grinned at her and winked his good eye. "B'lieve you would, miss. But 'twon't be necessary. I'm needin' the job."

She knew he was needing the work and she thought he would do her a good job. She rather liked the old cuss, anyway. He had an engaging wry grin, as if to take her into his piratical confidence.

That fall she didn't feel quite as though she were hanging on by her eyelids, but very nearly. As close as she tried to keep watch, the stores seemed to keep open more by the grace of God than by her own efforts. Houston, warned by General Arbuckle that the Supreme Court must pass on his claim of exemption, had bought a trading license, giving way grandiosely to the moment. "I do not at all concede my claim," he told the general, "but until the court hands down its decision, I will abide by the law." He had cut badly into Savanna's Cherokee trade from the day he opened his doors.

The trade with the Creeks was not as good, from the beginning, as she would have liked, but her principal worry continued to be the stores at Fort Smith and Crown Falls. David and Abe were both doubtful that she could continue to operate those stores, but she refused to be driven to the wall. "Thomas left me three stores to operate and I will operate them until the accounts show they are irredeemably in the red," she said stubbornly. "I have, I hope, the sense to recognize that moment when it comes—if it comes—and the sense to forego sentiment. But until it comes, I mean to keep the doors open."

XIII

Savanna sat with her chin propped in a palm and watched David Holt screw three bottles of wine deeper into the pail of ice. David had brought the wine. Preacher had furnished the ice by the simple expedient of collecting it from the edges of the pond. "How lucky," David said, twiddling the bottle necks, "to have ice the first week in April."

Savanna's jaw waggled as she tried to speak without removing it from her palm. The words came out half mangled. "Kizzy would not agree with you. She planted potatoes last week and has been praying for a mizzle to moistify her garden. Said the Lord got thickheaded as a jamb-rock and sent frost."

David's eyes twinkled. "I suppose the Lord is in high disfavor today."

Savanna uncupped her chin, grinning. "Oh, yes. She says, taking it up one side and down the other, He's so cross-grained He does about as much harm as He does good."

"She thinks she could do better?"

"Of course. At least she knows when the dirt needs dampening down. It wouldn't be slud over with no brickle of ice, neither. Just a little mizzle, soft as a youngling's hand a-pattin'. If a human body knows little blades and vines swivel when frostburned, it do look as if the Lord could keep it in mind."

"I need an interpreter."

"So does everybody but Kizzy." Savanna stretched lazily and yawned. "Did Abe say what time he'd be along?"

"No. Just said he'd be here. They only got back this morning." He gave the wine bottles another turn, then left them. "These should be about right by the time he comes." He filled his pipe and lit it with a coal, then mended the fire before sitting.

This was Savanna's birthday. She had asked David Holt to supper, saying, "If Abe is back, I'd like him to come too."

"I'll tell him," the surgeon had promised. "They're expected."

Savanna sat in the small rockingchair which had been her mother's and brooded over the fire. "I feel such a lot older than twenty-one, David."

The surgeon sucked on his pipe and watched her. There was a pale light in the room, the kind of light which, after a day of brilliant sun, gives added dimensions to objects, shadows and ledges and mouldings, so that there is the illusion of the day brightening instead of darkening. In the light, Savanna's face was profiled cleanly, the short, straight nose a pure delight, the soft, sweet mouth more thindrawn than he liked to see, the fine, deeply orbited dark eyes half shuttered against the light. Her inner weather was uncertain, he saw. She had been broody and introspective, for the most part, since he came. He might have teased her out of her mood—she usually responded to his quips—but he sensed that her needs were different today. Something about her birthday had set her thinking, and her thoughts plainly were painful.

The pipe bowl warmed in his hand as he drew on it. "Well," he said, "all of us have times when we feel old; especially when we are tired, or vexed, or things generally have gone ill with us. When we have been swimming too long against the current we begin to feel that time is against us too."

She refused that comfort.

"At home," she said, "on birthdays our mother always mixed up a cake and iced it, if she had it, with white sugar icing. There were little presents at the breakfast table and . . . " her voice broke a little, "—mother made everything so nice for us. My mother was such a lady, David. She valued good manners and proper ways and she tried to bring us up to value them too. None of us do, and she would dislike that so much. She believed, when I was born, that her daughter would be what

135

she had never been. Many times she told me how pleased she was to have a daughter—to train up in her ways and be a comfort to her. She meant me to be a gentle person, a lady like herself. She thought my life would follow along the same lines as hers—that I would be a loving wife and mother and homemaker. How disappointed she would be if she could see into what different lines it has fallen. How dreadful she would have thought me last night if she could have heard me screaming like a fishwife at those fools for meeting their drabs on my premises."

The rockingchair stopped its motion and Savanna's head came up, the long hoop earrings set to jingling suddenly. David could not help smiling. Touch a nerve and Savanna's head came up and the jingling of her earrings was a bell of warning. "It still makes me furious! And I could still scream! Fancy, David. Old Kanima brings his girls to loiter and wait in the woods and when the men leave my place, they meet them—behind my back this has been going on! Preacher came on the lot of them last night in the stable. They tumbled out of the loft, wenches still clinging to them, hay in their hair, their clothing still disarranged! Kizzy came and I went flying. I have never been in such a rage in my life! I stormed and shrieked at them like a shrew and if a man of them had opened his mouth to say one word I would have had McNulty throw him off the premises. There they stood, yawping like louts, caught outright, fumbling with their dress. It was enough to turn the stoutest stomach. They slunk away like dogs. I made Kanima round up his floozies and I drove them all away. I threatened to horsewhip the lot of them if they stepped foot on my land again. I was in such a rage that my head rocked with it and my throat ached from shrieking and screeching, but I will not allow them to turn my place into a doggery. I'll prohibit the premises to every Indian wench in the Territory before I allow it."

David puffed slowly. "The morals of the men . . ."

"Oh, damn their morals. I don't care a whit about their morals. They can bed with every Indian doxie in the country for all I care. But they shan't do it on my property. Oh, Lord," she collapsed and mourned, "mother never even *heard* the word doxie in her time. She would be so ashamed of me."

"Savanna, I doubt that."

"Yes, she would. She was so sweet and dear and she had such nice manners and ways. I wish I was more like her. I think so often of her and I know she would disapprove of me now."

It was time to end this, David thought. She was wallowing,

because it was her birthday, and old memories had been revived—and because, also, the affair of last night still smelled in her nostrils—in a sticky, sentimental morass of self-abasement. "How," he asked, "would your mother's sweetness and niceness deal with a sly, thieving Indian? How would it make trade with Creeks and Cherokees and Osages? How would it meet, asking no quarter and giving none, with Auguste Chouteau and Pete Crown? How would it deal with squalid squatters and the ragtag and bobtail that travels the Road? The first things sacrificed when you pit your wits against the people of this country, or any new country, are sweetness and niceness. You are lucky if you can save your honor—and your life. Your mother was never faced with the difficulties of your life."

Savanna gazed at him, blinking.

His voice moderated a little, his eyes growing twinkly, David said, "Tell me, Savanna, what would your mother have done had she been left alone as you were?"

"She would have managed—differently, perhaps, but she would have . . ."

David cut in quickly. "Yes, I can imagine how she would have managed. She would have gone back to Kentucky, or she would have starved genteelly to death, or she would have married again in helplessness. You will never do any of those things. You didn't go home to your father. You won't starve because you have enough wits not to starve. And you won't marry again, at least I hope you won't, until you are so crazy in love with a man you can't live without him."

"Which," she said, grimacing, "isn't likely. There aren't any more Thomases."

David had the quick thought that she needed no more Thomases, but he didn't go into that. He hadn't finished with her yet. "Just so," he said. "Get it into your head once and for all that you are not like your mother and never will be and leave off grieving about it. She was what she had to be and you are what you have to be. You had better be grateful that someone, somewhere in your family line, gave you enough spirit and heart and guts to make your own way, since it's what you have to do. You may not possess your mother's particular virtues, but you have virtues of your own. You are an admirable woman, Savanna, and you have done very well in very tough, dirty, lying and scheming circumstances. You've got your own kind of sweetness and niceness, too. They'll do, and they'll do better than your mother's kind in your situation. Quit belittling yourself."

Savanna's mouth quirked ruefully. "You don't leave much

137

skin when you set out to flay a body, do you?"

"Ordinarily," David said, grinning. "yours isn't tender. I don't like to see you go pawky and mushy. It's weakness and God knows you can't afford to be weak. Now, this thing about the men and old Kanima and his girls. You've got to make that stick, Savanna. Polly Walker can't be touched—she can run a doggery without fear. She's Indian and she's on her own land. But if there are enough complaints you can be closed up. Jolly can be made to revoke your lease, or the colonel can revoke your license."

"He wouldn't!"

"Not unless he had to, certainly. A few married men have been coming this winter, haven't they?"

"A few," Savanna admitted, adding defiantly, "why not? Their money is as good as anyone else's."

"Their wives might not appreciate their absence."

Savanna gave a short laugh. "Then let their wives mend their ways. A wandering husband usually has a reason to wander, and I don't intend to play nursemaid, but they're better off here than at Polly's. Luke Hammond has been once or twice, Havery and Bushmyer . . . I don't recall the others. They are all gentlemen. They make their purchases, play a little cards, drink a glass or two of wine and leave. They don't stay late."

"You can tell them they shouldn't come in the evening. They're good fellows and wouldn't want to see you get hurt."

Angrily Savanna stood, shoving the chair back hard. "David, I'll do nothing of the kind. This place is open to any person who behaves himself from the time the door is opened in the morning until it is closed and chained at ten o'clock at night. Let their wives forbid them. I won't. I mean to be discreet, but there is a line at which discretion becomes cowardice. Sweet heaven! Must I stand at the door and examine every man who enters? Must I say, Sir, does your wife know you're out tonight? I won't allow girls, and the country knows it. I won't allow drunkenness, and the country knows it. But there is another thing I won't allow—and that is to be told who my patrons are to be and how they are to come and go! The day I allow that, I have let the country itself put shackles on me and I may as well shut up shop. No—of course I won't do that."

David Holt spread his hands. "I see. Well, forgive me. I expect you're right."

Savanna pushed her hair back and sighed. "So many pitfalls, if you don't look sharp."

She walked to the window. The twilight was beginning to come on, softly blue. Outside, birds were twittering and the cow's bell gonged a time or two as she moved slowly about the pasture. A dog barked, up the road. Savanna leaned against the window, breathed on the pane and rubbed it with the heel of her hand.

David Holt watched her, his eyes a little sad and wistful. Nothing now was very easy for her. Wherever she turned there were problems and difficulties—all of her own making, true, for had she been less stubborn and valorous she might have taken an easier way—and he did not see how they could grow any less. They would, instead, increase almost inevitably. But she would have to bump her way along as best she could yet a while. She was not yet ready . . . the time was not yet ripe . . . He took a deep breath. But what a magnificent reward awaited a man's patience. He heard the slow clop of a horse in the road. "Abe?" he asked.

"Houston," Savanna said.

David joined her at the window. "He must have been deeply disappointed over the court's decision."

"The colonel doesn't think so. He thinks Houston simply tried to bluff him and the colonel wouldn't bluff."

David nodded. "I would give him credit for being too smart to believe that old British treaty would stand up in court. He must surely have known the government would not honor the Cherokee Nation as a sovereign power."

Savanna shrugged. "The colonel is probably right. He tried it on, to see how far he could go with the military. He got his trading license soon enough when the colonel forwarded his letter to the War Department."

"I wonder," David said musingly, "I wonder if everything he does in this country isn't a blind—that trading store, his friendship with the Indians, with Chouteau and Love—all simply a means to an end. Texas."

"Then I wish he'd get on with it," Savanna said brusquely. "That trading store is hurting me every day. I'd like to see him move on."

They turned from the window. The pallid light had gone and the room was growing dim. Savanna lit candles. "I wish Abe would come."

As if her wish had summoned him, there was a step in the dogtrot and Savanna hurried to the door. "You are late, Sergeant Lathrop."

Abe stood, blinking a little, burdened with a big rolled bundle. He was freshly shaved, his face clean and hard and brown, and he smelled of cold and bay rum and tobacco and leather. Savanna took in her breath. Abe laughed and thrust the bundle into her arms. She caught at it, almost dropped it,

139

and cried, "What in the world . . . ?"

"Birthday."

He sailed his cap across the room and followed it, limping and groaning, to stretch himself full length on the black bear rug in front of the fire. "God," he said, letting himself down easy, "I'm tired. Even my bones are tired. And don't tell me," he craned his neck to look at the surgeon, "don't tell me bones don't get tired, David. Mine do, and they are."

"Sure they get tired," David Holt said, "and you've been racking yours for more than thirty days. The wonder to me is that a few of 'em haven't cracked. Was it a good detail?"

Abe settled his head on the rug. "Damndest detail I ever drew."

Savanna had laid the bundle on the floor. She was struggling with its knots. Though they watched, neither man offered to help her. She would have refused. By myself, she had always said. She worried at the knots, tongue caught between her teeth, until the last one gave. Slowly, then, she unrolled the bundle, more quickly as its beauty became evident, her eyes widening with delight, until finally it lay flat and exposed—a blanket, a horse blanket, and the most beautiful horse blanket she had ever seen. She gasped and ran her hand over it. It was thick and heavy and fleecy, strong and tightly woven. The dyes were brilliant and gorgeous—red, black and blue, running in broad stripes around the saddle square. In each of the four corners a small running horse, so exquisitely done you could see his velvet motion, had been picked out in white and blue tiny beads. The saddle square was studded with double rows of flat silver disks. It was a magnificent blanket—arrogant, gaudy, heavy, and . . . "Comanche," Savanna said, flicking a look at Abe.

"You think so?"

"Come here, David. Of course it's Comanche. This silver is Spanish."

David poked at the silver disks. "I'd say so." He gave Abe a long, level look and whistled. "No wonder your bones are tired. Where have you been, man?"

"The detail," Abe droned, as if reading orders, "will proceed to the mouth of the Kiamichi River and will ascend the Kiamichi River not more than fifty miles from its confluence with the Red and determine which point thereon is best suited for the establishment of a cantonment."

Savanna eyed him shrewdly. He was as windburned and gaunt as she had ever seen him. His eyes were red-rimmed and watery, as only grit and sun could make them. There was no grit on the Kiamichi. It was soggy country. He had been on the plains and it was written all over his worn body and in his sore and rheumy eyes. "Did you have to kill the Comanche to get it, Abe?" she asked.

Abe rolled over on his side, laughing. "Lord, no! That was the last thing we were supposed—" he checked himself abruptly. "No. I traded with an Osage for it, who swore he had it off a Pawnee."

"You're a liar."

She spread the blanket carefully, smoothing out its folds. "Oh, heavens, but it's elegant, Abe. I love it. Won't the Duke be handsome wearing it?" Impulsively she caught it up and draped it around her shoulders. "I'd love to wear it myself. It just suits me and it'd certainly be handsomer on me than on a horse."

Play-acting, she struck a pose with her head well up, her eyes haughty, her mouth arrogant. She preened and posed and paced—and she was wholly unaware that, framed by the candles, she was suddenly as splendid and barbaric, as magnificent and savage, as any Comanche princess. The rough, springing black hair was unglossed by the candlelight, needing no shine to make it vibrant, curled and tense with life. Her face was flushed a little with pleasure and excitement and the skin glowed, ripened and bloomed. Her eyes were half shuttered, secret and mysterious, and as a slow, small smile curved her mouth it was as though she knew the whole of feminine mystery, isolated and inviolate, was shrouded within herself, the veil never to be removed and the mystery never to be known.

Abe caught his breath sharply and David Holt gave him a quick, queerly apprehensive look. "Take it off, Savanna," he growled. "It *is* meant for a horse, you know."

The spell was broken.

Savanna laughed and threw the blanket off, folded it and laid it on a chest. She sighed with satisfaction, stroked it and finally wrenched herself away from it. "The Comanches make such gorgeous things. I do thank you, Abe. It is a truly elegant birthday gift."

Abe drew his legs up and groaned as his knees creaked.

"What you need," Savanna said briskly, "is not that wine David is cooling but about three fingers of corn whiskey."

Abe squinted one eye at her. "Make it five, Savanna. Make it a whole damn glassful!"

Savanna felt warmly content sitting by the fire after supper—made a feast by David's gift of a bag of grouse and what Kizzy had been inspired to do with them—listening to the two

141

men talk. They were such satisfying friends, such fine men. Neither came up to Thomas for good talk, but she had never known anyone who did. Thomas had been unique. But David could spin a yarn extremely well and he was one of the jolliest of men, usually in high spirits and full of quips and jokes. She watched him now, telling an incident that had happened in North Carolina in his boyhood. He looked happily disreputable, shaggy and bearlike with his thick beard and rough head of hair. But it had been sweet of him to replace the old linsey jacket with a new one in her honor. It did not matter that within a week it would be just as shapeless and baggy as the old one. He had bothered to dress, a little, for the occasion.

He cares not a whit for his appearance, she thought, though he scrubs himself well and his linen is always fresh. If his person is clean the rest doesn't matter. Look at those boots, crusted over with old mud and dust and so patched they barely hold together, and those pants stuffed into the boots. He has mended the knee with a different color. He is as thoughtless of how he looks as a youngling, and more like a youngling than he knows, with that passion for wild country.

In those days Savanna was not equipped to probe much deeper than the surface man. On the surface, David Holt was a jovial man, humorous, even-tempered, easy-mannered, genial, cheerful, and with a flyaway readiness for sport of any kind, from racing to buffalo hunting. If he could get away, he was the first to join any party going to the mountains or onto the plains. Savanna knew how much he must have wanted to go on this last scout with Abe.

He knew how comical he looked jouncing along on his great gray nag, his elbows flapping and his beard flying, but he was always the first to laugh at the figure he cut and he poked so much fun at himself that no else thought of doing so. "Like Don Quixote," he said, "I tilt at windmills."

Only a few knew what he meant and Savanna was not among them. She had never heard of Don Quixote.

She thought David Holt wonderful; he made her laugh oftener than any man she knew and she adored having him with her. He was as comfortable as an old shoe and she took him as much for granted. He exuded confidence as a lamp gives off light, and it did not once occur to her that somewhere inside there was a vulnerable man. Thomas had told her once. "He is very lonely. There are not more than two or three men in the country with whom David can talk. I am one of them."

"Lonely? David Holt? He has more friends than anyone I know."

"He has more acquaintances."

Perhaps. But Savanna had always taken him as she found him.

She knew he cared passionately about the men who sickened at Gibson. She assumed all surgeons did that. She knew he hated the high rate of sickness at the fort and preached it was an unhealthy place. But where were you going to put a fort except on a river and near the Indians?

She knew that when he read the funeral service over a man he had not been able to save his face was grave and sad and, more often than not, grim. She thought this was because it fell his duty, and a duty that was always sad, to read the service. Gibson did not yet have a chaplain and in the absence of a chaplain it fell the duty of the post surgeon to read the service at funerals. It was enough to make any man not dedicated to religion sad, Savanna thought. She had no way of knowing that while David Holt was not dedicated to religion he was dedicated to humanity and that a little bit of himself died each time he lost a patient. He usually got very drunk afterwards.

If he had ever had a woman no one knew of it. He led a peculiarly monastic life for a man thrown in circumstances where the sex urge was the easiest thing in the world satisfied. Singularly incurious and imperceptive, Savanna did not even wonder why. It was simply David's way. That he might have been too fastidious did not once occur to her. That, with a shy ideal so pure it didn't even bear speaking of, he disciplined himself as harshly as a monk, would have been an idea so farfetched as to be ridiculous to her. Men, the men she knew, even Thomas, did not carry idealism that far. Before marrying her she knew that Thomas had had Indian girls when it pleased him. The knowledge hadn't bothered. Once married, he had stopped and that was what counted. If David Holt didn't take an Indian girl when he wanted one it was his own affair—they were plentifully available.

He was saying, now, "How did Bill do?"

Abe toyed with his glass. "Pretty well. The men don't like him much, but there's one thing certain," he grinned, "he sure dried out."

The colonel had finally reached the end of his patience with Bill Felt. He dismissed him from his staff and assigned him to field duty. He had been sent, second-in-command under Captain Hammond, on the detail Abe just completed.

As almost everybody had been, Savanna was relieved and glad when the colonel had acted at last. Bill Felt's situation had worsened so much that to be around him was to walk on eggs, tip-toeing carefully. Like most people with little to be proud of, he had a touchy pride that could not bear the shame he had

143

brought on himself. Unable to pay all of his gambling debts, he took to avoiding the men he still owed, who included several officers with whom he had formerly been intimate, and many of the traders. When thrown unavoidably with them his behavior varied so as to be unpredictable. He alternated between a surly taciturnity and an arrogant contempt.

He reached a point in his drinking where he was rarely sober and when sailing full before the wind his temper was so often violent and threatening that even the most patient and loyal of his associates had eventually to give him up. It was as though he meant deliberately and intentionally to ruin himself; and as if he meant by degrading himself to degrade all officers, make of rank itself an official shame.

Patently, the colonel had eventually to act.

"Probably swilling it down tonight to make up for it," David said.

"If he's swilling down corn whiskey tonight," Abe said, a twinkly gleam in his eye, "he's learned to make it himself. He didn't come back with us."

"Killed?" Savanna said quickly.

"No. Cap'n Hammond had orders to put the lieutenant in charge of the road-building detail. The old road to Towson has grown over and it has to be cleared and widened and corduroyed for the supply trains. When the road is finished, Bill Felt is to be transferred to Towson. The new Fort Towson is to be built of stone and it will take a long time to finish. I don't think Gibson will be seeing much of Lieutenant Felt for quite a while."

"Sent to Coventry, by God!" David Holt said.

Abe nodded.

"Good. Fine." Savanna's voice was crisp. "It will be a blessed relief for Margaret."

"I imagine," David said slowly, "that not a living soul on the post will miss him—not even his wife. That all will feel, as you do, it's a blessed relief to be rid of him. What a pity—what a pity."

"A pity!" Savanna cried, "he deserves it. He brought it on himself."

"Yes. Yes, he brought it on himself—this slow, tragic destruction of himself. I wonder . . . I wonder . . . I wonder if he could have helped it."

"But certainly. . . ." Savanna began hotly.

The surgeon moved his hand and Savanna hushed. When David got this dark, sad, troubled look she felt a little frightened. She had only seen it once or twice and had been quick to forget it, but witnessing it again, seeing the dark,

144

pained look in his eyes, her heart beat a little faster. It was as though something hurt him way inside, so deep inside he could barely get at it himself. His words came out so slowly, almost haltingly. "Were the seeds of destruction so strongly planted in Bill Felt, and were they so infinitely mutilating that he had finally to undergo the ultimate mutilation and lop himself, like a grape, from the vine that sustained him?"

"What vine?" Abe asked.

David's eyes widened. "The regiment. Bill Felt loved the regiment once."

"Oh, never," Savanna scoffed.

"But he did. You didn't know him when he first came to Gibson but Abe will remember. He wasn't a bad fellow then. He was weak, perhaps, and vain and shallow, loving ostentation and show. But he had promise. He was genial and cheerful, he had a good, quick mind. Yes, he had promise. The colonel would never have added him to his staff if he hadn't." The surgeon rubbed at his beard. "And he was a very hard worker. It seemed to me, though, that even then one could sense grimness in him. As if he knew the odds, not only in the army but in life, were against him and he meant to lick them. He took a great pride in being an officer. It meant more to him, somehow, than it did to the others. And he had an intense pride in being sent on a hard duty—to the Seventh, which has always drawn a hard duty and is proud of it. Did you ever hear Bill Felt complain about the heat or the cold, the dust, the wind, the dirt, the isolation?" David turned to Abe.

Abe's attention was riveted now. He shook his head slowly. "No. No. You have to give him that."

"Did he complain on this detail?"

Again Abe shook his head.

A long silence grew in the room, so long and so still that when a coal fell the soft sound was as startling as a clap of thunder. Savanna jerked and Abe turned his head quickly to see. Only David did not move. Gazing at the dying ember, he continued, at last. "I ought to have spent more time with him. For it was me he told . . . but I am always so occupied, so run here and there eternally, and by the time I was aware it was too late. He grew up in the most degrading and loathsome circumstances a man could know. His mother was a prostitute and he never had a father. He was a by-blow, the end result of a chance encounter between a woman who was bought and a man who was a passing stranger. He does not even know his real name. Felt is his mother's name. He finished last in his class at West Point because his schooling was so meager he
145

could never, with the hardest effort, make up his lack of preparation."

"How did he get into the Academy?" Abe asked.

"By cheating and lying and blackmailing a senator."

Savanna lay back in her chair. "Well, there you are. He never was any good."

"Did he ever have a chance to be? Never in his life has he known the assurance of the possession of anything in the world. Not love, or position, or honor, or even a name. He possessed finally the regiment, but with no assurance. It, too, might slip away from him. He couldn't lean, as other young officers do, on his background—for he had no background. He had to work relentlessly at the things they took for granted. No gentleman, he *had* to be one. He had to gamble, as they did, and race, and drink. And he had to marry a pretty girl. And eventually he had to have a son—but with no more name than he had."

"Oh, fiddle," Savanna said, "if he had to have all those things, he got them. He did have them. Why does he throw them away?"

"Because, my dear, not being a gentleman he had no instincts for restraint. There were no limits. In his efforts to be the perfect officer and gentleman, he overreached himself—then destruction, already set in motion, took over. He has lived on the naked rind of darkness all his life and it has finally enveloped him. That is tragedy, real tragedy, for tragedy does not lie in what happens to a man, but in what is fated to happen to him. Bill Felt was fated for destruction."

Abe had been listening intently. He leaned forward when David finished. "I don't believe that, David. I don't believe in destiny. I believe a man can make his own destiny. All Bill Felt needed to do when he overreached himself was take a good grip on himself, dig in and pay off. Why didn't he? One step at a time is all a man has to take and it doesn't have to lead him down. He can go in any direction he chooses. The mess he got himself into wasn't hopeless, but it's damn near hopeless now. He's seen to that himself, and it was Bill Felt did it, not destiny. If I believed that a man must be what he was born to be, that he couldn't change, I'd cut my throat, for in my own life—" He threw out his hands. "Can't an evil man desire to be good? Can't a hopeless man cling to one final thread of hope? Can't even a weak man find enough strength to make it serve him until he can grow more strength?"

Savanna's eyes turned on Abe now. She had never seen him so intense. His eyes had darkened to the color of gray ledgerock, and a patch of color showed high on each cheek. He leaned forward in his chair, his hands gripped between his knees. Something, something powerfully felt was moving him. His lips looked dry and he licked his tongue over them often. Her heart lurched and beat up in her throat. She did not like this. She did not like this direction in which David had led him. She must end it. But before she could speak or move, David was talking again.

"A man who desires to be good, and acts on it, is not evil, Abe. A man who can cling to a thread of hope is not hopeless. A man who can find the meagerest courage in his soul is not weak. But a man who has been given a dank and desolate heart, where the drama of life is really played out, cannot find these sustenances and hopelessness and destruction are inevitable for him."

Abe replied hotly. "And I say they are not! Listen to me. Bill Felt never had a father. Well, I would have been better off without the one I had. Do you know what my father did to me? He taught me to steal and beat me when I didn't steal enough. Bill Felt's mother was a whore. Mine was driven insane by cruelty. Bill Felt cheated and lied and blackmailed to get into the Academy. I lied and cheated and stole to get food. There isn't a meanness or misery Bill Felt ever knew that I haven't known, or any sordid sin. Don't talk to me about destiny. In the end I did," he hesitated the barest moment, then finished, "what I had to do. Bill Felt finished at West Point, last in his class, maybe, but he finished. He graduated and became an officer and a gentleman. I enlisted in the army and I am a sergeant and a scout. He is a poor officer and no gentleman. I am a damn good soldier and there are few Indians that are any better scouts. By his own bootstraps Bill Felt pulled himself up out of the gutter. By his own foolishness he is throwing himself straight back into it as fast as he can. By my own bootstraps I pulled myself up, too, but I'm throwing nothing away. What has fate to do with it?"

"Abe . . ."

Savanna's voice was choked and tight. She felt she *must* stop this. David had no right to make Abe draw back the curtain on his own past. Abe was too taut. There was a kind of leashed violence in him.

But already David was speaking again. "That is precisely what I mean." If there was any shock in what Abe had revealed David did not show it. His eyes were tender and full of compassion, his voice kindly. "Bill Felt's gutter was one kind. Yours was wholly different. But neither of you had any choice. His gutter gave him a dark soul and a dank heart. Yours put

147

iron in your soul and steel in your nerves. Did you choose your parents? Did Bill Felt?"

"I didn't get any iron or steel from my parents," Abe said curtly. "I've told you what they were. I got them for myself."

David was shaking his head. "No. Perhaps not from your parents, but from somewhere the seeds of iron and steel were planted—they were in your bloodstream and in your fibers and in your brain and in your nerves from the day you were conceived. So were your father's hair or your mother's eyes, your grandfather's chin, your grandmother's mouth. So were the seeds of destruction planted in Bill Felt, in his weakness, his vanity, his pride over the wrong things, his foolishness as you call it, along with his mother's prettiness, perhaps, his father's incapacity for drink . . ."

"You're saying," Abe cut in, "that a man cannot change his nature?"

"He cannot. No man can change what was born in him. Nature does not change. At best, what a man can do, and then only if it is given him to do it, is temper his nature and control and discipline it."

"If a man has been violent . . . ?"

"The seeds of violence are in him forever. He may curb them, control them, contain them rigidly, but they are there. They are a part of his essential nature. Part of his own peculiar manhood."

"Always a threat?"

"Oh, no, no. I don't mean that at all. Perhaps never a threat. They need never escape his leash if it is strong enough. But they will never cease to tug."

"Yes. Well, then . . . if the leash is strong enough. It has to be, doesn't it? And a man can see to that?" The pupils of Abe's eyes had grown so large they looked all black. They never moved from David's face.

"Some men," David said.

"One man."

David laughed softly. "The man you mean can see to it."

Abe laughed with him and they stood, their eyes meeting, strong and even tender with understanding. Something had been asked, something answered; trust given, faith returned.

Savanna felt as if she were suffocating. Now, now, she would end this. Pretending petulance she pushed herself out of her chair. "Do, please, let's give over this dull and serious talk. You are spoiling my birthday and giving me a headache."

Instantly, almost hilarious with release, they were eager to make amends. "Abe," David cried, "another glass of wine around. We haven't drunk the birthday toast yet. Savanna, forgive us. We have been unpardonably rude."

Abe brought the bottle, poured the glasses, and they bowed before her. The glasses clinked. David's eyes were merry. "To Savanna's earrings—may they never cease jingling."

Abe's eyes were glinted with mischief too. "To Savanna's Comanche blanket—may its colors never fade."

Savanna sputtered. "You are outrageous, both of you."

David aimed for her forehead with his birthday kiss, and pecked her nose.

Abe's aim was truer and for a brief moment his mouth was young and hard and hot against hers. She darted a quick look at him and compulsively put her hand over her mouth. She hadn't been kissed like that since—she hadn't—well, goodness, she hadn't *ever* been kissed like . . . Mercy!

David retrieved the moment. All earnest and serious now he lifted his glass. "To Savanna—'this garden that is forever fair.' "

XIV

The sky was dead ashes and the rain sieved down the windowpanes like dreary tears.

For the hundredth time Savanna paced to the window and looked out. She felt as cheerless as the day, unaccountably forlorn and sad. She felt almost disembodied, wraithlike, as though she had no place on earth to set her foot.

Restless, every room refused to have her and she had spent the entire afternoon walking distractedly about, unable to put her mind to any task or to comfort this prodding, urging, stirring sensation in her body.

I must be coming down with something, she thought. I have never in my life felt like this. But her nerves had been near the skin for three months. She had been jumpy and cross, not eating well, and for the first summer she could remember the heat had wilted her. She had wanted to push past everyone she knew, past every routine chore, to get near something . . . But what? To get where? To get still again, inside herself again. But how was that to be accomplished?

She was alone.

Preacher and Kizzy had gone to the cantonment. McNulty was in the store but he was napping. There was no trade because of the rain. She had changed her mind half a dozen times about going to Gibson with Preacher and Kizzy. First she would go, and she had dressed. Then, no, she had no business at Gibson and it was too hot and it looked like rain. But if she stayed at home—no, she was going to the cantonment in two days for the Fourth of July celebration. There were things to be done at home. There was no sense going today and again the day after tomorrow. Besides—very well, she would *not* go, and she let Preacher and Kizzy drive away in the wagon without her, and almost went running after them. What *had* got into her? She had been quickly decisive about things all her life. This kind of see-sawing about, making up her mind, changing it, making it up again was so unlike her that she felt she must be ailing. And she had done none of the things that needed to be done. Done nothing but pace like a chained animal, back and forth, back and forth.

Drawn compulsively to the window again she tried to gather her thoughts and determine what could be worrying her, bothering her to this uneasiness.

Not the fact that she had lately learned Auguste Chouteau was responsible for the affair of old Kanima and the girls in the spring, that he had bribed the old Indian and planted the girls to ruin her reputation. She had long ago nipped that in the bud, and she was still not afraid of Auguste Chouteau.

Not the fact that she had had such an excellent offer for the Duke, whom she no longer had the time to ride, that it was folly for her to turn it down. Captain Rogers must want him very badly to offer such a price, but she could not sell the horse. Not yet. She might have more time this fall, and Widgie worked him out every day. If she ever sold him she wished Abe might have him. Abe had never in his life owned a thoroughbred. But that was footless. He could never afford one.

And it was certainly not the fact that an attempt had been made to burn the store at Crown Falls. She expected that sort of thing. Parley Wade had found the fire in the storeroom and put it out before any damage had been done. As though it had been a joke, Parley had laughed. "Takes more'n a leetle fire to skeer me out, ma'am."

"Next time it may be more than a little one," she had warned.

"Won't be no next time, ma'am. I been steerin' clear of trouble on your account. Been holdin' my fire. But I aim to shoot the varmint that comes skulkin' about now."

"Do that," she had told him crisply.

If Pete Crown thought he could scare her out with fire he would learn she didn't scare any easier than Parley Wade. Let Parley cripple one of his Indians. That would teach him.

But when she had told Abe he had exploded. "You're going to get killed," he had stormed, "or get your man down there killed. You ought to sell that store, and the one at Fort Smith

150

too. You've got no business traipsing over the country, running into every risk and danger."

"I've been doing it for years," she said.

"Which don't mean you'll be safe to keep on doing it."

She had felt tempery and cross and irked that day and when Abe tried to tell her how to manage her affairs it was the last straw. She bellowed at him suddenly, "I wish you'd mind your own business and let me mind mine! What affair is it of yours? I can run my business by myself!"

The look he gave her would have frizzled a toadfrog. "There are some things you can't do by yourself. You'll learn that someday, but it may be too late." He had turned on his heel and walked away. "I wash my hands of you."

And good riddance, she thought now, pricked again by the remembered quarrel a month ago. She hadn't seen him since, but she didn't need Abe Lathrop or any other man.

There was the sucking sound of hoofs in the sloppy road and incuriously she glanced out. She shrugged. Houston again, and drunk. As she watched, the figure on horseback swayed and almost fell. He recovered his balance at the last moment but in so doing he fell forward on the animal's neck and clutched at his mane. This frightened the horse and he threw back his head and reared dangerously.

The loose, lumplike figure slumped to the ground and the horse, freed, galloped off down the road.

As unmoving as if he were dead, Houston lay, his face in the mud. He can't breathe, Savanna thought. He'll suffocate. He'll drown.

She snatched her scarlet cloak from its peg and threw it over her head. The rain was slacking, was not such a downpour, but it was still heavy.

She sloshed across the watery yard, remembering too late that she had on thin slippers. They were soaked after a dozen steps. Well, the harm was done. She fled on, holding her cloak against the wind and rain, shielding her eyes with her hand.

When she reached the fallen figure in the road she stopped. Gaunt of frame though he was, Houston was still a very big man. As inert as a sack of meal, and as helpless to help himself, how in the world was she going to move him? He was already struggling for breath and quickly she bent and turned his face. If she had something, she thought, to use for a pillow perhaps she could prop him up out of the mud. His horse coming home with an empty saddle would make Talahina send one of the slaves to look for him. It might not be too long before help arrived. But the horse might not go home, and already the great, craggy head was turning into the mud again. No, it

151

wouldn't be safe. Lying, as he had fallen, on his belly, his neck was twisted to one side. He would not, even in his stupor, leave it safely turned. She must drag him out of the mud.

She straddled him and scooped her hands down into the mud and under his armpits. By heaving mightily she could lift him only a very little. He was so limp and heavy. She struggled and slid him perhaps six inches before her hold slipped and she fell across him herself. A rope, she thought. I must get the rope from the barn.

She turned his head again and threw off her cloak to stuff it under his face. Then she ran to the barn for the long hempen rope which always hung there. She fled back, her hair blowing wet about her face and whipping wildly, her dress now sodden, her slippers as useless as if she wore none.

Back in the road she managed, by tugging and heaving and struggling, and no little use of her grandmother Tattie's oath, to turn the giant man on his back. Quickly she knotted the rope about his chest and slid it under his arms. Slipping, sliding, falling occasionally, damning him to perdition, she got him out of the road. She kept tugging on, out of breath, wetter than a drowned cat, madder than a hornet, until she had him sheltered to some extent under a tree. "There," she gasped, kicking angrily at one long, limp leg. "You can lie there the rest of the day for all of me. What a great hunk of clay you are, Houston."

She leaned against the tree to ease her breath and thought wearily she would probably come down of the lung fever herself from such a chill wetting. She didn't know why she had bothered, except you couldn't let even a cur-dog die if you could help it.

She looked at her mud-smeared dress, at her soggy, ruined slippers, and felt of her lank hair. Sweet Mariah, but she must look a mess. And she felt a mess. She'd have to take a bath all over to get rid of the mud, and that meant dragging in the heavy wooden tub and heating water. But somehow she felt better. She didn't particularly relish doing good deeds, especially in the rain and mud, but doing *something* had eased the restlessness in her. She felt more at peace than she had for days.

She bent to unknot the rope.

Houston moved and one hand went up slowly, as if weary beyond bearing, to cover his face on which the drip from the tree was seeping. In the hand was clutched a piece of paper —tightly clutched. Savanna, curious, unfolded the fingers carefully and took the paper from them. They released their hold unprotestingly.

152

She could make nothing of it. It was an ordinary sheet of writing paper, covered with figures, odd dots and dashes, fractions, variations of strange words—Latin, she thought likely. Gibberish, she thought, and started to toss it away. What could such an undecipherable mess of . . . ?

She stayed her hand, startled. Undecipherable—cipher.

Cipher—all that correspondence.

Wait—it might have some bearing. The colonel must see this.

She left the rope, forgot it entirely, and flew across the road and into the house. There was no time for a bath. She washed off as much of the mud as she could see and changed into her riding habit. She must take the paper to the colonel at once.

"I don't know what to make of it," she confessed when she had given it to him, "but I thought you would be interested in anything belonging to Houston."

The colonel was so agitated the paper shook in his hand. "My dear Savanna. My dear girl. It may be the key. It may be precisely what I have been needing. I cannot tell you now, but I have had a letter . . ."

Savanna felt needles of excitement prickling her skin. "It may be nothing, sir."

"Oh, of course. It may simply be scratching. Some men do such things when their hands are idle. He may have been at Chouteau's or Hugh Love's, drinking, his hands restless, and he may have been henscratching. But I'll put Captain Hammond onto it at once. He is our best cipher man. If it is a code he can determine it."

Savanna pushed her wet hair back. She had toweled it, but no amount of toweling would have dried it completely. It had been too thoroughly wet. "What good will it do you, sir, if it is a code?"

The colonel peered at her over his steel-rimmed spectacles. "Why, I shall begin censoring the man's correspondence. And I shall learn the truth about certain rumors."

"Can you do that?"

"Do what?"

"Censor his correspondence."

The old man smiled. "My dear, in Indian Territory the military is the law, and within discretionary limits the commandant at Gibson is the expression of the law. If necessary I think I may safely say that any man's correspondence comes within my discretionary limits."

He called for young Joyner who, entering and seeing Savanna, blushed uneasily. To put him at his ease Savanna quipped with him. "Where do you keep yourself, James? You haven't

153

been to see me in a coon's age. It must be all of—" She stopped, struck by the knowledge, quickly calculated, that it must be all of six months since James Joyner had last come to share a glass of wine with her. She had barely missed him, he had always been a nuisance, but it did seem curious now. As his face went a deeper red she laughed. "You have forsaken me, is that it? You have a new love?"

"Miss Savanna . . ." the boy stuttered.

She put her hand on his arm. "Why, James, it must be true. Oh, dear, and I have put my foot in it, haven't I? Who is she? Forgive me. Please. I don't begrudge it."

The red-faced young aide shifted from one foot to another so rapidly that he seemed to be doing a peculiar and stiff-legged dance. "Now, Miss Savanna . . ."

The colonel interrupted. "Whatever is the matter with you, Joyner? Stand still. You make me dizzy. And here—take this to Captain Hammond and ask him to go over it carefully. If it turns out to be a cipher I want it broken."

"Yes, sir."

The boy made a stumbling exit and the colonel watched him go, grumbling, "Young ass. Acts as if he had St. Vitus' dance. Don't know what has got into him."

He turned, then, and caught happily at Savanna's hands. "What an excellent head you have on your shoulders, my dear. I knew I could trust you to be alert."

A little wanly, her excitement dying down, Savanna said, "I'm going to be ill, sir, if I don't get home where I can change into some dry clothing."

"What?" He peered at her. "Bless my soul, child, you're quite damp, aren't you?"

"Well, sir, it's raining."

"Where is your cloak? You didn't ride two miles in the rain without your cloak, did you?"

Unable to contain it, Savanna giggled. "It's lying in the mud of the road, sir, in front of my house."

"Well, upon my word and honor, Savanna, what a queer place to leave it. Why on earth should it be in the mud of the road?"

He had not heard a word of her story, she realized. Bedazzled by the possibility of a cipher which would explain Houston's motives falling into his hands, the words had fallen on his ears but he had not listened. He muttered now, shaking his head, "I think both you and young Joyner must be addled today."

"Yes, sir," Savanna said, a fit of giggles threatening again. She inched her way to the door. "I expect it's the weather, sir."

154

Behind her, the colonel stuck his head out the door and shouted, "I shall buy you a new cloak, Savanna, but you must promise me not to be so careless with it."

Savanna ducked her head and fled. Oh, he was a such a fuzzy old darling. New cloak, indeed. He would never think of it again. She would have to rescue the old one and have Kizzy wash and mend it. But she did hope the paper was important. She did hope she had been helpful to him. He had done so much for the country, so unselfishly. He did deserve to have something done for him.

Going home she felt almost lighthearted.

She was going to think only of happy things, such as the Fourth of July at Gibson. She was going to be gay and giddy then. She had two new dresses for it, one for the daytime and the most elegant ball gown she had ever owned, as gold as the sun and so stiffly wired it would stand alone, for the evening. The satin was as smooth as skin. She was going to hang every bauble she owned on herself and ring like bells when she danced.

And David was going to be her escort. She might even get a little bit tipsy before the evening was over.

XV

General Arbuckle encouraged his people at Fort Gibson to make much of the Fourth of July. He was wise enough to know that in so lonely a place a good rousing spree occasionally, a splendid and gala celebration, was like a tonic. It relieved boredom and tedium, heated up the blood, put sparkle into eyes, and it made a great many men work very hard.

The Fourth furnished the most perfect occasion of the year, for who better than soldiers would do honor to the Nation's birth? Besides, the general was sentimental himself about the Fourth and thoroughly enjoyed all the preparations, the day itself, and the weariness that followed. He always had pleasant recollections of it later.

At Gibson, the celebration took the form of pageantry. There was the dress parade, the salute of the cannons, racing both morning and afternoon, the general's dinner to his staff and friends, amateur theatricals, fireworks, and the officers' and men's balls. It was a very full day and in addition to the military the post was always crowded with civilian visitors. It took a lot of getting ready for.

Benign, a little fuzzy, stooping, limping, the general went about watching the preparations. When the general was happy he liked to drone, under his breath, the only tune he knew, a

155

hymn—Bless the Lord, O My Soul. He droned because he had never learned the words. It was an invariable sign of his good temper. Humming and pottering he looked on while the trees were trimmed and the grass was cut, while every least particle of litter was swept up, while the buildings were freshly white-washed, while all were draped with bunting. He made certain the paths were newly graveled and raked, that the stockade was scrubbed and scoured so as to look and smell fit for the visitors. There was some grumbling when he ordered the ferry washed down and draped with bunting, also, but he knew what he wanted. "Many guests," he said, "will arrive from over the river."

The contagion spread and everybody worked furiously —windows were shined, floors scrubbed, horses were curried, stables cleaned, the blacksmith shop tidied, every building into which a guest could possibly poke his nose was neatened up. Personal paraphernalia was put in order, guns cleaned, swords polished, boots shined, uniforms pressed. Wives caught the fever and bought materials, made new frocks—something crisp and cool for the hot day, something as elegant as they could manage for the ball. They furbished up bonnets, looked speculatively at their slippers, bought new ones or sighed over old ones, were cross or gay according to their temperaments under pressure. Children went hiccupy and hysterical with ex-citement. Oh, it was a real jubilee, the Fourth of July at Fort Gibson, Arkansas Territory.

When Savanna arrived, at about nine in the morning, a throng was already gathered on the campus. She nodded to a hundred acquaintances as she threaded her way, Kizzy behind her bearing the carefully wrapped new ballgown, to Martha Short's house. Halfway there she was stopped by a little knot of officers' wives, who exclaimed over her new lawn day dress. "Savanna! How charming you look! Green is the perfect color for you. And isn't it accommodating of the weather to turn cool? Your sweet dress will hardly wilt today."

In the group were Captain Hammond's wife, Esther; John Haverty's wife, Ann; and Aaron Cleet's wife, Susan. Savanna guessed that some claws would scratch before they were done with her, for their husbands still came, occasionally, to her place in the evening. They would not easily forgive her for that. She sent Kizzy ahead and turned to the women. "The rain was well timed, certainly. We have never had a more perfect day for the Fourth."

Esther Hammond was a tall rail of a woman, perpetually worn from the mothering of six children. Savanna knew she hated this duty at Gibson and vowed if Luke did not get himself transferred she meant to take her children and go home. She never did, and she never would, but she never quit threatening it. If I were Luke Hammond, thought Savana, I'd make her go so I could have some peace. Esther said now, "Yes, isn't it fine? So nice to know the track won't be dusty for the races. Are you riding today, Savanna?"

Amused, for the clawing was beginning, Savanna laughed.

"Oh, no. I have given up riding, along with many other gay and giddy things of my green youth."

"It isn't true then that you have sold your horse to Captain Rogers?"

Of course they had heard, as doubtless everyone in the country had, that she was in difficult straits and they had put their own definition on Roger's offer to buy the Duke. Thank heaven she had been sentimental enough and turned him down. "My goodness, no," she said. "Captain Rogers wants him but I am not prepared to sell. My boy, Widgie, will ride him today, as he will until I retire the Duke to stud."

They blushed at the bald use of the word, as she had known they would, and she smiled sweetly at them.

Esther, recovering first, lifted her brows and gave Savanna a sly look. "There is one thing you possess, my dear, that if you ever want to sell I would pawn my silverplate for."

"Now, what could that be, Esther?" Savanna was arch.

"If you ever want to part with your earrings, my dear, I rather fancy them."

Savanna laughed, throwing her head back so that the golden hoops rang. "Never. My Thomas gave them to me for a wedding present. I'll be hungry the day I let them go."

The woman's face flushed with anger and she turned aside.

John Haverty's wife was a small birdlike woman with a thin birdlike voice. She ailed. David had told Savanna that Ann Haverty like being ill. She had a tiny pursed-up mouth. "Have you heard," she asked, piping plaintively, "that Margaret Felt is going to the ball? She has the sweetest new gown—the palest, dearest blue. Won't she be exquisite? With that pale hair and those enormous blue eyes. Just like a china doll. But I must own I think it very queer of her to go without her husband. Don't you agree, Savanna? I wouldn't dream of going without John."

Savanna said, shortly, "It isn't Margaret's fault her husband was given field duty. And it's time she had some fun for a change."

She did not miss the oblique glances of the women before Ann Haverty said, "But, my dear, Margaret Felt does not lack fun. Lieutenant Joyner sees to that."

Savanna knew that when the general dismissed Bill Felt from his staff and assigned him to field duty he did so sadly and with some sense of guilt toward the young wife. With the great kindliness typical of him, he had made himself responsible for some of her comforts. Joyner, as his aide, had often been sent to bear small gifts or to do those things which were difficult for a woman to do about her place. So she said serenely, "Lieutenant Joyner acts for General Arbuckle."

"There are some things," Susan Cleet said, snickering, "a man does for himself."

"The general," Savanna said, "feels responsible for Margaret since Bill has been on field duty. James Joyner carries out the general's orders."

"One would think," came the tart reply, "it was James Joyner who felt responsible."

Savanna gathered her skirts. "Shall I see you at the general's dinner?"

They chorused they would and Susan Cleet added coyly, "Is your loyal swain escorting you to the ball?"

She meant David, but how wonderful, how terribly, monstrously, enormously wonderful to be able to say with casual deadliness, so blastingly, "Do you mean the general? But of course, ladies. Good morning."

Let *that* get around the country for a change!

What a lamb he had been to send that note. And just as she had learned that David had to go to Fort Smith and wouldn't get back in time for the Fourth. She had really been swizzled, but the general's note had saved the day.

> *My dear: Only today I learned of a tragic error that has been made. Two weeks ago I asked that young blatherskite, Henderson, who does most of my writing for me, to send you an invitation to be my honored guest at my usual dinner, and to open the ball with me. I learned an hour ago that the dunderhead had either forgotten it or neglected it. I hasten to rectify his stupidity but greatly fear I am too late. Send me, at once, by this messenger your reply and lift the anxiety from my poor old disturbed head . . .*

How sweet. Do you mean the general? But of course, ladies. Actually their jaws had dropped. Oh, joy, oh, bliss!

She strode briskly away, her head high and proud, her earrings jingling, her face a blaze of gloating pleasure, leaving utter ruin behind her. The cats!

Her briskness took another turn with Martha Short. "What have Joyner and Margaret Felt been up to?"

Martha Short was never dullwitted. She eyed Savanna shrewdly. "You've heard something."

"An insinuation that Joyner keeps her amused."

"I'm afraid he does."

"What does that mean?"

Martha broke out, "It's the general's fault, really. He has Margaret on his conscience and he sends Joyner with little presents of food, fresh meat, milk from his cow, a pat of new butter, things like that. The old fool is as blind as a bat to what he's done."

Savanna's brow furrowed. "But there's no real harm in that."

"The harm is in what it has led to. Joyner goes much too often now. The general doesn't send presents or messages every day. Far from it. But Joyner goes every day. And he is so simpleminded that he doesn't realize his feeble little excuses are seen through. He must cut her wood. He must see that she has water drawn. He must take her laundry. He must carry it back. He uses no sense at all. It's as though he simply couldn't stay away from her."

"I suppose," Savanna said thoughtfully, "it's her helplessness."

"When did you last see her?"

"I don't recall. A month ago, perhaps."

"Well, it may have been her helplessness in the beginning. I think Joyner is the kind of man who does like a woman to be frail and dependent. He was mad about you, of course, but he was bound to waken from that. You aren't at all the sort of woman he could marry. But Margaret has bloomed lately, just like a rose. She's put on some flesh and her eyes shine and she has color and is pretty again. Actually that gives them away as much as anything. If she's not in love I don't know love when I see it. And it's there, plain on her face, for the whole post to see."

Savanna groaned. "Lord, Lord, what fools we mortals be. Did you know she's going to the ball tonight?"

"Oh, yes, I knew she was going. She told me and showed me her new gown. She's as pleased as a child and so excited she can hardly contain it. But the worst thing is that the general has detailed Joyner to be her escort."

"Didn't you tell her she shouldn't allow that? With the whole post gawking and yapping?"

Martha shrugged. "*You* tell her. I didn't have the heart. The child is happy, Savanna, happy. She is bubbling with happiness, glowing with it, and if I am not wrong she is, so far, innocently happy. I don't think she has realized why she is so

159

happy yet. I don't believe she has defined it. She has simply accepted it. Someone is being nice to her. She is going to be gay again after all these long months of dreariness. Now, can you spoil it for her? Can you deliberately walk in there and topple all her pleasure into dust tonight? I can't."

"Well, I certainly would have thought you could."

"Oh, my bark has always been worse than my bite. I can't help wishing she could have this one night of pleasure. I know she must be warned eventually, but surely not until after tonight."

"It won't *be* pleasure," Savanna said. "You know what will happen. She'll be cut by the women and the men will be red-faced and awkward and ashamed and afraid to be nice to her. She will be hurt and bewildered and she'll be desperately unhappy. I wonder that the general could have been so tactless. But where men and women are concerned he's an old innocent himself—" She broke off, frowning, pondering a moment, then her face cleared. "The general, of course. It's really very simple. The general is my escort, Martha. I will simply make him ask James and Margaret to join us. We will be a party then and above suspicion." She broke into happy laughter. "We'll just make the general mend his own fences."

"That will be fine for tonight," Martha agreed, "but you will talk to her tomorrow, won't you, Savanna?"

Savanna worried an earring, then broke out vexedly, "What a pity anybody need talk to her. Something should happen to Bill Felt. He's no good to himself, or to Margaret, or to the boy."

"Nothing ever happens to that kind. I know. I've seen them before. What I'm most afraid of is that Bill will learn of it and there will be a tragedy. I've seen that happen before, too." She had been sitting but she now got up and took to pacing the floor. "If only an army post wasn't such a world in itself. We get sent to these dreadful places and we are cut off from everything we've ever known, everybody familiar and dear and loved and it happens, in time, that nothing exists for us but the post and the people on the post. We forget what home was like and we forget there are people in the world who are not army. We are focused so closely on ourselves. And there are always too many men and too few women. I have never been on a duty with Fred Short, at any post, that I have not seen at least one young officer fall in love with another officer's wife. She is near, he sees her constantly, he is cut off from his normal intercourse with young girls for there aren't any, and nearly always the wife is either neglected by her husband or thinks she is, or is bored with the tedium and loneliness. She is ripe for a new love, in any event. At Natchitoches the most promising young lieutenant in the regiment was called out to fight a duel because of his attentions to such a wife. She wasn't worth it but he was killed because of her. As useless as Bill Felt is, he might think it necessary to satisfy his honor by calling out young Joyner." She broke off. "Have you ever seen Joyner shoot?"

"No."

"How the boy got through the Academy is a wonder to me. He couldn't be a poorer shot if he had never had a gun in his hand. Felt is a dead shot. The boy wouldn't have a chance."

"Is there something you want me to do, Martha?"

Martha Short wheeled. "Yes. Speak to the general. He will listen to you, I believe. Make him give Joyner field duty and make him get Joyner off the post at once. Bill hasn't been home for more than two months. This has all begun to simmer since he was here last. He may be home again at any time. Joyner must not be here when Bill Felt comes. Do make the general understand that, Savanna."

"What about Margaret?"

"Perhaps I'd better talk to her after all. She's going to grieve, of course. She'll be unhappy and she'll lose her bloom and prettiness but she won't be half so unhappy as she would be if her husband killed the man she loves."

Savanna sighed. "How perfect it would be if some Pawnee lifted Bill Felt's blasted scalp."

Savanna dressed for the evening leisurely. She knew the value of a grand entrance. She meant to be the last woman to arrive at the general's dinner.

Kizzy helped her and when she was ready she went in to say goodbye to Fred and Martha. "Sure you won't change your mind about going?"

Martha shook her head. "Dinners and balls are, thank God, over for us. Savanna, no woman has a right to be as beautiful as you are. It isn't fair."

"Do you like my gown?" She whirled, sending her skirts flying.

"It's absolutely elegant. It is perfect for you."

The gown was cut quite low at the neck and shoulders and fitted tightly in the bodice, pointing up Savanna's slim waist and high, full bosom. It flared in graceful panels to the floor then. Its importance was its simplicity. Unerringly Savanna had known that the rich material could not stand any froufrou, nor did she want it to detract from herself. The color was exactly right for her ripe-honey skin. Her neck and shoulders

161

rose radiantly from the gold satin, soft, smooth, tawny and glowing. Her face was creamy, flushed enough to be pearly toned, the eyebrows blackly embossed, the mouth full and red, the long, tipped eyes magnificent.

She had been extravagant with bracelets and necklaces, hanging a dozen gold bangles on her arms and winding a chain of gold about her neck. The beautiful hoop earrings swayed from her lobes. Again her instinct had been unerring. Nothing but gold, dripping with gold, against a gold-toned skin. She looked rich and exotic, gorgeous and barbaric. Aladdin's lamp could have conjured her up.

"Are you going for Margaret?" Martha asked.

"No. She isn't coming to the dinner. She thinks she must stay with the boy until he is asleep. She will come when the ball begins."

Her entrance was as satisfying as she had wanted it to be, late, every eye turned on her when she paused in the doorway. There was a sort of stunned silence, the men gaping, their drinks suspended, the women gawking then slowly going stony, curdling with envy. No other woman in the country would have attempted such a gown or such an entrance. No other woman could have got away with it. She stood another moment, savoring her triumph, then a bevy of clamoring men surrounded her, hid her, claimed her, and her victory was complete.

Because of the heat and the number of guests it was the general's idea to have his dinner outdoors on the lawn back of his quarters. He had caused posts to be set up with flares attached and candles flickered down the long table.

The night was softly warm and there was a river smell on the air, a languorous, moist odor which was a little dank but pleasant in the nostrils. The dinner began.

Savanna was seated at the general's right with Major Hazen, the second-in-command now, across from her. Auguste Chouteau was at her elbow. As was always true of any social event on the post, there was a preponderance of men. It was impossible to find partners for them all. There weren't that many eligible girls.

Glancing down the long table Savanna nodded to Captain John Rogers, Captain Duval, who had become a merchant since his dismissal as Cherokee agent, and his wife. There were also Pierce Butler and his pretty young wife, Miranda— the Duvals' daughter. There was Mr. Dillard, a lawyer from Crawford Court House, and Anderson Quesenberry, all the prominent people from the area. Well below the salt sat Sam Houston, swaying but upright, wearing this night the uniform

162

to which he was entitled. Talahina was not with him.

Savanna felt happy and proud. The torchlight was kind to even the plainest woman and lent them all a touch of glamour. Their shoulders gleamed whitely, their jewels sparkled, their voices seemed softened and gentled by the wide, night air. The men were brave-looking in their spruced uniforms; their swords glanced and their boots gleamed. And the guests had nobly honored the occasion with dark coats, white linen and their best satin stocks. Savanna murmured to Auguste Chouteau, who was impeccable as always, his dark face saturnine, fastidious, quixotic: "We do the general proud, I believe."

He lifted an eyebrow. "None so proud as you, madame. You are beautiful tonight."

Savanna smiled. "I meant to be."

"You have an axe to grind?"

"Several of them and I'll begin with you. M'sieu', why did you set Kanima and his girls on me?"

The Frenchman's mouth curled with amusement. He made no attempt at equivocation. "It seemed a good idea at the time. But you are too clever, madame. I now think it was a mistake."

"I think it was too. That cat won't jump, sir. Don't try it again."

"*Non.*" He lifted his napkin and delicately touched it to his mouth. "The general's clear soup is always excellent, isn't it?"

"Excellent."

The general claimed her. He gallantly fetched up half a dozen of his impoverished, raggedly worn compliments, then, lowering his voice to little more than a mumble, said, "Savanna, I can relieve you of that chore I asked of you concerning Houston. It is no longer necessary."

Savanna's eyes widened questioningly but the general, with a small discreet gesture toward Chouteau, warned her. "Perhaps you can find it convenient to call on me tomorrow."

"Yes, sir. I meant to in any event. There is another matter I must take up with you."

"Shall we say ten in the morning, then?"

"Certainly, sir."

The general gave them a sumptuous dinner. He was something of a gourmet, not perhaps as fastidious as Auguste Chouteau, but he en·oyed good food and fine wines and his black woman, Delphy, had been taught to do wondrous things. He might live roughly, in a log house in the wilderness, but he had never allowed rusticity to dull his imagination. He gave them an excellent soup, pheasant, grouse, a saddle of venison, ham and turkey. There was asparagus and small lettuces from Delphy's garden. There were tiny new beans no thicker than a

163

sliver with roasted pecans sliced over them. There were great bowls of pickled walnuts. To finish there was a *bombe*, the secret of which only Delphy knew. The general always had it produced with a flourish.

The meal concluded, the old man stood, proud in the uniform he had worn all his adult life, and with great dignity lifted his glass in the first toast: "Gentlemen—the President of the United States!"

On their feet, the company drank and cheered. Immediately the big gun boomed. The toasts, the cheers, the boom of the gun for each toast, had become tradition and Savanna, as the toasts proceeded, always got a choked, lumpy feeling in the throat. They were so cavalier, so gallant, ignoring their isolation on the fringe of civilization, a tiny knot of people observing their traditions, being themselves for one night civilized again.

The final toast, the thirteenth, was drunk to "The Fair Sex," and most of the masculine eyes around the table turned, some openly, some slyly, on Savanna. She smiled radiantly and her eyes misted. At that moment she loved them all, felt protective and soft and proud. She was proud still to be a part of the regiment, the general's honored guest, the elegant first lady of the evening. God bless them all!

Then the general announced, somewhat portentously but with a fine glitter in his eyes, "I regret we cannot linger, but we must now adjourn to the council house. I believe my boys have some theatricals to perform and we are expected."

The council house was a rough slab structure built originally for holding Indian councils. It was floored and a stage had been built along one end. The cantonment had got into the way of using it for chapel services on Sunday and as a kind of recreation room, for theatricals and balls, on special occasions. The walls were draped with bunting and flags for the Fourth, and benches had been set around to accommodate the audience.

There was an unbelievable amount of talent among the men and the skits they put on were always hilarious. Written, produced, and acted by men, they were a little on the bawdy side, rather more coarse than would have gone down in any other place. But they hit home at familiar tender spots, poked fun, and satirized persons and events well known to the entire post. Savanna saw some of the women blushing at some of the jokes, hiding their eyes at some of the actions, stopping their ears at some of the songs, but she had a lusty pleasure in it all and when it was over went out humming the tune of the song which had provided the theme for the evening, around which every skit had been moulded, and which had been sung to the point of repetition. It was all about that fine Arkansas gentleman who lived close to the Choctaw line, who had a mighty fine estate of five or six thousand acres, and four or five dozen Negroes who would rather work than not, and such quantities of horses and cattle and pigs and other poultry that he never pretended to know how many he had got:

This fine Arkansas gentleman has built a splendid house
On the edge of a big prairie, extremely well populated with
    deer and hares and grouse;
And when he wants to feast his friends has nothing more to
    do
Than leave the pot-lid off, and the decently behaved birds
    fly straight into the pot, knowing he'll shoot them
    if they don't;
And he has a splendid stew,
    This fine Arkansas gentleman,
    Close to the Choctaw line!

The fine Arkansas gentleman makes several hundred bales,
Unless from drought or worse, a bad stand, or some other
    damned contingency, his crop is short or fails;
And when it's picked and ginned and baled, he puts it on a
    boat,
And gets aboard himself likewise, and charters the bar, and
    has a spree, while down to New Orleans he and his
    cotton float;
    This fine Arkansas gentleman,
    Close to the Choctaw line!

And when he gets to New Orleans, he sacks a clothing store
And puts up at the City Hotel, the St. Louis, the St. Charles,
    the Vernada, and all the other hotels in the city
    if he succeeds in finding any more.
Then he draws upon his merchant and goes about and treats
Every man from Kentucky, and Arkansas, and Alabama,
    Virginia, and the Choctaw Nation, and every other
    vagabond he meets;
    This fine Arkansas gentleman,
    Close to the Choctaw line!

The last time he was down there, when he thought of going
    back,
After staying about fifteen days, more or less, he discovered
    that by lending and by spending, and being a prey in

general to gamblers, hackmen, loafers, brokers, hoosiers, tailors, servants, and many other individuals, white and black,
He distributed his assets, and got rid of all his means,
And had nothing left to show for them, barring two or three headaches, an invincible thirst, and an extremely general and promiscuous acquaintance in the aforesaid New Orleans;
This fine Arkansas gentleman,
Close to the Choctaw line!

Now, how this gentleman got home is neither here nor there,
But I've been credibly informed that he swore worse than forty-seven pirates, and fiercely combed his hair;
And after he'd got safely home, they say he took an oath
That he'd never bet a cent again at any game of cards, and moreover, for want of decent advisers, he foreswore whiskey and women both;
This fine Arkansas gentleman,
Close to the Choctaw line!

This fine Arkansas gentleman went strong for Jackson and King,
And so came on to Washington to get a nice fat office, or some other equally comfortable thing;
But like him from Jerusalem that went to Jericho,
He fell among thieves again, and could not win a bet whether he coppered it or not, so his cash was bound to go;
This fine Arkansas gentleman,
Close to the Choctaw line!

So when his moneys all were gone, he took unto his bed,
And Dr. Reyburn physicked him, and the chamber-maid, who had a great affection for him, with her arm held up his head;
And all his friends came weeping round and bidding him adieu,
And two or three dozen preachers, whom he didn't know at all, and didn't care a damn if he didn't, came praying for him too.
This fine Arkansas gentleman.
Close to the Choctaw line!

They closed his eyes and laid him out all ready for the tomb,
And merely to console themselves they opened the biggest kind of a game right there in his own room.
But when he heard the checks, he flung the linen off his face,

166

And sung out, just precisely as he used to do when he was
   alive,
"Pridle, don't turn! Hold on!
I got twenty on the king, and copper on the ace!"
This fine Arkansas gentleman,
Close to the Choctaw line!

It occurred to Savanna, following her limping general out,
that the song said a great deal about the country and its more
assiduous gentlemen. Who had written it, she wondered, to
know so well where to point the chaffing finger? It fitted any
one of a dozen leading citizens well enough, and each of them
in some particular. Land, Negroes, cotton, cards, whiskey,
women, New Orleans—fine Arkansas gentlemen, all of them,
who indulged in that way of living. Dear me, she thought grinning, how it must have prickled, especially those who had
brought their wives!

While the benches were being shoved to the wall in pre-
paredness for the ball, and the regiment's band was on the
stage tootling and tuning, she went with James Joyner to fetch
Margaret. They were to meet the general at his quarters where,
needing refreshment, he had repaired. He had voiced no objection to inviting the pair. "But mind you, Savanna, don't be late.
Don't let that young lady preen and primp too long. We must
be on time for the grand march."

Margaret was as sweet as a fresh-picked flower in her pale,
sky-blue gown, her silvery-yellow hair piled atop her head with
little side curls before her ears, her eyes shining, her face fresh
with happiness. It did Savanna good to see her, but as she
listened to Margaret quipping with Joyner, saw her coquette
the tiniest bit with him, saw her love him with her glances, she
had a pang of pity for them both. Joyner would have been so
right for Margaret, with his nice young decencies, his shy
young ideals, his very great sense of honor and his inherent
goodness. It was such a pity. "You'll need a shawl for the
drafts between sets, Margaret," she reminded the girl.

Margaret brought it and Joyner laid it, with a lover's linger-
ing hands, about her shoulders. She gave him a happy smile. I
must not let them out of my sight, Savanna thought. They
must at all times be where they can be seen.

Sounds from one of the mess halls came across the campus.
Its windows were open and smoky light showed through. They
heard men and women laughing, there was a hoarse shout,
some stomping, and a chorus of yells and then a fiddle began
to scrape. "The men," Joyner said, "are in good form tonight."

"Is that where they are having their dance?" Margaret
asked.

167

"Yes."

"We must hurry," Savanna said, "we can't keep the general waiting."

She didn't want to think about the enlisted men's dance, where Abe Lathrop was, and perhaps . . . and perhaps . . .

In his quarters, the general insisted on another glass around before they went to the ball. What with the wine of the dinner barely faded, Savanna's head was a little giddy when they set out. She felt flushed and warm, a little loose-jointed and floaty. Amused at being tipsy she giggled and leaned more heavily than she intended on the general's arm. Sweet heaven, don't let me fall flat on my face, she prayed.

They stood outside the door waiting for the fanfare which would signal the beginning of the grand march. Savanna raised her hot cheeks to the small wind, smelled the river smell, felt her hair lift and blow. She smiled when the general stole a kiss, just below her ear. She could spare it. It was the loveliest night, the softest night, the starriest night. A meteor fell, scattering a a long tail of blazing embers. Make a wish, quick. Quick! I wish—I wish—her eyes went across the campus to the lighted mess hall where whoops and shouts were so wild and loud the scrape of the fiddle was almost drowned—she wished—the trumpets blared, the drums rolled, the general straightened, gave his coat a tug, bowed to Savanna and offered his arm. "My lady."

Savanna took his arm and moved forward through the doorway with him. She held herself as straight as an arrow, her black, curly head high. As she moved, slowly, the golden bell of her skirt flowed about her feet and the bells of her earrings and bracelets were set ringing.

She was a whole Fourth of July celebration herself, and she knew it. It was what she had intended to be.

XVI

With a gallant and surprising spurt of energy the general whirled Savanna into the set which followed the grand march but he was glad, then, to release her to the younger men. "Have a good time, my dear. I shall claim you for supper."

Instantly she was surrounded and besieged.

She cast quickly about and saw that Joyner was releasing Margaret to a small but flattering knot of similar men. She grinned when she saw that John Haverty was among them. Better to risk a wife's displeasure than the general's. Margaret Felt's presence with the general and Savanna was an order—I approve of this girl, she is my guest, so behave toward her accordingly. Margaret would be all right now.

Savanna chose Auguste Chouteau and laid her hand on his arm. Tonight she had no enemies and no one danced a quadrille more divinely.

Like a lovely golden moth, then, she drifted from one pair of blue- or black-sleeved arms to another—from Chouteau to Captain Rogers, to Duval, Hammond, Cleet, Haverty, Joyner, to Elias Rector and Pierce Butler and even, astonishingly, to Sam Houston's wooden embrace. It was heavenly. Never had there been such a ball. Never had the band played more splendidly. Never had she had so many partners. Never had the punch been more delicious. She kept warm and a little giddy with it, flirted outrageously, forgot everything on earth but the band's wonderful music (no wonder the general took such pride in it), men's arms about her, men's whispered words, "Madame, you are beautiful tonight."

"Savanna, you dance divinely."

"You are enchanting."

"Savanna, the next set is mine."

"No, mine. She has danced twice with you already."

"Are there bells on your dress, Savanna?"

"Gold is what men die for, they say, Savanna. Isn't it dangerous of you to wear gold tonight?"

In a dream, a drifting, swaying, music-lulled, whisper-lulled dream, Savanna danced, listened, smiled, took her pleasure. In a dream she saw Margaret occasionally floating past; saw Esther Hammond, who hadn't an ear for a tune, treading doggedly; saw Ann Haverty, sitting mostly, fanning against the smoke and the heat; saw Susan Cleet, herself as pretty as a china doll, whirling angrily—her husband was squiffed and was dancing too often with Savanna. She smiled. It couldn't have mattered less.

She only roused from her tranced state when the band rested for the interval. Major Hazen had been her partner and he seated her and took her fan, agitating the air in front of her face. Savanna turned her head from side to side to feel the air. She was more heated than she had realized.

Couples still filled the floor, walking about aimlessly, meeting and joining to talk, moving on together, slipping outside to the cooler air, in groups or by couples. Idly Savanna watched them. If the general could be found she would like to walk outside too. She cast about seeking him, and suddenly realized that Margaret's blue gown was gone. Quickly she surveyed the room. Joyner was absent too. She got up suddenly, so suddenly that the major, bent over her, was taken unawares and was jolted by her head. She clutched him. "I'm so sorry, sir. I've

169

just remembered an errand I must do in the interval. There isn't much time. Thank you so much for taking such excellent care of me."

She threw the words at him and even as she spoke was easing past him. She left him, still waving her fan about, his mouth gaping. The young fools! They would be missed in a matter of moments. Already the clot of people on the floor was thinning. She moved swiftly through the people still standing about, flinging them her apologies. "I'm sorry, may I pass? I do beg your pardon. I'm sorry. Forgive me."

She reached the door. But where on earth to look for them? A dozen paths led away from the council house. They could have taken any one of them. Other people were parading the graveled walks, slowly, and she would look such an idiot dashing about peering at every face. The moon had set and the lights from the council house illuminated only the shortest distance. Every path trod into gloom within fifty feet.

She walked rapidly down one path, bumped an embracing couple, mumbled an apology, bumped another, and was cursed. It was hopeless. She returned to the doorway. She would never find them this way. She had to think. Where would Joyner have taken Margaret? Which path would he have chosen? Or if no path, what other place? The deep shadows under the trees? The garden back of the house? The river? Oh, surely he would be more discreet.

It was hopeless to think. There were too many places. She didn't know where to begin. But they must be found. She had to find them. Before the interval was over they must be found and they must enter the council house with her, safely in her company, as if she had strolled out with them, been with them all the time.

She felt frantic with indecision. Someone had to help. One of the officers. She whirled, and stopped without taking a step. Which officer? It needed only one other person to know for this indiscretion to run like a wind around the post. She couldn't think of a married officer who could be trusted not to tell his wife, nor a bachelor one who wouldn't delight in snickering it around his quarters. The general? Then Joyner would be in trouble. Oh, Lord, why had they been so foolish? She could have shaken them until their teeth chattered. The general's wing didn't shelter all the dark places on the post. Joyner, certainly, should have known better. Was he, for tonight, so carried away he could forget? Had he drunk too much? Had Margaret? Great gobs of mud, what a sweet and broiling mess this was going to be if she didn't find them. And she was standing there like a dithering idiot. There *had* to be

170

someone who could be trusted, who could help her—some man. Well, of course!

She ordered her face, lifted her skirt gracefully, swished her silk handkerchief as if fanning, and walked quite deliberately and slowly down the path which led across the campus. She kept her head down, hoped she looked composed, idle, interested only in cooling herself. But when the darkness enveloped her she hiked up her skirt and ran fleetly. Instantly her bracelets were set to jangling and she dropped her skirt to clutch them. Oh, damn—why did she always have to hang herself with clanging baubles? She sounded like a blacksmith's iron.

She did not stop running, however, until the mess hall loomed ahead and the grass was patched with light from the open door and windows. She slowed then and tried to ease her breathing. Lord, what a rout they were having here. She hoped Abe could be found easily. Every drunken, leering man there would pass his tongue over her, guessing at her reasons for coming. Thank heaven if they had an interval here it was over. The noise and the whooping and the scraping was going on as though it would never quit.

She stood outside the door, careful to avoid the light, trying to think what to do now. She had made no plan. She had simply thought Abe must help her find Margaret and Joyner. But it wasn't going to be as simple as that, she saw.

A man stumbled down the steps, lurched against her, grabbed at her and pulled her up against him. Before she could fight loose he brushed a sour mouth against her neck. She could have screamed it was so loathsome, but she fought him off silently, thrusting him away so fiercely that he lost his balance and fell, then lay where he had fallen, heaving. It made her feel sick herself. She scrubbed at her neck viciously. It would take a bath to rid herself of his foulness.

She circled the mess hall looking for a window low enough to peer through, but they were all so high it would have taken a very tall man to see over their edges. She gnawed a knuckle, thinking. She would have to go inside, then. There was nothing else for it. Perhaps she would have only to step barely inside. From the sound of it there was such a mob that if she could only slide inside the door and stand there quietly perhaps she could find Abe, catch his eye and beckon him out.

She was itching to hurry, for there was so little time, but she made herself squeeze patiently through the people jamming the door, and then edge inchingly along the wall. Once inside the thick air struck her. The smells, blended and strengthened by heat, of sweat, whiskey, dust, smoke, that peculiar dank smell of Indians, the sour smell of men's unwashed bodies, and something sweet and sickening like patchouli hit her full in the face. She wrinkled her nose—God's britches, what a stink! She had had too much of the punch and the foul odors made her queasy. She put up her handkerchief. Over the square of silk she looked about.

What a parade of people, color, sound, there was here. There was every sort of human being in this place. Indians and Indian girls, trappers, hunters, soldiers, settlers, laundresses, floozies from Fort Smith, they sat around on the floor, leaned on the walls, or draped themselves on each other. With not much restraint to begin with, and that little abandoned by drink, they were openly amorous. Couples braced along the wall clung mouth to mouth, loose and enveloped; women sprawled across the legs of men and men sprawled on the bosoms and knees of women. Hands reached and groped and felt, women evaded screeching and laughing hoarsely; men cursed and reached again.

There was Sebe Hawkins with a fat witch of a woman, his eyes vacant, his face gone silly and flat, his clothing disordered. The woman's hair had fallen and her bodice was torn. Savanna wondered if they had bothered to go outside to the dark.

There were Ellie and Dickson, both reeling, both shouting raucously, and laughing. There was the Texan clutching a Creek girl who was squat and greasy, fumbling with the girl's skirt band. There was Polly Walker, who ran the doggery, with a man Savanna had seen in the stocks a short time before. Polly had brought her girls to the post and the mess hall had been turned into a doggery. For the first time Savanna understood why such a place was so called. It slandered animals, she thought, for bitches were in heat only in season.

In the small space left in the middle of the floor four couples were doing a wild, flinging square, the women's calico skirts flying, their hair falling, their feet often lifted clear of the floor by strenuous arms, then touching again, stomping, and trodding, and stepping.

Abe was not among them, nor had she yet caught sight of him. She began a systematic search, taking the people one by one as best she could and separate them.

When a group standing directly across from her straggled apart she found him, and wished at once she had not. Such a wild, exquisite pain coursed through her as to make her clutch her side and bend with it for ease. It was as though an iron fist had clawed at her heart. Bitterly she thought how little chance she had of catching his eye.

He was standing, half leaning, elbow propped, against the

172

logs, loose and easy, one arm pulling so close to him that she was melted into him, the little halfbreed laundress.

The moment she saw his face, thin, brown, hard-jutted, Savanna knew how beloved it was, for her heart opened and received it as though, untenanted too long, it was now full again. She was not even much surprised, except that she had been blind so long. There was an instant's glad singing, and then anguish again.

She hurt so—not with just a grieving hurt, as she had done at her mother's death and at Thomas's, but with a sharp, stabbing hurt in her chest, as physical as a throbbing tooth. She squeezed her eyes shut. What was it that made her hurt so bad?

They were not clutched in the lewd embrace all around them. They were simply standing there, very close, but easily. The girl was fitted against him as if she knew his bones and knew where were the best places to rest her soft flesh. He was loosely braced, as though he knew how best to rest her, knew exactly how she was formed and accommodated her. They were so comfy and old-shoe, in the way married people come to be comfy with each other, from long experience and intimate knowledge. And at that moment Savanna knew what had stabbed her. They did have long experience and intimate knowledge of each other. All men grabbed, occasionally, at a woman, and she wouldn't have minded that. But Abe had no need to grab. This woman was his any time and all the time he wanted her and she had been his for so long there was no strangeness left for him. They could stand close and with no urgency because their urgencies were worn with time.

Savanna wondered why her face should feel numb, stony, as if she had ridden a long way in an icy wind and it had lost its feeling. And how could one be cold in July, as she was cold, perishing cold and shivering with it, so aguish that even her head was palsied. She turned away, feeling her legs so weak she thought they would fail her. Blindly she pushed her way through people and was again in the air and the dark, the blessed dark. She stumbled a few steps, drinking in the sweet, reedy smell from the river. The river! Without thinking, everything but her own physical need forgotten, she had an instinct to get to the river. She must hear its purl and murmur and bathe her hands and face in it and let its slow current take with it, away and gone with the water, her pain.

Her feet groped the path, feeling for it, to a private place she had often sought—where the bank sloped gently and there was a wide flat rocky ledge the water lapped. She had always liked to go there and sit, idle, thinking, letting the water soothe her.

173

It was so very dark. She had lost all sense of time, did not know how far she had come, but she kept going, slowly, instinct directing her. At last the ground sloped under her feet and then she came out on the rock. The water here was like a gentle surf. It swelled up and slid a little way on the rock, then sighed away. Savanna sighed, hearing it, and found the log on which she used to sit. The pain was abating a little and she could straighten. What, she wondered, made hearts wobble so? Her heart felt wounded and bruised.

The cold which had shaken her was gone and she felt hot now. She dipped her hands in the water and held them there, grateful for the coolness. Then she bathed her face and lifted it for the soft river air to dry. The sky was so black, so black. The prickling stars were like spangles sewed to a huge black cloth. The stillness by the river, broken only by the river's sounds, was hushed and, she felt, nearly holy. Her knotted nerves were soothed and a feeling of languor crept over her.

It did no good, she thought sadly, to deny one's right to suffering. She had no call to be hurt by Abe. She did not own him. But suffering came where it would, as love did, without asking leave. She wondered a little, hurting again, why in everything else in life one could take care, in some degree, against effect—only in love one could not. It came, striking without notice. Some it blessed, some it blasted, but every man in the whole swarming world was in debt to it. It was a force so uncertain that no man in his right senses would have trafficked with it, but all men did. It mocked and maddened. It relieved and it grieved. It shamed and it stole. It procreated, was devoted and faithful. As wayward as the wind it came and stayed, or lingered and fled. Once in a while it made of two people one flesh until death parted them.

She bit on her fist to keep from crying out. It could have done that with her and Abe—oh, it could have, and been wild and savage and sweet and dear. Why must it have been Abe? Why not young Joyner? Why not David? Why not, even, the general? Why Abe Lathrop, with his soft mole-fur hair and his hard, brown face, and his cool gray eyes? Why the one man in the world she couldn't have because he already had what he wanted? She washed her hands together, an agony of helplessness and loss taking her, breaking and defeating her, until she put her head on the log and cried and cried and cried.

When she had done she felt weary and exhausted, but she washed her face again, patting the water against its puffiness and heat. Then she stood, straightening her shoulders, tilting up her chin. The movement swayed her earrings against her cheeks, set their hoops to tinkling. She touched them. Well, then. She had not asked to love Abe Lathrop, but she did. She could not have Abe Lathrop, so she must live without him. She would have to go through her days seeing him often, and with a silent, aching emptiness inside her. But since there was nothing else to be done, she had to do it, and since she had to do it, she would do it. But, as she faced it squarely, she would do it so steeled that not he nor anyone else would ever know it. She would keep what she felt private and she would face her world and his with pride. No one should ever know and no one would ever say about her, poor Savanna. It would rake her nerves raw, but they were her nerves and she would have to learn to salve them. She had to begin tonight, she knew, by going back to the ball. She winced from that—it would be torment—but it had to be done. And she might as well get used to dancing with light feet and a heart so heavy that it creaked and heaved.

She hadn't done very well by Margaret and Joyner, either. What a faithless chaperon she had been.

She had started up the bank when she heard the creak of an oarlock and almost immediately a woman's laugh. She whirled around, peering in the dark, and called softly, "Margaret?"

There was absolute silence.

"Margaret? It's Savanna. Joyner, put the boat in here."

When the boat touched she grasped Margaret's arm roughly. "What in the name of God do you think you're doing? Have you taken leave of your senses, Margaret?"

Young Joyner spoke up. "Now, see here, Savanna. . . ."

"Shut up. *You* should have had more sense if Margaret didn't. Get out of that boat, both of you."

Margaret, clambering out, was bewildered. "But, Savanna, we only meant to get cool. We thought of the river—and James borrowed a skiff. Everyone else was taking the air."

"Everyone else had a right to. You and James don't. What you have done is beyond foolishness, it's insane! Everyone on the post will be talking—your husband may hear it. What do you think will happen then? Do you want him to call James out? Do you want James killed?"

Margaret gave a gasp and young Joyner swore. "By God, no one would dare—"

"The entire post would dare. Now, come with me. Margaret, we'll go by your home. I look a frump from searching all over for you and doubtless you can stand a little repair. Then the three of us will march right back to that ball. And we shall say, and bear me out, that all of us, the three of us, have been at your place all along. Your dress needed mending and we found the boy wakeful. With any luck at all we can bring it off."

She could not tell, later, whether they had or not. She noticed a few sidewise glances, a few whispering knots, but the general accepted her explanation for an hour's absence readily enough and Savanna saw to it that Margaret and Joyner had supper with them.

She ached all over and was eager for the evening to end, but she kept her back straight and a smile fastened on her face. The ball had gone as flat as her stomach, which coiled warningly when she tried to put food into it. She toyed with her plate, danced the last set with the general, and felt wonderfully relieved when he was persuaded to let Joyner see both herself and Margaret home.

In bed at last, she felt a revulsion for the post and everyone on it. She wished she was at home and she meant to go there as soon as possible tomorrow. What she had to do was get to herself, alone. She felt lax and lethargic but she knew how to deal with that. The medicine for that was hard physical work. She would clean out the store and whitewash it the moment she got home. Oh, Lord, if only she could go right now. If only she could get up out of this bed and saddle Sal and ride right away. Why hadn't she gone home with Preacher and Kizzy this afternoon? Why had she stayed for the ball? Why didn't she ever have any sense about herself? Like a ninny she had clutched at a night's pleasure and see what it had brought her. She wouldn't have known—wouldn't have seen—but, then—it would have come some time. It was, she knew now, what had been ailing her since the night of her birthday. That kiss—if she had had any gumption at all—should have told her.

She twisted and tossed, slept not at all, and the night was very long.

XVII

The next morning she was wan and depressed.

A sleepless night, swarmed with thoughts and emotions, with grief and hurt, had drained her. But she had a businesslike gift of cutting her losses which stood her in good stead and she put on the green lawn dress, brushed her hair, washed her face, and methodically went through with breakfast and an hour of talk with Martha.

Unemotionally she told Martha about Margaret and Joyner and they agreed she must tell the general this morning and he must assign the boy to the field immediately. A scouting detail was being readied at the moment and Joyner must go with it. He would be kept in the field at least two months. It was the surest way of spiking gossip. And while Savanna was with the general, Martha would speak with Margaret. She must know why Joyner was being sent away. "They can't be trusted," Savanna said tiredly. "They simply cannot be trusted to hide their feelings or to behave sanely."

She wondered if she could have been trusted to hide hers, if it were Abe and herself. Nothing stood in the way of her and Abe—nothing but a halfbreed girl named Jolie Perrier, but if Abe loved her, and he certainly must, she was as big as Bill Felt.

Feeling so dead that it was as though she had got outside herself and was watching her body act and talk, she listened to the general. "I've got him, Savanna, I've got him, just like that!" He slowly squeezed his fist and shook it, "Just like that. He can do nothing now. I've got him exactly where I want him, penned and hemmed, right inside the palm of my hand. He is powerless now."

Dully Savanna said, "Who, sir?"

"Houston, of course!" The general moved his head too quickly, and moaned. Like everyone else he had taken too much to drink the night before. He clutched his temples. "Why do men commit the folly of drunkenness?"

Savanna smiled, the effort seeming stiff to her. "I have a little head myself this morning, sir."

The general peered at her. "I thought you were looking paler than usual." He waggled a finger at her. "Don't make a habit of it, my dear. Don't make a habit of it."

"I shan't, sir. Not until next Fourth of July."

"Once a year is often enough for a pretty girl. Now, what was I saying?"

"That you had Houston in the palm of your hand."

"Yes. Well. So I have. And it was that cipher of yours, my dear. It proved to be precisely the key I needed."

"I'm glad, sir, if it was helpful."

"Helpful! Helpful! It delivered the man into my hands. Oh, I have heard rumors, had my suspicions. But I have not before had proof and I do have now. Even the President has been alarmed about the extent of the rumors in Washington. Gossip has it that Houston has quietly been enlisting recruits to form an expedition. His avowed intention was to form a separate and independent government in Texas with himself at the head of it. It appears that he toured Baltimore, Philadelphia, New York and Boston in an effort to gain funds and that he went so far as to enlist emigrants. The President was so disturbed over the conversation of one man, who was approached by Houston at Brown's Hotel in Washington, that he had him write out his conversations with Houston, and he then forwarded them to me. The man said that Houston had enlisted several thousand persons and that each man enlisted was required to pay thirty dollars into a common fund to finance the expedition. At a given signal, it seems, they were all to repair to an appointed place on the Mississippi and from there converge on Texas. Houston was to take with him from here the entire Cherokee Nation and as many Creeks and Choctaws and Osages as he could recruit. The Indians were to form his army. I placed him under surveillance at once when I had the President's letter. But his activities were not overly suspicious, as you know. However, that extensive correspondence continued to trouble me. But I had no reason, nor right, to interfere with it. When Captain Hammond broke the cipher, though, I was free to examine a letter Houston had placed in the post. The rumors are not without foundation. He does have his eye on Texas!"

"How do you propose to stop him, sir?"

"Oh, I don't propose to stop him. Texas can have him. What I do propose is that he shall not take one solitary Indian with him. I so informed him last night. I informed him that we had full knowledge of his cipher and that in the future every letter he writes or receives will be censored. I am within my rights, now. Having been a military man himself, he understood at once that for all practical purposes he is under arrest. I informed him that his home would be kept under guard, that every movement he makes will be closely watched, and that he can neither write nor receive letters privately any longer. He is finished, Savanna—done, through, finished. He might as well be in the guardhouse as far as any effectiveness is concerned. Perhaps you noticed that he was not himself last night. I think he was stunned, to say the least."

"I only thought him drunk, sir."

"Well, he was that, too. But from now on Sam Houston will be nothing more than a drunken Indian trader here in the Territory."

Savanna stirred. "Well, I wish he would leave the Territory. Since he got his trading license he has been cutting into my Cherokee trade considerably. It would be good riddance for me if he would leave."

"I expect him to. I expect him to." The general eyed her solicitously. "But I warned you, my dear."

"Yes." Savanna shrugged. "So did David Holt. I expect I should have listened. But I did not. And I'll manage in some way. I don't cry quits very easily."

Then as unemotionally as she had related it to Martha Short, she told the general about Margaret Felt and young Joyner and the conclusion which she and Martha had reached.

The general's creased old face showed concern. "But I depend on Joyner a great deal," he said. Then he smiled a bit apologetically. "He makes an old man's life a little easier. I should have to make do with that stupid young chatterbox, Henderson, if I sent Joyner away."

"Yes, sir. But wouldn't it be better to do without him for a few months than to lose him permanently?"

"Are they in love, Savanna, or is it just a fancy?"

"I believe they are in love, sir—quite deeply in love. They cannot be left near each other."

The general sighed. "Yes. Well. A pity. A man's usefulness, and Joyner is very useful to me, cut off because he falls in love with the wrong person."

For the first time that morning Savanna winced. "I don't suppose he wished for it, sir."

"No. No, I don't suppose he did. Very well, my dear. I will see that Joyner leaves with this detail. I don't know how I shall put up with that idiot Henderson until Joyner returns. Is it your thinking they will recover from this feeling by then?"

"No, sir. I don't believe they will recover at all—not, in any event, as long as they are circumstanced where they will see each other constantly."

"Then where is the virtue in sending Joyner away?"

Savanna smiled. "It will give you time, sir, to transfer Bill Felt."

The general raised his bushy eyebrows. "I must lose Felt, too?"

"Will he be any great loss?"

"He is doing surprisingly well at Towson. I am beginning to be hopeful of him—but, well, we shall just have to take care of things, shan't we? Thank you, my dear, for advising me."

He took her to the door where a rising spurt of energy caught her and she left, walking briskly.

It served her until she reached her own home and then it left her as suddenly as it had come, left her more spent than before. Drearily she undressed and went to bed, feeling she would never rest again. But her body betrayed her and sleep overtook her almost instantly. She slept deeply and soundly the balance of the day and through the night.

"Plumb worrit 'bout you," Kizzy said the next morning. "Ain't ever seed you sleep so long."

"I was never so tired," she told the black woman. "I danced the whole night through."

Kizzy grunted. "Ah tuk notice yo' slippahs was 'bout woah thoo. Mus' not set down de whole evenin'."

"Once or twice. Kizzy, I'm going to clean the store today.

179

Get buckets and hot water and soap and tell Preacher to mix some whitewash."

"I got to wash today."

"You can wash tomorrow."

"Dis my washday."

"Don't stand there yapping at me! I said you could wash tomorrow!"

"Yessum."

Kizzy stalked away muttering about people that came home from sociables in a bad temper and stirred up a hornets' nest, disturbing folks from their work. Acted like they didn't know one day from another. She didn't think much of it and it misput her a right smart.

Savanna ignored her. She put on an old and faded dress, wrapped her head in a rag and made herself a big brushy broom. She would set Kizzy and McNulty to cleaning the store. She would take the outside and do the whitewashing. She felt exactly like whitewashing today. She could splash and slosh and make as big a mess as she liked. She could work off some of this temper Kizzy objected to.

It was typical of Savanna that as her soreness of heart eased, her temper should rise. She was beginning to be angry, with herself, with Abe, with the whole set of circumstances. What business had he to keep an Indian girl so faithfully? Why wasn't he content with a light-of-love as other men were? If he loved her enough to keep her for years, why hadn't he married her—legally, before a preacher, as decent men did? She doubted he had even bought the girl the Indian way. Abe wouldn't part with horses for a girl, not if she knew him. No, he had simply reached out and taken himself a handy doxie, but he had no right to keep a doxie as if she were a wife. What she should have done the other night was to march right across that room and confront him. She couldn't think why she hadn't. What had possessed her to creep away? Her face grew hot at the memory of her pain and tears. Who was Abe Lathrop to make her run away and cry? She could do very well without him. She could do very well without any man! She'd just as lieve the whole male sex vanished from the earth. All she'd ever had from them was trouble!

As she raged to herself, she worked violently, making great sweeps with the broom and sloshing the whitewash recklessly. The angrier she grew, the more violently she worked until the windows, as well as the walls, were splashed and she herself was spattered from head to foot. She was hot, too, and she kept wiping at her sweaty face, smearing the whitewash until she looked painted with it.

She had no idea he was near until he laughed. "What in blue blazes are you doing?"

She jerked about. She was so furious at the sight of him that her bosom heaved and her eyes blazed. "You've got eyes. Can't you see?"

"You're getting more on yourself than on the walls. Here, let me have that brush."

"You touch this brush and I'll hit you with it! Just leave me alone. I'm whitewashing this wall and I don't need your help."

"Still feeling independent, aren't you? Well, you're doing a hell of a job on that wall." He leaned lazily against a tree and grinned.

It infuriated her. She switched around and sloshed the broom in the bucket, then swiped fiercely at the logs. The brush broom hung on a splinter and she yanked at it angrily. Never in her life had she been more vexed.

Abe's voice behind her was drawly. "You do make the biggest messes of things, Savanna."

Enraged, she gave a tremendous jerk at the broom and it came loose suddenly, tearing the splinter with it. She lost her balance, stumbled back and sprawled on the ground. She lost her hold on the broom's handle and as if personally vengeful the brush, too fully loaded, slapped her squarely in the face. She couldn't see, for her eyes were full, her mouth was full and the loathsome mixture dripped from her forehead to her chin. But she could hear and what she heard was one gleeful whoop from Abe and then uproarious shouts of uncontrollable laughter. It was monstrous! It was unbearable! It was the last humiliation!

She thrust herself up from the ground and flew at him, screeching hysterically, fighting and kicking and clawing and biting and scratching. She would kill him! She would claw his eyes out! He retreated, fending her off as best as he could, trying to grab one of the flying fists or kicking feet. But she was like a hurricane blowing all about him and he had much to do to protect himself. She doubled her fists like a man punching, her brothers had taught her that, and she made his face sting again and again. His shins were cut from her blunt-toed heavy shoes. It was like trying to clutch an eel out of a barrel to get a grip on her. He staggered back until he was again against a tree, where he braced himself. When she tried to butt him, he found a handful of hair and held on.

He sank his fist deep into her hair and slowly pulled her off. She did not leave off her flaying and kicking until her neck was so twisted it looked as if it would break. He held it that way, for to loose her until she was spent was only to start the battle again. Abe's breath came rapidly and his nose was unbelievably tender. One eye felt as though it might be closing too. What a little devil she was when roused. "Cry quits?" he said, looking down at her.

She slumped against him and went slack. Thinking it a trick, he held her away, but he felt her shoulders shake. Loosing her hair he lifted her chin and saw that she was crying—crying with her eyes tight shut, the tears seeping from under the lids and meshing the long lashes that lay against her cheeks. He held her and rocked her a little. "Don't cry, Savanna."

Her head fell back against his arm and slowly, drawn irresistibly by the woeful white-spattered little face and the sweet crumpled young mouth, he bent his head until his lips touched hers. She gave no sign for a moment, then surely and certainly she answered, her mouth softening, the lips parting slightly. Her arms moved to close around his neck. Abe shut his own eyes, tightened his arms until she swayed, bent a little back, and they stood, tranced and lost, for so long it was as though they slept, mouths joined, locked forever.

When finally, for breath, Abe let her go, Savanna still leaned slackly against him. Her face, under its coat of whitewash, had gone tender and her eyes were liquid, soft with a faraway dream. "Well," Abe said, "well—now. This calls for a little explaining, I think."

The softness went and the dark, tipped eyes grew hot. "It does nothing of the kind. You took advantage of me."

"Oh, did I? You needn't have kissed back. You did, you know, and very expertly."

"You should know!" she snapped at him. "You are the expert at making love."

"So." He looked at her gravely, then his face broke into a smile which was so winsome, so dear, that Savanna's heart was stabbed again. "You know, do you?"

"Know what? If you mean I know about your Indian floozy, it's common knowledge."

"I expect it is. I've never tried to hide it."

Oh, he was brazen and contemptible. She could have taken a horsewhip to him, welted him so his back would be scarred for life. How could she have let him touch her when he had come straight from Jolie Perrier!

The sun struck through the leaves and just touched his head. She melted. She could have snatched the dear head to her heart and pillowed it there forever, never let it go. "I hate you, Abe Lathrop! I wish you would go away and never come back. I don't want to see you again, ever!"

He took her wrist and when she would have jerked it away

held it with an iron firmness. "I am not going until we have talked about this. You cannot kiss a man as you kissed me, Savanna, and hate him. That's your temper getting the best of you. But it was your heart speaking when you kissed me. Now sit here beside me and tell me what this is all about."

"I won't."

He did not argue with her. He simply picked her up and deposited her on the grass beneath the tree and held her there. She was totally helpless. "You will tell me," he said, "or I will keep you here until you do."

"You can't."

"I can, and I will. Now—why were you so angry with me? What have I done?"

Savanna glared at him, hating him and at the same time loving him so much she could have gone into the house with him at that moment. She had the queer thought that animals must mate with the violence and passion, part hate, part love, she was feeling. "That girl," she said, "I saw you—" She broke off because she could not trust her voice.

"But I have told you I made no effort to hide it."

"I didn't know . . ." Savanna burst out, then bit her lip.

"You said it was common knowledge."

She shook her head, miserably. "I didn't know—until the other night. Not for sure."

"What happened that night? Take your hands down from your face, Savanna. You can't talk through your hands."

"Leave me alone!"

"I won't leave you alone. What happened that night?" No one had ever spoken to her with such sharpness. She might have been a recruit, subject to his authority.

Well, she wasn't going to be put in the stocks. She raised her head and looked at him defiantly. "I went to the men's ball at the messhall to find you."

"Yes. I knew you'd been there."

"Well, God's britches!" she burst out, "if you knew, why are you making me tell you?"

"I want to know what happened. All I know is that you came."

"How do you know that?"

"For God's sake, you don't suppose you could come to that place and not be seen, do you? Half a dozen people saw you."

"Who?"

"It doesn't matter. It happens that it was Sebe Hawkins who told me. He thought you might have been looking for me."

"Well, I was."

"I tried to find you as soon as he told me, but you'd gone. I went over to the officers' ball and looked in. You were having supper. So I supposed it hadn't amounted to much. You seemed gay enough."

Savanna gazed at him bitterly. Gay! Her heart had been breaking. What an actress she must really be. "If you must know," she told him, "I needed you badly." She told him briefly about Margaret Felt and young Joyner. "But I found them, finally, down by the river."

He accepted the story mildly, made a few comments, said he understood Joyner was being sent on the detail.

"Are you going?" Savanna asked quickly.

"Not this time. It's a routine field trip—nothing important—just shoving some squatters off Choctaw lands."

He spoke so easily that he caught her unprepared when he asked, "What made you think of the river?"

All her misery returned, everything she had seen and felt and done that dreadful night. She began to cry helplessly and to sob out the story between swipes at her eyes, sniffles of her nose, and jerky, short breaths. ". . . and you just stood there . . . and that girl was leaning against you . . . and you looked as smug as the cat that's just licked the cream." She snubbed and then wailed, "You looked just like you'd been married to her all your life!"

She buried her nose in his shoulder, hiccuping, clinging to his shirt. He held her. "What did you do, Savanna?"

"I went away," she said forlornly.

"You went to the river," he said, his voice very gentle, "because you always did go to the river when you were troubled or hurt. You didn't go to find Margaret Felt at all, did you?"

"No. I forgot all about Margaret and Joyner." She looked up at him, her face all smeared with whitewash and tears, her eyes still bright with them, the lashes stuck together. "Well, what would you have done? How would you have felt if you had just seen . . . ?"

"What would I have done? If I'd just seen you with a man?" His voice rasped suddenly and became like cold iron. "I would have killed him."

She didn't take his meaning directly. Still involved with her own feelings, her mouth tightened. "That's what I felt like doing to that girl."

"Why didn't you?"

"Well, good Lord, Abe, if you love her, what good—?"

"Who said I loved her?"

"But you've lived with her for years!"

"And a very comfortable arrangement it's been, too. It happens that love doesn't enter into it, however."

184

Savanna sat up straight. "You're a blackguard, Abe Lathrop."

He laughed easily. "Perhaps. But Jolie understands."

Savanna shot him a look from under her lashes. "I'll bet she loves you."

Abe shrugged. "Oh, she's fond of me—used to me. She'd be better off married."

"Who'd have her now?" Savanna's voice was caustic.

"Offhand I can think of a dozen men, without going into the tribe. There her value has not depreciated at all."

"You're disgusting. How can you take such things so lightly?"

"Better lightly, don't you think, than too earnestly—unless, of course, you mean business. Which I don't and never did. Our arrangement was very simple. She accommodated me and I accommodated her until one or the other wanted it to end. I'll break it off at once."

Savanna's eyes flamed at him. "Not on my account you don't! I don't even intend to be friends with you any more."

"I don't intend to be friends with you, either, Savanna," he said softly. "I intend to be your husband." He got up, stretched yawningly, scrubbed at his face, then gave her a hand up. "If you'll wash that mess off your face and change your dress we'll ride up to the Mission right now. I happen to know that Preacher Chapman is there."

"I think," Savanna said, staring at him, "you have lost your senses. You surely didn't ride up here today with that in mind."

"No. I came to find out what happened the other night. But it's a good idea, don't you think? Seeing that I love you and you love me, I don't suppose you want to live in sin. And if we're going to be married, there's no point in waiting, is there?"

"I haven't said I'd marry you!"

He took her in his arms, leaned his forehead against hers and said, his mouth only inches from hers, "But you will, won't you, Savanna?" He kissed her. "If you won't," punctuating his words with short, sweet touches of his mouth so that she could hardly think what he was saying, "you'll be sorry—I don't mean—to let you—go. I love you—and I mean—to take you—tonight—married or not—so you had—better—marry me—today."

He would. She knew he would, and she would let him. She felt as weak as a kitten. She wanted him as badly as he wanted her.

The green core of her young will rose within her and hardened with purpose. I will have this man. I *will* have him. She rejoiced in her savage yearning for him and felt that her fate had found her. For this she had been born; for this given the tinge of guttersnipe, the coarse vein that could be bawdy and lusty; for this she had been tried and taught to endure; for this she had been tutored by the tender, fading passion of a gentle man. Everything in her life had been preparing her for this day, all things leading to this end.

Fiercely, exultantly, she did what she had been longing to do and snatched his head against her, cradled and held it. "Hush," she said, "just hush now."

She let her unbridled hands make free with his hair and roamed her lips over his face, over his closed eyes, the weathered wrinkles at their corners, over the hard brown skin lean over his bones, to the wide, ripe, full, young mouth. How wonderful that it was young!

Seeing one eye beginning to swell, the skin about it already yellowing, she giggled. "You're going to have a black eye, darling."

Against her throat he murmured. "I know. Don't think I won't pay you back, my girl."

She lifted her head and took such a breath his head was jolted. Ah, let him. Let him! How joyfully she would receive it!

It was a shock to her to see Kizzy standing in the doorway. The black woman stood there struck so dumb, her mouth so gaped, her eyes so whitely rolled, that Savanna gulped, giggled, and choked. "Kizzy is going to have a spasm," she whispered to Abe.

She called to her. "It's all right, Kizzy. Mister Abe and I are going to be married this morning."

XVIII

The satiety of the night hours did not dull Abe's consciousness that he must leave at dawn, and he woke from light, brief sleep just as daylight began to bleach the sky.

Careful not to wake Savanna he slid from the bed and moved to the window. It would be hot later but just now the air was its freshest and felt cool on his bare skin. He took a deep, lung-stretching breath and his mouth and nose were filled with the sweet scent of honeysuckle, the pungent smell of wood-smoke coming from Kizzy's cabin, and the faint swampy smell which all land near rivers retains.

In the big mahogany bed behind him Savanna stirred and he turned, moving back into the gloom of the room.

Reticence was not only a natural trait in Abe Lathrop, it had been trained into him early and, finding it served him well, not only in childhood when stealth and wariness were necessary, but in all other circumstances as well, he had retained it. Reticence did not mean, however, that he was inarticulate. There was never any stuttering and stammering in his mind. It worked sharply, lucidly, and cleanly. He stood now and watched Savanna and thought.

When a man marries, he thought, he knows he will discover some things impossible to know sooner about his wife. He had known Savanna was high-spirited, full of determination, stubborn, tempery, generous, loyal, and lively. He knew she had a zesty appetite for pleasure and was gifted with a fine humor. He knew her face was beautiful and he supposed that through all the clothing women wore which so effectively hid any intimate knowledge of their figures, she had a good body.

He had not been prepared at all for the wanton loveliness of her flesh, and his first sight of it had shaken him profoundly. It was flawless, perfect, and as voluptuous as a ripe peach. Nor had he been prepared for the violent passion waiting within it to be unleashed. He had not supposed she would be cold. After all, she had been married. But he had not expected the vehemence of her passion which, even with his greater experience, he had been hard put to it to cope with adequately.

She stretched in her sleep, the gesture of lifting her full breasts and arching her back into the flowing, beautiful curves of hips and thighs. Even in sleep it was offering and voluptuous. Abe smiled. He had married himself quite a woman.

A rooster crowed in the chickenyard and there was the heavy gush of water as a horse in the barnlot relieved himself. Savanna turned on her side and moved her arms toward the place he had left. "Abe?"

He went to her, ran his fingers up the arch of her back, and kissed her. "Reveille soon. I've got to go."

Her arms closed about his neck.

"No." He put them away and left the bed. He dressed quickly, kissed her again, spanked her lightly, and left.

He did not say when he would be back, or if he would be back, or if she should join him at the post for a few days, or if she should begin to make ready to move permanently to the post. She didn't mind. He would be back or he would fetch her where he was. She did not mind anything at all now. Spent with love, drugged with it, she only smiled drowsily when she heard the door close. She felt replete and utterly slack, sleepy, wholly satisfied, blissfully content. During the night of love she had dozed only in snatches. She turned again and closed her eyes and was instantly asleep.

The dusk had fallen when he returned. "Got a month's

leave," he told her, grinning, snatching her off her feet and devouring her. "Won't have to leave at daylight for a while."

He couldn't wait for her until he had eaten, nor would she have had him wait. She was as insatiable, as demanding, as he. Stirred, barely awakened by an old man's tender, exquisite way of making love, she was savagely ready for a young man's violence. She turned violent herself, wanting his hard and bruising quickness, his impatience.

She dozed a little afterward and was brought out of it by Abe's laughter. She rubbed her eyes and grumbled at him, then sat up and fanned with the sheet. "Lord, but it's hot. This room is like a sweat bath. What's funny?"

Abe rolled over on his stomach, his lean, lovely, beautiful, hard, young stomach and braced himself on his elbow. "The general."

"What's he done?"

"Nothing. It was the way he took the news. He was caught so flatfooted when he heard we were married all he could do was stutter. He looked like a bag of wind collapsed. He managed to stammer out some good wishes but he was mightily astounded. I guess he was pretty fond of you."

Savanna felt a pang of remorse. "We should have taken longer, Abe—observed the proprieties."

He looked at her from the corner of his eyes. "For the old man to get used to the idea? What's it matter?"

She couldn't think of why it should have mattered except that he had always been so kind to her and she felt a little guilty at taking him so by surprise. With Abe, she saw, that didn't count.

He was musing again. "It is sort of silly, isn't it? That you should marry a sergeant when you could have had a general."

Savanna denied it immediately. "I married a man, not a sergeant. It's only incidental what you are."

"You'd have been mighty comfortable with the old man."

"Pish. What do you think I am now?"

He eyed her comically. "Offhand, I'd say you should be feeling a little battered."

"Dolt!"

It delighted her that through that first week together Abe came to find her when it pleased him. Thomas had been too contained, too conscious of his dignity, too fearful of the ridiculous, ever to use the daylight hours. But Abe had neither dignity nor fear and when he strode into the house, swept her up and locked the door behind them, she exulted in his hunger and fed her own starved passion.

But she slowly learned, also, that in more ways than making

188

love Abe Lathrop was not another Thomas Brook.

She had always known that he could be hard, even implacable. She had watched him too often break a horse and handle his men. It came, however, as a surprise that he could be equally implacable with her.

In the second week of their marriage she butted her head straight into its stone wall. He brought up, one afternoon, the matter of her stores. "I would like you to sell the two at Fort Smith and the Falls."

"Now, Abe," she said impatiently, "don't begin on that again. We have been over all that ground before."

"We'll go over it again."

"We'll only quarrel," she warned.

"No, we won't quarrel," he said. "There is nothing to quarrel about."

"Just as much as before," she said tartly.

"No. Before you were not my wife."

"What's being your wife got to do with it? They're my stores, not yours."

"But *you* are my wife and I won't have my wife traipsing over the country."

"I can't *run* the stores without traipsing over the country." Her temper was rising already. "I've tried to tell you that."

"Which is just the point. You can't run them without traipsing and I won't have my wife traipsing. So—sell the stores."

"Well, I won't! I can't!"

"Why can't you?"

"Very well," she stormed at him, "if you will keep on at me about it you can have the truth. Parley makes money for me at the Falls and until the place is better established I have to have the money he makes. And there is still some hope the Fort Smith store will pick up. Thomas always believed . . ."

"Thomas is dead," Abe said brutally. "Sell both the stores, Savanna."

"You can't tell me what I have to do, Abe Lathrop!"

When she was angry Savanna's eyes looked as though a fire had been lit in them, the splintered sparks hot enough to burn.

They did not burn her husband. "I *can* tell you what to do and I am telling you." He did not raise his voice at all but it was as cold as winter sleet.

She could not brook restraint and it made her furious for him to stand there so dead still and cold telling her already, in less than a month, what she should do. Husband or no husband, she wouldn't have it. The stores were hers and none of his affair. Nobody was going to tell her what she could or could not do! She glared at him. "You can tell all you like, but I won't do it. I will not!"

He shrugged. "Very well."

He went out. She heard him cross the dogtrot into their bedroom and heard him thumping about in there. Presently he came out carrying his belongings. She flew to the door. "Abe! Where are you going?"

His step didn't hesitate. Over his shoulder he threw at her, "Back to the post. I'm leaving you."

She went running after him, pulling at his arm. "Abe, you can't do that. Think what people would say."

"I don't give a damn what people say." He tore loose from her and went on to the stable.

She followed him. "Abe, you're the meanest thing on earth. Making all this fuss over the stores and shaming me in front of everybody."

He led his horse into the stall. "You don't have to be shamed. If you are, it's your own doing. But you may as well learn right now I mean what I say." He picked up the saddle blanket and threw it on. "Sell the stores or I go."

She felt blindly for the post behind her, a sudden draining and weakening sensation in her legs making her afraid they were going to give way under her. She was sick with dismay and raked by fear. He was furious with her, she could tell. His face was stony, the jaws jutted, the mouth tight. His eyes, when he glanced at her, were as cold and hard as ledgerock. He meant it. He really meant he would leave her if she did not sell the stores. He would do this thing. He was precisely that angry with her.

He hefted the saddle onto the horse's back. It was his own mustang. In the generosity of her first great joy and love, when she would have given him the earth and moon if she could, she had made him a gift of the Duke. As happy as a little boy with the thoroughbred he had been riding him daily since. This morning, however, he was turning his back on her gift as he was turning it on her. He meant to go and he meant to take nothing of hers with him—nothing, she thought miserably, but her heart.

How could he be so angry with her? How could he be so heartless? It would set everyone to talking—she shoved hard against the post, standing away from it, struck with the thought. Sweet heaven, if he went she would be the laughingstock of the whole country. Savanna Brook, married less than two weeks and her husband walks out on her, leaves her! The talk would run as wild as prairie fire and as uncontrollable; there would be a thousand rumors and conjectures—why, what

190

happened, who was to blame, did they fight, will they make it up? She had heard them before with far less cause.

And there would be pitying looks and sly looks and malicious and catty looks. She would be the butt of the coarsest and crudest kind of laughter and jokes. She could hear them now, obscene and bawdy, snickering that Abe must like dark meat best after all—that Miss Proud wasn't so good in bed, maybe—that Jolie Perrier was right fancy and hard to follow. It made her writhe to think of the lewd things that were certain to be bandied about.

And with what satisfaction some people would say, well, I guess that'll learn her. I guess she knows she's nobody's pampered pet now. Guess she's found out she can't have her own way with everybody. She ran into a stone wall with Abe. She sure got her comeuppance. She sure found out nobody pushes Abe Lathrop around.

Her jaw squared.

Nobody had tried to push Abe Lathrop around, but Abe Lathrop was doing his best to push her around and nobody pushed Savanna Brook, either. If Abe thought he could bend her to his will by riding out of her life, let him. Bend? Savanna Brook? Sell her stores because he didn't want her riding about the country? Who did he think he was? Nobody could tell her what to do with her property, and nobody could forbid her to do what she pleased. Let the country talk—let it laugh. It had talked and laughed before. She could stand it. She didn't need Abe Lathrop. She didn't need anybody. She could manage by herself!

As Abe led the mustang outside she followed him, her tears dried and her own jaw jutted, her face now as set as his, her eyes hot with indignation. "If you leave," she said, as he prepared to mount the horse, "you needn't think you can come back."

He gave her a long level look but said nothing. He swung into the saddle and rode away without another word or without a backward glance.

She watched him go, her heart sick and sore. There, she thought woefully, went the wreck of her love and her hopes and her happiness. Such a little time of happiness and love, and so soon over. The tears flowed again, but she wiped them away angrily, snubbed them back. The terms were too hard. She wouldn't give in. If she never saw him again she wouldn't give in. He had no right to ask her. He knew nothing about business, had often said so. It wasn't fair of him.

She squared her shoulders and marched into the house and went stoically about her work for the rest of the day.

Her pride and anger sustained her until night. Then, in the big, wide bed, the memories of their hours there together haunting her, his pillow, his place beside her so empty, she felt a deep and desolate crying within her. She was so lonely, so lost without him. She had already got so used to him she didn't see how she was ever going to do without him.

Her mind went round and round the whole affair. Thomas had never cared what she did. He had been proud of her spirit. Never in their time together had he tried to thwart her. Why couldn't Abe have the same pride in her? Why did he have to be so cussedly proud himself? He didn't have an ounce of business sense. All he knew, and admitted it was all he knew, was the army and horses, and a little petty thieving. But it ought to be clear to anyone, even a child, that with as many traders as there were in the country nowadays one store wasn't enough. You had to have a string of them. Look at the Chouteau string, stretching from St. Louis to the Rockies, and look at all the irons Captain Rogers had in the fire—land, the tavern, the cotton gin, his store. Look at Hugh Love and every other trader in the business. She might do as well to sell the store at Fort Smith—it was actually costing her money—but she couldn't sell the store at the Falls. This place on the Road would give them a place to live and furnish them with bacon and beans, but for money to operate she had to have the store at the Falls. If he just hadn't got so angry all at once. If he had only listened to her!

The night was dark and hot and she twisted restlessly about as her thoughts fled down the gloomy paths now opened before her. She was wretched and miserable and heartsick and lonely. She flounced and thought: Well, I'll just have to get used to it. I can't do what he wants. I don't dare.

She did not sleep until just before morning when, exhausted finally, she dropped off, Abe's pillow clutched to her for comfort.

She was roused when he shoved her roughly. "Move over."

She was awake instantly, the dear voice heard and received in her heart even through sleep. Obediently, wordlessly, she made room for him, a pulse of exultation surging through her. He had come back. He did love her. He couldn't go away from her and stay.

In the wan, pale light of the dawn she watched him undress and come into the bed where he lay very straight, careful not to touch her. He was extremely tired and his eyes were bloodshot and dust-rimmed. And he was not happy. His face was as set and fixed as it had been when he left. But he was here. He was here! She waited, wanting more than anything to touch him, to clasp the mole-furred head to her and cover the dear, drawn face with her kisses. But she did not. She lay as straight as he, as careful not to touch.

He turned his head on the pillow finally and looked at her. "You are not to believe," he said, slowly and wearily, "that I have come crawling back to you. I haven't. But I married you and I made some vows that are bigger than anger and pride."

For once in her life some instinct for silence governed Savanna and she kept quiet. She simply looked at him and waited.

"A man's got no right," he went on, scrubbing his face with his hands, "to walk away from his promises and vows. You are the stubbornest, most bullheaded female the Lord ever made, but I knew that before and I married you anyway. You are my wife. The only thing is that I've not been married long enough but that I forgot it yesterday. I forgot I'm not free to walk away now. I said in front of Preacher Chapman that I would cherish you and protect you until death parted us. I didn't promise that lightly even though I forgot it yesterday. I wish you would believe I was trying to protect you when I asked you to sell the stores."

She touched his arm. "I believe it, darling."

"Well, then—you know. I won't ask it again."

With a rush she gathered him in and when she had cried and he had soothed her and she had offered to sell at least the store at Fort Smith and he had agreed she might keep the store at the Falls, they made love and because they had been parted and had been hurt and had been cruel to each other, it was wonderfully rapturous and exquisite and wholly transporting.

They believed that no two people in the world had ever loved as they did, and they believed they had done all the harm to each other they could ever do and they were forever safe and secure now.

Neither of them knew that buried very deep in Savanna's subconscious was a new knowledge—that she was stronger than the hardest, strongest man she had ever known.

XIX

Abe went with her to Fort Smith, where Captain Rogers bought the store.

The deed done she found it was a relief to have it over. "I'm well quit of it," she said.

"I think you are, Mrs. Lathrop," the captain said.

It was the first time she had been called by her new name. She said it over to herself, mulling it so that she missed the rest of what was said. Savanna Lathrop—Savanna Lathrop. It wasn't quite as pretty as Savanna Brook, but no matter. She tossed it aside. Abe redeemed it. She would have taken his name if it had been Turnipseed.

They stayed the night with her father but arose early the next morning for the journey home. A pea-soup fog, usual in the river bottoms, shrouded the country and made the trees look as if they were swimming in it. Feeling wraithlike herself, Savanna rode by Abe's side, silent, her mind taking many turnings and twistings.

They had never discussed where they were going to live. She knew it must be at the trading post, but did Abe? She told herself he couldn't be thinking to move her to the cantonment, for where on the cantonment could they live? It would be the quarter, of course, along with Ellie and Dickson, the laundresses, the other enlisted people, the hunters and trappers.

Brought up short by this knowledge she realized for the first time that Officers' Row was no longer open to her. Major Thomas Brook's wife had, without question, belonged in the upper circle. Major Thomas Brook's widow had continued to belong. Sergeant Abe Lathrop's wife would not. Closed to her now were the dinners and balls, the inner ring of officers and wives at the races, at sociables, the warm gossiping hoop of rank. She hadn't given it a thought before. She, Savanna Fowler Brook, had been welcome anywhere. But Savanna Lathrop had come down a peg in the world. With a pang she realized she had danced her last time as the general's partner, had sat at his right hand at his famous dinners the last time.

But fiercely she thrust it away from her. It didn't matter at all. Abe was worth a hundred dinners and balls and sociables, and he was worth any place on Officers' Row. Of course he might—it did happen—win a field commission one day. But it didn't matter.

She rode up beside him. "Abe, have you thought where we are to live?" She might as well settle it now, though she felt a little fearful after the explosion over the stores.

He gave her an amused glance. "In your home, of course. Where did you suppose?"

She laughed. "That was my idea too. Do you mean to live on the post and come home on Sundays?"

"No. I'll get leave to live off the post. Ride back and forth."

Savanna sighed with relief. "I'm glad. I wouldn't like your being away all week."

"I wouldn't like it either. It's going to be a damned nuisance leaving your warm bed every morning. But if it's warm for me when I return I'll try not to mind too much."

He rode close to kiss her, then restless rode ahead, kicking the Duke into a canter. He was eager to get home, she thought. Oh, what did any of it matter? They could cross their bridges as they came to them. She was eager to get home too. Kizzy would have a good meal for them and there would be two or three hours before the men from the post began to gather for the evening. Her heart beat up at the thought of those hours. She wished their nights weren't cluttered with the nuisance of the men until ten o'clock. But they couldn't afford to discourage them. It was plain that more than ever now she needed their trade.

But they found David waiting for them, fuming the house with his pipe. If the news waiting for him when he got back from Fort Smith had jolted him in any way, it didn't show. He was cheerful, shabby, jovial and joking with them. "The instant I turn my back," he said chidingly, "you take advantage. Why didn't you let a fellow know?"

Abe said casually, "Didn't know ourselves. Just happened."

"Bang—like that."

"Bang," Savanna agreed, looking across at Abe, amused at exactly how banglike it had been. She was so single-minded in her love there was room for no one but Abe. No room even for David. She felt prickled and vexed to find him there.

"Well," David said, chuckling around his pipe, "you stole a march on everyone. The whole post is set by its ears—nothing else being talked about. I feel a bit sorry for the general. He's going about looking as if he's lost his last friend."

"Fiddle," Savanna said, drawing up chairs and getting out a bottle, "when a man reaches his age he's too set in his ways to change. He don't really want to marry."

"He thought he did, and he thought he wanted to marry you."

"Just a notion," Savanna said, pouring the wine.

"A notion he's had since Thomas died. A notion held that long gets to be a habit."

"Well, even if I hadn't married Abe I wouldn't have considered the general. One old man . . ." she broke off, appalled at what she had been about to say. How could she have forgotten Thomas's kindness and goodness? One old man was enough, indeed! Thomas had rescued her from the dreariest life on earth, given her everything within his power, treated her gently and tenderly and set her up in business. She owed him everything she had. All her life she ought to hold him in honor for what he had done for her. But, sweet heaven, what a monstrous and wonderful difference!

Abe was looking comfortable and a little smug. She scowled

195

at him. "But don't take all the credit to yourself, my boy. It was my doing. I *could* have had him, or a dozen others."

Abe laughed at her scowl, stretched his legs and yawned.

She had to touch him. She had to lay her hand on him. She went quickly to him and with no regard for David's presence, as unabashed as though she and Abe had been alone, kissed him lingeringly. "You're a wretch, Abe Lathrop, a miserable wretch," she murmured. "I don't know why I love you, but I do. Madly."

Neither she nor Abe saw the quick clench of the surgeon's teeth on his pipestem, or heard the little snap as it broke.

Nothing else she could have done would have shown him more plainly his place in her affections. Friend, tried and trusted friend. So good a friend, so peacefully and placidly accepted that she need not be reticent with her new husband before him. Like the furniture sitting about the room, like the air she breathed, like the horse she rode, a part of her life, even perhaps a necessary part of her life, but barely to be given a thought to. He took the broken pipe and tossed it into the empty fireplace. Carefully he made his face a mask.

Savanna lifted her head and pushed her hair back. David was standing, as if there were a fire, hands locked behind him, teetering on his heels and toes. She grinned at him. "Have you seen Martha?"

He nodded.

"What did she say about us?"

"Nothing much. Said she hoped you knew what you were doing."

Savanna laughed. "I expect she knows the sparks will fly. Living with this scamp," she tapped Abe on the head, "I may burn the house down." She stretched her arms above her head and sighed gustily. "Lord, but I'm tired."

"I'll go," David offered. "I only meant to stop by. I've been to Three Forks."

"No, no," Savanna said, "you'll stay for supper."

For some reason she now wanted him to stay. She felt lax and slack, her hunger for Abe suddenly gone. "I'll tell Kizzy."

They persuaded him and over the meal he told them gossip and the latest news. Nothing much. Everybody was in the doldrums with the heat. The general had held a council with the heads of the Osages, Cherokees and Creeks. No one knew why.

Savanna knew. The general was cementing his relationship with the tribes—putting the skids under Sam Houston.

And Sam Houston had gone to Tennessee. His mother was dying. No one knew when he would return. Talahina was running the trading post.

Savanna sat up straight at the next piece of news. The detail had returned. "But they were to be gone two months," she said.

"Just a rumor some squatters were down there. There had been, but they had already moved out. The detail took a look around and didn't think it necessary to follow. They came on back to Gibson."

Savanna groaned. "Oh, great gobs of mud!"

David looked at her queerly. "What's it matter, Savanna?"

Abe told him about Margaret Felt and young Joyner. "Savanna talked the general into sending Joyner on the detail to get him out of the way," he concluded.

David pulled at his beard speculatively. He shook his head. "I don't know whether it's wise to try to play God, Savanna."

"Do you want to see Joyner killed? He will be, if Bill Felt calls him out."

"Don't you think perhaps Joyner and Margaret should be consulted, Savanna? Must you take this out of their hands for them?"

"Oh, God's britches! They haven't any strength in them." She could never understand a tendency for weighing and balancing. When you could see, as plain as the nose on your face, that a thing was so, that something must be done about it, then it was her policy to do something immediately. That was her way and she was convinced it was the best way. "They won't be able to stay away from each other."

"You don't know that. You can't be certain of it."

"They didn't before."

"But they weren't aware then. Since that time Martha has talked to Margaret and the general has spoken to Joyner."

"Oh, I don't know what reason the general gave for sending Joyner away. He may have given none. He didn't say what he meant to do."

"But Martha did speak to Margaret?"

"She said she would."

"You don't know positively that she did?"

"Well—no."

"You don't know of a certainty, then, that either of those young people has been warned."

"Well, I certainly spoke my mind to them the night I found them on the river. They've had one good strong warning."

David sighed. "Perhaps that will be enough. I wouldn't go meddling any further, Savanna. People aren't chess pieces to be moved about on a board."

"She also had a notion the general should transfer Felt," Abe put in.

"Oh, now, Savanna," David said, "don't try to take over the

197

military completely. Major Hazen reports that Bill is doing pretty well at Towson. He has his right to a chance, too. Transferring him right now might send him off again."

"I shouldn't be surprised if it did," Savanna said bitterly. "In fact I would expect it to, but I don't think Bill Felt is worth risking trouble over."

"Why are you so certain Felt will be coming home?"

"Because he's due a relief, for heaven's sake!"

"He didn't take his last relief."

"Which doesn't mean he won't take his next one. If he's squaring up as you say he is his conscience may get to bothering him about his wife. If Joyner is not here when he comes, and if by some good fortune his relief is delayed a while, the gossip may have died down by then. But if Joyner remains at Gibson neither he nor Margaret will have the sense to keep away from each other. The whole post will be buzzing with talk. No. Joyner must be kept away from Gibson until the general has transferred Bill Felt. It is the only answer and I know it."

The two men looked at each other and smiled. She felt very strongly about this. Always stubborn, not easily swayed from a conviction, she knew trouble was going to come out of this. The men were not so sure. By their smiles Savanna knew they thought she was creating a tempest in a teapot. She stood abruptly, angrily. "You are both as blind as bats. When Joyner has been killed and Bill Felt cashiered, you will regret it."

XX

One morning in the middle of August, about six weeks after she was married, Savanna felt dull and cross and her stomach was so queasy that the odors from the kitchen made her want to heave. She wished Abe didn't have to leave so early. He breakfasted in the men's mess and she always had to face an empty table at the morning meal. One of the best things about being married was having breakfast together. But there was no help for it. It was either get up in the middle of the night, and who wanted to eat then, or leave the situation as it was.

She sat at the table and picked at the food, finally shoving the plate aside.

When this had happened four mornings in a row Kizzy looked at her askance. "Been missin' yo' brekfus' too many times," she said. "You gwine lose yo' flesh, you doan tek keer."

"When I eat in the morning it makes me sick," Savanna said petulantly, "and don't start carping at me. It won't hurt me to lose a little flesh."

Kizzy stopped in her tracks and stared at her. "You eats hearty 'nuff at dinner an' supper. Huccome jes' brekfus' mek you sick?"

"How would I know? It just does, that's all. I can't even stand to smell it. I'm bilious, I guess."

"Has you missed yo' health?" Kizzy asked shrewdly.

"Missed my . . ." Savanna's eyes rounded on the black woman wonderingly. "I don't know. When Thomas died I quit keeping up . . . God's britches, Kizzy, it *has* been a long time!"

Kizzy chuckled. "You ain't got de bile, Miss Savanna. You has got a youngun makin'. You is in de family way, dat's whut. Heavin' yo' brekfus', missin' yo' health. Dem's de signs, all right."

Frowning, Savanna was counting on her fingers. Finished, her hand slowly went to her mouth and her eyes got as round as saucers. "The last time was in June, Kizzy."

The black woman yelped shrilly with laughter and said coarsely, "You done took, Miss Savanna, de fust time you is covered. Jes' lak a good brood mare." She gave Savanna an oblique, randy look. "You sho' got yo'self a diff'runt man dis time. Got yo'self a good stud man. Dat Mistah Abe, he quick on de leap." She shook her frizzy head and her face creaked with an admiring grin.

Slowly Savanna grinned back at her. That Mister Abe!

Her stomach gave a convulsive heave and she fled. "I'm going to lie down."

She had mixed emotions about this new knowledge. She had to think about it. It was going to take some getting used to. She lay flat on her back because her stomach seemed to act up less in that position, and pondered.

It was odd, she thought, that she hadn't given a fleeting thought to the possibility of a child. She had grown too used, perhaps, to never having to think about it. It was true, as she had told Kizzy, that she had paid little attention to what the black woman called her health, even when married to Thomas, for she had slowly come to the conviction they would have no children. Since his death her monthly periods had simply been a nuisance to her. Sweet heaven, the last time had been the middle of June. She placed it by the discomfort that had kept her from helping in the garden when Preacher and Kizzy planted the second crop of corn. She had been nearly due again, then, when she was married. She giggled. By George, Kizzy was right. She had taken on the first cover. She was more than a little proud of that.

But it would be inconvenient, just the same. She needed to give all her attention to the stores. A baby was certainly going to complicate things. Abe was away at the fort all day and knew nothing of trading anyhow. It all fell to her as it had always done.

She had never got as much of the Indian trade as she had hoped. The Cherokees went to Houston's and though some of the Creeks came to her, more of them were faithful to Chouteau. Another thing bothered her, too. Since her marriage there had been a falling off in the number of men who came at night from the post. She didn't know why. They had always been completely respectful to her, not one of them ever making free with her, so she couldn't understand why her marriage should make any difference. But it was making a difference, a little, and she didn't know what to do about it. It wasn't the best time in the world to be having a baby.

But, she faced it squarely, nothing under God's heaven was as irrevocable as a man's seed planted. One way or another it had to grow and come to term. There was absolutely nothing to be done about it. She would have to manage in some way. And, as always when faced with the inevitable, she knew she could do what she had to do.

Her mind wandered away from the problem the fact presented and she thought, grinning ruefully, of Margaret Felt's prediction. Just wait and see. Well, she had waited and now she was seeing. Her boast that nothing could make her lose her appetite had been mighty premature. She certainly couldn't get breakfast down these days.

She remembered then how Margaret had looked carrying her boy. Lord, Lord, she hoped she wouldn't be sick like that and turn sallow, get frowsy and slack and have dark circles under her eyes. The hope had no more than framed itself in her mind than determination followed. She wouldn't do it. She wouldn't have it. She might heave her breakfast but in the morning she was going to get it down, every bite of it. She wouldn't knuckle under to a heaving stomach. She had too much to do to be sick and ailing, and she would see to it that she didn't get slack and whichaway. She was going to have a baby—but having a baby wasn't going to turn her life topsy-turvy.

She was going to have a baby.

Suddenly a tremendous pride and pleasure and joy surged through her. She and Abe had made a baby! She felt a lusty glee that their couplings and tumblings should be so soon fruitful. There was something wonderfully right about it. They had certainly given breeding every chance—she laughed to herself, remembering. How could such wantonness not be fruitful? She locked her arms behind her head. That Mister Abe! Wasn't it

200

exactly like him to seed her at once? Quickly. Impatiently. Violently.

She rolled over on her side and her hands, with a kind of sensuous pleasure, stroked her stomach. It hadn't changed. It was flat and hard, difficult to believe that already a child was making. But Abe's seed and hers were joined and even now springing with new life. The sweet and overpowering sense of it awed her. They had done this, she and Abe. Out of their love they had done this—made life.

She hadn't thought much about it before. It was such an old story—people married, coupled, had children. But this was herself, and Abe, and this child rooted was theirs. It would grow in her body, swell and stretch her body, feed on her, and when its time came it would tear itself free of her and a new, fresh life would be born. Her heart jumped and thudded. They had done this—she and Abe!

She turned again, smoothing her flatness, wishing she already bulged, wanting to push her bulge proudly before the whole country. Let everyone know, she thought passionately, how we've spent our hours and what is the consequence. She wasn't going to hide her bulge away in shame. She was going to jut this child as proudly as she jutted her chin. She was going to say with her bulge, look what I carry—the fruits of love— the end to which all couplings are meant to lead! Sweet heaven, she hadn't known it would be like this!

Savanna had never known her grandmother Tattie Cartwright and she had no knowledge of that woman's fierce joy in bearing, but in that moment of lusty, earthy pride and exultation, Tattie would have recognized herself and she would have said, with equal pride, "Just like me, that one. She likes herself when she's bearing."

XXI

Savanna's morning sickness didn't amount to much. By the end of September it had passed. Kizzy told her she was lucky. "Some it lasts de whole time an' most it lasts fer months. Jes' plain lucky, you is."

Her general health was always excellent and apparently her body needed only to make the adjustment to the changes required of it, which it did quickly. But much of her luck was her own determination. She had no patience with illness. Though her stomach roiled and heaved, she made herself get up on her feet, stay up on her feet, and keep on about her business.

The heat lasted long and that bothered her as much as any thing else. When the first mizzly, cool day came she decided to go to the fort. She was tired of being cooped up, she said. She wanted to see people, listen to women's backchat, visit Martha and Margaret. She had only been to the fort once since she had married. It was high time she caught up.

Everyone on the place, Kizzy, Preacher, McNulty, and Abe, humored her these days. Kizzy soothed her because she fearfully believed a woman bearing needed humoring lest harm come to her or the child. She faithfully supplied Savanna's cravings for sour and salty foods, bore her tempers, fetched and carried for her. Preacher humored her because Kizzy laid down the law to him. Abe humored her because he was as deeply proud of their achievement as Savanna. He thought she was a wonder to take so quickly and had earned a right to a little spoiling. And McNulty humored her because Abe laid down the law to him. She became a little brattish, but not much. At her most unreasonable she was able to break off, hitch up her humor, and laugh at herself.

Abe always went to Gibson early so he had gone when she determined to go. No one gainsaid her. Kizzy did tell her she couldn't ride the mare. "Yo' ridin' days is ovah," she said. "Preacher kin tek you in de wagon. You ain't gwine bounce dat chile 'round on no hawse."

That was the worst of this bearing, Savanna thought. It hampered you so. You couldn't do this, you couldn't do that, because of the child. But she didn't want anything to happen to this child either so beyond a little fussing and fuming she followed Kizzy's orders.

Later, she didn't know why, she went to Margaret Felt's first. It was a reversal of her habit of going straight to Martha's. Something vague tugged at her and directed her to Margaret's.

She hadn't seen the girl since the Fourth of July. The one time she had visited Gibson since, Margaret had not answered her knock. The curtains were drawn and Savanna supposed she was not at home. But she knew the girl must be deeply unhappy these days. Young Joyner had stayed in camp only one week. He had been in Fort Smith ever since. Abe had told her that Joyner himself had asked for field duty again after the week at Gibson. A detail had always to be kept at Fort Smith near the Choctaw agency and usually the duty was rotated. Abe understood that Joyner had asked not to be relieved, however. Savanna had felt a deep relief when Abe had come home with this news. Now it only remained for the general to transfer Bill Felt out of the Territory and on her last visit to the cantonment he had promised he would do that as soon as he conveniently could arrange it.

The curtains were drawn at Margaret's today and no one answered when she knocked, but finding the door unlocked she pushed it opened and went in, calling as she did, "Margaret?"

There was a small sound, like a kitten mewling, from the next room and she followed it. What she saw appalled her. Margaret was curled on the bed in one of her shapeless sacks, her hair stringy and hanging, her face haggard and hollow-cheeked. Her eyes were dull and empty-looking. Savanna would have thought her tipsy but she knew Margaret never took anything but a sip or two of wine at a party.

When Savanna entered the room Margaret looked at her, the expression of her face unchanging. There was no word, no smile, no apparent recognition. There was not even a shifting of her curled, coiled position on the bed.

Savanna went to her quickly. "Margaret, what's wrong?"

The girl acted as though she had not heard. Her eyes, fixed on the door, did not follow Savanna across the room. She continued to stare woodenly at the door. Coming near her, Savanna caught the stench of vomit and her nostrils quivered. Her own stomach was none too predictable yet. The bed was fouled and the front of the girl's garment. Savanna took her shoulder and shook it. "Margaret? How long have you been ill?"

The girl shuddered at her touch and drew away.

Savanna straightened. She laid her things aside and went to the kitchen. When she came back she was carrying a basin of water and a towel. She bathed the girl's hands and face. Margaret suffered it listlessly, as if it were being done to someone else, but when Savanna tried to lift the soiled garment over her head she clutched it and held on, crying, "No. No, I have to wear this."

"I'll get a clean one for you, Margaret."

"No. This is the only one I have."

"You have half a dozen nightshifts, Margaret. Let me find a clean one."

"No! I have to wear this!"

She was so vehement that Savanna left it alone. It was, she saw, one of the sacks Margaret had worn before her baby was born. She wondered, absently, why Margaret had dragged it out to put on. She had vowed to Savanna she never wanted to see one of the shapeless things again. Such a strange thing to do, Savanna thought.

She looked about the room for the little boy. He was always near Margaret. Perhaps he was asleep in the cradle. But it was empty, and the room was empty of him too. "Where is little Bill?" she asked.

Margaret looked at her wonderingly. "Little Bill?"

"Your baby, Margaret!" Sweet heaven, was the girl gone daft?

Margaret puzzled her brows together. "He was here—my baby? But I don't have my baby yet. That's why . . ." She gave over the attempt to talk and plucked twitchingly at the loose sack enveloping her.

Savanna gazed at her. She was wandering, no doubt about it. Fever, probably. She must go for David, but first she must find the boy. She went to look for him, uneasiness rising within her. It was so queer—Margaret hadn't felt hot. She didn't have a chill. But she had vomited a dreadful amount. And this weird stupor, as if she couldn't make her mind work. Saying she didn't have her baby yet.

She found the child in the next room, come to no harm. He was beginning to toddle and he had wandered away, crawled under the table and with his thumb in mouth for comfort had gone to sleep. Savanna didn't disturb him. He was as well off there as anywhere for the time being.

She went back to Margaret and sat down on the bed beside her, taking her hand. "Margaret, what is it? What has happened?"

The girl shifted her eyes, then, and looked at Savanna. "Do I know you? I don't know you," she said, her voice thick and labored. "I never saw you before."

Frightened now, Savanna laid the limp hand down. She picked up her bonnet. "I'm going for the surgeon, Margaret," she said, "but I'll be back in a few minutes. Lie still, darling, and rest."

She hated to leave the girl alone but she couldn't cope with this. It was too eerie and strange.

She took another peek at the child and heaved a sigh that he was still asleep. She was out the door before she remembered that David was in the mountains hunting. Abe had told her so a few days before. Oh, Lord. Well, she hurried her steps, Martha must come. Margaret was too queer and she didn't have the least idea what to do. Somebody had to come.

She found the sutler's house empty, wandered through the rooms, calling, and then went into the store. "Where are Major Short and Mrs. Short?" she asked their store man.

"Fort Smith. Went yesterday."

Savanna yanked her bonnet off angrily. Wasn't there anybody on this post? Had everyone gone away? Even Abe, she remembered, was out on detail today. Esther Hammond? Susan Cleet? For no reason she could identify she shrank from having them see Margaret in this condition. She had a crazy feeling that whatever was at the bottom of this was something

204

they ought not to know. What it was, she did not yet know herself, but it was all too peculiar.

She stood in the doorway and fanned herself with the bonnet. It was still drizzling but not enough to be called a rain, and the morning was warming fast. She had hurried and her face was beaded with sweat.

The storekeeper watched her, wondering, and finally said, "Is something wrong, Miss Savanna? Could I help?"

It pulled her out of her daze. She would just have to manage as best she could. "No, Garrett. No, thank you. I meant to visit Mrs. Short, that's all." She strove for nonchalance, not knowing exactly why she did. "I think I'll just go back to Mrs. Felt's."

"Yes, ma'am."

"When will the Shorts be home?"

"Not for a week. Some goods got mislaid at Fort Smith. They thought Cap'n Rogers might have unloaded them with his."

"Yes. Very well. Tell them I called, please."

"Yes, ma'am."

She marched back to the Felts' cabin.

Margaret had not moved since she left her. Her face was still slack, her eyes empty, still fixed staringly on the doorway. Savanna wondered what she should do. Feed her? Kizzy always made a sick person eat. Something to eat, Kizzy said, never hurt anybody.

The boy was still sleeping, though he stirred a little when Savanna went through to the kitchen. There was a pot of stew on the hearth. The sight of it stopped Savanna. Margaret hadn't been too ill yesterday to make a pot of stew. Whatever had happened, it had occurred since yesterday. In the condition she was in right now she could never have made stew, or anything else.

Savanna raked the ashes, fed the fire, and stopped again. The fire was not an old one. The ashes were full of coals, big chunky coals, the kind a breakfast fire would have made. Left from yesterday the ashes would have been only faintly warm. And the boy, she recollected, was dressed. He had not been neglected since yesterday. One thing at a time Savanna tracked this weird illness of Margaret's to the morning, and since breakfast at that. She swung the soup pot over the fire. She put fresh water into the basin and went back into the bedroom.

Gently she eased Margaret Felt into a flat position in the bed and began to bathe her face and hands, and her arms to the shoulder. Rythmically she rubbed, massaged, stroked, her strokes always upward on the arms. She had a vague recollec-

205

tion of hearing, somewhere, some time, that the blood should be moved toward the heart in cases of . . . well, in general. It was a good idea. She watched the wan, haggard girl for some sign of bettering, but for a long time it did not come. Savanna worked away not knowing whether she was doing good or harm.

The child wakened and came stumbling in, whimpering. Savanna took him on her lap and gave over the bathing. He wasn't comforted and kept struggling to reach his mother. It dawned on Savanna finally that he was hungry. Margaret had not weaned him yet. Maybe . . . maybe she could nurse him. She put the boy in the cradle, where he set up a howl which she didn't bother trying to hush. She piled pillows behind Margaret and raised her, then taking the child she laid him in Margaret's arms. Eagerly the boy snatched at her garment, picking at it, trying to reach the full breast beneath.

To her sickening, weakening horror, Savanna saw Margaret look at the child as if she had never seen him before. The girl's face was puzzled, her brows wrinkled with a frown. She looked helplessly up at Savanna. Dear Lord, Savanna thought, she doesn't even know her own child! And her breasts so full the front of her gown is wet with their leak.

The boy, frustrated, set to weeping and wailing, still picking at the front of his mother's gown. Well, there was no reason he should go hungry, Savanna determined, because his mother's mind was wandering. Firmly she untied the neck band of Margaret's sack and drew it down to uncover the breast. The boy snatched it, nuzzled it and began to draw on it in great gulping sucks, kneading the firm, swollen flesh as Savanna had seen puppies and kittens do. She stepped back, feeling relieved.

Margaret was watching the child, still puzzled evidently, but passive. Then all of a sudden, so suddenly Savanna had no time to prevent her, she snatched her breast away from him, hid it inside the garment, and shoved the baby from her lap. Only the fact that she was in bed saved him from falling. He rolled over her knees and came to no harm on the far side of the bed, save that his meal so rudely taken from him he was angry and he howled fit to raise the dead. Margaret's eyes blazed at Savanna. "How vulgar of you! How dare you set a child to my breast!"

Without a word, feeling words hopeless, Savanna lifted the indignant little boy and carried him on her hip to the kitchen. She made him a sugar-tit which comforted him a little and laid him in his cradle. She hoped he would sleep again.

She brought a bowl of soup and one spoonful at a time fed it to Margaret. Like a young bird the girl opened her mouth obediently and swallowed the soup until the entire bowl was finished. Then Savanna took the pillows away and made her comfortable. She saw with relief that the staring eyes were closing and soon, by the regular breathing, she knew that Margaret Felt slept.

While Margaret slept Savanna found Preacher and sent him for Kizzy. "Tell her to come straightway. I need her."

"Yessum."

"And hurry. Don't waste any time."

"No'm."

She then tidied the house which Margaret kept so well it needed little tidying, but she could not sit still and hold her hands. When the boy wakened he was whimpering and gnawing his knuckles. Savanna cast caution to the winds and fed him soup also. It surely wouldn't kill him. Then she made a pen of chairs—she didn't want him escaping and wandering out of the house—and set him in it with his small, fat fingers dabbed with molasses. She handed him a downy feather and watched, amused at his fascination with it as he concentrated on trying to transfer the feather from one sticky finger to another. She had learned that from Lena. "It'll keep 'em quiet for hours," Lena had said.

She was beginning to expect Kizzy and Preacher when Margaret roused.

The girl stirred and stretched, moaned a little, then came fully awake. She looked better, Savanna thought, a little rested and refreshed, but best of all the light of reason was in her eyes. "Savanna!" she said, "what are you doing here? When did you come?" She pushed herself up in bed, looked bewilderedly at its rumpled state, at the soiled wrapper on herself, looked about the room. "Why am I in bed? What time is it?" She thrust her legs over the side of the bed.

Savanna stayed her. "You have been ill, darling. I've been here all morning. I found you ill. It's nearly midday now."

"But I've got to get up. Where's Billy?"

"He's playing—in the next room. He's all right, Margaret. I don't think you'd better get up. Do you remember at all what happened? What made you sick?"

The great violet-blue eyes went dark with anguish as Savanna's questions made her remember, and one hand pressed against her mouth. The other clutched Savanna. "Don't leave me. Please don't leave me, Savanna. I'm so scared."

"I'm not going to leave you, Margaret." Savanna sat on the bed beside her. "I'm not going to leave you. Why are you so scared?"

"Bill's coming home."

"But why should that . . . how do you know?"

"The general sent a note this morning. That's the last thing I remember, Savanna. When I read that note I think I fainted. I don't know what happened after that."

"Well, you were sick, darling. That wrapper is foul with vomit, but you wouldn't let me take it off. You said you had to wear it, and you were—well, your mind was wandering a little."

Margaret pulled her hand away and covered her face, shaking her head from side to side like an animal in pain. "What am I going to do? What's going to happen to me?"

"Nothing is going to happen to you, Margaret," Savanna said, trying to comfort the girl. "What *could* happen to you? You had a shock of some sort but it didn't last very long. As soon as you had some food and slept a little you were all right again. It's nothing to worry about."

"You don't know. Bill will kill me. He will *kill* me!"

"Oh, nonsense, Margaret. Bill may be mean and hateful but he isn't violent. Why on earth should you be so frightened of him?"

Margaret's voice was so whispery that Savanna had to lean close to hear her and its strained whisper somehow made it more desperate. "He will. I tell you he will. You don't know . . ."

"What don't I know?"

"Savanna, he can't come now! He *can't* come! James has gone, and I'm going to have a baby, and Bill will know . . ." She broke off, the fear in her eyes so dark and deep that Savanna thought her mind had snapped again. "He will kill me. He will kill me. He said he would. He said he would. He will kill me." The whispery voice died away.

Savanna sat like a pillar of salt.

God in heaven, what a sweet mess young love had got these two innocents in!

But, of course. That was why Joyner had asked for field duty again. During his week at Gibson they had lost their heads and he, at least, had realized belatedly they could not trust themselves.

And of course Margaret had proved fertile.

What agonies she must have gone through here alone— James absent. How she must have wanted his comfort. How much cudgeling she must have put her mind through seeking some way out. She must not have told a soul yet. Martha wouldn't have left her alone had she known. She must simply, since knowing, have hidden herself away here, hoping against hope perhaps it would prove untrue, trying to wish the fact

208

away, hoping James would return but not having the courage or the wit to take steps to bring him back, hoping something would happen to lift her out of the straits in which she was plunged.

That was Margaret's way—to shrink, to back away from facts, to appeal helplessly for help. "How do you know you're going to have a baby?" Savanna asked, finally.

Margaret looked piteously at her. "It's just like last time."

"You've missed?"

Margaret nodded.

"And you're sick in the mornings. How often," she went on ruthlessly, "were you with James?"

The color washed up into Margaret's face, then receded and left it sallow and hollow-cheeked again. "I don't know."

"You must know. You couldn't forget. More than once?"

Margaret's eyes were pleading. "Savanna, we couldn't help it. We tried. We said each time . . ."

"It was several times then."

Margaret stretched out her hand and took Savanna's, gripped it tightly. "We didn't mean to. We did try. But he couldn't stay away and if he had I would have sent for him. Savanna, we do love each other so much."

Could she have stayed away from Abe, Savanna wondered—and was gentle. "I'm sure you do."

She rose, paced the floor, trying to think. "When did you hear Bill was coming?"

"This morning. It made me frantic, Savanna. I can't bear to see him again. I can't—I simply can't." She began weeping.

"How long since he was home?"

"Six months."

"What's bringing him now?"

"I don't know." Margaret was wringing her hands, her face crumpled and wet. "I don't know. Something the general has ordered. He sent a note over by the Henderson boy and the note said Bill would be home Wednesday."

The general had ordered Bill Felt back to Gibson to transfer him, of course. Oh, Lord, why hadn't she kept her mouth shut. There would have been time—but she made the general promise—and Bill was coming—and there was no way in the world to lay this child to Bill Felt. Don't meddle, Savanna, don't meddle. But she had. And what on earth was she to do now?

It would set him wild, of course. It would set any man wild. There was no hiding the pregnancy and in no time he would learn, for he would either wring it out of Margaret or hear it from a dozen people eager to tell him, who the man was. And there was literally no telling what he might do then. That he would call Joyner out, she did not doubt for a second. Any man would. That he might do physical harm to Margaret was also entirely possible.

Obviously, then, Margaret could not be left alone to face him. She must be protected.

She halted her pacing and turned swiftly to the girl in bed. "Get up, Margaret, and dress. I'll pack your clothing and the baby's."

Looking dazed but hopeful because of the authority in Savanna's voice, Margaret obeyed. "Where are we going, Savanna?"

"I am taking you home with me."

Shuddering, Margaret dropped the shapeless sack around her feet. "Why do you suppose I put that dreadful thing on? My mind *must* have been wandering. Oh, Savanna, what would I do without you? You are so strong and sure. Everything comes all right when you are with me. Nothing very bad can happen as long as I have you."

"You might," Savanna said bitterly, "have listened to me when I warned you and James."

"Don't . . . don't."

Savanna wished she was as strong as Margaret thought her. Everything was far from coming out all right yet. But in her frail way Margaret was eased. The load of decision had been shifted from her own helpless shoulders. Just as Kizzy felt her world was safe as long as Savanna ordered life for her, Margaret was feeling safe with Savanna taking the responsibility for her.

Taking Margaret home with her was only a temporary solution, but Savanna forbore saying so. Bill Felt would follow her there. He was certain to. And he would follow her with knowledge of what she had done and he would have to be faced. But at least Margaret would not face him alone. With Savanna and Abe and with Preacher and McNulty, Margaret would not be in any physical danger. She could think no further than that. When Abe came home they would work something out. They would decide.

She packed clothing and made parcels and hustled Margaret about.

Everything ready, she left Margaret a few minutes while she ran to the general's quarters. She went straight to the point there, telling the old man the blunt truth and she badgered him into promising, as far as it was within his power, to keep Bill Felt from going to find young Joyner.

The general was greatly shocked.

He was really an old innocent at heart. Ladies and gentlemen did not behave in such fashion. It had not occurred to him that Margaret Felt and Joyner might get themselves into . . . well, might get themselves into such straits. He had rather romanticized their love. Hopeless love appealed to him. He had felt great sympathy for them, but it stopped short of approving the physical act of love. He had expected them to renounce their love—sadly, grievingly perhaps, but firmly nonetheless. He had expected them to keep it a pure and shining thing.

Savanna set him straight in the plainest possible terms. "What you should do," she concluded, "is send Bill Felt straight back to Towson and transfer him from there."

The general stiffened. "Savanna, really, I am still the commandant of this cantonment."

"Oh, General Arbuckle—can't you see? We have got to play for time. Bill Felt cannot come here to Gibson and learn what has happened. You *must* keep him away!"

Tiredly the old man capitulated. "Very well, my dear. I will do what I can. I will intercept him if possible."

Vaguely Savanna noticed that the door to his private quarters was slightly ajar when she left, but she was too distraught to give it her attention. She believed she had done the best she could to save the situation. Margaret was waiting. Kizzy and Preacher should have arrived. She had to get Margaret away from Gibson and then, tomorrow or the next day or the next day or the next, she and Abe must decide what to do next.

XXII

Abe was stormily angry when he came home that night and found Margaret and young Bill in the upper bedroom.

"Do you have any idea what you have done?" he raged at Savanna.

Tightly she replied, "I have brought my friend home with me for her protection."

"And her protection may very well cost me my army connections."

"Abe!"

"Hasn't it once entered your pretty head, Savanna, that Bill Felt is my superior officer?"

Oh, my God, Savanna thought, her heart missing a beat. Not until that moment had she realized what she might be doing to Abe. If Bill Felt followed his wife here and Abe was present, if Bill Felt threatened his wife physically, or threatened Savanna, Abe would have to interfere. Being the man he was, he could do no less. But if he opened his mouth to an officer he would be court-martialed. If he laid a hand on an officer he would be drummed out of the service. How could she have been so blind. But—what else could she have done? Her mind ferreted around for a solution. "You simply must stay at the post. Don't come home. You can't run the risk of being here if he comes."

"And leave you to face him alone? Two helpless women?"

"I'm not so helpless," Savanna said staunchly. "I can handle Bill Felt."

Abe said a coarse four-lettered word contemptuously. "You think you can handle anything. Let me remind you that you are carrying a child too—a child who is much more important to me than Margaret Felt's. Even if I were willing to let you risk yourself do you think I would let you risk him?"

In her great absorption in Margaret's problem Savanna had forgotten she was going to have a baby too. She looked mournfully at Abe. "I've made a big mess of things, haven't I? You ought to keep me penned, darling. When I run loose I get into trouble."

Abe shrugged. "Well, it's done. I'll have to try to think of something. What I'm most afraid of is that if the general doesn't intercept him he may come during the day when I'm on duty. I can't get any more leave . . ."

"Oh, no. You mustn't be here. You must not. Abe, can't you send for the Shorts? Or David? Or get the general to take Margaret into his quarters and protect her? Or Captain Hammond?" She was wildly suggesting and she knew it, but she was so appalled at what she had done to Abe that she was casting recklessly about.

"Oh, be quiet," Abe said. "Let me think. Put it out of your mind, now. I'll handle it."

"Abe," she said, feeling as small as the smallest thing on earth and as helpless as a squashed beetle, "Abe, I *am* terribly sorry. I didn't think—you know that. I didn't once think of anything but Margaret."

"I know that, Savanna," he said, his voice a little warmer, giving her a brief smile, "I know that. I know it was the goodness of your heart. But you do think, Savanna, that you alone in all creation can manage things and solve things."

"I know," she said forlornly, "I know. But what else could I have done? David was gone. Martha was gone. I couldn't turn her over to the wolves on the post, could I?"

"Being you, I don't suppose you could. But you're terribly shortsighted. None of this need have occurred if you hadn't been."

212

With some spirit Savanna said, "I did everything I could!"

"And all of it wrong. If you and Martha hadn't tried to take over the military and order it around, if you had simply encouraged Margaret to go for a visit to her people when it all first began, likely nothing more would have happened. A year in the east, away from Joyner, might have solved the whole problem. It would have given the general time to transfer Felt or Joyner, in any event. But no, you and Martha, two of a kind, had the only solution and you browbeat the general into believing it too."

The solution was so simple that Savanna could not think why it hadn't occurred to her. Send Margaret away, of course. She and Martha had concentrated on sending two men away. She clutched her stomach. "I'm going to be sick." She didn't know which nauseated her the most, her heaving stomach or her sick remorse that they had been so blind.

"Go and be sick, but don't heave up that boy."

She gave Abe a stricken look and fled.

She didn't know what Abe did.

She knew he talked to McNulty and Preacher. She saw McNulty cleaning the gun that was always handy in the store, and loading it. She suspected Preacher had done the same thing in the smithy. She wasn't afraid, she told herself, with McNulty and Preacher on guard. What she hoped and prayed was that Abe would not be at home if, or when, Bill Felt came.

Two tense, uneasy days went by.

Margaret, wholly unaware of the trouble she was causing, the danger she had created, was almost blithe in her relief. She was no longer alone. She was with Savanna. Savanna wouldn't let anything happen to her. Savanna would tell her what to do and everything would be all right. She didn't have to see Bill and he would soon be going back to Towson and perhaps James would be coming home to Gibson. Something would be worked out so that she could be happy with James again. Savanna would take care of it.

Savanna watched Margaret being helpful about the house, bright in her manner now, and cheerful to the point of singing occasionally, and wondered if the girl's mind wasn't really a little weak. How could she so easily put her troubles out of it otherwise?

It didn't occur to Savanna that Margaret did not once think that her husband might follow her here. Away herself from the home to which he might come, in her mind certain that she would not have to see him, she felt blessedly at peace and as easily as water runs off a duck's back she slid her future onto Savanna's shoulders.

It had been a Monday when Savanna brought Margaret home with her. When Wednesday passed with no angry husband arriving, Savanna's spirits rose a little. She was almost convinced that General Arbuckle had been able to intercept Bill Felt and send him back to Towson. Abe could not pick up any gossip at the post, so the general had evidently kept it all very quiet.

By Friday Savanna was certain all was well. Abe was inclined to agree. He had the military mind with its great respect for orders and he knew Bill Felt had it too. "Unless something happened to him on the way," he said, "he would have been here by Wednesday night. The general must have handled it all right."

When he came home that night he had good news. "The general called me in to see him today. He told me he had sent Henderson to meet Bill with the new orders. He was to report back to Towson without coming on to Gibson, and from there he was to take a detail out to the Wichitas. That will keep him busy two months. He says for us to get Margaret on the next boat headed east. He says when Bill gets his leave next spring they can fight it out between themselves back home. He'll transfer Bill out before his leave comes due."

They both felt a great sense of deliverance. Savanna, particularly, was giddy with relief. She promised to talk with Margaret the next day about leaving.

"And the next time," Abe warned her sternly, "try to remember that you aren't the only person on earth with a mind and a will. Let someone else decide a few things."

She vowed she would.

XXIII

At noon the next day, Savanna and Margaret sat at the table for the big midday meal.

It was a bright, sun-spangled day after two days of rain and Savanna felt fine. She had talked with Margaret and as a result Margaret's eyes were red-rimmed from weeping. She knew she had to go but she wished with all her heart she need not. She mourned constantly that she would never see James again.

"Maybe you will," Savanna said. "Maybe Bill will be killed on this scout." She did not mean to be brutal but her relief was so exquiste and keen she felt reckless.

"Oh, no, Savanna!"

"Well, sweet heaven, Margaret, it's the only way you'll ever be with James."

"But that would be to wish . . ."

"You don't know what you wish," Savanna said curtly. "You're so wishy-washy you just drift like a leaf on the Verdigris. You want James but you don't want Bill out of your way. How in the name of heaven do you think you're ever going to have James?"

Margaret's eyes brimmed again. She didn't know how all this had come about. She hadn't meant any harm. She only loved James so much. She didn't care whether she ever saw Bill again or not, but she couldn't bring herself to wish he would be killed. The idea itself shocked her. She didn't honestly know what she wanted except, wistfully, that everything would somehow turn out all right and she and James could be together again.

Widgie came flying through the door, his eyes rolling whitely. "Miss Savanna! De Duke done got out de pasture. Him an' dat mare mustang done knocked down de fence an' got clean away. Ain't no tellin' whur dey at."

"And what were you doing when they got away?" Savanna yelped at him. "You're supposed to watch the pasture!"

"I got to eat," the boy whimpered.

"Do you have to use your eyes to eat with?"

Great gobs of mud! There was no telling where the animals had got to. Abe had warned her yesterday the mare was in season. They wanted the Duke to cover her, but not this way. He could come to harm running free—cut himself, scratch himself, he might even break a leg. He would have to be found.

Savanna threw her napkin on the table. "I'll have to go with Preacher and McNulty, Margaret."

"Can I help?" Margaret said.

"You'd be in the way," Savanna said flatly. "Stay here with Kizzy. Widgie, come with me. I'm going to skin you one of these days."

"Yessum, Miss Savanna, yessum."

McNulty saddled Sal for her and for two hours she combed the woods methodically with the men. There was no trace of the horses. They had swum the river, then, and were headed for the prairies. This was what she had been fearing. "McNulty," she said, pulling up at the river bank, "you and Preacher work up the opposite bank and go at least ten miles in both directions onto the prairie. Don't come home until you find them. Abe will join you tonight."

"Yes, ma'am." McNulty touched his cap. "We'll find 'em, Miss Savanna. Don't you worry none."

She herself was bone weary and could do no more. "I'm going back to the house."

She watched until they had swum their horses across the

river, saw them deploy right and left, then she turned Sal toward home. Dear Lord, if it wasn't one thing it was another. Abe would be frantic. He prized the Duke more than any horse he had ever had. He would whip Widgie, too, unless she could intervene. She couldn't let the little light-skinned boy be snaked. He was too little and too young yet.

Tiredly she set herself to meet Abe's anger, and with resentment wondered why it was always she who had everything to face, everything to decide, everything to bear. How had it come about that all those close to her relied on her, expected her to carry their burdens? She only meant to carry her own but, she grimaced wryly, it looked as though if you carried your own they inevitably became intermixed with a hundred others. There were Preacher and Kizzy and Widgie for whom she would be responsible to her dying day; and old Parley down at the Falls, and McNulty and Margaret and her boy and, yes, she had to confess it, Abe. As strong as he was, he was not nearly as competent at earning their way as she. Without her management and her income they would have been reduced to living in the quarter on his sergeant's pay, and it was a mighty poor reduction. Those who would be free, she thought pensively, pay a pretty penny for it.

She rode into the barn lot, unsaddled the mare and turned her loose in the pasture. Angling across the yard to the front door she noticed a strange horse tied to the hitching rail. At almost the same moment she noticed the horse she heard Margaret scream, and as she came around the corner of the house she saw Margaret crouched in a fence corner where she had been hanging the baby's napkins on the rails to dry, her husband advancing on her.

Savanna had thought that if this moment came she would be scared witless. She had built up a dread of it until even to think of it made her ill. She had felt that if the time came to face Bill Felt her heart would fail her and her stomach would betray her. Nothing of the sort happened at all. Her eye took in Margaret, crouched and quailing, her ear heard Bill Felt's loud, threatening voice and, already exasperated, already out of sorts and hot and irked and weary, it was simply the final vexation. Her temper rose in a swift fury that drove her blindly and as fast as she could run to the fence corner. She would not have this. She was not going to have Bill Felt on her place badgering poor Margaret and shouting at her and threatening her. She would have him thrown off at once!

She screamed for McNulty, forgetting he wasn't there, and catapulted herself into Bill Felt's back, butting him off balance with her head. "Get out of here!" she screeched at him. "Get off my place! I won't have you here! Get on your horse and get out of this yard!" She went to flailing and kicking.

But Bill Felt was a very big man and the months at Towson had made him hard and very tough. He slapped her aside as if she had been a droning insect, a gnat or mosquito, a distraction perhaps but nothing to bother about. His big hand hit hard and she fell against the fence, brought up out of breath, a great pain racked across her side. She sobbed for air and hung onto the fence.

Margaret was cowering, her hands over her face, whimpering pleadingly, "Don't, Bill . . . please don't . . . please, Bill . . . please . . ." She was backed into the angle of the snake-rail fence and could retreat no farther.

He stood where he was, a great hulk of a man, swaying a little on his feet, his eyes fixed on his wife. He had grown quite brown during the summer; he looked leaner, the paunch of his stomach now gone. Savanna could not see his face and eyes, but she could see how taut his muscles were, stretching the cord of his shirt, bulging the thighs of his buckskins. He stood there, swaying like an angry bull, his arms hanging loosely, the hands flexing, tightening into balls, then loosening. The big head hung forward on the neck, the shoulders hunched up around it. They were immense shoulders, as blocky as an ox's. He took one step forward. "Take your hands down, Margaret," he said, his voice pitched very low now, deadly level and cold. "Take your hands down and look at me. Or can you look at the man you have cuckolded?"

He waited, but Margaret only sobbed. Suddenly the voice rose in a spiraling, frenetic snarl, lashed out at her. "I said take your hands down and look at me! Goddammit, do what I tell you!"

Margaret shuddered and dropped her hands. She could not yet open her eyes. She leaned faintly against the fence. "Open your eyes," Bill Felt commanded. "Open them before I slap them so far back in your head you'll never see again!"

Margaret's head went back against the fence post as though she could no longer hold it erect without help. Very slowly she opened her eyes. Savanna could not see what Margaret saw when her eyelids rose, but she could see Margaret's face change. It had worn dread and fright, but they were a normal dread and fear. Her face had been crumpled, like a child's, drained of color, the mouth drawn down pitiably. As Savanna watched, her breath still coming hard, she saw a mask of such horror and terror stiffen over Margaret's face that a deep and terrifying fear shafted through her own body. God in heaven, what did the man mean to do?

217

He took one more step forward, his hands clenching and unclenching, the big head and shoulders swaying angrily. "Now!" he said. "Now, tell me yourself what you have done. Tell me."

Margaret made no sound. Like someone charmed she stood against the fence, her eyes fixed on her husband. The horror and terror had frozen on her face. It was as though they had been permanently carved into it.

Bill Felt's big head was suddenly thrust forward. "Tell me!" he roared. "Henderson has already told me, but I am going to hear it from you."

Margaret stood unmoving. Even her eyes were now unmoving, fixed on her husband stark and staring.

Savanna's hand clutched the fence rail so hard the split wood bit into her palms. Henderson, of course! The young, vain, cheap, vaunting chatterbox and gossip. Why hadn't she persuaded the general to send Abe to intercept Bill Felt? Why had they left it to the general? Blind. Blind as bats! But why had the general told Henderson?

Bill Felt's voice went very soft suddenly, soft and gentle and persuasive. "Don't be afraid to tell me, Margaret. I know it all. You needn't be afraid to tell me all of it. Henderson knew it. He heard Savanna tell the general. He heard every word of it. He was in the next room and the door was open and your friend's voice carries very well. Henderson didn't miss a word. And he told me every word he heard. He thought I should know. And so I do know. But I want you to tell me yourself, Margaret. I am going to make you condemn yourself," his voice rose in the whining snarl again, "as the cheap, lying, fornicating whore you are! You are going to tell me or I will choke it out of you word by filthy word!" The voice softened horribly. "Then I'm going to kill you, Margaret, I'm going to kill you. With these hands," he lifted them up and shook them at her, the fists clenched tight, "with these hands I'm going to choke the last breath out of your bitch's body and Joyner's bastard will die with you!"

He rocked on his feet and dropped his hands. "And when I have done with you I'm going to kill your fine friend Savanna. I am going to break that proud neck of hers too. She's to blame for all my troubles. She began them—she and her damned Kentucky horse." The snarl rose again, and rose, and a cold wind blew across Savanna's neck and she felt the short hairs rise like the hackles of a dog. "Everything would have been fine if it hadn't been for her. I had my plans. I could have paid my debts. I could have held up my head. She ruined me. She ruined me." The man took a step forward and teetered

218

dangerously. "And now she has ruined you. You were a decent woman until you let her be your friend. *She* has ruined you—made a whore of you." His big arm chopped up and down suddenly. "And she did it to heap one more shame on me, one more disgrace." The rasping, snarling voice became cunning. "She thought I wouldn't know. She thought I wasn't clever enough to see what she was doing. She thought she could fool me. But she can't. Bill Felt is smarter than she thought he was and she hasn't fooled him at all. She isn't going to have her way in this. Her proud head isn't going to be proud much longer, for I'm going to break her neck and her proud head will hang as low as a dog's. Margaret! Look at me!"

The seeds of destruction, Savanna thought wildly—the seeds of destruction. Oh, David, David! The man was stark, raving mad! She had to do something. She had to find somebody to help! She slid a foot or two along the fence and then with horror she remembered there was nobody to find. There was only Kizzy in the house. They were three women at the mercy of a madman. McNulty and Preacher were ten miles away. She thrust her hand over her mouth to keep from screaming in her own swift terror.

Margaret swayed a little as her husband took one more step toward her and even from where she stood Savanna could see that the girl's eyes were slowly glazing. They looked as though she were being hypnotized. She looked exactly as she had that day she had stared so fixedly at the door, looking even then to see Bill Felt standing there. Savanna recognized the unseeing stare. Oh, God, Margaret couldn't answer him if she would, she thought—she's gone out of her mind again. I've got to do something. I've got to do something! What! What can I do? Help me, somebody! Please help me—mother—David—Abe —somebody come. McNulty—Preacher. Somebody, please, please come. Somebody, please come!

She wrenched her mind back from hysteria. There was nobody. There was nobody but herself, Savanna. Only Savanna.

Keeping her eyes fixed on his back, she began inching her way along the fence. Don't let him turn around. Make him keep looking at Margaret. Make him so intent on Margaret he doesn't think of me. Don't let him see me. Her hand felt the post. This was the end of one section of rails. The next section bent away from the house. Here she must leave the fence. Here she must make a dash for the house, the store, the gun in the store.

She took one stealthy step away from the fence. If Bill Felt turned the slightest degree he would see her. Don't let him turn. Don't let her feet make a sound. Quiet—quiet—one step and then another, one small step as quietly as a cat stepping on grass, and then another. Thank God Margaret had gone into a stupor. She couldn't give her away by looking startled. One step, one more step, another step, and still Bill Felt's voice raged on, now high and snarling, now low, soft, persuasive.

She was a dozen feet behind him now. Four more steps and there was a hedge of honeysuckle vines. Behind it was the path, and two dozen steps up the path was the door. Let her get safely behind the hedge. Let her get safely up the path. Let her get safely to the door. And let the gun be there. Even if it wasn't loaded, let it be there where McNulty kept it. She knew how to load it and she knew how to shoot it. Just let her get there safely and let her get her hands on the gun. Don't let McNulty have it with him!

Three steps, two steps, one step.

She was behind the hedge. She felt so weak and dizzy suddenly she thought she was going to collapse and her side hurt her so bad. The vines were tough and stout and she braced herself against them. Over them Bill Felt's voice was roaring again, mounting and mounting in raging hysteria. Savanna pushed away and peered through the vines. She dropped them, then, and ran, careless of noise, careless of pain, careless of everything but urgency. Bill Felt had come very near to Margaret. He was almost near enough to close his hands about her throat.

The bell on the door tinkled as Savanna fled through it. The gun! Ah, God be praised it was there, on the pegs by the door. She grabbed it down, made certain it was loaded, and sped back out the door and down the path. As she came from behind the honeysuckle vines again Margaret screamed—one long, wailing scream which was choked off into a terrible liquid gurgle. The gurgle was forced slowly, then more slowly, into silence.

Savanna lifted the gun and took careful aim. As she pulled the trigger she heard David's clear, distinct voice saying in her ear, the seeds of destruction—the seeds of destruction.

XXIV

She lay on her bed, propped with half a dozen pillows. She felt, she thought, pretty well considering it was the first day she had been allowed to put her feet to the floor in ten days. And it was so good to be dressed again. Savanna was like her mother. She could not abide a bed except for its natural purposes. She did not admit that illness was one of them.

Martha Short's knitting needles clicked and Piney Fowler's little rocker swayed easily, its small creak a counterpoint to the click of her needles.

This was not Martha's first visit since the tragedy.

She had come immediately, with Abe, and stayed three watchful days to see if any ill came of Savanna's fall against the fence. She had not left until she was certain the combination of shock and fall had worked no bodily injury except two broken ribs.

At first she and Kizzy had been sure the baby would be lost. They could not see how, after what Savanna had been through, it could live. When it did, when there was never the slightest sign of trouble, they agreed it must be the lustiest boy ever planted. "Ain't nothin' gwine shake him loose, now," Kizzy said. "If his maw shootin' a man an' gittin' two ribs busted doan drap him fum de limb, ain't nothin' gwine ha'm he. He gots a good, tight hold."

Savanna herself was proud of him.

More anxious than Kizzy or Martha during the three uneasy, watchful days, she had raged at herself for losing her head. Temper again. When was she ever going to learn to think coolly? It had been a lunatic thing to do—bolting in to fight Bill Felt physically—to risk hurt to herself or the child. She ought to have gone for the gun at once. But when she went into such a rage her mind always went light and white with heat and she had to strike out blindly. It was God's mercy she had only two broken ribs out of it.

"The mistake we made," Martha said, breaking the silence, "was in thinking Bill Felt was a gentleman."

Savanna punched a pillow higher under her head. "Nearly everything we did was a mistake, Martha."

"No." Martha Short shook her head, "No—not everything. Our concern was no mistake. Men laugh at women's instincts and women's intuitions, but our instincts were right and our intuition of trouble was right. We knew something had to be done. And if they didn't want us meddling, they should have done it. No. Everything we did was based on the assumption Bill Felt would behave like a gentleman. Any other officer would have called out young Joyner and killed him, and then he would have quietly sent his wife away and got himself transferred. Failing that, he might have killed himself. But we couldn't know Bill Felt would go berserk. How could we have known he hated you so much? Or what that fool Henderson's talebearing would do to him?"

"There were signs," Savanna said sadly. "I knew them. I knew them. But I am too heedless. I knew Bill Felt had never

221

liked me, and I knew that winning that race ruined him. David and Abe told me, afterward."

Martha looked up from her knitting. "Would you have let him win if you'd known before?"

Savanna's mouth set stubbornly. "You know I wouldn't. I had too much at stake myself. And I wouldn't know how to lose a horserace if I wanted to. I've been beaten, but never purposely. I run the best race I can. You know that, Bill Felt knew it, and everyone else knows it." Her hand hit flat against the patchwork quilt drawn over her knees. "I say if you can't stand the gaff you've got no business chancing being hooked. If Bill Felt couldn't afford to be licked, he shouldn't have risked it. What I should not have done though," she continued, "was to buy the horse from him. I am sorry I did that. That was pure greediness in me. He was a beautiful animal and I wanted him. But that was piling on too much. Margaret told me that would make him hate me. I laid on the last straw by buying the horse And got no good of him. He turned out to be an oat burner, which was about what I deserved. No. No, I wouldn't have thrown the race. My pride equaled his that day."

Martha stretched her knitting over her knees and smoothed it. It was a blanket for Savanna's baby. "I didn't think so. I didn't think so. Well," she added reflectively, "nobody's got a monopoly on pride. I wouldn't give a fig for a human being without it. And who's to say it would have turned out any better in the end?" She gathered up the white fleece and resumed knitting. "Something, some day, would have sent him mad anyhow very likely."

Savanna was moved to tell Martha the story of Bill Felt. It could not hurt him now and she knew it would go no further. "It was heedless of me to forget that story, Martha." She concluded, "It was another sign and another warning. I should have known that when he learned Margaret was in the family way by Joyner he would see his mother, the prostitute, in her. He must always have been dreadfully ashamed of his mother, perhaps hated her. Now, Margaret was following in her footsteps and Margaret had more power to shame and disgrace him than his mother ever had. Margaret was his wife."

"Do you think Margaret knew about his mother?"

"She never said. But I think she did. She said Bill would kill her. I think he may have told her something of her and that may have been when he warned Margaret he would kill her if she was ever unfaithful. I didn't believe that, either, when Margaret told me. I thought it was just more of her spinelessness. I never once was afraid he would come here with murder in his heart. I thought the worst he would do would be to rage at her, perhaps beat her if he could, and I meant to stop that before it could start. The greatest fear I had," she admitted wryly, "was for Abe, once I'd got Margaret here. I was terrified that Abe would be here if Bill came and would do something he'd be cashiered for. Heedless, heedless," she said, shaking her head, "that's me. I never think until it's too late."

It wasn't easy to live with the knowledge she had killed a man, insane though he was. It was still, ten long days later, a heavy burden to her. The memory of it was burned on her mind. She had raised the gun, taken careful aim at the broad, bull-like back, pulled the trigger, and in one second a living, breathing man had become a corpse. It still made her shudder. She was too realistic not to know the necessity had come to her door and she could have done nothing else, given the circumstances. But in spite of realism she had these morbid spells of guilt. If she hadn't done this—if she hadn't done that—if, if, if . . .

"Think no more of it than if he had been a mad dog," Abe told her roughly, "for that is what he was. Crazy and insane. It was the only way you could save Margaret's life and your own. When he had finished Margaret he meant to kill you. Didn't he say so? Didn't you hear him say so? He blamed you for everything. What else could you do?"

"Nothing," she agreed, "nothing. I had to do it. But, Abe, he fell so slowly. He stiffened at first and his hands flew up and then he twisted around a little. And his knees buckled and it looked as if he just sagged down a little bit at a time, so slowly, and it took so long for him to hit the ground. I thought . . ."

Abe's face was somber. "You thought men died instantly. Sometimes they do. Sometimes they don't." He gathered her hands into his. "Put it out of your mind. You did a brave thing. Margaret would have been dead in another five seconds. Would you rather it had been her?"

"Of course not. But it wouldn't have been I that killed Margaret."

"Yes, it would. If you could have saved her and didn't, out of squeamishness, it would have been you as much as if you'd pulled the trigger on her. Put it out of your mind. It's the only way you can live with it. It's what I've done all these years."

Savanna looked at him, her mind only slowly taking in what he had said.

He nodded. "I killed a man too. My own father. And I was big enough and strong enough that I might have done differently. I could have pulled him off my mother and beaten him to a pulp. But I killed him instead. I was tired of the brute. It wasn't safe to leave my mother alone and I simply wanted him dead and out of her way and mine."

Savanna drew a long breath. "That's when you joined the army?"

"Yes. My mother died of the beating he had given her. I expect she was dying when I killed him, though I didn't know it. Sometimes what you have to do, Savanna, is so ugly it leaves a scar, but if you haven't the guts to do it the scar would be bigger and uglier. I thought I was saving my mother's life, and you did save Margaret's. I would do it again and so would you. We aren't tender people, Savanna. We are gutsy and tough. We do what we have to do. And the scars don't maim us. You did what had to be done."

It was a comfort to know that was true, but she would be glad when the details faded, became less clear and distinct. She could still smell the smoke of the gun and it sickened her as it had that day. She had flung it down. The pain in her side had come sharp and stabbing and she bent like an old woman to ease it. She had walked toward Bill Felt and Margaret. She did not know if she had saved Margaret. When Bill's hands were loosed from the girl's throat she had fallen back against the fence and had slid down it into a sitting position, but her neck was strangely angled. Dully, Savanna thought it looked broken.

She went first to Bill and looked at him. There was yet no feeling except relief that he was no longer a threat. He lay on his back and his face was still bloated with anger, the color not yet faded. His eyes stared wide and menacingly. His mouth stretched over his teeth and they seemed bared like fangs. Savanna shivered. This was the face Margaret had looked into and from which she had retreated into mindlessness. Seeing it, even dead, Savanna thought it no wonder that Margaret had quietly lost her reason. It had been a blessing that she could.

Holding her side against the pain, Savanna knelt and listened for a heartbeat. There was no wound in the chest. She had aimed at the great, broad back, just under the shoulders. The bullet had thudded home and stayed there where it had been received. He was dead—fatefully, perhaps predestinatedly, but certainly irrevocably, dead. Bill Felt had come to the end of the sinuous, twisting, dark, desolate road which life had started him on in a whorehouse in a city alley.

Still numbed against any regret for her own part in bringing him to that end, she left him lying where he was and went to Margaret. As dull as her mind was and as badly as her side hurt she saw at once that Margaret's chest was rising and falling with regular intervals. She was not killed, then.

Savanna was suddenly and violently sick. She leaned her

head against the fence and let her stomach empty itself. When she had finished and again opened her eyes, Kizzy was beside her. The black woman braced her. "Whyn't you call me? Whyn't you yell fer Kizzy? You ain't in no shape to be skeered dis way."

Savanna made a gesture toward Bill Felt. "I killed him."

"I done see you did." Kizzy wasted no time on Bill Felt. "Miss Marg'ret ain't bad hurt. I done see dat, too. But is you? Whut he do to you?"

"Knocked me against the fence. I think maybe I've got some broken ribs, Kizzy. Help me get Margaret in the house."

"You ain't gwine he'p nobody. Ah git Widgie he'p me git Miss Marg'ret in de house. Ah gwine git you in de house fust an' git you in de baid. You got mebbe some'pin more broke dan ribs. Be lucky you doan drap dat chile."

It was the first time Savanna had thought of the possibility of injury to the child. She denied it instantly, for she could not harbor the thought. "No! It's just my side." But she went with Kizzy into the house and allowed herself to be put to bed, her feet raised on pillows higher than her head. "Wouldn't I hurt in my belly, Kizzy?"

"Dunno yit. Ain't gwine hurt none keepin' you feets up. You lay dere an' doan move. Ah gwine het up some salt an' put on yo' belly. Den I gits Miss Marg'ret to baid. Do, Lawd, two wimmens in de fambly way an' bofe liable to slip 'em."

When she had taken the precautions she knew how to take, Kizzy hunted out Widgie, hidden under the house, to help her with Margaret, with whom she took the same precautions. Coming back to Savanna later she said, "She be all right now. Ain't been knocked 'round none. She comin' 'round. Her th'oat right soah, but it be fine in a day or two."

Savanna nodded.

Margaret would have no memory of that shot. Her wandering mind had at least been spared that. She would not, all her life, have to carry with her the remembered sight of Bill Felt falling, dying, crumpling on the ground. A slow chill shook Savanna, then, uncontrollably. Kizzy brought blankets and piled them on and built a fire and still the chill shook her. Neither she nor Kizzy realized that it was reaction. Both were frightened, terrified, that it was the onset of miscarriage.

Kizzy poured hot tea down Savanna, put hot stones around her, warmed blankets and wrapped them about her, until the chill broke and she sweated. She felt sleepy then, but before she slept there was one more thing to be done. "Send Widgie for Abe."

Abe had to come, and he had to take Bill Felt away.

225

Later, when they could bear to talk about the entire thing, all of it, Abe had inserted the one note of humor in it. He told how Widgie, stuck like a small brown monkey on Sal's back, had come pounding into the cantonment yelling as though a band of Comanches was on his trail. Everyone on the post had come running out, each with his own alarms in his heart. Some had thought the Osages had taken to the warpath. Some had been certain fire had broken out in Savanna's store. Some had wondered if the Creeks had risen against the Cherokees. But none, no one at all, could have thought of what had actually occurred.

Only Abe guessed a little.

He was at the sutler's store, comfortable, a cud of tobacco in his cheek, talking idly with Fred Short. Hearing Widgie's yells, he was outside instantly, and seeing Widgie his mind went instantly to Bill Felt and a great current of fear ran through him. But fear was never paralyzing to Abe. It always, instead, made him act, and he ran to meet the boy now.

At about the same moment, the mare ran under some low-hanging limbs of a big elm tree and Widgie was raked off as cleanly as if a hand had scooped him from the saddle. When Abe reached him he was lying breathless on the ground. Abe had to pound air into his lungs before he could learn the boy's message.

Abe had come, bringing Martha, because Savanna's chill had scared Kizzy witless and Widgie was infected with his mother's fear. "Miss Savanna gwine slip de baby, my mam say. Say you come quick."

Kizzy had given Savanna a dose of laudanum and she was asleep when Abe and Martha got there. While she slept Abe put Bill Felt's body on the wagon, draped it with a blanket and took it to the cantonment where he had somberly related to the general as much as Kizzy had told him of the events.

When Savanna roused, much later, Martha Short had found the broken ribs and bound Savanna's chest tightly, hoping a sharp end had not punctured a lung, hoping the child had not been killed by the fall.

At the end of three days, when it became apparent that the ribs had done no internal injury and that the fall had not harmed the child, Martha went home. Kizzy could deal with Savanna's discomfort and keep her in bed until the ribs had healed. Martha came back every day or two, however, to help while away the idle hours.

And other people came, amazingly kind, rallying around her—Talahina, Auguste Chouteau, Hugh Love, old Parley Wade, Preacher Chapman and his wife. Preacher Chapman brought good wishes from the entire mission and some of their late fall apples which were so crisp and cold and juicy.

General Arbuckle came and stood by her bed and held her hand. He was so grieved, so terribly grieved and he felt himself so much at fault. "I should have listened to you sooner. I should have acted much more quickly. Savanna, if you had been harmed I should never have forgiven myself."

She took some comfort from his words and much comfort from his concern.

Even the women she disliked most at the post had come —Esther Hammond, Ann Haverty, Susan Cleet—though instinctively Savanna felt they came out of curiosity rather than friendliness. For of course the entire country knew the truth now. Henderson was incapable of holding his tongue and having with its looseness, its avid necessity to wag, set into motion the train of tragic events he had to salve his conscience by sharing the enormity of his private knowledge.

Though they brought peace offerings in the way of soup and pies and cakes they wanted to see how Savanna bore herself, having killed a man. And they wanted to see Margaret. They wanted to see how a woman who had been unfaithful to her husband and was going to bear another man's child carried herself when she had caused his death.

There had been so many who had caused his death, and they not the least among them. Watching them in her room Savanna wanted to tell them so. She wanted to say to them—you, too, are guilty. With your cruel tongues and your stiff-necked virtues and your self-righteousness, you are like vultures. You don't frighten me. I have never been afraid of you. But men like Bill Felt and women like Margaret Felt are terribly afraid of women like you. And with reason. You, and your husbands who cannot control you, can drive pride to shame, anger to murder, and fearfulness to insanity.

She would not let them see Margaret. Let them see her instead. Let them wonder how it felt to kill a man. But they would not lick their eyes over Margaret. Nor would she discuss Margaret except to say she was recovering rapidly though not yet able to leave her room. She took an astringent satisfaction in thwarting them.

Margaret had recovered, less rapidly than Kizzy had predicted, but with no real difficulty. Her neck was badly bruised and the white skin was patched with blue and purple and brown spots. She had trouble swallowing for several days but that slowly passed too. What was most encouraging was that her mind was clear again. But Abe was convinced it was the shallowest, the flightiest mind he had ever known.

When he thought her well enough to hear the truth he had told her and she had wept a little. "Poor Bill. Poor Bill." But her tears had dried quickly in a following thought. "Now I can marry James!"

She had made no secret of her joy. Not once did the enormity of what she had caused mar the vapid innocence which was her childish guard against the world. She did not blame Savanna, but neither did she enter at all into the necessity into which Savanna had been thrust. She felt no guilt. She was sorry Savanna was ill. Was she feeling better? Could she go downstairs and visit her? Could she help care for her?

"No," Abe said, feeling an abrupt revulsion for the girl. "Just leave her alone. You've done her enough harm."

But that, too, was beyond her comprehension. She? Harmed Savanna? She only loved Savanna. How could she have brought her harm?

On the fifth day, when Savanna was free of pain unless she moved too suddenly, young Joyner came. The general, he said, had sent for him.

Savanna was appalled at his appearance. Where he had been a well-padded young man, his face round and smooth, he was now almost as lean as Abe, as brown, and the face was gaunt and sallow. His eyes were sunk deep in their sockets as though he had not slept for a month. His mouth trembled when he tried to speak and he had to make the greatest effort to bring out the stumbling, halting words he could manage. He was sorry—so sorry—but he hadn't known. She knew that, didn't she? He would not have gone away on field duty had he known.

"Of course you wouldn't," Savanna said. "Nobody blames you, James. Except," she added, "for being so foolish."

"Yes. Yes, I was that, Savanna. I find it hard to pardon myself for it. But I . . . I . . ."

Savanna could not hold resentment against him. He had been silly and irresponsible, but he was young and it had been for love's sweet sake. "I know," she said, "you couldn't help it."

Joyner moved his feet restlessly, hung his head so as not to meet her eyes. "Well, I could have . . . any man can, I guess. But I—well, I didn't."

"Oh, James, it's done. And now you'll have to mend it. Recriminations will get you nowhere. You want to see Margaret, don't you?"

"If I may."

Savanna laughed. "If you may! She has been expecting you every day. It's a wonder she didn't see you riding up and come tearing out to meet you. Her room is on the right at the top of the stairs. Knock first. She's in the habit of napping in the afternoon and she may not be dressed." Savanna's eyes sparkled. "You may prefer her that way, however."

The slow color rose in the boy's face then receded, leaving the skin sallow and jaundiced. Without a word, he went out.

Savanna thought the lovers would have so much to say to each other they would be closeted for hours, but Joyner returned shortly, Margaret clinging to his arm, beaming radiantly. "Oh, Savanna, the most wonderful thing has happened! James is going to take me home! We are leaving on the next steamer. Oh, I did so dread the journey alone. I knew you and Abe would make me go and I didn't know *how* I would manage with all those trunks and boxes and little Billy. All those changes to make—boats and stages. But James is going with me. I can't quite believe it yet." She squeezed his arm and looked up at him, her happiness bubbling and glowing.

Savanna darted a quick, questioning look at the boy.

He nodded. "The general . . . has suggested that I accompany Margaret east."

Something was wrong. Margaret was radiant, but Joyner was plainly not happy. His face wore a haunted look, a deathly defeated look. There was no relief, or joy, or love, or serenity on it. His eyes were burned holes in a strained, parchment skin. Savanna had the quick fear that he did not, after all, love Margaret. In this testing perhaps he was learning that what he had thought was love was simply a gawky, adolescent infatuation and he was dismayed at a future which must include Margaret.

She put the thought down quickly. He was tired. Of course he was tired and he had been terribly shocked, and he was so honest he had blamed himself, perhaps, out of all proportion. And he may have had, too, a bout with the intermittent. No need making a bugbear out of the way he looked. She said swiftly, "How kind of the general. Margaret would have had a miserable journey alone. Will you be able to stay long enough to see her through . . ." She shifted ground quickly, "Will you be able to see her settled?"

Joyner's full girlish mouth quivered. He moistened his lips. "I think . . . it . . . yes, very likely."

Margaret squealed. "James! You didn't tell me! Oh, you'll be with me when the baby comes! Darling, darling!" She flung herself on him.

Above Margaret's head Savanna saw him close his eyes and the look of terrible, desperate grief which settled over his face horrified her. He could no longer contain it. He could no longer hide it. As she watched, two slow tears slid from be-

229

neath the covering eyelids and trembled on the cheekbone, then taking a crooked furrow to the mouth were absorbed. A great shudder ran over his frame, but almost immediately he controlled it. He gently put Margaret aside, kissed her lightly, and left without saying another word. Something is dreadfully wrong, Savanna thought, dreadfully, dreadfully wrong.

XXV

She learned what was wrong that night.

David Holt came.

Savanna's first feeling was one of shrinking from seeing him. She couldn't bear it if David went into one of his broody, reflective moods and began pondering fate and seeds of destruction again. Those words were branded on her mind now.

But he was bouncing with the health and energy these hunts always renewed in him. His head was bushy with his uncut hair, and amazingly he had shaved off his beard. Savanna stared at him unbelievingly. "When did you do that?" Why, he was a handsome man without all that brush of hair on his face. You could see the shape of his chin and his jaw, and his mouth was just plain sweet. Lord, Lord the things men did to themselves.

He had done it, he told her, the first day of the hunt so his face would brown over evenly and he wouldn't look like a whitefaced clown. "Do you like it?"

"Well, of course I like it. You have no idea what an improvement it is. I've always wondered what you were hiding."

"Thought maybe I had a harelip, eh? Or no chin. Just laziness, Savanna, just laziness. I hate to shave."

She kept watching him across the room. She felt as though she were looking at a newly discovered person. He was David, but he was David in a new dimension.

He made no comment on the tragedy save to berate her soundly for breaking two ribs in her delicate condition. Didn't she know she might have lost the baby? And he wanted to see those ribs at once. Very likely they hadn't been set properly and she would be lopsided the rest of her life. And had there been any sign of trouble? Had she had any pain? Had there been tenderness here and here—any tinge of blood? He had come, he said, the instant he returned. Fine patient she was, knocking herself about the moment he wasn't there to see to her.

He took her breath away. "Fine doctor you are," she jeered, beginning to enjoy him, "going off on your own pleasure at such a time."

"It saved my life," he said, twinkling, "it quite literally saved my life. I was perishing at the hospital. And I brought you something."

Savanna shoved up on her pillows and winced immediately. "Oh, drat these ribs. What? What did you bring me?"

"A white buffalo robe."

Abe looked at him quizzically. "You didn't find an albino buffalo in the mountains, David."

"No," David laughed. "I sure didn't. I've not been anywhere near the mountains."

"Let him tell where he's been after I've seen the robe, Abe," Savanna said impatiently. "I want to see it. I've never seen a white skin."

It wasn't actually white—it was more the color of rich cream, but David told her it would bleach if she put it out in the dew and the sun. Albino buffaloes were so rare that few white men ever saw one in an entire lifetime of hunting. Indians believed they were sacred and an Indian would not kill one. But David had stood in no awe, knowing the cause of the lack of coloration. "When I saw him," he said, "I thought of what a fine rug he'd make for the boy to play on."

"Savanna will never let him play on it," Abe said, grinning, "she'll be afraid he'll puke on it."

"Oh, go boil your head," Savanna said. "It will wash, won't it?"

When she had finished admiring the skin Kizzy took it away, for the smell was still strong and musky.

The men ate, and away from Savanna said what was in their minds and hearts to say about the tragedy. "She's taking it well?" David asked of Savanna's part.

"Pretty well," Abe said. "She had a spell of blaming herself right hard. But that's about passed."

"Yes. Yes, she would do that. But she's got a healthy body and a healthy mind. She's too sensible to brood long. Savanna," he said, chuckling, "has a precious gift of being able to forgive herself."

This was a little profound for Abe but he trusted David Holt and his long knowledge of Savanna. If David said it was a precious gift, it was a precious gift and it was Savanna's good fortune to possess it. "Did she come to any harm, David? I'm still a little uneasy about that."

"The baby? No. None at all." And David said almost precisely what Kizzy had said. "That one has got a good tight hold and will hang on till his time comes. No need to worry about him."

Kizzy warned them that Savanna was growing restless and

wanted their company in her room.

Abe did not yet know, for he had come with David, that young Joyner had been that day. Savanna told him. She repeated what Joyner had told her. "So I suppose that ends the whole affair," she said. "They leave on the next packet. When is it due?"

"The day after tomorrow," Abe said.

"Oh, good heavens! Margaret will never be ready."

"Oh, yes, she will," Abe said sharply. "I mean to see to that. I want that young woman out of your life and out of mine. She'll be on that boat as sure as God made sour apples."

They laughed at his determination.

Then Savanna said, "Poor James is not very happy about it. He looked really dreadful. He looked miserable about it, actually. I would have thought he would be relieved that she is free now. It was shocking to see him."

The laughter fled from David's eyes and they looked sad. "He has good reason to be miserable. The general asked for his resignation. The boy is through in the army."

"Oh, no!" The hurt shocked all through Savanna. "Why, the army was his whole life. He loved the service. Why, that means his entire career is finished. Oh, what good does that do? What on earth made the general do it?"

"Well, by God," Abe said explosively, "if you can't see it you're stupid, Savanna. The old man is right. If a man can't control himself how can he be trusted to control other men. Joyner was an officer. In the natural course of things he could expect promotion. Someday he would rate a field command and men's lives would depend on him. If he couldn't command himself what good would he be in a pinch? The old man fumbles around sometimes but he knows what kind of officers we've got to have out here. He was dead right!"

Savanna was silenced.

They were right—the general and Abe—of course they were right. But she could not help feeling that young James Joyner was a lamb sacrificed on the altar of the frontier.

David's comment was as near as he came that night to being reflective. "One man killed. One man's career broken. One woman's peace of heart endangered. Out of it all has come one shallow girl's happiness which may or may not endure and whose worth is entirely questionable." The full, rumbling voice broke a little. "The ways of the Lord are indeed mysterious, aren't they?"

XXVI

On the evening of the fifth of April, the day before her twenty-second birthday, Savanna ate heartily and hugely of Kizzy's good supper—a roast fowl, boiled beans, new spring onions and fried johnnycakes. "You're going to bust," Abe told her, looking at her heaped plate.

"Then I'll bust," she said. "I'm perishing. I'm always hungry these days."

Kizzy, passing the hot bread, chuckled. "Dat boy tek de most ob it. Miss Savanna jus' git whut's left."

Savanna's time was almost due.

She and Kizzy had figured it would fall between the sixth and the sixteenth. In the past month she had become enormous. She was swaybacked with the jutting child and she waddled like a duck when she walked. Hoisting herself out of a chair she heaved and puffed.

"My God," Abe said, "you look like a steam packet pushing a scow!"

Savanna stuck her tongue out at him, patted her bulge lovingly and said, "That's a boy I'm making for you."

None of them doubted the child would be a boy and Abe and Savanna had had many arguments about a name for him. Savanna wanted to call him Abraham, but Abe would have none of it. "It's been burden enough for me," he said, "I won't saddle another kid with it."

They had finally settled on John Cassius, for Savanna's favorite uncle, Johnny Fowler, and for her grandfather Cartwright. She knew her uncle very slightly and her grandfather not at all, but she had heard much of both and her ignorance of them only increased her admiration. She felt strongly this boy should bear an illustrious name. Abe had no objection.

Savanna loved this supper hour when Abe came home from the cantonment and shared with her whatever news he had learned through the day. She looked forward to it all day and was like a child watching out the window when the time neared. If Abe was late she was petulant, so he took care to come home, as nearly as he could, exactly on time.

Just now the entire countryside was buzzing with news from Washington about Sam Houston.

Having been balked of his Texas scheme by General Arbuckle, Houston had appeared to disintegrate gradually before the very eyes of the country. Always a heavy drinker, he was now never entirely sober. He drifted aimlessly about the country, buttonholing whomever he could find to listen to talk about various grandiose plans—an expedition to the Rocky Mountains—a trading station on the prairies—a return to Tennessee to storm the political circles again—but he was brushed off by all. Often his horse came home without him nowadays and the faithful Talahina would ride out to find him. He could be seen lying beside the road where he had fallen many mornings and it spoke for the contempt in which he was held that few would take the time to help him home. Even his most loyal friends, the Cherokees, fell away from him and in ridicule called him the Big Drunk.

It was a sad and sorry sight.

Then he had once again made his way to Washington. What had happened in that city was a seven-day wonder. Hearing that Senator Stansbery had made discrediting remarks about him, Houston accosted the man on the street and had beaten him with his cane. He had then been held for trial by the Senate. The Territory had waited with unconcealed interest for the results of the trial.

"Acquitted," Abe told Savanna at the supper table. "And he is the President's darling again."

"Texas," Savanna said, "move over and make room for Sam Houston. You think he'll bother to come back to the Territory, Abe?"

"Well, there's Talahina," Abe said, "and his property . . . sure he'll come back."

Savanna leaned forward. "But he'll not take an Indian out of here. The general said he would see to that. I'll bet you a new suit of buckskins to a buffalo robe if he comes back here he'll ride away alone. Not Talahina or even a body servant with him."

Abe shrugged. "No bet. The general has crocked him with the Indians."

"David said what Sam Houston wanted was an empire."

"He's got some ideas about what Andrew Jackson wants, too."

"What's that?"

"Texas."

Savanna's eyes grew thoughtful. "Well, David was right about the expedition. Does he think the President is going to let Sam Houston take Texas for him now?"

Abe pushed his chair back. "No. He thinks Jackson will send Houston to Texas as his personal representative now—to feel out the ground. And David says that some day, when the Texas rebellion comes, Sam Houston will be on the Rio

Grande flapping his wings and crowing right along with the rest of them."

Many years later Savanna was to remember David's prediction, for Sam Houston was on the Rio Grande and he did flap his wings and crow mighty big.

She was uncomfortable from the big meal and went to bed early. Around midnight she wakened Abe. "I've got a dreadful bellyache, Abe."

Abe rolled over only half awake and mumbled. "You ate enough to make a horse have the bellyache."

"I was hungry. *Do* something, Abe!"

"What the hell can I do? It's your belly."

"Heat some salt and put it in a bag. Maybe that would help."

Grumbling, Abe crawled out of bed. Only when he was standing on his feet did it occur to him this might be more than a common bellyache. "Hey," he said, "reckon it's your time?"

"Light a candle," Savanna snapped at him.

He fumbled about and got his pants on, went for a coal from the kitchen fire and lit the candle on the bedstand. He and Savanna both looked at her prominent bulge as if it should tell them something. "Don't look any different," Abe said. His face was suddenly scared-looking. "How's it supposed to commence?"

"With a bellyache, Kizzy says. You'd better call her."

"And go for David."

"You're afraid," Savanna accused, laughing. "You're afraid this boy's coming and you'll have to catch him."

"Not with Kizzy here," Abe said.

Kizzy questioned Savanna and learning the pain was almost constant rolled her eyes. "Do, Jesus, Mistah Abe, you ain't gwine hab time to git de doctah. Dat boy on his way an' 'bout to git heah."

Abe was alarmed. "I'm going, anyhow."

Savanna, who was clinging to Kizzy's hands, threw him an impatient look and said, pantingly, "Bosh! Kizzy and I can manage this."

Abe was stubborn. "I'm going."

"Well, go, then! Just get out of here and let us get on with it!"

When he and David Holt arrived an hour and a half later Savanna was propped up on her pillows eating soup. "You're too late," she accused them, waving the spoon at them. "There they are."

"They?" Abe said stupidly.

Kizzy bustled in, cackling with relieved, hysterical laughter. "Yassuh—Miss Savanna done got twins. She done brung two

235

boy chillen. Ain't she de beatin'est in de worl'?" She threw back the white shawl Martha Short had knitted. "Dere dey is! Two de fines' boy babies I evah seed."

David came forward and peered at them, then he whooped joyously. "Well, by God! Savanna always has done things bigger and better than anyone else. She wasn't satisfied with one youngun. She had to get two at one whack!"

"Twins," Abe mumbled, still too astounded to take it in.

Savanna leaned back against her pillows. "And no trouble at all. Kizzy will tell you. Not more than an hour to bring them both."

She was immensely proud of herself. Her face was glowing and she reflected an opulent satisfaction. Not only had she and Abe produced a youngling nine months to a day from their wedding, but they had stolen a march on every married couple in the country and produced two. Let that record stand until it could be matched!

David wanted to see to Savanna but she wouldn't have it. "Kizzy and I took care of everything. I'm fine."

"But, Savanna . . ."

"Fiddlesticks. I've helped my mares when they foaled, and the cows, and what I didn't know Kizzy did. I won't have you fumbling around."

Helpless, David laughed. "Just so. There's nothing you can't do, is there?" He turned to Abe. "Since we aren't needed here perhaps we'd better adjourn to the other room and fortify ourselves with a few drinks. If we drink enough perhaps we can forget how lowly and unnecessary the males of this world actually are."

Abe pushed up to the bed and looked at the infants. "Twins," he said, shoving wildly at his hair. "By God, two of 'em! No wonder you looked like a steam packet pushing a scow. Where'd they find the room?"

David shook his head. "I'd say they weigh near eight pounds each. Lord, Savanna, you do the damndest things."

Savanna beamed at them both, then she cut a look at Kizzy and winked. "That Mister Abe," she murmured.

Kizzy's grin stretched to her ears. "Yessum. Ain't he de ring-tailed coon?"

The sun broke in the window and slanted a beam across Savanna's bed—a rich, mellow, domestic beam. In its light both babies stirred.

"Which one came first?" David asked.

"This one." Savanna touched the thick-thatched, black-headed one.

"Wouldn't you know?" the surgeon grinned. "Bet he's going

236

to be just like his mother, always pushing and shoving."

"He's John Cassius," Savanna said. "And this one," touching the sandy-haired boy, "is David Abraham."

"No." A look of pain swept across David Holt's face. "No, I can't allow it, Savanna. Don't crock the boy with my name."

"Nor mine," Abe said just as staunchly. "I've already told you that."

"But I want to," Savanna wailed, "I want him named for the two of you."

Neither man could be moved, though she stormed and blustered and even wept.

In the end, days later, she named the child Matthew Arbuckle, quickly explaining the Matthew was for her father—the general couldn't have the whole honor.

It turned out that the names Savanna was so proud to give them were not very important, for in the way of families the world over diminutives were soon created and all their lives the Lathrop twins were to be known as Jonce and Buck, until in the mists of time they themselves forgot they had ever been given any others.

XXVII

For Savanna, caught up in the demands of her babies, her home, her business operations, days blurred and the weeks and even months merged until they had little meaning for her. She only knew that Jonce was hungry or Buck was weeping; that Jonce had the sniffles and Buck had a rash; that Jonce had cut a tooth and Buck had cut two. She would not have believed that babies could be so demanding. She was proud of her swollen breasts, which provided all the milk the boys required, but she was sometimes vexed at the time it took.

"If they'd just nurse at the same time," she fumed at Abe, "but no, they're never hungry together. It's first one then the other until I feel as though all I do is sit and let a youngun tug at me."

"Get a wet-nurse," Abe said. "Martha knows a Creek girl . . ."

But Savanna would have none of that. "I'll raise my boys myself," she said crisply.

"Then quit fussing about it," Abe advised.

Nagging at the back of her mind, also, were her business problems. She was deeply concerned about the trade in the home store. With slow, strangling persistence Auguste Chouteau was squeezing the Creek trade away from her. She had never had as much of it as she had hoped when she chose her location. And on her other side, Talahina kept a fast hold on the Cherokee trade.

To make it worse, the drop-off from the post which she had noticed when she and Abe were first married continued. During the time she was heavy with the twins it had become so pronounced as to alarm her. And now, now that she was not only married but a mother, the trade from the cantonment had become almost infinitesimal. Where once the big room had been packed every night, now only a handful of the faithful gathered and occasionally, once or twice a week, it was wholly empty. It frightened her and she fumed at Abe about this, too. "They were glad enough to come when I wasn't married."

"Maybe you shouldn't have married."

"Maybe I shouldn't," she snapped at him.

Later she amended this. "Seriously, Abe, why should it matter? They never made trouble for me, not even the enlisted men. They came here and drank a little wine and played cards a little, spent their money, made no difficulty for me. Why should it matter that I'm married now and have two children? What difference does it make to them? Not a one of them wanted to marry me. Not a one of them tried to make love to me. I can't understand it."

Nor could Abe, who shrugged it off.

It was David who tried to explain it to her. "It's just human nature, Savanna. Perhaps they didn't make love to you, but you were a widow. There was no man in your life. You were pretty, you were not married, and though some of them were married themselves I expect it gave them a feeling of mild roistering, maybe fired their sense of rebellion against their wives and their own dull and duped selves, to ride over here to a young widow's for the evening. Now you've got not only a man but two boys. Whatever you made them feel is gone. You're just another trader now and you don't offer them as much as the others do."

"Are you proposing I should keep girls here for them? Is it your intention I should sell whiskey here?"

"Naturally not," David said. "I'm just trying to tell you the way the men feel now."

"But what am I to do, David?" she cried. "Only the fact that Parley Wade still makes money for me at the Falls is keeping me going."

David stirred uneasily. "Shouldn't Abe advise you on matters like this?"

"Oh, Abe." She dismissed her husband with a shrug. It was eloquent of a small disenchantment. "Abe has no more

238

business head on him than the twins. He'd only say do what you want, it's your affair."

"I expect," David said, making a steeple of his fingers, "you've reminded him of that often enough."

"Well, of course I have. Nobody can run my affairs for me."

"But you're asking my advice now."

"Oh, well, David, you're different. You're . . . you're . . ."

"Never mind," the surgeon said, wincing. "Savanna, your stocks are pretty badly run down."

"I know it. But I have no money."

"Why don't you borrow on the store at the Falls?"

"Go in debt?" She was instantly horrified. "God's britches, David, do you have any idea what debt has always done to me? Didn't the boys and I work our fingers to the bone to pay off father's debt? And didn't Thomas's debt nearly worry the life out of me? You must be out of your mind to suggest such a thing. My stores are clear and they're going to stay that way."

"But you can't do business without goods. You're enough of a businesswoman to know that."

"Oh, I do know it—and I'll manage somehow. I'll move some of Parley's goods. I'll find a way."

When David had gone she sat before the fire and brooded. Wearily and a little sadly she had to confess she had not chosen a location as well as she might. And not the least of her regret was the fact that she had gone against the counsel of men who had her good at heart. She had been warned it was not a good location. But in her usual strong-willed way she had disregarded their counsel. She thought now she might better have listened to General Arbuckle and David.

What it amounted to was that the home store had become little more than a home. She had principally to depend for trade on travelers on the Road and they were chancy. Their income, for it never occurred to her to put any reliance on Abe, came from the store at Crown Falls and it was only God's mercy that Parley Wade continued to provide them with a profit from that store. She prayed that nothing would happen to him or the store. What *would* they have done if she had listened to Abe and sold it? They would have been living in want, and many months they came perilously near it anyhow. She kept it a careful secret from Abe that the last time she had gone to the Falls she had been shot at. He would have instantly made her quit going, and without her careful hand old Parley might fail her too.

Abe's pay was a pittance. It barely provided feed for his string of horses which it never occurred to him to give up. To Savanna's credit it never occurred to her either. Abe was her

239

husband. She did not question what he wanted. Though she was sometimes vexed that he took no responsibility for their living, she tried to keep a firm check on any resentment. She managed this capably enough unless she was weary and worried. Then she did wish she could transfer some part of her heavy load to his shoulders. It would have slipped off like water sliding over a dam, she knew, so she never tried it.

Her difficulties pressing her that year she lent only half an ear to the events occurring about her. Almost uninterested she learned that Captain Bonneville had finally left on his Rocky Mountain expedition in May. The twins were little more than a month old and she was still obsessed by them. "He left from Fort Osage," Abe told her.

Vaguely she wondered if in those vast distances to the west he might meet with Manifee and she wished, a little, she had given him a message before he left Gibson.

When Union Mission closed its school a few weeks later she felt some regret but not much. The school had never attracted Osage children as the missionaries had hoped it would, as Dwight had attracted Cherokees, and in its twelve years of existence had boarded only a meager total of one hundred and fifty-four children. What regret she felt was for the teachers who had struggled so valiantly for so long and with so little sympathy from the white settlers. She heard they were moving up the Osage Trail to Harmony.

When Sam Houston returned from Washington in the summer she pricked up her ears and was delighted when the general, stopping one day as he returned to the cantonment from Three Forks, told her that Houston would soon be leaving the country. Dryly the old man said, "He has a personal commission from the President to represent him in Texas. I am to issue him a passport when he has wound up his affairs."

"Always Texas," Savanna said, laughing.

"Always Texas," the general agreed. "But he leads no expedition. In fact he goes entirely alone. Not one person shall go with him."

"Not even Talahina?"

"My dear," the old man said, smiling, "I don't think Sam Houston wants Talahina to go with him. She has served her purpose."

Savanna was glad to see the last of the gaunt, hard-drinking, brooding Sam Houston. As was the entire country. Texas, they all said, could have him. Savanna felt sorry of Talahina who, gossip said, was prostrate with grief at being abandoned. Houston, who had used her to his own ends, was not quite heartless enough to leave her helpless. He gave her what he could—the land he had come by, which was Cherokee land anyhow; the home he had built; the stock; what was left of his trading goods; and his black people. He left her, the country had to admit, better off, save for her broken heart, than he had found her. When he rode south to the border he took with him, as the general had promised, no one. He had only a change of clothing and one horse—a bobtailed nag which he rode.

Elias Rector, a fine Arkansas gentleman from Fort Smith, met him on the Choctaw Road and reported later that Houston cut such a sorry figure on his bob-tailed nag that he persuaded him to change steeds. Rector said he had not wanted anyone to leave Arkansas looking so ridiculous. It might, he thought, reflect on the Territory's hospitality!

And that was the end of Sam Houston in Indian Territory.

XXVIII

Savanna was startled out of her own preoccupation when Abe came home one day in September with word that a regiment of Rangers had reported to General Arbuckle that day.

"Rangers?" she asked. "What are they?"

"Mounted troops. They're the Arkansas Mounted Rangers. They were recruited for the Blackhawk War but the war's over so they were ordered to report to Gibson."

"Well, upon my word and honor!" In Savanna's experience only officers were mounted, and scouts, of course. A mounted regiment was something new under the sun. "What's the general going to do with them?"

"Use them for details on the prairies."

"What does the Regiment think of them?" The Regiment, naturally, was the Seventh Infantry.

"Don't like 'em. They're the funniest crew you ever saw, Savanna. Not a uniform in the crowd. Just wear whatever they've got—mostly buckskins. Don't know the first thing about drill or formation. Just a ragtag and bobtail bunch Jesse Bean picked up. Mostly loafers and no-goods, I expect, but man they can shoot, and they can ride. And they're mounted. They got good horses."

Savanna caught the note of envy. Though he was loyal to the Seventh, Abe off a horse was only half a man. "You mean," she said, "they're going to be Regular Army? Is the Army going to have a mounted corps?"

"Seems as though." Abe sighed regretfully. "Sort of wish I could transfer to them. David is."

"You can't mean that. I don't believe it. David is too loyal to the Seventh."

"Don't you believe it. He doesn't owe the Seventh anything. He's not even Army. Besides, they've not done too well by David. He's had a Post Surgeon's job at an Assistant's pay. A lot of work and very little money. He don't feel any special loyalty. And you know how he loves to lope that nag of his across the country. Surgeon to the Rangers is a job hand-made for David. He can see to their health and get his fill of traveling and hunting at the same time. Anyway, he's resigned and applied for the post with the Rangers. And," he chuckled, "the general couldn't be madder with him."

"Oh, Lord, he'll send him to Coventry."

"No, he won't. He can't. David's a civilian. Lord, I wish my enlistment was up."

"Abe, you don't know what you're saying! You've been with the Seventh since your first enlistment."

"Which may be too long."

"Oh, sweet heaven, men are such fools. You're Army, Abe, you're Army! Would you throw that away?"

"Like a shot—if I could join the Rangers."

"I don't know what's got into you."

She felt bewildered. She had taken it as a basic premise that any future Abe had lay with the Seventh. But here he was willing to barter it away. "The Rangers may not last," she warned him. "They're here apparently because nobody knew what to do with them. They may be disbanded tomorrow. The Seventh is here to stay. It's had a splendid past. It will always have a future. I don't know what's got into you."

"Savanna, you're just more of a man with a horse under you. I've been lucky. I've scouted, so I've ridden where other men have walked. But if the Army is going to mount regulars there won't be a man wouldn't rather be in a mounted company than on foot. They'll flock to it. If they're going to mount regulars, it won't be any time till the Infantry's the stepchild of the whole army. I don't want to be a stepchild. In the past, only an officer was mounted. The rest slogged along on foot. Don't you see that if the men are going to be mounted too it's a real step up for them? Cavalry, Savanna, cavalry. I've heard of the cavalry regiments in Europe, but we've never had cavalry in the United States Army. This is the first. There won't be a man that won't want to join up with them. Just to get a horse under him. Just to get up out of the mud and the dirt and the slogging on foot. How do you think a man feels standing up to his knees in mud when an officer rides by? Great God, Savanna, every man who ever knew the feeling of a horse between his legs will want to join up with the Rangers!"

Nothing more was said of it, for Abe's enlistment was up not until December of the following year, but it stuck like a burr in Savanna's mind. It was just one more thing, one more nagging, prickling uncertainty with which to cope. She didn't want him to leave the Regiment but if the Rangers were still at Gibson when his enlistment was up, she was certain he would. She prayed they would be disbanded and tried to forget it.

The entire country was alarmed and disturbed about this time, also, by the general's failing health. Gossip had it that he was going to retire soon—as soon as he could be replaced. Gibson without General Matthew Arbuckle? It was unthinkable. So accustomed had the Territory become to the tall stooping old figure, the patient, far-seeing, kind, friendly old man, that they were thrown into dismay by the very idea his hand might no longer be on the reins that guided them.

And the Army was capable of sending anybody. They might send a man no one could get along with. The Indians would be certain to be restless and hard to manage. But undeniably his health was bad. He had asthma, recurring bouts of the intermittent fever, and his ancient enemy, the gout, pestered him constantly now. Wheezing and shaking his head he admitted he ought to retire. "Ought to let some young fellow take over," he said, "I'm no good to the country or my people any longer."

But he was so beloved no one quite believed him and all urged him to stay his hand. Wait a year, they advised him. Don't be hasty. Your health may improve. "But my age will not," he said, sadly.

His retirement hung over them like a threat.

In October of that year, 1832, there was a stir of excitement when there arrived at the post some travelers from the east. They indentified themselves to the general as Henry Ellsworth, a commissioner appointed by the President to look into Indian affairs with the hope of inducing the Plains Indians to move into the Territory, and his guests Washington Irving, a young Swiss nobleman, Count Pourtalès, and his tutor.

Savanna had never heard of Washington Irving. "Who's he?"

"Writes books, they say."

"What's he doing out here?"

"Wants to make a journey onto the prairie," Abe said. "And the general is arranging for the whole party to join the Rangers and spend a month or so out there."

"Foolish," Savanna snapped.

Abe grinned. "The fellow says he's tired of writing about

243

Europe. Wants some pure American grist for his mill for a change."

"He'll get it," Savanna said, "and a chance to lose his scalp besides."

"Oh, no, the Rangers will protect his scalp."

David went with the expedition and when it returned six weeks later he was ecstatic about his experiences. "Never had so much fun in my life. Wild horses, buffalo, storms, lightning, stampedes, prairie fires, saddle sores, the cross-timbers, everything. I had a bonny, bonny time, Savanna love."

"You look it," she said. "I never saw you so brown and lean. What happened to your paunch?"

"Lost it. Lost it on venison roasts and buffalo hump and wild turkey. And riding three hundred and sixty miles."

"Did your author get enough material for another book?" Abe asked. He had been so envious he could hardly stand it when the expedition had left and he had had to stay behind. "What's he like?"

"Oh, a gentleman, definitely. Pretty soft. Used to more comfort than he got on the prairies, but he didn't complain too much. He got the best of everything, naturally. Cap'n Bean was ordered to see that he did. But the real man of the bunch, Abe, was that commissioner, that Henry Ellsworth. Nothing shocked Irving. Not even the Osages. They were all just local color to him. Everything shocked Ellsworth, but my God he was tough. He never once complained, though he was horrified. Irving got peevish sometimes—especially the week we wandered around in the cross-timbers. You know what they're like, Abe. Growth so thick and tough they tear a man out of the saddle. Irving's clothes were ripped off his back and he didn't like it at all. Didn't see why we had to go through them. But Ellsworth never said a word. He was the first one in the saddle of a morning and the last one off at night. He wrote up his journal every night. Took him so long he must have put in everything that was said or done all day. But he was on government business and Irving was out for pleasure. Makes a difference, I guess."

With many a chuckle David told how the young Swiss count, Pourtalès, had chased Osages all over the prairie trying to find himself an Osage girl. Chouteau had filled him full of tales about their ardor. None of them could know that thirty years later the same Swiss count, not so young now, would be one of the world's foremost oceanographers and that a certain basin off the Florida coast would be called the Pourtalès Plateau. At the moment he was simply a lively figure of fun.

"Did he find one?" Abe asked.

"No. He finally gave it up and went along with us peacefully. But he never ceased sighing over his lost pleasures."

More seriously Abe asked, "Did Ellsworth have any luck with the Plains Indians?"

"No. We had to turn back before we got to the Comanches. The only Indians we saw were some mangy Osages. Irving was mightily disappointed."

"Well, that's just too bad," Savanna said dryly. "Looks like you could have arranged at least one Indian fight for him, seeing he had come so far for something to write about."

"Ah, Savanna . . ."

Some years later Savanna's husband handed her a book which had come in the day's post. It's title was *A Tour on the Prairies,* and its author was Washington Irving. "He dressed it up a right smart," her husband said, "and made it sound romantic and all, but I reckon that's an author's right."

The year of 1833 was marked by General Arbuckle's patient efforts to persuade the Osages to move up into the Kansas Territory where a reservation for them had been set aside. They were finished in their ancestral home, pushed out by the eastern Indians the government was moving in increasing numbers onto the land that had been theirs since time began. They were loath to leave it and it took much counciling and much patience. It was not accomplished that year, but Abe was away from home constantly, riding with the general's party all over the country, from one council to another.

The year was marked also by a great flood in the spring which damaged every trading house on the Verdigris, including Savanna's. There was one frightening week when she expected the house and all the other buildings to be swept off their foundations. Abe wanted her to go to the cantonment but she stubbornly refused. "I've got to see to things," she said.

"You'll be drowned," he stormed at her. "And then what'll you see to?"

"The heavenly angels, I expect," she said. "I won't go, Abe. Don't mention it again, for I won't go."

The waters lapped about her doorway and Kizzy rolled her eyes and spent most of her time on her knees, but the flood never came into the house and as the waters slowly receded Savanna was contemptuous of Abe and Kizzy both for wanting to flee in the face of the flood. "I told you," she said. "You see, nothing happened."

"You're the bullheadest woman the Lord ever made, Savanna," Abe said, "and it's no credit to you the flood didn't wash you clean down the river."

"It didn't, and that's good enough for me," Savanna snapped at him.

They seemed always snapping at each other nowadays.

During the summer there was talk that Captain Rogers was trying to get the cantonment moved back to Fort Smith. "Why?" Savanna asked David, who had stopped by to see about the summer sniffles the twins were afflicted with. "What good would it do over there?"

"It would do Captain Rogers a lot of good," David said dryly. "He has bought up all the land around the old stockade. If he could sell it to the government at ten times what he paid for it, he'd be a rich man."

"I hope," Savanna said, "the government has got more sense."

"Oh, I look for it to come to pass in time. Men with money can get their way, you know. The captain's got a right smart by now."

But the great event of the year came about in December when Savanna's twins were a husky year and a half old.

On the seventeenth of the month, on a cold, blowy, snowy day, there arrived at Gibson five companies of Dragoons—the first cavalry regiment ever authorized by the Congress of the United States.

They were a seven days' wonder to the entire country, for each Company was mounted differently. In A Company every man's horse was a bay; in B Company the horses were cream; in C, they were gray; in D, they were black; in E, they were chestnut. No one had ever seen so magnificent a turnout as these men who made up the First Dragoons. Even General Arbuckle, soon to be replaced at Gibson, was a little awed by them. Their commanding officer was Henry Dodge. Their lieutenant colonel was Stephen Watts Kearny. One of the young lieutenants, fresh out of West Point, was Jefferson Davis.

They were arrogant young men and they refused to be quartered in the old stockade on the post. Instead they pitched their tents half a mile south of the garrison and set about building their own quarters.

"I'm going with them," Abe told Savanna. "I can't stick it with the Seventh any longer."

"Abe!"

"Savanna, I'm half horse myself. I can't stick with a foot-slogging outfit any longer. You ought to see them! They're the most wonderful outfit in the Army. The Infantry is out of date. It's out of style and out of fashion. I want to go with the Dragoons. I'm going to go with them! The Cavalry is going to

246

be the Army now. And my enlistment is up. When I re-enlist, it will be with the First Dragoons."

There was no swaying him, and Savanna knew it.

When she saw the Dragoons on parade she quit trying. For they *were* wonderful. With Sebe Hawkins' bugle, for he, too, had been wooed to them, blowing their formations, with the guidons flying in the breeze, with the gorgeous horses in perfect alignment, with the men so straight in the saddle with their long Dragoon stirrup, her own emotions were moved until a lump formed in her throat. The Seventh was dull and prosaic beside them and she couldn't find it in her heart to blame Abe. Times were changing. The Seventh had had a long history on the frontier and it had served faithfully and well, but there was a magic about the Dragoons which no infantry regiment could match. The wheeling horses, matched by companies; the blowing pennons; the silver-toned trumpet echoing the hills and the river and the prairies; the bright, neat blue uniforms; the straight backs; the trimmed hats; the gleaming sword belted under the braided sashes; it was all too picturesque, too gallant, too romantic to resist. The day of the Infantry was over. The day of the Cavalry had dawned. It was a new urge, a new time, a new era. Savanna felt it, bosom heaving, and told Abe, "Yes, you belong with them."

It was a proud day when he put the yellow cord on his hat, sewed his sergeant's stripes on his blue sleeves and lined the Duke up with E Company's chestnuts. Savanna could not help feeling that he was a little glad to be living on the post again. Colonel Dodge, contemptuous of the old general's loose and easy rein on his men, granted no special privileges. Abe would get home only on weekends hereafter and not every weekend at that. Savanna suspected that babies and business and home had become dull for Abe. He was so proud of being a Dragoon that it was as though his entire life had been recharged. It was full of excitement again.

She missed him, but she was too hard-pressed to miss him much. And something had happened to that fine ardor of their first married days. Maybe she was too tired, too worried. Maybe Abe was too bored. Maybe it was simply that you cannot live on the top of the wave all the time.

The Arkansas Mounted Rangers, six straggling unkempt companies, were merged with the Dragoons, which brought it to full regimental numbers. Oh, it was the proudest outfit! Gibson had never seen anything like it, and many hearts were hurt by it. A man on a horse was so much superior to a man on foot. The Seventh had always been a proud regiment, but the First Dragoons made them feel humbled and dust-bitten. Captain Hammond, watching the Dragoons ride out one day, guidons fluttering, mounts prancing, swords flashing, said bitterly to Savanna, "They will make history. The Seventh will be forgotten."

Loyal still, Savanna flashed a quick reply. "No. The Seventh will never be forgotten."

But it was.

There was no way at that time anyone could know that the First Dragoons, the first cavalry regiment of the United States Army, recruited and trained at Jefferson Barracks in the year 1833, ordered to its first duty at Fort Gibson, Arkansas Territory, would have a proud and continuous history for over one hundred years; that some of its officers would become immortal; that men like Robert E. Lee, Jefferson Davis, Braxton Bragg, Zachary Taylor, Henry Dodge, Henry Leavenworth, Stephen Watts Kearny would go down in history. There was no way anyone could know the First Dragoons would fight its country's battles in Mexico, in the War between the States, in Europe, until a century later it would be absorbed in a more modern cavalry, the Third Armored Division at Fort Knox, Kentucky. No man who ever served with the First Dragoons ever forgot it no matter to what heights of fame and fortune he attained. It was the first and the proudest cavalry regiment in the land. Its glory was never dimmed, its fame never faded.

Though her emotions were mixed in the beginning and she was jealous for the Seventh, in later years Savanna was always proud that Abe had served with the Dragoons.

In the winter of 1833, however, she had her hands full with her own affairs. The twins were growing rapidly and they were lively boys who took a deal of care. That winter, too, she gave up all trading at the home store except for the travelers on the Texas Road. She placed no order for the spring trade and hoped only to dispose of the stock on hand. She even let McNulty go, who immediately enlisted in the Dragoons also.

That winter, also, General Arbuckle finally handed in his resignation and it was learned that General Henry Leavenworth would arrive in the spring to take command at Gibson. People wondered what he would be like. "He's a fine officer," their own general assured them. "I've served with him. He'll do a good duty here and you'll like him."

The country wasn't so sure. They meant to keep a very close eye on General Henry Leavenworth. They consoled themselves that it wouldn't be too bad. They were not wholly losing their own general. He was giving up the command but he wasn't leaving the country. His heart would still be with them. He meant to live on his plantation, Arbuckle's Island. He would be near if he was needed.

Times were changing—times were changing.

There was even talk that the eastern part of the Territory wanted to break away and enter the Union, become the state of Arkansas. What would be left? Why, the Indian Territory of course. It had always been there. It was older than any white settlement. Spiritedly the people around Fort Gibson said: Let them go. We'll have the best; we always have—we always will.

It was a slow winter, but in its inexorable way time passed.

On a gusty, rainy Sunday late in March, Abe came home unexpectedly around midday. He had been home the Sunday before and Savanna did not expect him again for several weeks. She had thought if the rain quit she might ride over to the post and see him, but the rain held on and she had given it up.

The twins were making such a racket on the floor at her feet that she did not hear Abe and was startled when he flung open the door. She jumped up. "Abe!"

And then she stood where she was, for he was not alone. Clinging to him, trying to hide behind him, was a very small, very thin, very wet and very badly frightened little Indian girl. "What on earth . . . Abe!"

Abe struggled inside with the child, who fled immediately to the farthest corner of the room and crouched there coweringly. He took off his hat and shook it free of water, hung it on a peg and shrugged out of his dripping coat. "She's Kioway," he explained. "I bought her off a trader passing through. Fellow named Perkins."

"For heaven's sake, why? What are you going to do with her?"

Abe looked a little embarrassed. "She was so little and scared and she looked so starved—I thought maybe you could feed her up and teach her something and she could be a little help to you some day. Just took a notion, I guess. I hate to see anything mistreated and you can tell she has been."

"The trader mistreated her?"

"Don't think so. He hadn't had her but a day or two. Said he couldn't get her to eat. Too scared, I reckon. He bought her from an Osage that captured her. Don't know why the Osage didn't kill her, but he didn't. His women had knocked her about some, though. Perkins said he bought her cheap with the notion of taking her to his woman, but he didn't believe she'd live till he got her there. Said she hadn't eaten a bite since he'd had her and the Lord knows how long before."

Savanna looked helplessly at the child and was then galvanized into action. "My God, she's probably covered with lice! They'll be on the bed—the twins'll get 'em! Come here, girl. What's her name, Abe?"

"Don't know."

Savanna flung him an exasperated look and hurried across the room.

The child moaned and shook her head, then dashed past Savanna to the bed and scrabbled under it like a frightened pup. Savanna wheeled and yelled at Abe, "Get her out of there! There'll be lice all over the bed!"

The twins, thinking it a lark, were running wildly about now also. She didn't want them near the Indian child. Savanna grabbed at them uselessly. "Kizzy!" she shouted.

She corralled the twins and shoved them through the door. "Go to Kizzy," she told them. "Go on. Go to the kitchen."

They did not like being thrust out of the room so unceremoniously and set up an uproar of their own. Savanna cuffed them lightly and yelled again for Kizzy who, finally hearing, came down the dogtrot on the run. "Whut happen? Whut gwine on in heah. Soun' lak jedgment day done come."

"It has. Mister Abe has brought home an Indian child. Take the twins to the kitchen and fasten them up. Come back here then and help me give the girl a bath to get the vermin off. Hurry!"

"Yessum." Kizzy herded the angry and yelling twins ahead of her. "Whut Mistah Abe want wid a little Injun?"

"Don't ask me. Just do what I told you."

Abe was dragging the child from under the bed by her heels. He handled her with a little roughness because she was kicking and clawing and scratching. "God," he said, puffing when he finally had her out and firmly held, "she must be kin to you. Here, take her."

Though she was vexed with Abe for buying the child and bringing her home, when Savanna saw the look of sheer terror on the little girl's face, saw her heart beating flutteringly in her throat and her narrow, small chest heaving with her breath, saw the bruises from blows on her thin, shanky legs, she was reminded of a stray dog which had been so abused and starved it shrank from any touch. Her vexation ebbed away, and pity for the child filled her. It was done. There was no use crying over spilled milk. She and Kizzy would have to do their best for the child.

She went toward the girl quietly, smiling at her. "What a welcome we have given her. I'm ashamed, Abe."

Abe looked at her and grinned. When Savanna's voice was warm and friendly as it was now, everything was going to be all right. He had cursed himself all the way home for buying the child. She would be a nuisance fo Savanna, at least for a while. And he was almost certain Savanna would be angry with him. It had been the purest impulse. He simply couldn't stand the pitiable condition of the little girl. And Savanna did have a big heart when it was touched. Her first anger over, he had banked on her being as moved as he had been.

Savanna put her hand on the child's shoulder and felt trembling run through the whole slight frame. "She's so cold, Abe. And so wet and dirty."

"And so hungry. I've not been able to get her to eat yet, either."

Savanna tried to take the child's hand, but it was snatched away, and she cowered against Abe. He looked apologetically at Savanna. "Women have done the abusing of her. She's more afraid of them than men."

Not wanting to frighten the child any further, Savanna was puzzling what to do—she had to be bathed and dressed; she had to be fed; but if she was going to run and shake and cower and quake at every touch it was going to be pretty difficult.

"Maybe . . ." Abe was starting to say, when Kizzy came in.

"I got de boys eatin' dere dinnah. Now, whut's dis youngin' heah?"

With one long, appraising look the black woman took in the child's fear, her hungriness, her bruises, her filth. "Po' little baby. Po' little mistreated t'ing." Before the child knew what she was about, Kizzy swung her up in her arms. "You jes' leab dis little youngin' to me, Miss Savanna. Ah knows whut to do. Ah gwine wash her an' git her somepin to eat, an' put her to baid." She was cuddling the child, unafraid of vermin, her cheek against the little girl's ragged, filthy hair. "Po' little baby."

The child, wild-eyed and rigid, made squirming efforts to get loose, but the soft, coaxing tones of Kizzy's voice slowly reassured her. She quit squirming, though she remained stiff and fearful.

"Ain't nothin' gwine hurt you no more," the black woman murmured, rubbing her cheek up and down against the child's. "Ain't nothin' ever gwine hurt you no more. Kizzy's got you. Kizzy gwine tek keer ob you now. Kizzy ain't got no girl chillen. You gwine be Kizzy's little girl chile now."

She carried the child away and Savanna and Abe looked at each other wonderingly. "Well," Savanna said, on an out-blown breath, "I guess that settles that."

Abe chuckled. "Simple, wasn't it? Who'd have thought Kizzy would adopt her?"

251

XXIX

Aware of how foolish it sounded, and always meaning to give her a name, they called her Sugar. It was what Kizzy called the child. "Whur's mah sugah?" Kizzy would cry if the child was ever out of her sight.

It was marvelous to behold the love the black woman lavished on the child. Without neglecting Savanna's boys, or her own Widgie, she yet had plenty of time and devotion for the little girl. She kept her clean, fed her, watched over her and kept her out of Savanna's way. She took over all the care of her and was jealous if Savanna tried to do anything for the child herself. "No need you wearyin' yo'self 'bout dat chile," she would say. "I do fer her."

Slowly the little girl put on weight, filled out, grew less and less fearful though she would always run and hide if strangers came about, and Savanna and Kizzy realized she was going to be pretty some day. "Don't spoil her," Savanna warned Kizzy.

Kizzy scowled. "Needs spoilin', dat one. Been 'bused too long."

"You know what I mean, Kizzy. She has to learn to work."

"In good time—in good time." Kizzy was lofty about her management of the child.

They could not determine her age. She might have been eight, nine, ten, but they doubted she was older for she was unformed even when she had put on some flesh. "Health ain't commenced on her," Kizzy pronounced after several months. "She 'bout ten, I'd say."

Kizzy's one grief with regard to the child was that either she could not talk or she would not. She tried speaking to her in the smattering of Cherokee and Osage she knew, but the girl would only stare at her. She tried English, but a blunt, uncomprehending stare was the only response she ever got from the child. "Ah doan b'lieve she *kin* talk," Kizzy told Savanna.

"Maybe she's been too badly frightened," Savanna said. "I've heard of people being struck dumb."

"She ain't skeered now."

Slowly the child had got over her deepest fear. She manifested a measure of trust in Kizzy, though she still eyed Savanna askance occasionally, especially when she raised her voice at one of the boys or at Abe or Kizzy. At such times she would cringe and slide silently away.

For all her love, Kizzy was not perceptive enough to notice the sad look in the little girl's eyes sometimes. Savanna caught it once in a while, a sort of lost, longing look, when the round black eyes went searching about, liquid with some inner emotion she could not release.

It puzzled Savanna until she came upon the child looking at the horses in the pasture one day. She helped the little girl onto the top rail of the fence and pointed to the horses. "Horses," she said, in an effort to get the child to repeat it after her. "Horses."

The child made a guttural sound in her throat and as she, too, pointed at the horses, an exalted look lit her small face. She pointed again at the horses, then making a long, sweeping gesture with her arms, she pointed west. Why, she wants to go home, Savanna thought, she's homesick.

The gesture had been unmistakable. Horses, and then the long, long ride west toward home.

Troubled, Savanna spoke to Abe about it. But he shrugged it off. "Well, she'll just have to forget it. How the hell can she go home?"

The way was provided, sooner than they could have expected.

General Leavenworth arrived at Gibson in April. By June the entire country knew that the Dragoons were being readied for a long expedition onto the plains. Abe told Savanna they were going to the Wichita Mountains to treat with the Plains Indians. A little uncomfortably he said the general wanted to buy Sugar. "Well, he can't do it," Savanna said tartly. "Kizzy would have a conniption fit. Besides, I wouldn't sell her myself."

"He don't want her for himself. He wants to take her back to her people. And you said she was homesick."

"But, Abe . . ."

"He's buying a couple of Comanche girls from the Osages and a Pawnee girl they've got. It's his opinion if they take these prisoners home it will have a good effect on the tribes and they'll parley quicker. But he wants Sugar for a trade. The Kioways have got a white boy they took about a year ago. If the general takes Sugar back to them he thinks they would trade and he's promised the boy's folks to try to get him back."

Savanna knew it was important that the expedition have every advantage it could. The troops couldn't know beforehand how they would be received. They would be taking an excellent chance of being met with arrows and bullets. If word could be sent ahead by scouts and runners that they were bringing prisoners home, the Indians would be much more likely to be friendly and meet in council. It was important, also, she knew, for the expedition to succeed if at all possible. The Comanches, Pawnees, Kiowas, Wichitas were making the

Santa Fe Trail a deadly road for wagon trains. Even at that moment one company of Dragoons was on its way west escorting a train across the prairies. David Holt, in high good spirits, had gone with them. And the Plains Indians ranged so far, raided so ruthlessly, that white settlements even in the southern edge of the Territory were threatened and none in Texas were safe.

But Savanna had never been so torn.

The child ought to be allowed to go home. She might even sicken and die if kept here. Indians did when they became hopeless. And it would helpful to the general and the expedition. It was the only sensible thing, even the humane thing, to do—except for Kizzy. "It would tear her heart out to take the girl away from her, Abe," Savanna said. "You haven't watched her with her the way I have. She must have been wanting a little girl to love for years. She dotes on that child like she was her own. It would be cruel and I don't think she would ever forgive us, to take her away from her."

"Which do you want to be cruel to, the girl or Kizzy?" Abe said. "It's cruel to keep the girl if she's as homesick as you say she is. And Kizzy is a grown woman and can manage for herself. You oughtn't to have let Kizzy take her over, anyhow. If you'd taken care of her yourself Kizzy wouldn't have got so attached to her."

"Oh, God's britches!" Savanna retorted hotly, "you saw what happened. How could I have helped it?"

"Well, you'll have to do the best you can to make Kizzy understand. It's not exactly an order from the general but it's near enough I've not got much choice. He wants Sugar and if you don't give her up I'll be in trouble."

They wrangled irritably for another half an hour, each accusing the other of creating the problem, Abe by bringing the child home in the first place, Savanna by allowing Kizzy to grow so fond of her, until finally Abe flung himself out of the house, shouting that he washed his hands of the whole affair.

Savanna watched him ride away, thinking bitterly it was exactly like him—saddle her with the responsibility and then wash his hands of it.

They had no choice, she knew. When a commanding officer makes a suggestion it amounts to an order however he may word it. But she put off telling Kizzy until there was barely a week left before the expedition was due to leave.

The advance units of the expedition hoped to leave on the twelfth of June. It was late to be taking to the field and General Arbuckle, the experienced and knowledgeable old hand on the frontier, would have got the troops underway a month earlier

254

at the least. It was a very long journey they had to make and as they advanced onto the prairies the grass and game would both be diminishing. Water would also present a problem for in midsummer many of the small streams would be dry. The troops were green, unacclimated yet; the beautiful horses were largely thoroughbreds. There was much about this proposed expedition which troubled the old hands on the post.

Though he was proud of the Dragoons and proud of belonging to a crack regiment, Abe felt too much emphasis had been put on spit and polish. Jesse Bean's Rangers could have taken to the field with half the trouble. Both Colonel Dodge and General Leavenworth insisted on perfection and Abe knew all too well that perfection in drill, battle array, fatigue dress, equipment, and maneuvers would not serve them half so well as an early start and better knowledge of the country through which they must pass.

Finally, the first week in June, with Abe due to leave with the advance companies on the twelfth, Savanna approached Kizzy. She was almost sick with apprehension. And her heart dropped when she saw the stony look on the black woman's face at her first words. She persevered, however, for she had no alternative. "They will take her back to her own people, Kizzy. You know any child belongs with its parents. Sugar isn't really happy here. She wants to go home. It is best for her."

With majestic dignity Kizzy ignored Savanna. She was combing the little girl's hair. She braided ribbons into the coarse black locks as if the child had been a Negro—braided many tiny plaits and let them stand up stiffly from the scalp exactly as she did her own hair and would have done that of her own child. Savanna had a wild and hysterical moment of wondering what the girl's parents would think when they saw her in a calico dress with her hair braided into a dozen little plaits. Would they know her? Would they refuse her? Would they deny her? She looked nothing like any Indian child they must surely have ever seen.

Without replying, saying nothing at all, Kizzy went on with her careful braiding. Her face was wiped of all expression. The most stoical Indian could not have presented a more expressionless visage to his enemies. Savanna felt as though she were speaking to an image, a stone and unresponding image.

Having, finally, exhausted all her reasons, having gone successively through pity, sympathy, a few tears, Savanna stood, anger sweeping her. "Well, that's all I've got to say. Abe has promised we would have Sugar at Gibson on the fifteenth. She will travel with the other Indian girls in the wagons. Abe is going ahead with the advance companies but the general won't

255

leave with the wagons until later. So you just make sure her clothes are ready, Kizzy."

Kizzy did not even look at her, did not so much as give her a glance to indicate she heard. Irked, provoked, feeling guilty, and angry because of the necessity for guilt, Savanna swept out of the kitchen. Oh, drat the United States Government anyhow, drat General Leavenworth, drat Abe, and drat all Indians! How had she ever got herself into such a mess? Kizzy oughtn't to have to give the child up. Great gobs of mud, men could create the biggest messes. She would have to keep an eye on the child and Kizzy. She wouldn't put it past the woman to run away with the girl. And she had promised Abe faithfully to have Sugar at Gibson by the fifteenth.

Early on the morning of the twelfth Abe left with the advance companies. Savanna did not see him go. He was at home the evening before, though he did not spend the night, and she knew the troops would leave at sunup. As she watched the sun rise over the eastern hills that morning she knew what was taking place at Gibson. She knew Sebe was blowing Assembly. In her mind's eye she could see E Company forming, the chestnut horses beautiful and glossy and stamping and throwing their heads about, the troops clean and hard-looking and brown and lean. Formed, she knew Sebe would blow the Advance and the gates would be thrown wide and four abreast and company deep, E Company would trot through and take the trail to the Washita. Abe would be riding the Duke far out ahead. Ah, she wished she could go—she wished she could go, just once.

Kizzy, to Savanna's surprise, made no move to hide the Kiowa girl or to run away with her. Instead she washed and ironed the three calico dresses she had made for the child. She cooked bread and meat and put them up in small parcels. "You needn't do that," Savanna told her. "General Leavenworth will provide food for the girls."

Kizzy ignored her. She had not spoken one word to Savanna since the subject had been broached to her. Unhappily, Savanna wondered if Kizzy would ever speak to her again, would ever love her.

On the night of the thirteenth Savanna went into the kitchen to make certain the Kiowa girl was ready to leave. "Tell Preacher I'll want the wagon in the morning," she said. "I'll take Sugar to Gibson and turn her over to General Leavenworth then."

"I'se gwine wid you," Kizzy said, breaking her silence.

Savanna put her hand on the black woman's shoulder. "Kizzy, don't do that. Tell Sugar goodbye here."

"I'se gwine wid you," Kizzy repeated, as if Savanna had not

spoken, "an I'se gwine wid dis chile—tek her to her folks."

Savanna thought she had not heard aright. "What did you say?"

"You heared me." Kizzy was lowering and scowling. "Ah said I'se gwine tek mah Sugah to her folks. Ah ain't gwine hab her skeered no more. Ah gwine go wid her. She got to go back, ah is gwine tek her. Ah ain't gwine let her go wid no ahmy folks. Dey skeer her. Ah gwine go wid mah Sugah an' ah ain't gwine let nobody hab nothin' to do wid her twill she gits whur her folks is at."

"Have you lost your mind, Kizzy?"

"You kin think so, does you lak. But mah li'l sugah ain't kwine be skeered no moah. She done be skeered too much. I aim see she ain't neber skeered no moah. Ah knows she got to go. Ah knows hit's best fer her to go. But I'se gwine wid her an' I'se gwine see her own ma holdin' her ahms 'foah I turns loose ob her. She mine twill den."

"The general won't allow it!" Savanna was aghast.

"He doan, he ain't gwine tek mah li'l chile."

Oh, Lord, and Abe was two days out on the road!

Savanna begged and she pleaded, she stormed and she raged. Kizzy was adamant. Where her sugar went, she went. "Ah ain't gwine let de ahmy hab mah sugah. Dey skeer de life outen her. I'se gwine wid her."

Finally, seeing that she could make no dent in Kizzy's purpose short of snatching the child bodily from her, Savanna saddled and rode to the post to see General Leavenworth.

How she wished he was her old friend. General Arbuckle would have understood. General Arbuckle would have chuckled with her over the difficulty and he would have set his wits to take care of it. "Well, now, let's see," he would have said in his ruminative way, "we can't hurt Kizzy's feelings, can we?" and he would have thought his way through to a conclusion which would have accomodated Kizzy, have satisfied the ends desired, and would have lifted the burden from Savanna's shoulders.

Henry Leavenworth, now commanding officer at Fort Gibson, was an unknown quantity to her. Abe said he was strictly spit and polish, gruff, cool, contained, difficult to approach. Maybe he *had* built Fort Leavenworth up in the Kansas Territory. Maybe he *was* one of the Army's top military men. But Savanna would have traded him and the entire First Dragoons at that moment to have Matthew Arbuckle behind the desk at Gibson again.

He was courteous to her.

He heard her out, though she felt as silly as a schoolgirl

making her first speech as she explained the situation. "That's the way it is, sir. She loves the child dearly. She isn't willing to turn her over to the Dragoons."

"This woman," the general said, making a temple of his fingers, "is your housekeeper?"

"She is more than that, sir. It's true she is black and I own her as far as the law is concerned, but . . ."

"She is a slave, then."

"Yes, sir. She and her husband, Preacher, belonged to my husband. When he died they became my property. But she is very independent and she is a very valuable person. There is more between us than owner and slave, sir, there is love, and there is respect, and . . ."

The general hemmed and hawed.

Savanna knew he was thinking that she had spoiled the wench and that it was after all a simple matter. Tell the woman the child must go.

Savanna felt an intense dislike for him, but she made herself wait patiently. She glanced idly out the window. A wagon driven by one of the enlisted men lumbered by. An idea popped into her mind and she blurted it out on impulse. "Sir, would you allow me to take my wagon and man as far as the Washita? I know you can't be pestered with a black woman, but if I take my own wagon, if I look after the girl . . . perhaps I could persuade Kizzy by the time we reach the end of the road . . ."

The general eyed her coldly. "You are presently the wife of Sergeant Lathrop, are you not?"

Savanna steeled herself and drew herself up proudly. An enlisted man's wife asking a favor! "Yes, sir. Sergeant Lathrop is my husband now."

"Sergeant Lathrop is not in the main body of the expedition," the general said dryly.

The implication was plain that he thought the entire story a fabrication, that like some lovesick girl she wanted to accompany her husband as far as she could. She made herself smile even though she flushed with anger. "My goodness, sir, my husband is the last person I would want to see. I assure you I only want a little time—my husband will know nothing of my presence. I would not interfere with his duties. If you will give me permission to attach my wagon to the supply train I will not seek him out." She did not add that Abe would probably be in a towering rage with her and it would be well for her to avoid him in any event.

She leaned a little forward over the desk. "I would be no bother to you, sir. You can depend upon it. I will take my

258

black man and my own supplies."

"You know that the wagons go no further than the mouth of the Washita, do you not?"

The fool, she thought. In the direction of the Wichitas the cross-timbers had to be traversed. There wasn't a wagon built that could travel that trail. Everybody in the country knew that. "Yes, sir," she said levelly.

It occurred to her, at about that moment, that the general could not actually prevent her from going to the mouth of the Washita. He could refuse to allow her to join his wagon train, but the road was open. Nothing could keep her from taking her own wagon, her own black people, her own supplies, and going to Towson. She sat up straighter, her shoulders braced, her pulse beating fast. She would do it! She would do this thing! She thrust her head up, the movement jingling her earrings. She had not worn them for months—not since the twins were old enough to be fascinated by them and grab for them. A torn ear lobe had finally driven her to take them out. She had put them on this morning in an effort to look her best for this conversation with the general. She touched the golden hoop in her right ear. It felt smooth and cool and somehow reassuring. She would not leave her earrings off, ever again. She would wear them as she used to do. The twins must be taught to leave them alone.

The general was tapping his fingers on the desk edge.

Savanna's mind raced on as she waited. She would take the twins to her father's and leave them with Lena. She would have Preacher put new tires on the wagon and strengthen its frame. There was plenty of dried beef and salt and cornmeal. They could load the wagon with ample stores and she and Preacher could share the driving. Kizzy and the Kiowa girl could find nests for themselves in the provisions. She wondered if the canvas of the tent had suffered from its long storage. Kizzy could patch it if it had. She must remember, too, to take medicines. The heat would be bad, and one of them might have chills and fever before it was over.

She clutched her knowledge that nothing could prevent her going exultantly. It would be better to have permission.

"You realize, Mrs. Lathrop," the general spoke at last, "that it is only because we badly need this girl that I entertain the thought of allowing you to accompany the expedition as far as the Washita at all." He smiled briefly. "I expect what I should do is simply commandeer the girl."

Savanna met his look coolly. "Sir, I doubt that could be done. She is private property. She was bought, not given. I would not sell her, but I will freely give her to you if I may have the time I need to persuade Kizzy."

"Oh," the general said dryly, "I think we could evade the technicalities under the circumstances."

"The papers are in my name, sir," Savanna insisted stubbornly. "My husband gave her to me."

"Women don't have property in their own names."

"I do, sir." Savanna said quietly. "I have a great deal of property in my own name." She did not know the law on it, but just let anyone, this general, Abe, or anyone else try to get anything that belonged to her away from her. She would show them whether a woman could have property in her own name!

"Well," General Leavenworth said, spreading his hands, "it's an academic question. I shouldn't like doing it. You realize, Mrs. Lathrop, that even to the Washita is not an easy journey. If you fall behind I can't vouch for what might happen. I think you might have to be abandoned."

Savanna kept from smiling. Lord in heaven, a plain road, wide enough for wagons, a rough journey? Let him abandon her. She and Preacher and Kizzy could manage. "I'll take that risk, sir."

The general finally smiled warmly at her. "I believe you will." He rose to see her to the door. "This is most unusual, of course. But you people in this country seem to do so many unusual things. I am not yet accustomed to your ways and I may regret allowing this, but we do need your Kiowa girl. I am extremely anxious to have the exchange of prisoners with that tribe for they hold the little Martin boy, and they may also have information about the Ranger, Abbé."

The summer before, the Rangers had made a scout onto the prairies and they had run into a small band of Kiowas. There followed a running fight which lasted less than an hour but when it was over a Ranger, Abbé, was missing. Nothing had been heard of him until recently when an Osage visiting the cantonment said the Kiowas still had him.

"Yes, sir," Savanna said.

Holding the door for her, the general said, "I am as loath as you to force your black woman against her will, but I do have your promise, do I not, that the girl will be turned over to me at Washita?"

"You have, sir."

"Very well, then." He smiled down at her. "I think perhaps I should make you a member of my staff. I have already included the young artist who wants to paint Indians."

"Who is that, sir?"

"A young man by the name of Catlin. He has come espe-

260

cially to go on this expedition so he may see Plains Indians firsthand and paint them."

"Is he daft?"

"No. But artists seem to be a peculiar breed of people. We leave at sunrise the day after tomorrow, madam, and if you are not prompt we shall have to leave without you."

"I shall be here," Savanna assured him.

She sped down the steps. There was no time to waste.

Months later, when it was all over and she was under the necessity of examining her motives, Savanna could with truth tell herself that that morning, in General Leavenworth's quarters, they had been pure and innocent. She had meant to go as far as the Washita. She had wanted only to give Kizzy a little extension of time. She had wanted only to be generous and kind, and there was no danger, of any sort, on the road from Gibson to the mouth of the Washita.

She could not account, even to herself, for the fact that she had put up extra provisions in the small, tough, rawhide cases Abe liked on a scout, or that she had driven the usual team of two horses and tied to the tail of the wagon two extra mustangs.

XXX

As far as the mouth of the Washita, where the advance companies had laid out a camp for General Leavenworth, who himself was going no farther, there was the road which Bill Felt had helped to build. The wagons had little difficulty. The road was rough but passable. The wagons rumbled along raising a great dust on the dry trail, but if there was such a quantity of dust that Savanna, at the end of the long train, was constantly powdered with it, at least there was no mud into which the wheels could sink to the hubs. She was grateful for that.

At the last the twins had been left with Martha Short. There was no time to take or to send them to her father's. Martha strongly disapproved of this venture but unable to persuade Savanna she volunteered to care for the children. Savanna could leave them with an easy mind. Martha doted on the two boys and was always glad of an opportunity to have them to herself.

Savanna also left Widgie at Martha's, adjuring him to be helpful. The house and store she simply closed and locked. There was now so little trade it couldn't matter.

This was the main body of the expedition, with General

Leavenworth, Colonel Dodge, Lieutenant Colonel Kearny leading. The troops followed and the supply train trailed the troops.

From the day the expedition left Gibson it was hard pressed by sickness. Savanna had an uneasy feeling it would have been good to have David Holt on this expedition. He knew these chills and fevers so well. But David was far away, jouncing his gray nag, as disreputable-looking as ever probably, along the Santa Fe Trail. He had been loyal to his ragged but joyous Ranger company as long as it existed but he had gone along with it when it was absorbed into the Dragoons. As a civilian he was loosely attached to the company and he was having his fill of adventures. Savanna could see David jouncing plumb to Santa Fe, as happy as a boy let out of school.

There was a post surgeon at Gibson now and the Dragoons not only had their own surgeon but each company had some sort of medical man attached. But they were all ignorant of this intermittent fever and puzzled by its alternating chills and fever. The men were so dreadfully sick all at once and as the troops and the train slowly made their fifteen miles each day more and more reported sick and were sent back to Gibson. If only mildly ill they were told to fall in behind the wagons.

By the time the expedition reached the Washita forty men were abjectly tailing the train in the dust and at least that many more had been sent back to Gibson. It did not augur well for the expedition and it was not a happy troop. It was too hot and the men were not accustomed to such heat. They were not properly uniformed for it. They sweated through the heavy wool and it then chafed and irritated their skins, some men breaking out with an itching, maddening rash. The beautiful mounts lathered quickly, though the men tried to save them, and were then crusted over with dust which caked and hardened and turned them into scarecrows. Looking at them, Savanna thought how much better it would have been to mount the entire troop on mustangs. These beautiful animals were going to die like flies if water and grass got scarce. A mustang would lean down until you could count his ribs, but he would keep going. She gave her own four mustangs an approving glance. She liked a fine thoroughbred as well as anybody, but a thoroughbred was too tender, too nervous, too fine-boned for a long haul. It took a mustang when endurance counted, and in this relentless heat endurance was going to count.

They drew into the camp at Washita late one evening. The advance companies were waiting and Savanna was suddenly frightened that Abe would find her out. She drew her wagon away from the others into a woodsy place and told Preacher and Kizzy to make camp. She did some unobtrusive reconnoitering, searching out some man of Abe's company to question. She found Sebe Hawkins, whose mouth dropped open at seeing her. "Miss Savanna! What you doin' here?"

"Hush. The general gave me permission. Where's Abe, Sebe?"

"Up ahead a couple of days. He know you're with the troops?"

"No. And when you see him don't tell him."

Sebe grinned. "Sure, Miss Savanna, I'll keep my trap shut."

Since the day she rescued his horn from the river he would have done anything for her. He did not even need to know why she was here and Savanna saw no necessity for enlightening him or for telling him she would return home from here. She had learned what she wanted to know. Abe was not in the camp.

That night the general came to Savanna's fire. "We shall rest the troops here for three days, Mrs. Lathrop, in the hope that some of the sick will mend and can continue the journey. I feel certain that some are too ill, however, and must be sent back to Fort Gibson. You can return with them."

"Yes, sir."

"I am going no farther, as you know. I will remain in camp here until the expedition returns. Colonel Dodge will take command in the field. I trust you are prepared to hand over the Kiowa girl at this time."

Savanna swallowed hard. She was not. She had said nothing more to Kizzy and Kizzy was happy in the assumption all was well. "Yes, sir," she said. "Tonight?"

"No, no. Sometime before you leave. Give her into Colonel Dodge's care." The general mopped his florid, sweaty face. "This heat—is it always this hot in June, Mrs. Lathrop?"

"Usually it is, sir." She could not forbear adding, "April is the best month to take to the field, sir."

"Yes. Well I did not arrive until the twenty-eighth of April. I could hardly lead a command onto the plains that month."

"No, sir."

Looking past her into the coals of Kizzy's supper fire, his mind on another of his problems, he said, "There are so many sick—I don't like it. That young Mr. Catlin, the painter chap, has the chill today. What is this sickness so prevalent here, Mrs. Lathrop?"

"The intermittent fever, sir. It comes and it goes. One day you will be well, the next day you're shaking with an ague and then your fever parches you. If you stay here long enough

263

you're bound to have it, and if you ever have it once it comes back on you from time to time. We don't honestly know what causes it, but there's a saying in the Territory that if the Indians don't get you the intermittent will." She grinned at him contagiously.

"I can believe it."

When he had gone, Kizzy came up, her lower lip thrust out and her eyes suspicious. "Who dat?"

"The general."

"What he want?"

Well, she had to be told sometime. "He wants Sugar. This is as far as we can go. He has just ordered me to turn the girl over to Colonel Dodge."

Kizzy was up in arms instantly. "You ain't gwine do dat! You done promise you ain't. You done tole me I could gib her into her own ma's hands. You ain't gwine lie to me lak dat, Miss Savanna."

"I didn't lie to you. I never did tell you we were going all the way with the expedition. I can't help it if you thought . . ."

"Yessum, ah thunk it. Huccome we hitch up de team an' come dis fur? Huccome we cain't go no furder?"

"Oh, God's britches, Kizzy, orders are orders. The general isn't going to allow us to go any further with the troops. Do you think I can ride clear to the Wichita Mountains with the girl by myself?"

"Yessum." The outthrust lower lip was sulky. "Did you make up yo' mind, you sho' could."

"Well, I'm not that kind of a fool. You've simply got to make up your mind that Sugar has to be turned over to Colonel Dodge tomorrow or the next day." She was short with the black woman because she did feel such pity for her. She ought never, she thought now, have given in to her at all. She should have been firm from the beginning. This delay and postponement did not alter the inevitable, had only raised Kizzy's hopes and then dashed them again.

Kizzy glowered at her and stalked away to the pallet where the Indian child lay asleep. Savanna watched her lie down beside the child and gather her close. Sweet heaven, she could get herself into the biggest messes!

She went to her own bed but could not go to sleep. Here on the Washita the heat was close and steamy. No air was stirring and the night felt like a dark blanket wrapped about her. She felt prickly and restless and unhappy with a sense of desolation unfamiliar to her. What was the matter with her?

She turned and stared at the coals of the fire, sighing. She had enjoyed this journey. She was sorry it was over. She

264

couldn't remember when she had waked in the morning with such eagerness and freshness, ready to hitch up, drive on, keep moving. Drab and unexciting it may have been to the troops but it had provided a wonderful world of change for her. Her days at home were so blunted with repetition, the same things done over and over again in the same ways, the same worries, fears, problems, nagging frustrations always besetting her. She had shed them on this journey as a snake sheds his skin. Once again she had felt the keen, sharp edge of zest, the kind of glowing expectancy which had used to buoy her and send her charging into a new day as if to seize it and wring it dry of its promises. Now it was over, and tomorrow or the next day she must turn back and pick up the same old load again.

She sat up suddenly.

God in heaven, what had happened to her? Her life had become precisely what she had never wanted it to become, a jail of house walls, meals, cows, chickens, children. Even her zeal for business had been blunted and become instead a dragging and worrying thing of hanging on from season to season. Her mind and her body and her whole life had become heavy and dull, unlit by any glow of expectation, drab and shadowed by the eternal sameness of it. How had she ever got herself into such a fix?

She threw her blanket aside, pulled on her shoes, and walked to the river. It was a sluggish stream, muddy and warm, but it was a river, with water flowing steadily toward some confluence with other water. However slowly, it moved continuously . . . flowing, restless water. She sat on a log and dipped her hands into it, felt the slow current pull at them.

What had happened to her? What had happened?

It had been such a radiant, splendid world with Thomas to provide its brilliance, such a beautiful, sparkling world to hold so lightly in her hands. Every day had been so bonny, so full of pleasant things and new excitements and new interests. She had never thought to lose that splendid world—but she had.

Where had she erred? What had she done wrong? Where had the eagerness and the splendor gone? Abe? Was it being married to Abe? But that, at first, had been the most splendid thing of all. When had that exultant, insatiable hunger of theirs for each other gone? When had it become easily sated instead, of no great moment to either, a quick mating, a sudden tensing and release and quickly forgotten?

Why were they content to live apart for weeks at a time? And she was as content as Abe, she knew. His rare visits home had become more of a nuisance to her than a joy. In the beginning a sudden, unexpected glimpse of Abe any place had sent the blood lurching into her heart and love for him had streamed through her nerves. Now when he came riding home her first reaction was one of quick irritation. Lord, she would think, he'll have a bag of dirty clothes to wash, and he'll want a big supper tonight, and he'll spit tobacco juice all over the floor and it will have to be scoured tomorrow. She had even become so accustomed to the bed to herself that she no longer slept well with Abe beside her. He took up too much room and his body was too warm, and he snored.

Curiously, she wondered when this disenchantment with home and husband and yes, even the babies—she loved them dearly but they were not dreadfully exciting—had begun. And she could not place an exact time. It had slowly crept up on her and enveloped her in its gray, drab fog of duty and burdens and monotony. And she was so weary of it. Sweet heaven, she was so weary of it!

She jerked her hands from the water and stood abruptly, filled with an angry rebellion. It was her life and she could not escape it, but she did not want to go back to it yet. She did not want to go home! She did not want to hitch up tomorrow or the next day and take the trail back to Gibson. What she wanted was to keep going on a new trail, to face west and go on and on and on!

Do you think I can ride clear to the Wichita Mountains by myself?

Yessum. Did you make up yo' mind, you sho' could.

Oh, she could. She could!

She was filled suddenly with a wild elation. All her life she had wanted to venture onto the prairies. All her life the plains had haunted her and filled her imagination with dreams of long, long distances, high blue skies, herds of buffalo, and little bunches of wild, free horses. All her life she had rebelled against her woman's fate of being left behind. She had kicked and squalled when Abe took Manifee onto the prairies to hunt wild horses. She had nagged at Thomas and badgered David. She had threatened them all with what a woman could do some day. And what had she done? Become a prisoner of a woman's usual fate.

She looked across the river. A half-moon hung, meshed in the treetops on the opposite bank. She was very near the plains. She would never be any nearer, she knew that now. Just there beyond the river a few miles lay the cross-timbers; and beyond the belt of timber was the long downland of the prairies, that slow-tilting land that reached clear and unobstructed to the shining western mountains. She would never again be so near, for at home once more her duties would close around her and

266

she would never get free of them again.

In that moment she determined she would have this thing she had wanted for so long; she would have this great adventure before going back and forever closing the door on all adventure.

Sharply, coolly, her mind began to work. All the details of a clever scheme fell into place as though they had been clear to her and planned all along. They came full-fledged into her mind, shaped and clean.

She was well provisioned and she had four tough young mustangs. She had Kizzy and Preacher. She did not know the trails on the plains but she would follow the troop and the troop would leave signs a mile wide that any idiot could follow. She would stay behind, just far enough to be out of sight, but not so far as to lose the trail.

They would leave tonight, she decided. They would hitch up and take the road back to Gibson. They would follow it for a few miles and then they would hide the wagon in the woods and lie low themselves until the expedition had left Camp Washita. Then they would circle around, out of sight, and follow the troop.

The general would be angry, of course. He would be angry at her disobedience and at her failure to deliver the Kiowa child. Very likely he would send after her, but if she could not be found he would have to get on with the business at hand. If she gave the child up to Colonel Dodge just before they reached the Wichitas, the end would have been served just as well. She did not believe, in that event, that Abe would be made to suffer for her rebellion. He could be made uncomfortable but surely he could not be held accountable for a disobedient wife. He would be furious with her, of course. She shrugged that off. The day when Abe's anger could disturb her was long past.

Swiftly she went to waken Kizzy and Preacher, thankful that her camp was outside the circle of guards. Quietly the black people stole about doing as she told them. When all was ready, when Kizzy and Preacher and the Indian child were all in the wagon, she told them to wait.

Sebe Hawkins was on guard at the horse corral. For some reason she did not try to fathom Savanna went to him and told him what she meant to do. Even in the dark she knew he was grinning. "Yes, ma'am. I'll keep my trap shut."

If Miss Savanna wanted to go to the Wichitas, Sebe Hawkins wasn't going to stand in her way.

XXXI

It worked so easily and so beautifully that Savanna could scarcely believe it.

She took great care to go a full five miles back on the trail before stopping. The sun was up by then and Preacher, grinning from ear to ear and full of importance, hid the wagon in a thicket and made a camp for them in a copse where no passerby could spy them out.

Kizzy was singing, mumbling in undertone an ancient hymn of her own people. Miss Savanna had found a way—Miss Savanna had found a way—Miss Savanna could always find a way—Miss Savanna was going to lead them on. With the blindness of ignorance Kizzy thought that Miss Savanna could pass a miracle. The hymn she sang was endless, repetitive and mournful, something about crying holy unto the Lord, but Savanna liked hearing her. When Kizzy sang all was well with her. Mournful as the words and music might be, the impulse to lift her voice meant she was feeling fine. Savanna wanted Kizzy to feel fine right now.

They had a dull two days hiding out, but on the morning of the third day they could gleefully take to the trail.

All went well until they came to the cross-timbers. The trail of the troops was broad and plain and for sixty miles Savanna followed it easily. Then the trail entered, open, wide, still easy to follow, into the first sparse woods of the timbers. Savanna had heard for years about this broad belt of woods. She knew Abe had a healthy respect for it and disliked it, always dreaded a passage of it. "It's the worst piece of country I've ever seen," he had said more than once. "The brush grows as thick as blackberry brambles, all whichaway, but it's as hard as iron. It tears clean through an animal's hide and plucks a man's clothes off his back. You're lucky to come out whole. And it's a bad place to get lost, too. You've got to have your wits about you when there's no sun or you're liable to wander for days. Even the Indians get lost in it."

But Savanna entered the timbers confidently. Abe or another scout would have marked it plain for the passage. All she had to do when it got thicker was to watch for the blazed trees.

But within a mile she was hopelessly confused. There was no path left. And there was no trail marked. No trees had been blazed. She must have lost the way somehow, she thought, but she did not know where. She had been following along where hoofprints showed and in the beginning there were many.

Then the growth became so thick the ground itself was lost to sight and only an occasional hoofprint could be seen. She thought then she must watch for the blazed trees. It bewildered her that there were none. What were scouts for? Why hadn't they marked the way? How had the troops gone through here?

She had never seen anything like this close-grown timber. She had seen blowdowns on her father's farm, and she had seen treelaps. She knew how distorting to the senses a wide belt of uprooted and tangled trees could be. She had seen such bands of timber blown down before a tornado. But not by any stretch of the imagination could anyone know what this impenetrable forest, grown up with thorn and ironwood and brambles, was like. Unless you saw it for yourself you couldn't believe how it actually was.

She stopped her little party to reconnoiter. Savanna was leading; Kizzy, with Sugar perched in front of her, followed and Preacher, leading the pack horse, trailed at the rear.

"Is we lost, Miss Savanna?" Kizzy asked, but without real apprehension.

"No," Savanna said curtly, "but stay here—right here. Don't move, do you hear? I want to see which way the trail goes here and you mustn't get lost from me."

Preacher was no more use than a child would have been. He had no natural talent for tracking and had picked up none. He had been Thomas's body servant for years and after that his work had always been the chores about the place. Trustingly both black people sank onto the tussock of grass to rest, fanned themselves and looked with wide eyes at their surroundings. "Spooky, ain't it?" Preacher said.

Savanna left them and made her way on foot to the right, then to the left. If there was a trail she had lost it. She tried to backtrack and pick it up but she got only torn clothing, briar scratches, and cramps in her legs for her pains. Why hadn't the trail been marked? And how did you get through such a massive maze without a trail?

Not until she had rejoined Kizzy and Preacher and sunk herself onto the ground, hot and a little frightened and exhausted, did it occur to her that one of the scouts, probably Abe, had met the Dragoons at the entrance and piloted them through. It was that bad then—so bad that you couldn't even trust a marked trail.

She opened one of the buckskin bags and got out some dried beef. "Eat it," she told Kizzy and Preacher, "we may not be able to camp in this mess tonight."

Kizzy fed the Indian child. "Is you skeered, Miss Savanna?"

"No. But we've got to find our way through this. All of you

269

eat enough of that jerky to keep you going because I don't
mean to stop again for a long time."

"You fin' de path?"

"There isn't any. But we've got the sun and I know we've got
to keep heading west."

Having puzzled out why the trail wasn't marked, having
acknowledged she couldn't depend on a trail, that she must
pick out what hoofmarks she could, look for pieces of cloth
torn from packs and uniforms, she felt better. It was a lot
worse than she had imagined, but if the Dragoons had gone
through she could follow. There would be trampled bushes,
there would be occasional high places clean of thicket where
their passage would show, and, as her own torn clothing
plainly indicated, there would be patches of cloth clinging to
brambles and growth.

They mounted and went ahead.

Savanna was wearing her riding habit. The material was
heavy and thick. She believed it would protect her against anything, but within two hours the sleeves had been ripped and
torn until they hung in shreds. The skirt had lost jagged
squares and about the hem it was beginning to look fringed.
No one would possibly have known beforehand what was to be
encountered in this belt of timber! She recalled David's story
of Washington Irving and how he had rebelled against the constant brambles and thickets and had sworn at the Rangers for
leading them into it.

Drawing up her horse for a breathing spell she looked about
her. She had a naturally good sense of direction and the sun
was her guide. What she was most afraid of was that the sun
would be clouded over before they got to the other side of this
belt. She was afraid she might start circling then, and she knew
it was possible to be lost for days in the maze which looked
alike on every side. Fifty miles of it! They were certain to have
one cloudy day before they got through.

But maybe they wouldn't. Maybe they would be lucky and
find more open stretches. Abe had said there were a few.
Maybe they would make better time tomorrow. She wouldn't
give up yet. Doggedly she went on.

As the timbers gloomed toward evening Savanna was infected with something like panic. What had she got herself into? And Kizzy and Preacher and the little Indian girl. If there
was just someone with them who could watch out and look for
sign with more confidence than she felt—someone to decide
which way to go around this impenetrable thicket, right or left,
she never knew which way was best. But she had to decide. She
had to peer carefully, get off her horse and look at the ground,

see if it was firm, for strangely there were boggy, swampy places in the forest, see which way led to the fewest obstructions. Sometimes it was impossible to decide. Either way was so bad it couldn't have made any difference. But she had to take one way or the other, impossible or not. You couldn't stand still.

Exhausted finally, bramble-torn, as hot as though they had been steamed under cover, Kizzy moaning with the pain of her scratches and worried about her Sugar, Preacher fretful and beginning to be scared, she halted her little train and made camp on a small knoll which for a circumference of perhaps fifty feet stood in the clear. Dark was coming on. Saddles off and the horses crowding onto the knoll with them, Savanna lay on her blanket and gave thanks that above her the sky was clear. Through the interstices of the trees she saw a star or two. You couldn't by any means see the whole heavens, but you could pick out a pinpoint of light here and there. If clouds covered the sky, she didn't know what they would do.

Briefly before she closed her eyes she wondered if the twins were well, if they were giving Martha trouble, if Widgie was being helpful. She grinned, thinking this was going to be a longer time than Martha had bargained for, but the twins were to her what her own grandchildren would have been and she wouldn't mind.

The sun was still shining the next morning. They ate quickly and were on the way.

Toward the middle of the morning there was a wonderful piece of luck. They came onto the trail of the Dragoons. There was no path, but it was evident a large body of horsemen had passed here. The undergrowth was trampled in big patches, badly broken, and there were signs of stopping for food and to breathe the horses. She found scraps of meat and bread that had been thrown aside. There were horse droppings and in one clearing the marks of many hoofprints where animals had milled about for hours.

She took a deep breath of relief. In some way, she now realized, she had got clear off the path. She had taken a wrong turning at some confusing place and then followed a smaller party, Indians perhaps, that had preceded the Dragoons. In the exuberance of relief she gave a delighted whoop. "Here's the path, Preacher, and it will be easy to follow. We've been lost."

"Done figgered it. Done figgered you didn't know whur you was at," Kizzy said.

Savanna wheeled on her. "You hush your sass."

"Yessum," Kizzy said, but with no meekness.

The trail was easy enough to follow, but it was no easy trail.

It was still hard to get through. Fighting the wall of undergrowth and the ever clutching brambles hour after hour all day, Savanna began to feel a frantic need to see the sky and the open country. She didn't like this closed-in, dark, gloomy belt of timber at all. She would be glad to see the last of it. She had no idea how far they had come, and while she was grateful she had found the Dragoons' trail, she wished they would reach the western fringe of these woods quickly.

She had no idea, either, how far ahead the Dragoons were. She had lost a considerable amount of time meandering around and they may have drawn a full day, or even two, ahead of her. She began to feel a tenderness for the troops she hadn't felt before. It would be good to catch them up. Not, she told herself, so near as to be in sight, but near enough she could see their dust by day and their fires by night.

They were four days in the timbers. The Dragoons had been piloted through the narrowest, easiest belt to cross, but it was still a wearisome crossing. When Savanna's little party emerged, suddenly and quite unexpectedly, into the open, never had a barren prairie looked so good. She felt like getting down off her horse and touching the ground. It had been so long since there had been room to make that simple gesture. How good it was to see open country again—to see nothing but space ahead. How wonderful the sky looked. She discovered a new dimension in it, an immensity she had not before appreciated. From horizon to horizon it stretched, more capacious than anything else in the world, bigger and more far-reaching than the planet itself.

She was distracted by the moaning of the Kiowa child, who was struggling in Kizzy's arms. "Now, hesh, Sugah, hesh. It be all right. It be fine now. We is thoo de woods, now." Kizzy was trying to comfort her, thinking the child was frightened.

Instantly, Savanna knew better. "Let her get down, Kizzy. She wants down." The child's face wore the same radiant look it had worn on the day she had pointed to the horses and made that sweeping gesture westward. "Let her down a minute. She knows she's going home."

Released, the little girl ran about, circling, snooping like a coon hound. She scrabbled in the short grass and dust, then fled ahead, circling again, bent so that her small nose was almost touching the earth.

Wonderingly, Savanna watched her. Why, the child herself could have led them to the Wichitas, she thought. This prairie was homeland to her. She was excited by the signs of the troops, and she knew, finally, where they were leading.

It was late and they camped on the spot. They rested wel

272

that night, but got an early start the next morning. Savanna wanted the comforting sight of the long rooster-tail of dust behind the expedition and their supper smokes at night. So she hurried Kizzy and Preacher along, driving the mustangs hard.

The grass was very burnt and dry and the watering places were few. Most of the small streams had gone completely underground so that they had to dig for water at night, and while it was fine to have the trail of the troops ahead of her, it was discouraging to come on their camping places and find the water exhausted or roiled with their great corral of animals.

Still, recuperated, she was able to find much pleasure in the country itself. It was so vast, so unending. She had thought it would be flat and level. Instead it was rolling. It was like a great swelling sea, the billows of land breasting up so that you rarely had a great, far-reaching view of it until you topped one of the infinite rises. Then it was magnificent.

She had the surging thrill of seeing a small herd of buffalo one day, and she made camp immediately and harried Preacher into going with her to try to shoot one of the huge, awkward beasts. Preacher, she found, was terrified of them.

She ranged alongside and fired and fired, but she had had no experience of shooting buffalo and didn't know where to aim. Angry at herself, her gun, and Preacher, she gave it up when the herd stampeded; but she was still glad she had seen a buffalo herd and glad she had tried to kill one. It was something she had always wanted to do. She wished Manifee had been with her. He would have killed that big bull.

Her mind turned more and more to her brother as the days passed, and linked with him, marching with him and with her across the country, was David. She did not seek a reason for this, but she felt it. It was Abe who had taught Manifee the prairies, but Abe only used the land, he did not love it; afraid of it, distrusting it, he wrested its secrets from it to use against it. David had a passion for it, a love and understanding of it, as Manifee had had. Looking about her when they camped she would think, they have hunted over all this land. They know its look and feel, its breath and heart. It's their kind of country. She wished they were with her, to talk at night, to tell her about the land.

It was hotter than she had expected, and the grass was drier and the water scarcer, but it was still the most exciting, the most tingling and thrilling and heart-stopping land she had ever seen. She was glad she had come. And when, within a week, they came up with the troops, she had lost any fear she might have felt; she could even remember the cross-timbers with composure. It had been bad, but they had got through.

273

They could slow down now.

She followed the great dust cloud by day and when the troops camped at night she dropped back far enough that the tiny fire she allowed would not be seen by them. She gave thanks for the heaving swells, then. Beyond any one of them was a dip in which she could make her own camp unseen.

Slowly the land was flattening out, but it was now cut across by narrow and deep, unexpected gullies. These were invariably dry. Savanna's greatest problem now was always water. They would come up to one of these dry washes and scrabble about in its bottom, sometimes finding a little moisture, but as often as not finding nothing but more dry sand. She could not approach the troops to share a waterhole. She had to make do with what she could find. Kizzy and Preacher were always thirsty, but the Kiowa girl never complained. She seemed always these days to have her eyes fixed strainingly ahead. But she was helpful. Often it was she who found the only place they dug that yielded water. Savanna thought her touched in the head when she wandered out once and came back with her skirt tail full of dried buffalo dung. But when she saw the quick, easy fire the chips made, and wood was becoming so very scarce, she patted the child's head in gratitude.

Her provisions were holding out very well, supplemented by the small game she could kill occasionally. They were doing all right, she told herself. They were managing. Nearly always their night camp had a little water and always over the rise was the reassuring glow of the Dragoons' fires. She was troubled a little because the troops were making such slow progress. She wondered why. Some days they made as little as fifteen miles. For mounted troops, she thought, that was extremely slow. She had no way of knowing that the expedition was beginning to feel the slow attrition of illness.

Ahead of her men were sick and suffering. The movement of the troop was geared to the ability of sick men, more than half the regiment now, to mount and ride. All Savanna knew was that a day's travel was very short. From one camp to the next there was never any urgency. She could have done much better herself. Her mustangs were leaning down but they were still faring well, still tough and capable for a long day's hard ride. She wondered, but she adjusted her pace to that of the troop, loafed along, enjoying every day, leaning down herself and turning as brown as her own shoe leather. She was made for this, she thought exultantly; she was made for this hard, tough life on the prairie. Not once did she look back and regret. She forgot she was a wife and a mother, a storekeeper—she even forgot she was a woman. She woke each morning with a glad expectancy, the old bubble of joy, which had been absent for so long, risen in her throat again. She was tireless, bouncy with energy, ready each day to take to the saddle again, ready to ride, looking westward, hoping each day for the loom of the Wichitas on the horizon. Oh, they had been wrong to say a woman did not belong on the plains. She belonged as naturally as a wild mustang. This was her land, and she had always known it. She had come into her birthright.

XXXII

They had been out of the timbers and on the plains fourteen days.

It was a beautiful morning.

The night before it had rained a little, an hour of cooling, grateful moisture soaking instantly into the packed, hot, dried earth. The parched grass had drunk it like a sponge. The sunrise was clear and cool and Savanna sniffed the air happily. It was free of dust, free of heat, free of dryness. It was going to be a wonderful day on the trail.

They broke camp early. Kizzy made breakfast and packed the cooking equipment. Preacher caught up the mustangs and loaded the pack horse. Savanna saddled and mounted. Kizzy lifted her child up and then she and Preacher strung along in their own easygoing fashion. They were lazy with an ancient memory of energy-saving laziness.

They had been on the trail an hour, perhaps, and were moving up a long, slow swell, so gradual that it was only by the feeling in the saddle she could tell they were rising, when Savanna thought she saw a mounted figure far ahead, at the crest of the rise. She stared, was uncertain, and then was sure she had been mistaken. The distances, the sun, the shimmering heat, all combined to distort vision badly and she had already learned that on certain days the carcass of a buffalo might look as big as a house and a pile of horse droppings would take on the size of a great boulder. A bush, perhaps, she thought, momentarily thrown up out of proportion on the horizon. She dismissed it from her mind. Her only uneasiness was that it might have been a scout, drifting behind the troop, hunting perhaps.

There was a little more distance between her party and the troop these last days because the land was growing so flat she was afraid to camp too near. She could tell by the dust now that they were perhaps five, seven, miles ahead of her.

They plodded on, Kizzy's voice softly rising in a mournful tune. She broke off now and then to mumble, "Lawd, Lawd, but I'se hongry fer some good vittles. Ah could eat half a side of a hawg right dis minnit!"

Savanna paid her no mind. She had gone a little pensive, remembering a thing David had said to her once—that every time he went onto the plains he was like Antaeus, touching the earth his strength was renewed. She didn't know who Antaeus was, but she sensed what David meant. Her own strength had been renewed by this journey over this cruel, stark, beautiful land. She felt a soft wish that he was here and not five hundred miles away in Santa Fe.

From behind her, Kizzy's hymn was choked off abruptly, there was the guttural moan of the Kiowa child, and then Kizzy's high screech of terror.

"My God!" Savanna whirled to see what had happened. Kizzy was in mortal fear of snakes and there were rattlers by the hundreds on these plains. Every night Preacher had to beat the camp site carefully and kill four or five before Kizzy would trust herself to her blankets. Her horse, Savanna thought wildly, must have stepped into a nest of them.

But Kizzy was goggle-eyed, gray with terror, and pointing. She gaggled, trying to speak, but could only choke and point. Following Kizzy's palsied finger, Savanna's own heart rose in her throat. Over the rise and coming very rapidly was a small party of Indians. From the corner of her eye, she saw that the Indian girl was struggling with Kizzy's hands. "Hold on to her," she yelled at the black woman.

Her mind functioned quickly. Automatically she had pulled up. Now she called to Kizzy and Preacher, "Get off the horses—quick! Preacher! Bring them up close. Form them head to tail in a circle. Get the guns out."

She didn't reason why she did these things. There wasn't time. But old memories of Abe's and David's stories of Indian scrapes stood her in good stead. Surprised, you used your horses for a barricade. You never banged away wildly at charging Indians. There was always a good chance they were peaceful, simply showing off. But anyhow you held your fire. One at a time you shot, so that your guns were never empty at once.

Preacher and Kizzy moved quickly for once and the ring of horses was swiftly formed. Kizzy deposited her child in the middle of the packs. "Stay dere, Sugah. Doan move."

Then, glimpsing the Indians again, her courage deserted her and she clutched Savanna's skirt and moaned. "We be killed. We be killed."

"Give her a gun, Preacher," Savanna said. "Let go of me, Kizzy. Fire when I tell you, and reload instantly. Kizzy, all you have to do is aim and pull the trigger."

"Oh, Gawd, Miss Savanna, ah ain't neber shot a gun in my life. Whut I'll do is kill myself."

"I'll kill you myself if you don't do what I tell you! Now, let go of me. Stand over there behind your horse. Rest your gun on his rump. And for God's sake don't fire until I give the word. We'll all be killed if our guns are empty at the same time."

She was scared. She was so scared she was shaking as though she had the ague. She didn't know a thing about Plains Indians except that usually they were dangerous. She had no idea what tribe this little band belonged to. She didn't know for certain they were hostile, but they acted as if they were. It was a very small party—she could only count ten—but they were riding like demons let out of hell down the long slope, and ten of them was seven more than they numbered.

Without sequence, even as she ordered Kizzy and Preacher to dismount and form the horses into a barricade, her mind raced to a dozen other things. If she was killed here, and her heart squeezed—well, Martha would have to raise her babies. They would be left motherless. Her business would be left without a manager. Her home would be left empty. Called up by her racing mind and speeding swiftly through it, like visions in a dream, were her father and mother, Lena and her babies, her brothers. Her whole world which she had thought so dull and drab and colorless was imaged in her mind, her friends—Martha, her own old general, even Auguste Chouteau and Talahina, the women at the post, Widgie, Parley Wade —and the rivers and the hills and the blackjacks and the tall elms, the dusty Texas Road, the logs of her home, the Creek who had built it, David Holt. Here her mind quit racing; it stopped and clutched that stout, stalwart figure and held on to it. She would have given the world to have had him standing beside her. There was no time to think why in this last desperate stand of her life she wished most for him. It was simply so. He would know what to do, and he wouldn't be cross with her. He would understand precisely what she had been about. Like Thomas, he would know what had moved her. He would grin at her and wink and quip and he would say, "Darling, it will be all right."

As she watched the Indians form a shouting, whooping, arrow-flying circle about her little party, their intent clear now, she had one fleeting second to wonder why in her mind David should have called her darling. There wasn't time to ponder it. She only knew it would have been so, and that because it would have been so it would have been a great strength and armor to her.

She was too busy to think any more, or to feel any more. Some cool corner of her mind took charge and she fired, reloaded, ordered Preacher to fire and reload, ordered Kizzy to fire, and directed her sights on another Indian herself. She wouldn't have bet a farthing that Kizzy or Preacher would be worth their salt in a situation like this, but they had miraculously steadied. She would have expected Kizzy to have tantrums and hysterics and Preacher to wilt like a scalded cat. They did neither. They fired and loaded and Preacher laid out their extra ammunition coolly. "Dey's plenty, Miss Savanna. Don't bother none 'bout runnin' out."

The Indians were without guns. They had only arrows but Savanna learned quickly how effective arrows could be. A mustang went down, pierced through, the first time the Indians made their flying, ringing charge. "Kizzy!" Savanna screamed. "Pile the packs in the gap and get down behind them!"

It was satisfying to see Kizzy scramble to obey.

As the Indians circled again, more widely, it was an intense pleasure to her to see one of their horses go down. Savanna whooped at Preacher who had brought him down. "Good man! Good! Good! That's what we want."

She had heard Abe and David say that an Indian unhorsed was helpless.

Preacher grinned. "Git de man, Miss Savanna."

Drawing the running Indian into the center of her sight, Savanna pulled the trigger with a rising sense of exultation. She yelled like an Indian herself when the man went down.

They stood their ground steadily.

Savanna had no idea how long the Indians would hang on and there wasn't time to wonder about it. The three of them, herself, Kizzy and Preacher, had simply to fire, reload, and fire again as the savages charged them again and again. There was a supreme moment when Kizzy knocked an Indian off his horse. She brandished her gun and whooped and Savanna laughed. If they got through this, she thought, there would be no living with the black woman. She would be so proud it would be Kizzy who gave the orders!

The sun beat down relentlessly and there wasn't a cloud in the sky. Nor was there any dust plume from the troops. Far ahead at the day's beginning, they would have drawn miles farther by now. Unaware of what was happening behind them, they would be plodding along.

She was so thirsty. Her mouth felt as though it were wadded with cotton. They had water, but not too much. They had to ration it out. Savanna gave them each a mouthful around, told them to hold it before swallowing, but when she had swallowed her own mouthful she felt as though she had only wetted her tongue.

Occasionally the Indians withdrew, recovering their dead, by this time amounting to four, but they always returned to the attack. When they withdrew finally, Savanna would not at first believe it. She waited tensely for the next charge over the crest of the rise. She kept Kizzy and Preacher taut beside her. "Wait," she said, "wait. They may be plotting some surprise."

When an hour had passed and they had not returned, she laid down her gun. Four Indians had fallen. All her life she had heard that Indians would not risk many casualties. Perhaps these had had enough.

Collapsing, her legs now strangely limber and weak, she looked about and took in the full extent of the hurt done them. Three of the mustangs were down, two dead and another whiffling with pain. "Kill him, Preacher," she said wearily.

She reached for the water bag and drank thirstily, for the first time allowing herself as much as a cupful of water. She loosened her bodice and looked up at the sun. She was surprised to see it stood near its zenith. They had stood the Indians off all morning, then. It did not seem possible. The time had seemed at once so long it might have been a week and so brief it might have been an hour. She had lost all count of it, had not been aware of its passing. There had been time only for aiming, firing, and reloading to aim and fire again.

Kizzy was scrabbling in one of the packs, handing out dried beef to her child, to Savanna, to Preacher. "Whut we gwine do now, Miss Savanna? De hawses daid—all but one. How we gwine go on?"

"I don't know. I don't know. I'll have to think about it."

She gnawed on the tough beef and thought. They were unhorsed in the middle of the prairie. The troop was far ahead. Afoot, they could go no farther, nor could they go back. The Indians might return. Their predicament was just about as bad as it could be. They were wholly helpless.

With a deep-souled weariness that sagged her shoulders she knew there was only one thing to be done. Preacher must ride the remaining horse and catch up the troop. He must find Abe and bring him here. From the corral Abe must furnish fresh mounts for them and she must face his anger and her own shame and disgrace. This was the end of her adventure. Abe would never forgive her for this. And Colonel Dodge was going to be very angry. Feeling sore and battered and hotter than she ever remembered in all her life, she pulled herself up off the ground. No use putting it off. She had to pay for her folly and her recklessness. She remembered a saying of her

279

mother's. "If you're going to dance, you must be willing to pay the piper."

She had to pay the piper now.

"Preacher," she said, "take the horse and catch up the troops. Find Mister Abe. Tell him what's happened. Tell him to bring fresh mounts and hurry."

"No'm. Ah ain't gwine leab you."

"If you don't, we'll all die. It's the only chance we have."

"Whut'll you do whilst I'se gone?"

"The best we can. If there's another attack we'll try to stand them off. But I think they have gone. We're afoot now, Preacher, and helpless. You'll have to ride hard. The longer it takes you, the longer Kizzy and Sugar and I will be left here alone. They shouldn't be more than ten miles ahead. If you have to kill the mustang, catch them up quickly. We'll stay right here."

Still reluctant, but the need seeping finally into his head, Preacher rode away and Savanna set herself to get through the hours of waiting as best she could. The worst of it, she thought, would be the heat. There was no shade and she didn't know why riding in the sun and sitting in the sun were two such widely different things. You were in the sun either way. Why should it be so much less hot riding?

But there was no shelter.

And they were so thirsty. There was so little water left in the buckskin bag. Soon, too, the dead mustangs began to swell and to smell, and before long a skein of buzzards were circling overhead.

As the hours moved on, she began to feel as if the whole thing were a dreadful nightmare. She would wake up soon and find it all a bad dream. There would be her cool bedroom and the wide bed and the smooth white sheets, and the gloom of shade about her house, and this whole vast prairie, with its glare of sun and its immense sky and its eternal rise and swell of land and its lack of water and the Indian attack, would be only something she had dreamed in her sleep. The twins would be calling her. She must waken and rise and go to them.

She knew she was a little delirious then, and she made a hard effort to come back to reality. She *was* here, there *had* been an Indian attack, and she did have yet to get herself and Kizzy and Preacher out of this mess. She could not afford the solace of a wandering mind.

She opened a pouch and chewed on more jerky, making Kizzy, the Kiowa child clutched to her, gnaw on a string of it also. "We've got to keep up our strength," she told her.

"Yessum." Obediently Kizzy chewed and chewed and

swallowed. "You reckon we'se gwine git out ob dis place, Miss Savanna?"

"Certainly."

Kizzy grinned at her. If Miss Savanna said so, Kizzy knew it was so. Miss Savanna could always fix everything. She dropped her dried beef and closed her eyes.

Savanna struggled to keep her own eyes open.

She failed. The next thing she knew she was being jogged out of a deep, sound sleep. At first she thought the earth was shaking beneath her. Then she thought the Indians were attacking again. Wildly she struggled up and grabbed for her gun. But it was Abe, out of nowhere, and without Preacher.

"You little fool!" he shouted at her. "What in God's name are you doing here? What did you think you were doing? What has happened to you?"

Savanna clawed at him, still only half awake. She felt stupefied. "Where's Preacher? I sent him for you."

"I haven't seen him." Abe shook her again. "Get your tongue going. You've been attacked—that's plain. But what brought you here? Why did you come?"

"Abe . . ."

"Don't lie to me now!"

She whimpered under his rough grasp. "It was Kizzy. She didn't want to let Sugar go."

"That's not the truth. You could have settled with Kizzy. All you had to do was hand the girl over to General Leavenworth. We thought you'd taken her home. Look at me, and tell me the truth!"

"I've told you—it was Kizzy. She wouldn't even speak to me. She went around like a stone statue. She said if she could take Sugar back to her people and hand her over herself, she would . . ." Her voice trailed off. Looking up at Abe she recoiled. What was in his eyes at that moment was very close to hatred. "Abe, truly, I didn't know . . ."

"No," he said bitterly, "you never know. You never know anything but what you want for yourself. You never think about anyone but yourself. For years you've been begging someone to bring you onto the plains. Nobody ever would. So you found a way to bring yourself. You didn't think what the danger would be. You didn't think I might be cashiered over your foolishness. You didn't think of that when you got us mixed up with Bill Felt. You do exactly what you want to do. You always do. There has never been a time in your life when you haven't thought you could do anything you wanted to do—by yourself. Well, this time it hasn't worked. By yourself, you've got your black people, yourself, and me, into a hell of a

281

lot of trouble. You've never been anything," he finished contemptuously, "but trouble in your whole life."

"Abe . . . I don't always think . . ."

"Oh, shut up! I don't want to talk about it. Now tell me what's happened here. How many were in that band? How were they dressed? What did they look like?"

As best she could remember she told him, falteringly.

"Pawnees," he said succinctly. "And they'll be back. They've got you crippled and they know it. Where's Preacher?"

"I sent him for you."

"I haven't seen him. That fool bugler, Sebe Hawkins, was hunting this morning and he thought he heard firing back on the trail. He came to find me and confessed that he had known all along you were following. So help me God, I'll have his goddamned horn taken away from him and I'll have him drummed out of the service. I ought to have him drawn and quartered. The only excuse for him is that when the Lord passed out the brains to humanity he was hiding behind a door and didn't get his share. But I'll break him, I swear I will!"

Savanna had never seen Abe so angry. She had known he would be riled. She had known he would scold and carry on. But she hadn't thought he would be so mad he would hate her for her folly. When he looked at her it was as though he was seeing snakes or scorpions or rats. He had no use for her. He thought she was no good at all.

The last of her courage ebbed away and she quailed. "What are we going to do now?"

"You and Kizzy are going to take my horse and find the troops. They are ahead about eight miles. They're camped because we have so many sick we've got to leave them behind and we're trying to build some sort of shelter for them. When you get there, stay! Find E Company and tell Captain Northrop you're my wife. He may skin you alive and I'd beat him to it if I could, but he'll make you as comfortable as he can. Savanna, so help me, I will never forget this. You've done a lot of loony things since I've known you, but this is the craziest. And what you've done has not only endangered your own life, and Kizzy's and Preacher's, but it has put the whole troop in danger. That little band of Pawnees may be scouts out ahead of the whole tribe. With half of the regiment sick, what chance would we have of standing off a thousand Pawnees? Besides that, you may have endangered the whole mission. If Colonel Dodge isn't able to treat with the other Plains Indians, it may be your fault. I hope to God that for once you've got your comeuppance! And you're lucky to be alive."

"Abe! Aren't you glad I am?"

"Right now I don't know. I'm too mad. Right now all I'm worried about is the Regiment—and Preacher."

He started picking up the packs scattered about and then discarded them. "Hell! Wake Kizzy and the girl and get on that horse and get going!"

"But what will you do? You can't stay here without a horse. How will you get back to camp?"

"Let me take care of myself, will you? When you get to camp tell the captain to send me a horse. I'm going to look around for Preacher but I won't wander far from this place."

Bile rose in Savanna's throat. "Abe, I'm so sorry . . ."

He thrust her hand away. "Shut up. The only time you're ever sorry is when you're in trouble and somebody has to get you out of it. Get on the horse and start moving."

He shook Kizzy awake.

"Abe," Savanna pleaded, "it's too big a load for the horse."

"Well, kill the horse. One horse doesn't matter now. And don't stop for anything until you reach the camp, understand?"

"Yes, I understand."

He slapped the mustang on the rump.

Savanna whipped up the horse and left the sad remains of her own little victory, tarnished now and without laurels, behind her. She felt sick inside. What had she done? Whatever was going to happen to her and to Abe? What had happened to Preacher? What was going to be the dreadful result of her folly? What a fool, what a fool she had been!

She learned one of the results that night when they brought Abe's body into camp.

Caught alone, on foot, he had had no chance when the Pawnees attacked again. He had been run down and killed.

The full cup of her bitterness and remorse ran over when she saw his slack face, the scalp missing, the muscles lax and ruined and loose. This, this human being reduced to a mutilated corpse, was the dreadful result of her folly. Little Miss By-Myself had done this thing herself. By myself had caught up with her. There was no appeal from her own court of justice and no rock left in the land to hide behind. She had done this thing. No one but Savanna was responsible.

Looking at Abe her blood went as cold as a frozen river.

She turned away, unable to weep. She did not know how she could live with herself the rest of her life. She wished it had been herself the Pawnees had killed.

XXXIII

They buried Abe in the place called Camp Comanche.

Over the poor mutilated body, with tears streaming down his face, Sebe Hawkins blew the saddest horn he had ever blown. The wounded, grieving, melancholy notes, slowed to the muffled drum, bled into the bright, clean morning air, hung there achingly, and were driven by the prairie wind toward the shining mountains. They were as clear, as full, as articulate as ever, until the final note, which cracked and could not be recovered. Sebe dropped his horn and fled, and was never reproved.

Savanna looked and heard, but she was like one walking in an anguished dream. She had stood beside the grave of Thomas Brook and felt her heart break in two. But she had made the gesture he asked of her. She had lifted her head bravely, raised an arm, lifted her chin, so that he might hear the jangle of her baubles.

Abe had never asked anything of her. He had simply taken what he would. He had no poetry or music in his soul to make sweet gestures or pretty songs. But for a little time, for all too brief a time, he had sung the Song of Solomon with his beautiful young body. He had needed no words with his youth and his passion.

As the sabers flashed and the rifles echoed, Savanna knew she would never hear that exquisite song in quite that way again so long as she lived. She would never again know for any man that insatiable hunger and thirst which Abe had roused and fed. She would never again soar as she had done to such blinding heights of pain and ecstasy and rapture. Only Abe could have shown her the way to that sublimity. It had not lasted, but maybe it never lasted longer than it had with them. Maybe it was not to be borne any longer. Maybe it was too piercingly, too blindingly, too dangerously sweet to endure.

As she watched the first shovel of dry, sandy soil fall onto the blanketed form she was fiercely glad she had known the radiance and the rapture and the sublimity. In her heart had always lived Thomas's kindness, his gentleness and goodness. In her heart, also, would always live Abe's hard, ruthless young flame.

Then such pain as she had not felt since her mother died caught her in the throat, cut with a knifelike keenness, and she choked as if the stab were bleeding. She put up her hand and closed her eyes. She swayed, sickened. She had killed him. By her willfulness she had killed him. Oh, God, oh, God, how could she bear it? How could she live with it all her life?

And for the first time in her life, Savanna swooned and fainted dead away.

XXXIV

She was not allowed to go on with the troops.

Twenty sick men were being left in Camp Comanche and Colonel Dodge ordered her to stay there. He treated her very gently; he was neither gruff nor angry, and she was grateful. But he was very firm. "I am not certain, he said, "you will be any better off here, but having got yourself into this situation, Mrs. Lathrop, it's a chance you have to take. At least there will be a detail of men to offer some protection. Lieutenant Prescott will be in command." He added bitterly, "I trust enough of these sick will recover to be useful also. The expedition has been plagued with these chills and fevers and half the men are shaking and burning. But those who can must go on."

Dully Savanna accepted his orders.

Only after the main body of troops had left did it occur to her that she might as well make herself useful. She could help nurse these men. There was no catastrophe so great that mornings didn't dawn, people didn't have to be seen to, food had to be cooked and eaten and pots and pans washed; hearts must continue to beat however slowly and sadly, guilt must be borne and, coarsely and bitterly Savanna thought, bladders and bowels must continue to function.

The little Kiowa girl went with the expedition and, as numb with grief as Savanna, Kizzy let her go tearlessly. Her passion for the child had dulled, for Preacher was a casualty too. He was never seen or heard of again. Lieutenant Prescott thought he had been taken by the Pawnees. He tried to comfort Kizzy. He told her that all Indians had a fondness of black people and that they didn't torture or kill them. Preacher had probably, he assured her, been made a member of the Pawnee tribe by now. Someday they would find him and exchange him. But Kizzy wouldn't be comforted. "He done daid. He done daid. Ah knows it by de way mah heart done slowed down."

It was a disastrous expedition, only successful in part.

Decimated by the fever, with sick camps strung all across the plains, Colonel Dodge did meet with the Kiowas, at least one band of Comanches, and some few Pawnees. He held council with them for several days and was able to exchange Kizzy's Sugar for the little white boy, whom he found in good health. He learned that Abbé, the Ranger, had been taken prisoner, traded from one band to another, tortured finally and killed.

The Indians agreed to send delegates to Fort Gibson for a big council, but more disillusioned than he cared to admit, Colonel Dodge did not think they much meant it, nor that much would come of it if they went. But he was ordered to make the effort. Meeting the Plains Indians on their own grounds he saw better than Washington how improbable it was to persuade them to any different way of life. They lived for warring and raiding. It was all they knew. They could conceive of no other way of life, nor wanted any other.

He had also to confess, at least to himself, that they were better off than the poorer civilization Indians. They were handsomer, they were prouder, they were stronger. They dressed better and they lived better, they rode handsomer ponies (stolen from the Spanish) and they were wholly satisfied with their way of life. He could not see how the government, short of going to war against them, could ever change them much. They would have to be conquered, he believed, not persuaded.

But he did as he was ordered.

Then came the long, slow, dreadfully difficult journey home with half the men on litters, so many dying and having to be left along the trail that only the regimental journal had the count.

The young artist, Catlin, never quit sketching and painting. When fever was burning him up, he painted. When he was shaking so that the brush in his hands could barely be held, he painted. When he couldn't get up off his litter, he rolled over, took the sketchbook in his hands and limned in the lines of the mountains against the sun, the long sweep and swell of the prairies, the horses watering in a stream, a Dragoon postured beside a campfire, an Indian in war dress astride a horse. Done, he would groan and relapse to his chilling and burning again. He did not believe he would live to see Fort Gibson again, and he barely did.

One of the lonely graves left on the plains was that of Sebe Hawkins.

He sickened toward the close of one day and though Savanna and Kizzy worked over him the entire night, he died before the sun rose the next morning. He was too exhausted to rally. There was no Reveille that morning and Taps was not blown when he was buried. Fiercely Savanna demanded that his bugle be buried with him. "No one," she told Colonel Dodge, the tears blinding her and her voice choking, "no one shall ever blow Sebe Hawkins' trumpet again!"

"But, Mrs. Lathrop . . ."

"It was his! It was his! He bought it! It did not belong to the Regiment! They shall not have it! I tell you, no one but Sebe Hawkins can blow that horn!"

She was near hysterics.

Colonel Dodge gave in. The expedition was in such shambles it did not really matter whether they had a bugler.

As with all the graves, every trace was erased so that Indians and wild animals might not find them. But just before the troop wound eastward after the sad task, Savanna found a pretty colored pebble in a dry wash nearby. She laid it at what she thought was Sebe Hawkins' head. "Only Gabriel," she told him, "will ever blow a sweeter horn, Sebe. Talk to him when you get up there. Maybe he'll let you blow the last trump."

Savanna and Kizzy both were ill, also, of the fever, though neither of them had it as severely as the men. For some reason the intermittent never struck a woman as hard as it did men. But the two of them were miserable enough, and grateful they could creep along on the back of a shambling nag instead of footing it.

There were mounts in plenty, as men died like flies, but they were mostly scarecrow animals that could barely move. There was nothing left of the smart, sharp Dragoon Regiment which had left Fort Gibson. The men were gaunt, sick, their uniforms in shreds, their beautiful thoroughbreds now gaunt sticks. Even the pennons were bedraggled from the constant, hard-blowing, hot, dry wind.

Savanna had to shoot the Duke one weary night. He was too sick and too starved and too exhausted to go on.

As if to mock all they had been through, they learned when they finally reached Camp Washita that General Leavenworth himself was dead. The camp, seeing their dust miles away, sent a messenger to intercept the expedition with the news. "He made a scout after you'd left around the edge of the cross-timbers. A runner reached us with the news he had collapsed and could ride no longer. We sent an ambulance for him, but he died in the ambulance before he reached the Camp."

It appeared to Savanna, hearing the news, as though fate itself had condemned this expedition, that it should never have been made, and that made stubbornly and too late in the season it had been doomed from the beginning. With no real interest, in the dull way she looked at all things nowadays, she wondered who the new commanding officer at Gibson would be. It couldn't possibly matter, she thought.

When they reached Gibson finally she went directly to Martha Short's, who was so appalled at her condition that she put her immediately to bed. Savanna knew she looked like a hag and a witch. She had made some effort to keep clean, though no effort could really manage it. She was in rags; she was as thin as a broomstick; her eyes were sunken with great purple bruises under them, and her hair was so tangled and matted Martha cut most of it off. "You couldn't bear having it combed," she said.

Savanna's eyes filled weakly with tears when the twins were brought to her. They were fat and brown and healthy. Martha had taken excellent care of them. But they were subdued by this mother they barely recognized. They stood away and looked at her with round eyes, not wanting much to go near her. "Poor little orphans," Savanna wept.

"Now, Savanna," Martha was brisk, "eat this soup. You must get your strength back."

Savanna turned her head to the wall. "Why? It ought to have been me killed on the prairies instead of Abe. I've got no right to be living."

"Fiddlesticks. Don't let me hear you talk like that again. What's done is done. You have these boys to live for. Get your chin up out of the muck, Savanna, and put a little straightness into your backbone. I know you've been through a dreadful time. I know it must have been hell on earth. And you had the guts to go through with it. I'm not going to say 'I told you so' about your foolishness. You know how foolish it was. But it's done. It's finished. You've got to live. Now, eat this soup and begin from this day to get hold of yourself."

It was good to hear Martha's scolding voice. Martha was so sensible, so frank, so good.

Slowly she mended until a day when she could leave her bed. On that day Gibson learned that their beloved General Arbuckle had been persuaded to return. There simply was no one else and he had to be recalled. He groaned and complained that he was not able, he was not well enough, but he had never been a man to shirk his duty. Gibson had to have a commanding officer at once and he was just sixty miles down the river on his plantation.

He called on Savanna immediately. She wept to see him. She did love him so much, though not at all in the way he would have liked. He was such a stooping, fuzzy, benevolent, dear, good man. Wheezing with asthma, wincing with gout, he stooped to hold her hand. "Well, my dear, I hear you have been a bad child."

"Oh, you'll never know, sir. You'll never know how bad I've

been." The tears rushed and she made no effort to stop them. She had to confess how bad she had been to everybody who would listen.

Always abashed by tears, the general cleared his throat, coughed, mumbled something, then taking his courage in his hands he wiped her tears with his own handkerchief and patted her shoulder. "There, there, Savanna. It wasn't wise—it wasn't wise, but it wasn't all that bad. I should not have chided you."

"Oh, you should. Abe would be alive today if it hadn't been for me. I killed him. I killed him, sir." She twisted his handkerchief into a wet knot and gently he took it away from her.

"Now, that's impossible to know."

"No, it isn't. *I* know. He came to help us when we had been attacked. He made Kizzy and me ride on to the camp and he stayed behind afoot. When they attacked again he didn't have a chance, sir. They ran him down and killed him." She hiccuped and the tears poured again. "And, sir, the worst was—they took his hair—his beautiful hair."

So uncomfortable he twisted and turned in his chair, the general knew nothing to do but pat and mumble and wipe tears and pat and mumble some more. He said "There, there," half a hundred times.

Finally Savanna was wept out, exhausted and weak, and Martha came to take her back to bed. She looked with a scowling anxiety at the general and he shook his head. Martha nodded and took Savanna away.

For two weeks she felt like a vegetable, a very weak, turnip-like vegetable. Then, in spite of herself, her strong constitution began to assert itself. Nature had given her a good body which could stand a great deal of abuse and then come back resiliently to its healthy condition.

Food began to taste good to her again. She could walk about the house and grounds without feeling as though she were going to keel over at the next step. She began to be interested in her boys, to enjoy them again, to romp a little with them. Her face took on some color and the dark bruises under her eyes began to fade. Her hair, very short, standing brushily about her head, amused her and she began to have some concern about her clothing and general appearance.

Kizzy had not stopped at Gibson. Widgie was all she had left now and she wanted to gather him up and take him home. Savanna allowed it. While Savanna was mending, Fred Short rode up a time or two to see how they were faring and reported that though the place was grown up in weeds the stock seemed to be in good condition, the house was all in one piece, and Kizzy had taken command and was making some progress on setting things in order. He brought Savanna some clothing she had asked for.

There came the day, however, when she had been at Martha's for a month, when she knew she must leave. She was physically strong enough; she had got control of her weak weeping spells, and though she was still so sad she felt broken into parts, she had to pick up the pieces of her life and go on.

The one person she felt might have been able to help patch it back together again was still very far away. And there was no assurance he would ever return. The Indians might have killed him, too.

The morning Savanna left, Martha seemed uncomfortable about something. She bustled about like a distraught hen whose chickens have got too big, packing things, forgetting things, admonishing the twins and five minutes later admonishing them again about the same things. Savanna put it down to regret at giving them up. Childless, Martha spent on them the devotion she would have given children or grandchildren of her own. Naturally she was grieved to see them go, and of course her home would be very quiet and lonely now. Of course she would not know, for a time, what to do with herself.

Widgie came with the wagon. Under Kizzy's directions he had recovered it from the thicket in which it had been hidden; and Martha went out with Savanna. She helped the twins in, got them settled, scolded them gruffly and told them to be good boys, mind their manners, help their mother. Just beyond two years old, still babies, they didn't make much sense of what she said, but they felt the tenderness behind the gruffness and they grinned widely at her words and nodded. She kissed them both.

Then she stepped back and looked up over the wheel at Savanna. Her eyes were sorrowful and troubled. "There's a thing you've got to know, dear."

Savanna had the reins in her hands already. "Yes, Martha?"

"Your place at the Falls—the store at Crown Falls—it's been burned down, Savanna."

Savanna let the lines drop. Oh, God, wasn't trouble ever going to leave her alone? "Burned down?"

"To the ground, Savanna. There's nothing left at all. Not even a whole piece of log. I've dreaded telling you. You've had so much to bear. I've put it off as long as I could. I was afraid the general had told you the other day when I heard you crying so hard, but he said he hadn't. Savanna . . ."

She made a movement of warding off Martha's sympathy.

A sort of iron band of acceptance settled over her soul. This, too, had to be. This, too, was part of her fate. This, too, had to happen to her. She had to be reduced to nothing. She had to be brought down to scrabbling and to having literally nothing left but a few acres of rented land and a roof over her head. This was where all her pride, her determination, her will, her energy, had brought her. To nothing. She did not even feel any resentment. This was simply part of the pattern, one more thread in the web of her destiny. In that moment Savanna's youth fled and a woman was born.

"When did it burn?" she asked.

"Not more than a week after you left," Martha said. "I don't recall the exact time, but it wasn't long after you'd gone. The worst of it, Savanna. . . ."

Savanna knew what she was going to say. "Parley was killed."

Martha nodded. "He had been drinking, they said. He didn't even wake up. He was burned along with the store."

Well—she had let him sell alcohol. She had known he drank it thirstily. This was simply one more thing to be laid at her door. Great God, who else was she going to destroy? The twins? Kizzy? Widgie? Martha? Everyone she loved?

She picked up the reins and her head slowly came up.

Watching her, Martha Short saw her face harden, saw the determined chin jut and lift, saw the mouth firm. She's going to be all right, Martha thought. She's going to be all right. Nothing, nothing in the world can trample Savanna into the ground and keep her there. She's got her chin up again. She'll lick whatever comes now. She's going to be all right.

But what Savanna was thinking, was resolving, was that she would not hurt anyone again—would not again impose her will on anyone. She would never again run the risk of maiming and destroying. Her pride and her willfulness had taken too great a toll—Bill Felt, Abe, old Parley, Preacher, and, yes, she had to own it, even Thomas Brook. Misguided, often with good intentions, but always self-willed, always self-centered, always Miss By-Myself, she had sown a whirlwind and reaped destruction. She could find no self-forgiveness. She could only try to atone.

It was the bleakest moment of her life. She reached the nadir of darkness.

One of the twins whimpered. The sun was hot and he was thirsty. Martha brought him a drink of water. Savanna said goodbye and headed her team for home.

XXXV

That night she sat late in the big, empty room where so many men had used to gather.

The tables and chairs were haunted by the ghosts of men who had come and gone. Some had been transferred. Some simply now stayed away. But so many had died. She could see Abe's lean body sprawled at the corner table, and David, stocky and comfortable, filling the easiest chair. Heart burning, she learned that going away from pain was as hard as facing it. For you really never knew what was ahead, but you could never forget what was behind.

She turned to her desk, pinching the candle which was guttering.

She had to take stock.

She had a home for her family. There was a roof over their heads. Her health was restored enough that she could work. She would grow stronger as time passed. She had a bit of land. She was not in debt. But—she faced it squarely—these were almost her total assets. With them, she had somehow to make a new beginning.

She had to begin with no money and without any source of income. She had relied on the store at the Falls and it was gone. She had only the meagerest handful of goods on the shelves of the store at home. The lot wouldn't have brought twenty dollars, she figured.

There were four helpless people depending on her. Kizzy was capable and helpful but only when Savanna was in charge. There wasn't an ounce of responsibility in her. She hadn't been trained to responsibility. Widgie was simply a flutter-brained boy. He could do what he was told, within limits, but without orders he chased butterflies and sat in the sun. The twins were babies. Of the five people in her home, four were wholly dependent. She alone was responsible.

She went to bed, finally, aching not only with the weariness of exertion on a fever-weakened body, but with the gray weariness of desolation. She had reached the pit of hope and a strange deathly silence lay upon her heart. All of her life she had faced whatever came with a strong, resilient faith in herself and life. Difficulties, hardships, setbacks, had always been a challenge to her. She had always fought hard. But tonight, so tired her bones hurt, she felt no challenge. She felt beaten and licked and broken. She had no desire to fight. She wished she could close her eyes and never open them again.

But even as she wished it, she knew she must get up in the

morning and drudge on and, with a last pulling together of her nerve and her courage, she knew she would. Winter was coming on. They had to eat. She had to see, somehow, that her family was fed during the cold months. In the morning she would take stock of the smokehouse and larder. When she had done that she would know better how to plan; she would know better what she must do.

In the larder she found a dozen strings of dried beef, each containing perhaps twenty strips. There was a quarter of a barrel of flour. There was perhaps a peck of dried apples left over from the winter before. None, of course, had been dried this summer. There was no meal. There was less than ten pounds of sugar. There was soap, and there was one stand of rendered lard. There was no coffee. There was no molasses. There was no pork at all.

Grimly she surveyed the scant store. She had stripped the larder for provisions to take onto the prairie. She had expected to buy what they needed when they returned—meal, flour, sugar, some hogs to kill—but she couldn't buy now.

She turned away, her mind gnawing at what could be done. They would simply have to do without flour and sugar. There was a late apple tree that might yield as much as another bushel of dried apples and she'd lick Widgie within an inch of his life if she caught him stealing them now. Kizzy's cow would be fresh in January and they would have milk and butter then. The hens would lay a few eggs maybe, though they had a pesky way of quitting when the cold set in. And though they had no pork meat, they needn't suffer. There was always game.

Like a blow the thought struck her that there was no one to hunt it now. For years she had taken for granted the supply so plentiful that it was allowed to waste. But Abe was gone. And Preacher was gone. Widgie was worse than a fool with a gun. He'd kill himself if trusted with one. Her shoulders sagged. It was just one more thing she would have to do for herself, if it was done.

She wandered out into the yard and fought her way through a tangled maze of weeds and sprouts which had grown up while she was gone. There were so many problems and she was still so fever-worn. She leaned disconsolately on the garden fence and looked unhappily at the weeds. The place had always been kept so tidy, but now there wasn't even a path around the house. Only a few months of neglect during the hot, humid summer could turn any clearing near the woods into a jungle again. She must set Widgie to cleaning these weeds out. Snakes could take harbor in them and be a menace to the twins, and they also formed a fire hazard.

She turned about and looked absently at the garden. It was in worse shape than the yard, she thought. The weeds were higher than her head. And Kizzy was always so proud of her garden and always kept it so clean. It had been a good garden this spring—she straightened suddenly. Sweet heaven, what was she thinking about? There were potatoes buried in that mess of weeds, and pumpkins, and probably some corn. Only Kizzy would know what else. Great gobs of mud, her brain was as weedy as the garden not to have remembered.

She went scrambling for a hoe and rake, a briar blade and sickle, shouting at the same time for Kizzy.

Kizzy came running, her hand over her heart. "Whut now? What done tek place? You done been snakebit?"

"Lord, no!" Savanna handed her the sickle. "We're going to cut the weeds in the garden."

"Gracious Lawd, doan neber skeer me lak dat ag'in." Kizzy wiped her face with her apron. "We done had so much mizzable luck I made sho' somepin turr'ble done happen. Whut we gwine cut de weeds fur?"

"You planted a lot of potatoes, didn't you?"

"Sho' ah did, but you cain't find 'em now. Dey vines done daid. Weeds kivered 'em up."

Savanna was grim. "We'll find them. And we'll find anything else there is to find. Where's Widgie?"

"Mindin' de twins."

"Get him. Put the twins under that apple tree where we can keep an eye on them. We're going to work today like we've never worked before. And I don't want to hear a word out of you or Widgie. If you're going to eat this winter you'd better slash weeds till the last weed's gone."

"Yessum."

It took two days to clean up the garden. Because Kizzy was too thin and scrawny to handle the heavy briar blade, and Widgie too small, Savanna had to wield it herself. She wouldn't have believed it could be so heavy and such hard work. Most of the two days her arms were numb and her shoulders were cramped and her legs were trembling. But the moments of victory when they came across something that could be saved were worth it.

They found two rows of bean vines buried under the weeds, still fairly green and loaded with fat, succulent beans. Savanna gloated over them. "Kizzy, we'll dry them and snap them. They'll last a long time."

Twenty pumpkins made a respectable heap and there were some turnips. And there were many big yellow squashes, too big to be tender, most of them rotted on the under side, but

Savanna piled up every one. "Cut off the rotten parts. We'll slice them and dry them. They may be tough but they'll help keep us from going hungry."

Kizzy caught the infection and began to squall with delight when they made a discovery. She was beginning to remember where she had planted each thing. "Dey's some corn down at de fur end. Be dried up an' hard but we kin mek hominy outen it."

It was Widgie, though, who found the first dead, withered potato vine. He yelped and held it up. "Heah dey is. Heah's de taters!"

In the end, Savanna looked with gloating satisfaction at five bushels of potatoes, three barrels of corn, at pumpkins and turnips and squashes and beans laid out to dry or stored in the root cellar. It wasn't enough food; it wouldn't last them the winter; but it was so much more than she had thought to have. If they just had meat, they could eke it out. She doubted her ability to find game regularly. It was growing very scarce near the settlements and even the best hunters had to go far away for it. What they needed was meat they could count on.

If she just had some hogs. She had been foolish to quit keeping hogs because they rooted up the place, to depend on buying meat already slaughtered because she hated the mess. Right now, she thought, she would give the Duke if she still had him for two hogs fattened for killing. Oh, Lord, to have four sweet hams and four good shoulders, and thick slabs of side meat hanging in the smokehouse—and the jowls and sausage and ribs and backbones to eat fresh! Her mouth watered to think of it, and she brooded over it for days.

Fred Short stopped by one day and left a side of venison. He'd been hunting, he said. "Only got one. But Martha don't like deer meat very much. Thought maybe you'd enjoy some, this being the season."

"Are they scarce, Fred?"

"Getting scarcer all the time. I had to go clean to the Mountain Fork for this one."

Savanna wouldn't let a bite be eaten fresh. "We'll strip it and dry it," she said.

"Oh, Gawd," Kizzy moaned, "ain't nothin' tougher than deer jerky."

"You may be mighty glad to get it this winter," Savanna told her.

Auguste Chouteau came one day, his man behind him leading a pack horse. He was, he said, on the way to Gibson to take the steamer to St. Louis. He had some deer and elk. Would she accept a neighborly gift? Joyously and unsuspiciously, for

Chouteau always kept out many hunters, Savanna seized on it. This meat, too, was cut into strips and dried except for one haunch. They were all too hungry for fresh meat now. It was a luxury and she knew she shouldn't have allowed it, but she felt she could not bear to watch the heavenly juices of all that meat dry into the whang-tough strings which would still hold nourishment when eaten but would give so little pleasure. They all ate until they were gorged.

The next day Savanna heard that Talahina Houston had some fine fat hogs she wanted to sell. Talahina had remained at the Wigwam Neosho after Houston left and she continued to run the trading store. Her brother lived with her and he took care of her cattle and hogs and horses.

Savanna rode over to look at the hogs. They were all fat and healthy. On mast in her woods they would stay that way and with the first hard frost would be ready to kill. Choosing two, she asked what their price would be.

Talahina's brother answered. "Dose two? Fi' dollars."

Oh, it was cheap, cheap, but she no more had five dollars than she had wings with which to fly.

She rode home, her mind in a frenzy. She had to find five dollars somehow, in some way. There must be a way. There had to be. She had to buy those two pigs. There must be something she could raise money on. Something she could sell.

If she only had something to trade. If only she had enough goods . . . her thoughts flew to the store shelves. She hadn't been in the store but once since she got home. It had hurt her too much to see the empty shelves. She didn't even know what was left. Almost nothing—but if she made a pack of the things, and if she rode about the country with it, called among the Creeks, surely she could raise so small an amount as five dollars.

She made the old work horse plod as fast as he would and threw the reins to Widgie when she reached home. "Unsaddle him and turn into the pasture."

She raced into the store and dragged everything off the shelves. She piled them on the counter helterskelter until she had emptied the shelves and then she began sorting. Her heart sank. What Indians liked most was missing, of course. They had long since been gone. There were no needles, no calicoes, no domestics or strouding, no beads or bells or mirrors, and no awls. Slowly, one thing at a time, she made her inventory. There were three bolts of yard goods, all of them waterstained from a leak in the roof. There were two blankets, neither of them the good point-fours the Indians liked, which was why they were left. There were two iron kettles. There were six

296

pieces of crockery, all of them too small for an Indian woman's liking. There were eight skinning knives—the blades rusted and dull—but they were the most hopeful articles in the lot. That, that pitiful small heap, was all she had. That was all that was left of Savanna Fowler's once thriving store, of Savanna Fowler's three thriving trading posts.

She felt lightheaded considering the small pile. It couldn't be. This couldn't be all. Why, she had ordered skinning knives by the hundred dozens in her time! She had ordered strouding in three-hundred-lot bolts. She had ordered kettles by the dozens and crockery by the hundred barrels! She had made her rounds from one store to another and seen a thousand bolts of calicoes, kegs of nails, plows by the dozens, hundreds of barrels of flour, and domestics on her shelves. She had stored thirty, forty, fifty molasses in twenty dozen vats. This couldn't be all that Savanna Fowler had left of a once-proud empire! These, these mothy, trifling objects!

Nothing, not the empty larder, not the scrabbling in the garden, not the exhausted nights of cudgelling her brain, not any of these at all brought home to her the difference between what she once had had and what she had now been reduced to as did this meager pile of paltry trading goods. She flipped a blanket with a finger and sobbed . . . Dear God, dear God, how low she had fallen.

A few hard tears slipped from beneath her squeezed eyelids, but she wiped them away and set about making a pack. If this was all she had, it would have to do. The knives might sell, the crockery perhaps, and the kettles. If she was lucky some poor Indian who couldn't afford a point-four might buy a blanket. Bitterly she thought if he was too poor to buy a point-four, he would be so poor he could afford none at all.

The first day she peddled her goods she sold one kettle, one piece of crockery and one of the knives. She came home with four bits and a pot of tallow. She knew Talahina would give her only two bits for the tallow. Sensing her need, for when had the trader woman ever gone peddling before, the Indians drove hard bargains before parting with money and would part with no pelts for her poor goods.

The next day she sold two pieces of crockery and two knives. She came home again with four bits.

The third day she sold the remainder of the crockery and the other iron kettle. This time she had six bits.

She looked at the money when she had laid it on her desk. Three days and she had one dollar and seventy-five cents to show for her hard riding and begging and pleading. And the best of what she had to sell was gone now. The Indians wouldn't buy the yard goods. They weren't interested in the blankets. She had five knives left and three pieces of crockery. They would bring, at the most, another dollar. She leaned back in her chair and let her arms hang limp. Well. It was clear she wasn't going to raise five dollars this way.

Kizzy called her to supper and she answered that she wasn't hungry. "Feed the twins and put them to sleep. Leave something out and I'll eat before I go to bed."

Kizzy stuck her head in the door. "You gwine be sick you doan eat."

"Go away. I've got to think."

"Ain't gwine hab nothin' to think wid, you doan eat. Yo' brains gwine squish up."

"Let 'em squish. I'll eat. I told you to leave something out."

She paced back and forth across the big room. There had to be some way to raise the rest of the five dollars. It was such a trifling sum of money. What did she have to sell?

There were no horses. She had lost the Duke and her four mustangs on the prairie. She only had two old work nags left and they wouldn't bring a dollar apiece. Some of her dresses? Oh, but they were old and out of fashion. She hadn't bought any clothing since she married Abe. Even her gold satin ballgown was split at the folds. You had to wear silks and satins or time wore them out for you, and she had worn it so little. She hit her hands together. If only she hadn't given Thomas's uniforms away. Indians loved to deck themselves out in uniform coats. How ill-advised she had been to give all his possessions away. She hadn't even kept his sword.

Abe had left nothing. There were some worn old buckskins, but he had been buried in his Dragoon uniform. Even her Comanche blanket had been lost on the prairie. Oh, there was nothing, nothing.

Tired, her head aching, she drifted aimlessly across the dog-trot to her bedroom and threw herself across the bed. She could have wept. She needed those pigs so badly. It had become an obsession with her. They were so cheap, so cheap, and meat, pork meat hanging in the smoke-house, would make the difference between going hungry and well fed when the cold set in. There had to be some way to find the rest of the money. And if she didn't hurry Talahina would sell the pigs to someone else. She wouldn't wait much longer. But how was she going to do it? What way in the world was there?

Not once did it occur to her to borrow the money—from Martha and Fred, from General Arbuckle, or even from her own father. Not once did it occur to her to take her brood of living responsibilities and spend this hard winter in her father's home. Such ideas never once entered her mind. She had to find a way. She had to manage. She had to do something herself.

The room was chilly. It was late October and already there had been several light frosts. But she wasn't having a fire in her room yet. That was another thing she had to do. Wood must be got up for the winter. But she hadn't had time yet. So many things to do—so many things pressing in on her.

Feeling her arms go goose-pimply with chill she rolled over and half sat up to pull over her the quilt which lay folded at the foot of the bed. As she moved her earrings jingled. She never noticed the tinkle of her earrings ordinarily, she was so accustomed to it, but now the sound made her sit bolt upright. Her earrings! Of course! They were the most valuable things she possessed. Who was it who had said . . . Esther Hammond, that Fourth of July! There is one thing you have, Savanna, if you ever decide to sell I'd like to buy. She could hear the meaching, snide voice now. But, sweet heaven, what did it matter? If Esther would only buy them now she could be as meaching and snide as she liked.

She heaved herself off the bed and sped across the room to the dresser, hunting out the small wooden casket in which they had come. Of course, Esther might have been teasing. It would be just like her, but they *were* beautiful, and there *had* been a gleam of envy in Esther's eye. It was a hope, in any event.

She snatched the hoops from her ears and laid them on the dark velvet lining of the casket. There was a clutch at her heart when she saw their glisten against the velvet. They were so rich and so elegant and so exquisite. Oh, Thomas, Thomas, they were your wedding gift. You never meant them to leave me. They were to be my talisman and my courage and my pride. They were to jingle for you all my life. You were going to hear them in heaven. She touched them, fingered their smooth, cool surfaces. Then she resolutely closed the casket on them. Thomas would have understood. Thomas would have known she had to do it. Thomas would have known she had to have those pigs. They would eat these earrings many times over during the cold times.

The next morning she dressed hurriedly. She had no riding habit now. Bit by bit it had been strewn across the western plains. But she had a capacious skirt and she buttoned a short, fitted jacket over it. She thrust the casket containing the earrings into her pocket and hastened out to saddle. Going through the kitchen she said to Kizzy, "I'm going to Gibson. I'll be back this afternoon. Tend to things."

Kizzy scowled at her. "Whut you gwine to Gibson fur? You ain't got no bizness in Gibson."

"And you've got no business asking questions. Don't wait dinner for me, but I'll be home before supper."

Esther Hammond looked at the lovely baubles, a languid, unimpressed calm on her face. "My dear Savanna, I really don't know whether I want them or not."

Her hands clenched in the folds of her skirt, Savanna forced herself to appear unconcerned. She even managed a shrug. "Suit yourself, Esther."

The woman lifted one golden hoop from the casket and swayed it, making it tinkle. It rang like a gong in Savanna's ears—At the last, when they've finished blowing Taps over me, hold up your head, Savanna, and jingle your earrings and I swear that dead though I'll be I'll hear them—and she shivered.

Esther Hammond swung the bauble back and forth, her head leaned against the back of her chair, her eyes lazy-lidded and rapacious. The hand that held the beautiful, cool hoop was thin, veined and liver-spotted. It looked like a claw. The sweat broke out on Savanna's forehead.

Suddenly the woman leaned forward. "Why do you want to sell your earrings, Savanna?"

"Why . . ."

Esther Hammond's smile had venom in it. "You don't have a penny to your name, do you? You've lost your stores, haven't you? You've lost your horses, haven't you? You don't have enough food to eat, do you? You're going hungry, aren't you? You haven't bought any new dresses in years and you're wearing rags now, aren't you? And you've got to sell your earrings to feed your brats, don't you?"

No anger rose in Savanna. No bile surged to her throat. No hot color rushed to her face. No sharp retort came to her tongue. Instead she felt as though a rod of iron had braced her back all at once. God in heaven, what had brought her to the pass that meat should be more important than pride? What had made her, even for one moment, consider selling Thomas's earrings for two pigs? What had warped her judgment so badly that pork meat was such a necessity? Where was Savanna? What had happened to her? Who was this woman ready to crawl and cringe at her enemy's feet? Never in her life had Savanna Fowler crawled and cringed. What had got into her?

They weren't going to starve. They had food. They could eat tough squashes and pumpkins. They had potatoes and corn. And by God if her family wanted meat she would hunt it and provide it for them!

But even if they went hungry, she vowed in that moment,

300

even if they had nothing and she had to scrabble in the dirt like an animal to feed them, she would never again consider selling her earrings. There were some things too beautiful to sell—her golden hoops, her pride, her respect for herself.

Quietly she reached out her hand and took the earrings back. "I have changed my mind, Esther. They are not for sale, after all."

Esther Hammond's mouth popped open. "But you said . . ."

"Never mind what I said. They are not for sale."

With the woman watching, her mouth opening and sucking and closing like that of a catfish, Savanna latched the lovely baubles back into her ears. Then she stood and looked down on Esther Hammond. "They wouldn't look well on you, dear. You haven't the guts for them."

XXXVI

Leaving Esther Hammond's, Savanna was ferried across the river.

She meant to go directly home but when the old work nag plodded up the ramp she felt a strange reluctance to turn him into the road. Though there had been frost that morning, the day had warmed and now in the slanting beams of the sun she felt a need to use the most of it. She wanted to be alone a little longer.

There was a small waterfall off the trail a short way. She would go there, she decided. She had often gone there in the old days. She would sit beside it and she would think through what she had to do.

Deciding to walk, she led the horse into a thicket and tied him. Then she set out, taking her time. Inside her short, snug jacket she was warm and she felt a kind of peaceful acceptance, an unexpected clarity of vision which allowed her to loiter, enjoying the woods.

Coming at last to the small fall of water she sat beside it and cupping her hand drank of the icy water. It was good.

She leaned her head against the bole of a tree, a shaft of sunlight falling across her skirt, and listened to the swift, sliding music of the waterfall. How strange, she thought, it should have taken Esther Hammond's gloating hatred to shock her back inside her own skin. For she had got back into her own skin again. She was Savanna again, not a crumpled, broken, whipped, humiliated, guilt-ridden, whimpering woman going scrabbling about picking at the scraps of her life.

Ridden by horror into guilt, she had forgotten there is virtue in pride, if none in arrogance. She had forgotten there is virtue in strength of will, if none in willfulness. She had forgotten there is virtue in boldness, if none in recklessness. She had even forgotten there is virtue in anger, though none in temper.

She had been like a frantic animal, she thought, scared and scavenging and cowering. She had been salvaging. She had been scraping, trying to find the bottom of her barrel to use the last moldy dust of it. She had been rooting, like one of the hogs she had been willing to sell her earrings for, grubbing amidst the mast and the mud. Deep down inside her she knew she had thought it her penance, that she had somehow, in this way, to pay for all the harm she had done.

She had worn rue and sackcloth, taking on—with her usual extravagance and arrogance not even allowing guilt to another—all the guilt of all the weaknesses of all the men she believed she had hurt. Her mouth quirked wryly. The Lord knew she had not been blameless. But neither had any of them. If Thomas had died because they had moved to Gibson some part of the blame lay on her for her willful desire to live there; but some part of it lay on him, also. Thomas's weakness had been his fatherly wish to give her all things possible. He need only have been firm. He need not have listened to her.

And Abe . . . Abe, too, had had his weaknesses. When they had parted, it was he who came home. And he could never accept responsibility. He brought the Kiowa girl to her and then forgot her. If he had himself taken her to Colonel Dodge instead of leaving it for her to do, there would have been no occasion for her to think of following onto the prairies.

She had done things which made Bill Felt hate her—but she had not put the weakness for hate in him. In the end she had killed him, but there had been no intent of murder, as there had been in his heart.

She had left Parley Wade at Crown Falls, but she had not made him love corn whiskey.

No man is blameless. But no man can take on his own shoulders the guilt, the whole, total guilt of humanity. No man is God.

She sifted sand from a rock crevice through her fingers. What she had to do now, she knew, was to make the boldest venture of her life. She had to open the doors of her store again.

It frightened her to think of going into debt. All her life she had been scared of debt. She had been scared of it when she and the boys had worked so long to pay off their father's debt. She had been scared into scurrying and fretting and playing politics by the debt Thomas had left her. It held a dreadful terror for her. To be out of debt, to her, was always to be free.

Her head came up.

Well, she couldn't afford fear now. She had to go in debt, head over heels in debt, stock the shelves of her store again and go back into business. Tomorrow, in the morning, the very next day, she would go to Fort Smith and she would buy enough goods of Captain Rogers to open her doors. She would buy them on credit, without a penny in her pocket, with only her good name for paying as security, and as God was in his heaven, she would stump up the trade to pay him.

She would go to the post and she would talk to every man on it, tell them Savanna's place was open again and invite them to come. She would stock the things the men particularly liked and were short of. She would make the big room a merry place again, but this time it would be open to the enlisted men. Her friends, now, were the men. There wasn't a man who had been on the expedition who hadn't admired her courage—they had told her so—and there were many who would never forget her efforts to ease their pain on the racking journey back, who had felt her soothing hands on their faces. This time, she was going to bet on the men.

And she would take full packs, stuffed with the articles Indians wanted most, and she would invade Mr. Chouteau's Creek empire, and she would invade Talahina Houston's Cherokee empire. She would woo the Indians instead of waiting for them to come to her. There wasn't much dignity in being a peddler, but the dignity she felt inside her soul would serve her well.

What she had learned, she thought, sifting the sand through her fingers, feeling its grit and coolness, was that no man could take all sin and guilt unto himself, so no one could arrogate all pride and duty to himself. It had been the catchword of her life. By myself. But it had never been by herself. There had been her father and mother and brothers. There had been Thomas and David and Abe and her darling old general. There were always so many others. No one ever did things alone. Behind every move, every thought, every deed, every heartbeat, stood all the others, with friendship and love and faith and trust and hope, and forever shining over all the radiant miracle of God in his world.

Her eyes smarted with tears. Not by myself, Lord, not ever again by myself. Mine is the load and by grace and help I will carry it. But not by myself. With Kizzy, who has never betrayed me and who has so faithfully served me. With Widgie, whose feet have wings for me. With my babies, whose souls I do not possess. With the faith of Captain Rogers in my intention to pay. With the good will of the men at Gibson.

With the trust and the faith of the Creeks and Cherokees. With the friendship of Martha and Fred, and with the blessed dearness of my old general, who has never failed me. With all these. But never again by myself. Though I falter and stumble all the days of my life, let me never think by myself again.

She dropped the sand and her head went back against the tree. Her earrings made their small, belling tinkle. She smiled. May Savanna's earrings never cease to jingle. David had said that. She closed her eyes. With David most of all, Lord. With David. He would come home. He always came home. And this time she knew her heart.

The sun had moved up and slanted with a wintry paleness now across her face. It was thinner than it used to be, and in the green, forest-glinted light the skin had a luminous, pearly luster, a porcelain look of translucence. It had not ever before in her life been quite so delicately and hauntingly beautiful. There would always be, now, violet bruises under the great, dark eyes, but the bruises only enhanced their magnificent, liquid depth. Always vivid and mobile, always registering every emotion, her face now held a sort of refinement, a kind of clean, articulate harmony, as sweet, as clear, as defined as a note from Sebe Hawkins's horn. It was as though all the features, with their special qualities, had been pulled together and remolded.

She had had bitter experiences. They showed.

She had known transporting rapture. It showed.

She had known grief. She had known pain and harshness and worry and fear and trouble. She had known excitement and fun and laughter. They all showed.

But what showed most and dominated all else in the face across which the dying sun slanted was the essence of Savanna. And the essence was—valor.

She stood and brushed twigs from her skirt. She must go. They were waiting for her at home. They would be worried. She must not fail them.